HIGHLAND VENGEANCE

THE CELTIC BLOOD SERIES, BOOK 3

MELANIE KARSAK

CLOCKPUNK PRESS

Highland Vengeance

The Celtic Blood Series, Book 3

Editing by Becky Stephens Editing

Proofreading by Rare Bird Editing

Cover art by Damonza

Trigger Warning: Gentle reader, please be aware that this novel deals with the difficult topics surrounding violence toward women.

❀ Created with Vellum

For my readers

CHAPTER ONE

Macbeth.

Hover through the fog, the snow, the filthy air. There to meet with Macbeth.

Darkness wrapped around me as Ute took her torch and disappeared back into the castle.

"I'll take you myself. Let me refresh the horses," Tavis said, heading toward the stables.

I stood with Madelaine and Lulach in the dark. A swirl of light snowflakes fell all around us, dusting the ground.

"Corbie?" Madelaine whispered. I could hear the confusion in her voice.

I shook my head.

"I'll…I'll go get provisions ready?" she asked.

I nodded. "Yes. I'm coming in a moment."

Madelaine left me standing outside the keep. I stared up at the starry sky. Snowflakes fell on my face.

"Gillacoemgain," I whispered into the darkness.

I closed my eyes. A tear trickled down my cheek.

A raven flew overhead and landed on the castle ledge. It turned and cawed loudly at me.

Gently moving my cloak, I looked down at Lulach who was, much to my surprise, looking back at me. His eyes twinkled in the dark of night.

"See here, child," I whispered, motioning to the raven. "Hear now, sweet babe, hear how the raven calls."

Lulach pursed his lips and raised his brows at me.

I smiled at him and gently stroked the little red dart on his brow, a blessing from the faerie world.

The raven cawed loudly at me.

"Lulach the loved. Lulach the light. Remember that you are a child of Kenneth MacAlpin's line. Be strong, and drive your own destiny. You belong to no one. No man. No woman. No god. No goddess. You alone will choose what is right. Live with a free heart."

I glared at the raven. "He is a free spirit, not beholden to you or anyone else."

The raven flew from the ledge and landed on the ground before me, shifting into the red-robed Morrigu. Her eyes were stormy as she approached me, a fierce expression on her face.

I clutched Lulach tighter, stiffened my spine, and met her steely gaze. In my heart, I heard the wings of the raven and felt that dark presence fall over me, hooding my features. I was Gruoch, but I was more. I was Cerridwen, and with a stern expression, I met the gaze of the dark goddess advancing on me.

Then, something unexpected happened. She stopped. "Be careful what you wish for...Cerridwen."

We stood there under the dim light of the moon glaring at one another.

The Morrigu sneered. "Get you hence before Duncan finds you," she said, and with a swirl of cloaks, she disappeared back into the night.

I looked down at Lulach and leaned down to kiss him on his brow before safely concealing him under the warmth of my cloak once more.

I closed my eyes and listened to the beating of my heart, which thundered in time to the sound of raven's wings. Together, the raven and the woman, we would survive whatever came next.

CHAPTER TWO

I headed into the castle. The Morrigu was right. I needed to escape. Duncan would have a head start. Malcolm would have sent him to Aberdeen looking for me. I needed to get to Macbeth. And even as the thought crossed my mind, I felt the sting of guilt. Macbeth, or his men at least, had masterminded Gillacoemgain's death. I could take this chance to disappear, to run away. But at what cost to Lulach? My boy would have a claim to the throne of Scotland. My son could be king. Didn't I owe it to him to endure? Didn't I owe it to my country? My people? But I had to choose, my rapist or my husband's killer. Death in battle was a chance all warriors took and one Gillacoemgain had accepted. Would he begrudge my choice? Macbeth was his brother's son. What if Macbeth was more like his uncle than his father? Banquo saw something good in him. Didn't that count for something? In the end, I couldn't go to Duncan, couldn't put Lulach on his knee. Macbeth had warred against Gillacoemgain. The man I loved was dead. If Macbeth sought me, needed me, then Lulach and I had a better chance with him. But the guilt... I shook my head. I would have to live with it. I would have to betray Gillacoemgain's memory, which I held dear.

Inside the castle, I found Madelaine hurriedly packing supplies. "Send your fastest rider north. He must find Macbeth and tell him I'm coming."

Madelaine shook her head. "Are you certain?"

"Yes. It cannot be Duncan. One day I will explain. One day, but not now."

"Oh, my poor girl," she whispered, searching my face for answers. Finding none, she kissed me on the forehead then turned and began shouting orders.

I went to the chamber where I'd stayed before departing for the coven. There, I quickly grabbed the rest of my supplies and belted my sword.

Thora trotted nervously around me.

"We're on the run again," I told her. "If you are too tired, stay with Madelaine."

Thora wagged her tail.

"My lady," Ute said, entering the room carrying two satchels. "I have everything ready. But, my lady. Macbeth? He killed the mormaer."

"Yes. That is true. But I saw Duncan once, and he is quite hideous," I replied, trying desperately not to think about Gillacoemgain, to shut out the misery that wanted to insist itself upon me.

Ute stared at me.

"Do you have everything?"

She nodded. "My lady, the babies?"

I moved my coat to reveal Lulach who was now sleeping soundly. "This is Lulach. The other child did not survive. Let's head to the stables."

"Oh, my lady," Ute said, reaching out to comfort me. "I'm so sorry. The little one. The mormaer."

"Now is not the time to mourn our losses."

"Are you sure you can ride? You risk yourself riding hard so soon after giving birth."

"We have no choice."

"Stay here, lady. Send word to Prince Duncan. Let him fetch you here. If you wed him, you will be queen."

I shook my head. "We'll go home to Cawdor."

"I don't underst—"

"Ute. We must go. Now."

Sensing I was reluctant to share my reasons with her, she finally said, "Yes, my lady."

We went downstairs to the main hall. Madelaine had just returned from outside. "The rider left. There was news that Macbeth's men were on the Spey."

Kelpie waited, and a fresh horse was brought for Ute. Tavis stood ready with two heavily armed soldiers.

"These two men will join us," he told me. "They can be trusted. I wanted extra arms along…just in case." I could see the fear and worry on his face.

I looked at them.

"My lady," they said in unison, nodding to me.

I inclined my head to them.

Madelaine pulled me into a gentle embrace, moving the fabric to look once more at Lulach. "Little piece of life. Bless you, wee one. Oh, Corbie, are you certain?" she whispered to me.

"I cannot be given to Duncan. Not him."

"Then may the Goddess watch over you," she said then turned to Tavis. "Please, take care…of all of you."

He nodded, and I saw an anxious look pass between them.

Moving as best I could, I mounted Kelpie once more. Pain from my fresh birthing wounds shot across my body. Ute was right. It was dangerous to ride in such a condition, and a long ride could jeopardize my ability to bear again. But there was no choice. I felt yanked forward by the pull of fate. There was no resisting its tide.

We set off. It was late at night, and I was weary. Fat snowflakes fell. I was heading north once more, but not to my husband, not with both of my children. All that waited for me now was uncertainty.

I closed my eyes and imagined the sunshine, and Gillacoemgain, Lulach, Crearwy, and me all together in Cawdor. I saw us laughing, playing in the fields. I tasted wild strawberries and heard my husband's laughter. Overhead, I envisioned the falcons calling to their master. It was all joy and light. I forced myself to remember the dream, then I rode north knowing it was nothing more than a lie.

CHAPTER THREE

We rode through the night into morning. During the afternoon of the second day, we met the rider Madelaine had dispatched. He'd found Macbeth's army.

"Lord Macbeth asked you to ride to Lumphanan. He'd been told you were at Aberdeen and was headed in that direction."

"Very good," I said, well aware of the fact that Ute was shooting me questioning glances. I ignored her. "Please take some rest then ride ahead and let him know we are on our way."

The man nodded. "Of course. I must say, my lady, Lord Macbeth was surprised to hear from you."

"I'm certain he was," I replied. I knew my choices, my actions made no sense to anyone but me. But I didn't want to think about it anymore. I would meet Macbeth soon enough and take the measure of the man then. For now, I just needed to survive the ride.

We rested that night at our small camp in the woods. It was cold but didn't snow again. We sheltered in a grove of dense pine, their boughs making a tent overhead. There was a stream nearby. A strange, heavy fog rose from the water.

"Odd weather," Tavis said as he eyed the fog suspiciously. He reached out and moved his hand through the mist as if there were something tangible to catch.

"The water is warm," one of the soldiers said, nodding toward the stream. "Must be an underground spring."

"That explains the smell," the second soldier said. "Filthy air."

The other soldier laughed. "How can the air be filthy?"

"Don't know. Just smells…unclean."

"Just the stink of lime and the earth. Smells no worse than your breath."

Both men laughed.

Resting with my back against a tree, my head bobbing drowsily, I looked up.

"Sorry, Lady Gruoch," the first soldier said. "Didn't mean to wake you."

Filthy air? "No. No, I wasn't sleeping. Dangerous to sleep in the fog anyway."

The man nodded. "So my old granny used to tell me."

I nodded and peered into the mist. Exhausted, my body felt disconnected, my head felt lost between this world and the other. As I stared into the fog, shapes started to take form. I saw tall pillars, a cauldron, and the silhouette of two women.

"Ah, there now, the wind picked up something sweet. You smell that? Flowers," the soldier said.

Tavis reached out and gently jostled my leg. "Gruoch," he whispered. I heard the warning in his voice.

I turned and looked at him. The shapes in the mist receded.

"What? I don't smell anything," the second soldier replied.

"I smelled it too," Ute said sleepily. "Like lilacs."

"Wisteria," I whispered, looking at Tavis.

He smiled knowingly then went back to warming his hands by the fire. Apparently, Tavis knew much more about Epona's coven and the training that went on there than he let on.

My sleep that night was fitful. Between waking every few hours to care for Lulach to the horrible ache between my legs, when the sun rose again, I was in no mood to take to horseback. Only the thought of Duncan pursuing me moved me to rise. We struck camp and were back on the road again.

It was late in the afternoon when the village of Lumphanan appeared before us.

The village, comprised of no more than a dozen buildings, was surprisingly quiet. Chickens and goats meandered aimlessly while old wives tossed wash water out the front door. A boy chased a goose with a switch, and an old man fed turnip tops to pigs. The villagers eyed us curiously as we approached.

It quickly became evident that Macbeth had not yet arrived.

"The alehouse," I told Tavis, directing Kelpie toward a building at the edge of town.

We tied the horses at the trough then headed inside.

The musty scent of rancid ale, straw, and timbers filled the air. The barkeep barely looked up, but when he did, his eyes widened. He pulled out five mugs and began to pour. He eyed Thora who was leaning heavily against my leg. Then he looked away. She was lucky she had such good acquaintances. Tavis spoke in low tones, and the man directed us to a secluded table in the back corner. We slid into our seats. The guards sat facing the door.

A plump woman with a bright smile, her hair covered in a kerchief, brought us all steaming bowls of mutton stew. The heavenly smell of meat and winter vegetables made my mouth water.

Lulach stirred in his sleep. I adjusted him in the sling then patted him, settling him back down.

Tavis smiled at Lulach but said nothing. All of us exhausted, we ate in silence.

After we were done, Tavis and Ute dozed, their heads bobbing.

"I need to walk," I told the soldiers.

"We should come with you."

"No. You rest. I won't go far. Thora is coming. Right, Thora?" I said, gently tapping the sleeping dog with my foot. She was lying on her back, her tongue hanging out of her mouth. She opened her eyes and looked at me. "Come on, lazy," I told her.

"At least let one of us come along. I must insist, my lady," one of the soldiers said, rising.

He met my eyes. The expression pleaded with me not to argue.

I nodded to him.

Rewrapping my clothes tightly around me, I headed out. It was dusk. The skyline was streaked with deep red and vibrant orange colors. I looked out across the sloping hill behind the tavern. In the distance, I was surprised to see a standing stone near a raised bit of earth.

"Let's have a look," I said to the soldier, pointing toward the stone.

"Peel of Lumphanan," he replied, motioning to the raised ground. "Some say the rise used to support a fortress, others say it used to be an old temple."

Holding Lulach close, I crossed the snowy ground to the stone. There was but one menhir, and beside it on the ground, a clutch of rocks. I could feel the energy of the place. It felt old, sleeping, much the same way as Ynes Verleath did. I knew that if I closed my eyes, if I focused, I could see into the otherworld, see the past. But I was too tired. I walked to the stone and touched the tall monolith. Its power vibrated under my hand.

I wanted to get lost in the energy of the otherworld. I wanted to think of Ynes Verleath. I wanted to leave all my worries behind, but I could not.

I was a fool.

I closed my eyes. Tears rolled down my cheeks. Everything I'd loved had crumbled into ash. Gillacoemgain was gone. He was not the love of my soul, nor some figment of my imagination—which surely that was what my raven-haired man had been. He was just a man. And in that, he'd been a good husband. He'd been faithful and caring and kind. And now, he was dead. I sat waiting on his murderer to come claim me as a war prize. Had Duncan reached me first, Malcolm would have wed me to him and thereby solidified the boy's hold on the north. I couldn't let that happen. But to marry the man who'd killed my husband... what kind of woman was I?

I leaned against the stone and wept.

My body hurt.

My daughter had been taken from me.

My husband was dead.

Everything had been undone.

Behind me, I heard the jingling of rigging.

Thora growled low and mean.

I heard voices at the alehouse behind us, but I didn't move. Why bother? It would come, he would come, and then I would make what I could of my future.

The snow and frozen grass crunched under someone's feet as they neared. Only one person approached. I listened to the footfalls. It wasn't Tavis.

Was it Macbeth, or had he sent a messenger?

Thora growled again.

The footsteps stopped.

"My lord," the soldier who'd accompanied me said stiffly.

Someone spoke in a low tone to the soldier. I heard my guard retreat.

Metal armor clicked as the unfamiliar person approached. Thora growled and stepped toward the stranger. "I was told Lady Gruoch came this way. Instead, I found her familiar. Some mean looking teeth, lady," the man said, his voice filled with playfulness. I was in no mood for jokes.

"Heel, Thora," I said, motioning to her. Thora's reaction to the newcomer had not escaped my notice.

"Hello, Thora. I am Macbeth."

While Thora had stopped growling, she still stood with her hackles raised.

I stared at Macbeth's silhouette reflected on the standing stone. It twisted grotesquely.

"Lady Gruoch. Cousin. Thank you for riding north. I must admit, I'm puzzled by a woman who turns from the chosen successor of Scotland to join her husband's conqueror."

I frowned hard and clenched my hands into fists. Part of me wanted to turn around and bash his face in—well, most of me. I heard the angry beat of my heart. But then I reminded myself that I was the one who'd chosen to ride north. This was a nightmare of my own making. Calming myself, I said, "You avenged your father, as you no doubt thought was your right."

"It was my right. The cutthroat Gillacoemgain murdered his own brother, my father, over a square of land."

I bit my tongue. It took everything within me to remember my promise to Gillacoemgain and not spit out the truth at this pompous bastard. "You've had your blood. Are you satisfied now?"

"I am. But that explains my motives. What about yours. Don't you mourn your husband?"

The question enraged me. "How dare you ask me that! I loved Gillacoemgain. He was a good man," I replied sharply, turning on him.

When I finally got a look at him, however, whatever else I had intended to say faltered.

Him.

It was him.

"You," Macbeth whispered.

Sunlight shimmered down on Macbeth's raven-colored tresses. He looked just as I'd seen in my visions. The cut of his chin, the shape of his nose, his soft, blue eyes. It was him, my raven-haired man. He was real.

And he was…Macbeth?

"It's you," I replied, my voice shaking.

Macbeth stepped closer to me.

Thora growled.

"You're real. All those visions… I thought I was going mad, or maybe some fey thing had taken a fancy to me, but it's you," he said, coming closer. "You're real."

Thora bared her teeth and barked at him.

The sound woke Lulach from his sleep. He cried out in protest.

I looked away from Macbeth, turning my attention back to Lulach. "Sh, wee one. It's all right," I whispered softly, rocking Lulach.

"Is that the child of Gillacoemgain?"

Involuntarily, I clutched him tighter, moving my hands protectively over him. "Yes. This is Lulach. He's barely a week old."

"You rode so soon after bearing a child?"

It was not really a question. I didn't answer.

Macbeth's face softened, and he looked at me with pity. "I'll have a wagon arranged for you. My men are on the Spey. We can move slowly."

I eyed him closely. Macbeth was my raven-haired man in the flesh. I had run to my husband's killer to escape a fate worse than death. Against all possibility, I'd run to the very man I'd decided was nothing more than a phantom. Andraste had known it all along. But what manner of man was he? I didn't know. I'd seen him in my cauldron, no more. Had I run from the wolf to lie down with the bear?

"My lady," he said, offering his arm to me.

I stepped toward him but paused when Thora growled once more.

"Your dog, my lady," Macbeth said, eyeing Thora warily.

I cocked an eyebrow at her. Odd. Thora's sense of people was always very good. Perhaps she was just responding to my own mixed feelings.

"Enough, Thora," I said. I stepped in line beside him. Feeling wary due to Thora's reaction, I did not take his arm.

Her ears flat, Thora followed ruefully along behind us.

"Lady Gruoch, I am astounded to find you with such a small babe so newly born. You must be exhausted. I trust you are unhurt?" Macbeth asked as we walked back toward the alehouse.

In truth, I was tired to my very core, and my body ached miserably, but I would not have him know it. "I shall manage."

"I'm at a loss for words. Please don't worry. I'll make the arrangements for your comfort."

I felt desperately confused. I eyed Macbeth out of the corner of my eye, noticing that he was doing the same. How many times had I seen him in my cauldron? Now, here he was, in the flesh, with Gillacoemgain's blood on his hands.

Part of me hated him.

The other part of me, however, felt the smallest glimmer of hope.

Tavis and his men were waiting at the alehouse amongst Macbeth's men, all of whom were heavily armed. Macbeth ordered his soldiers to get a wagon ready.

Tavis eyed me nervously. "I should travel with you," he said.

I shook my head. "I cannot escape my fate. There is nothing more you can do. Please, ride back to Madelaine. Let her know I'm safe."

"But your little one," Tavis said, eyeing Macbeth warily.

"Corbie," he whispered, searching my face with that same fatherly expression I'd seen there before.

"I swear I'll be all right. Macbeth needs me to secure his claim. I won't come to any harm," I whispered, squeezing his hand reassuringly.

Tavis didn't look convinced, but he nodded and let me go.

"Make sure Lady Madelaine's men are provisioned," Macbeth ordered. His men moved off to follow their commander's orders.

Soon, the wagon was ready, and Ute, Thora, Lulach, and I were loaded in. Tavis stayed behind, watching as the cart drove out of sight.

I waved to him then turned and settled in as we set off north.

CHAPTER FOUR

Our small party met with Macbeth's larger force at the River Spey that night. The full moon was high in the sky. It was a cold night. A light dust of snow covered everything. The trees shimmered crystalline in the moonlight. I smelled the sweet scent of the river in the distance.

While Macbeth had ridden close throughout the day, there were too many ears around us to talk. The ride had been long, cold, and awkward. Ute was clearly displeased at the turn of events, and Thora watched Macbeth suspiciously. While Lulach mostly slept or rested against my chest, I knew well that my son had no business on the road. The sooner we got to Cawdor, the better.

When we reached the Spey, Macbeth left us. "I must see to my men, but I'll return soon. I'll do my best to have you and the little one back to Cawdor tonight."

"Thank you," I replied then watched him march off. The

soldiers nodded or bowed to him as he passed through the row of tents.

"Why don't you walk a little, my lady. Your body must ache. Our little lord is sleeping. I'll watch over him," Ute, who had been holding Lulach, told me.

"Are you certain?" More than anything, I wanted to move, to get some air, to get away from all the strange people. But I felt uncertain.

She nodded. "I don't want to move. Lulach and I will stay right here."

"Stay close to Ute," I told Thora, who was busy sniffing the ground. She kept nosing the air then the ground again. Something had captured her attention. "No adventures. I don't care what interesting thing you smell. Stay with the baby."

Thora gave me a muffled bark then jumped up into the wagon and settled in next to Ute and Lulach.

I crawled out slowly, in more pain that I'd expected. Kelpie, who'd been tied to the wagon, nickered at me.

"Rest, old friend," I said, patting him lightly on the nose.

Snatching a torch, I headed away from the party in the direction of the river. I just needed a minute alone. It was all so much to take in. I needed some air. Soon, I would be back at Cawdor. I needed to make my heart ready.

The sounds of the men drifted into the background as I headed toward the river. I could hear the water tumbling over the rocks. The forest shimmered with silver light. The air felt charged with energy. I stood still under the moonlight. I closed my eyes and breathed in the clean air. In and out. I soaked in the silence. I let nature surround me, comforting me like a blanket. I inhaled the frozen air, my nose and throat burning, then headed toward the river.

As I worked my way through the trees toward the water, the hair on the back of my neck rose. A strange sensation came over me. There was magic in the air. The snow sparkled liked jewels, the icy branches casting long shadows on the snowy ground. Magic filled the space around me. The tree limbs, covered in ice, twinkled. Moonlight illuminated the forest. I snubbed out the torch then gazed into the woods. I could practically feel the otherside near me. I closed my eyes and took a deep breath.

When I opened my eyes again, I saw movement amongst the trees. I looked closely and discovered a stag working his way toward the river. He exhaled deeply, causing steam to puff out his nose. He was a massive creature with a wide rack of horns. I had never seen such a magnificent beast before. He moved toward the water.

Wordlessly, I followed him as he trotted over a rise at the river's bank. It was fortuitous to find the King Stag in a winter forest, and I was in desperate need of guidance. The Stag God, the partner of the Great Mother, was a guide and protector. While he'd never appeared to me before, I knew of his magic. Surely, he would guide a widow with a broken heart, the mother of a fatherless son.

Moving from tree to tree, I edged toward the riverbank.

There, along the frozen shoreline, I found not the stag, but a man with his arms uplifted toward the moon.

Cernunnos, the Father God. Moonlight shone down on him. He glimmered with silver light.

I steadied myself and took a step toward him. When I did so, the ice between the stones at the river's edge cracked.

The god turned toward me. I expected to see him as he'd often been described: bright silver eyes, a massive beard, and the hint of antlers under a mop of hair. But what I found was quite different.

I gasped.

"Banquo?" I whispered, the word coming out of my mouth no heavier than the cloud of warm air that cushioned it.

He lowered his arms. Moonlight illuminated his face.

"Cerridwen?" Banquo breathed.

We stood there, both frozen, staring at one another.

Had we drifted between the worlds?

Banquo took a step toward me, the ice breaking under the weight of his footfalls.

No. We were in the real world.

This was real.

He was there.

He was right there.

"Banquo?"

Moving carefully, Banquo came to stand before me. Hands shaking, he reached out and touched my face. "Cerridwen," he whispered.

"This way, my lord. The tracks lead toward the river," a voice called from behind me.

I looked back. The gaudy orange light of a torch moved our way.

"Don't go," Banquo whispered.

I realized then that he believed I had walked between the worlds to meet him and that any minute now, I'd disappear back to Ynes Verleath.

"I..." I began, trying to think how I would explain, but there was not time.

The firelight and footsteps drew near.

"Stay with me. I'll keep you safe," Banquo whispered.

"Here, my lord," a soldier called, his torchlight breaking the otherworldly glow with its blinding light. "Is that you, Lord Banquo?" the soldier called.

"It is," Banquo said, and I heard a hard edge on his voice.

"Here," the soldier called into the woods behind him.

Macbeth appeared on the rise. He looked at me and Banquo and then smiled.

"Banquo," he called happily. "Well met, friend. Seems you've found the Lady of Moray. Lady Gruoch, your maid said you went off for a walk. I followed your footsteps here. I was worried."

"Lady of Moray?" Banquo whispered. I realized then that he had wrapped his arms protectively around my waist and had pulled me close to him.

"I... I just needed to move a bit," I answered, stepping away from Banquo's grasp. "By chance, I met the Thane of Lochaber, whom I knew in my youth."

Macbeth's brow furrowed. "That old teacher of yours

kept you in wide acquaintance, Banquo. You never mentioned you'd met the daughter of Boite."

I turned and faced Banquo who stood staring at me so intensely that his gaze nearly hurt. "The daughter of Boite," he whispered.

I felt like my heart was being sliced in half. I searched Banquo's face, my eyes begging his, screaming out in apology. Understanding, then pain, washed over his face, but he masked it at once. Standing so close to him, I saw the unshed tears that wet his eyes.

"As the lady said, just a passing meeting in our youth. Nothing more. It was many years ago," Banquo answered Macbeth in a light voice.

"My lady," Macbeth called. "We'll make for Cawdor. We'll have you by your own hearth one last time before we go to Inverness."

"Thank you," I replied, my eyes still on Banquo.

"Come, my lady," Banquo said, carefully taking my arm. "Let's get the daughter of Boite to Cawdor."

CHAPTER FIVE

We arrived at Cawdor in the dark of night. Banquo had ridden ahead of us along with the army. Apparently, he was chief amongst Macbeth's commanders. Macbeth stayed close to the little cart that carried me. Part of me suspected that Macbeth feared Duncan would send an ambush to wrestle me away. He was right to worry. Without me, his claim to the north—and even to the throne—was greatly weakened. Finally, I spotted the dark silhouette of Cawdor castle against the starry sky. Home. Home, but not to Gillacoemgain. I closed my eyes and rocked with the little wagon. I could not think of it, not now.

As we passed through the gates of the keep, Banquo was waiting to meet us.

"Banquo, will you see Lady Gruoch inside?" Macbeth asked as he dismounted.

"Of course," Banquo replied then turned to help me out

of the wagon. He placed his hand in mine, and when he did so, a sharp jolt shot through my body. The scars from our handfasting had brushed against one another.

"Very well. My lady, I must see to the men then I'll join you thereafter," Macbeth told me, clearly unaware of the suffering agony lingering between Banquo and me.

Banquo stiffened and kept his face blank, his eyes not meeting mine.

"Yes. Thank you, Macbeth," I said.

"My lady," Ute said, handing Lulach to me.

I took my tiny baby into my arms then moved to shelter him inside my cloak.

"Gruoch?" Banquo whispered aghast, staring down at the tiny bundle. He reached out and touched Lulach's cheek.

"This is Lulach, my boy, the son of Gillacoemgain."

Banquo's face went absolutely pale. "Little Lulach," he finally whispered. "Son of Gillacoemgain."

I looked at Banquo. He stared at the child as if in disbelief.

It was Thora who finally broke the tension between us. Barking excitedly, she jumped on Banquo and attempted to lick his face then wiggled all around his legs.

"Thora," he said, kneeling to pet her. Thora licked his cheeks and made happy whining sounds.

Banquo smiled and laughed lightly.

"My Lady of Moray!" someone called.

I looked up to find Tira, the young serving woman I'd once saved from Artos's clutches.

"Tira."

"Oh, my lady. Come in out of the cold. We were so worried for you," she said, beckoning me forward.

I tried to catch Banquo's eye, but he would not meet my gaze.

I went to the girl. "Tell me, how are you all? What has happened at Cawdor?"

"Standish laid down his arms when Macbeth's forces arrived. We've not been harmed," she told me.

I entered the castle to find my household waiting. My eyes searched the group for Eochaid. He was not amongst the others gathered there.

"Lady Gruoch," they called out upon seeing me.

"My lady!"

"Lady! How are you, lady?"

"Be at ease, my friends. I am well. I have ridden here with Macbeth. Tell me, is everyone all right?"

"Yes, my lady," Rhona reassured me.

"Standish?" I asked, looking around the room for the chief of Cawdor's sentinels.

"He's outside with Macbeth's men. Unharmed," Tira explained.

"My lady, your babies?" Rhona asked.

I smiled down at the tiny bundle I held then carefully handed Lulach to her. "Lord Lulach," I said.

"Thank the Goddess," Rhona whispered as the others pressed in to see. "Oh, my lady, how like you he looks. The other child?"

I shook my head. "Only one survived."

Beside me, Banquo stiffened.

"Oh, my lady," Tira said, tears coming to her eyes. "I'm so sorry. Such ill-omened times."

I nodded, swallowing hard to prevent the tears that wanted to break the surface. I turned to Ute. "Can you put Lulach down to sleep in my chamber, the one I used late in my pregnancy, assuming it has not been disturbed?"

"It's as you left it," Tira said. "I've already had the hearth lit. The chamber should be warm."

"Of course," Ute said then took Lulach from Rhona.

"Thank you. I have some matters to attend to, but I'll come very soon."

"Very well, my lady," she replied, looking relieved to be headed somewhere where she could rest. Lulach in her arms, Rhona following along behind her, Ute went upstairs, Thora following protectively behind them.

I turned to my household. "Please prepare what food you can for Macbeth's party. We've come under Macbeth's care in an inauspicious manner, but we will host him as is fitting in Moray."

Understanding, the staff nodded and headed back to work. The looks on their faces were glum. They would do as they were asked but with no joy.

"Tira," I called.

The girl paused. "My lady?"

"The boy, Eochaid, have you seen him?"

She stopped for a moment then shook her head. "No, my lady. Not since you went south."

I frowned. "If he does reappear, please send him to me at once."

"Of course."

I turned to Banquo. "My lord, will you assist me with something?" I asked, keeping my tone stiff and formal.

"Of course, Lady Gruoch," Banquo replied, his manner strange, as if he was desperately trying to rule himself—and failing.

I turned and led him upstairs. Wordlessly, Banquo and I went to the chamber I'd shared with Gillacoemgain, the only place in the castle where I knew we would not be disturbed. We entered the bedroom, and I shut the chamber door behind me. Before I could entirely turn around, Banquo pulled me tight against him.

I wrapped my arms around him, inhaling his woodsy scent. My mind was immediately flung back in time, and I remembered him under the trees, the love of my soul. Tears threatened. This was all too much, too much for a mere mortal woman to endure. I leaned my head against his chest and listened to the rhythm of his heart, its beat deep and comforting. I felt dizzy, and that odd old tremor that sometimes took over me threatened. I felt it shake me from the back of my neck. No. I could control it. I inhaled deeply and stepped back. Hot tears burned, but I closed my eyes, swallowed hard, then held them back.

Banquo held me by the arms and looked deeply into my eyes. "I never thought I would see you again," he said then shook his head. "You never told me who you were. You never told me you were the daughter of Boite. All the pieces of the mystery fall into place before my eyes. My Cerridwen, you are Gruoch, Daughter of Boite. Where have you been all these years?"

"But for the last year I've been here, with Gillacoemgain," I said. "And before that—"

"An ancient, lost place."

I nodded.

Banquo looked around the room. "I cannot imagine you the wife of such a man."

"He was not what people thought. He was a good man."

"Your son. He's such a small thing. And you lost a second child?"

Did I dare tell him the truth? There was too much risk in it. "Yes. I fled south when the war began. It was a hard ride."

"I'm so sorry."

I nodded.

"The wife of Gillacoemgain," he said then shook his head. "And the daughter of Boite. I never had a chance. Lochaber was nothing. When I reached for you, I reached for—"

"Scotland."

"And now?"

"And now I must wed Macbeth."

"You cannot!"

"I must."

"No. You will not. It cannot be. I can't allow it."

I stared at Banquo. "It…must be."

"But I've just found you."

"You forget yourself. Banquo, come to your senses. I *must* marry Macbeth. And *you* already have a wife."

Banquo stiffened. "As my father insisted."

"I've seen her. That day along the shore, I saw you both through the eyes of the raven. And you have a son as well?"

"I knew it was you. I knew it. Yes, that is my son. His name is Fleance. Cerridwen, what do we do? Now that I have you, I can't just give you over to Macbeth!"

"You must."

"I must," Banquo repeated absently.

I stared at my oldest love's face, his dark eyes, his curly brown hair, his strong jaw. I felt the soul inside him. My mind twisted. With every fiber of my being, I wanted to fall into his arms, plant kisses on his lips, and be who I really was. But I didn't. I couldn't. My mind was shattering. My hands began to shake.

"You have a wife and son. I have escaped marriage to Duncan by fleeing to Macbeth. I have a son who is the rightful heir to Moray. You must be the thane, and I must be the daughter of Boite and Lady of Moray. There is no other choice," I told Banquo.

"We could run away," Banquo said, clutching my hand feverishly.

"I am beholden to Lulach's fortune."

"Forget it. We'll raise him as a druid. We'll escape into the strongholds of the ancient faith and disappear."

"And what of Fleance?"

"I'll bring him."

"And take him from his mother?"

"No… I… I couldn't do that to Merna."

Finally, a name. "Merna. Is she a good wife?"

Banquo paused. "Yes," he said then sighed. When he looked at me again, there were tears welling in his eyes. "Cerridwen, what can we do?"

"We must wait until the next life to be together."

"How can you say that?"

"Search your heart."

Banquo shook his head. "It's not right. This is not the path. Cerridwen, I still love you!"

"And I still love you. But soon I will be Macbeth's wife, as I was Gillacoemgain's."

"I cannot bear it."

"You can, and you must. I must. We will bear it. In the least, we can be together."

"Like this?"

"This something is better than nothing."

"We are bound by spirit!" Banquo said, sticking out his hand to show the scar thereon.

I took his hand, pressing the scar on my palm against his. "Yes," I whispered, lacing my fingers in his.

Banquo stared at me. "Cerridwen," he whispered.

I shook my head. "Gruoch."

"No. My queen. My Boudicca. My Cerridwen. You'll never be Gruoch to me."

"This is the sad reality we must accept. I am Gruoch, Daughter of Boite and Lady of Moray. I am the mother of

Lulach, son of Gillacoemgain. You must know me as such. See me in this space."

"There are more places in this world than just this one," Banquo said then smiled.

"Yes. And in those spaces, you and Cerridwen are one."

"Always," he whispered.

"Always," I repeated.

From outside, Macbeth's voice rose up to the casement. "Where is the rider? I'll send word south to Malcolm. The Lady of Moray is mine."

CHAPTER SIX

Banquo left me shortly thereafter. I went to the window. The moon lit up the night's sky. In the torchlight, I could see Macbeth in the yard. I watched him as he read over dispatches, commanding his troops. A few moments later, Banquo appeared at his side. After the two had a brief discussion, Banquo set off in the direction of the stables. He cast a glance up at me. I lifted my hand. He smiled at me, a distressed expression on his face, then headed off.

How strange that we would find one another in this place, under these circumstances. Aridmis had once foretold that we would be reunited in the outside world. At the time, I'd hoped that meant we would be married. Now, it seemed, I was going to marry his lord and friend.

I gazed down at Macbeth. How many times had I seen him in my cauldron, visited him in spirit? He was my raven-haired man. Now, after I'd nearly forgotten him, he appeared. Sorrow swept over me. It was too much to bear. The loss of Gillacoemgain, finding Macbeth, and my unexpected reunion with Banquo…sometimes I felt like the Goddess was merciless. My body was torn and sore from childbirth. My breasts ached, overfull with milk. I felt weary and miserable.

Closing the shutters, I crossed the room and lit the candle sitting at Gillacoemgain's bedside. The room was alive with his memory: his clothes, his weapons, and even his smell permeated the place. I lay down on the bed for just a moment, breathing in his scent, a sweet mix of lavender and cedar. In the weeks to come, his smell would dissipate and be gone forever. I buried my face in his pillow.

"Gillacoemgain," I whispered. "I loved you."

A sharp pain shot across my head, and my body trembled, an odd metal taste filling my mouth. I closed my eyes and tried to force away the tremors that wanted to impose themselves on me. If I let them in, I would fall into the abyss. I tried…but I failed.

A tremor racked me hard. A stabbing ache blasted across my skull, making my ears ring. I clutched the blankets and breathed deeply, inhaling the last of Gillacoemgain. My body began to twitch. I gripped the blankets tighter, pressing my face into the bed, biting at the very fabric as I was struck violently. I twisted and shook. My back contorted. I could barely breathe. As I trembled, I opened my eyes just a crack, and at that moment I saw Gillacoemgain's shade reaching for me, trying desperately to help me. I closed my eyes, and everything went black.

"My lady?" I Ute called followed by a knock on the door. "My lady?"

"Yes... Yes, I'm here," I said, sitting up. The candle had burned low. I looked down at the bed to see blood on the coverlet.

Ute opened the door.

"My lady? Gruoch, are you all right?"

I looked down at the front of my dress. It was covered in blood.

"Your nose," Ute said, pulling out a cloth.

I wiped my hand under my nose. It was stained with blood.

"I feel sick," I told her.

She rushed across the room, returning with a pot.

Taking it from her hands, I vomited.

"What happened?" Ute asked.

"I don't know. My head aches," I said. My eyes hurt. It felt like someone was pressing them out from the inside.

"I was getting worried. Our little lord is looking for you. Tira is with him now. Are you sure you're all right?"

"I'll be fine now. It's just... It was too much riding. Too much everything. I'll be all right now."

Her arm around my waist, Ute led me back to the

chamber where I'd been staying before I'd gone south. There, I found Tira and Lulach.

"He's fussing for you, my lady," Tira said then looked up at me. It was then that she spotted the blood on my gown. "Oh, my lady! What happened?"

"Just a nosebleed."

Tira's brow furrowed with worry. She handed Lulach to me. "Feisty boy."

I smiled down at the baby.

"He looks like his father," Tira added. "I see our lord in his brow."

I hated to tell her that there was no way he could look like Gillacoemgain.

"Thank you," I said simply.

"My lady, I asked the other servants. No one has seen Eochaid. He probably ran off when the trouble started," Tira said.

"Thank you for inquiring," I replied. No doubt Eochaid had disappeared, but not to where they suspected.

I settled into a seat before the fire and set Lulach to my breast. I closed my eyes.

"Ute, please arrange for our things to be sent to Inverness. And check on the household staff. Some of them may want to come along. We won't need to keep many servants at Cawdor now, but I don't want them to be out of work. Any who wish to come may join us."

"Yes, my lady."

"Is Standish staying on as sentinel? If not, make sure the new sentinel knows that the closed wing of Cawdor must remain closed. No one—and I mean no one—may go there. Nothing should be disturbed therein, just as Gillacoemgain ordered. This is Lulach's castle now. We'll keep it as his father has always done."

"Yes, my lady," she said, laying a new dress on the end of the bed. "Can I help you change?"

"No, I'll be all right."

"Yes, my lady," she said with a curtsey then exited.

Drowsy, my head aching, I nursed Lulach into sleep. When he finally drifted off, I rose and laid him gently down on the bed. How sweet he looked, his small mouth working as if he were nursing in his sleep. He opened and closed his tiny hands. His breathing was slow and peaceful. Moving carefully, I lay down on the bed beside him, studying his face. As I looked at his brow, I thought about Tira's words. The shape of his forehead and angle of his eyebrows was rather like Gillacoemgain. And so was his chin. At least the deception would be more convincing if he did, by chance, have some looks reminiscent of Gillacoemgain. I kissed him on his brow then closed my eyes.

I must have fallen asleep then because I was startled when I heard a knock on the door.

"Lady Gruoch?" It was Macbeth.

Sleepy, I opened my eyes. My head still ached terribly. I rose, adjusted my stained gown, then went to the door.

"Macbeth?" I asked, opening the door. "What can I do for you?"

"I apologize," he said, looking me over. "I'm sure you were resting. We are preparing to leave for Inverness in the morning. I wanted to be sure you knew," he said, eyeing the room behind me. I realized then that he'd come with an excuse just to see me. I suppressed a frown. Though I was curious about him, about all those visions, I was in no condition for a visitor.

"Thank you. I've advised my maid to get everything ready."

He nodded. "I was wondering if I might have a few words."

I stared into his light-colored eyes. I realized then that he looked tired. My heart was moved with pity. "All right. Come in," I said, stepping back to open the door.

"Thank you."

I nodded then closed the door behind us.

Macbeth pulled off his heavy gloves and sat down near the fire. "Cawdor is being looked after," he told me. "Your people are being treated well. I saw your maid inquiring."

"They are good and loyal people."

Macbeth nodded then smiled. "Your little one is sleeping," he said, nodding toward Lulach.

"He is a strong piece of life. It's a lot of adventure for such a tiny babe."

Macbeth looked around the chamber. "Is this the chamber you shared with my uncle?"

The question made something in my spine stiffen. I hated the tone in Macbeth's voice, the contempt he held for the man I loved. But Macbeth thought Gillacoemgain a murderer, the man who'd killed his father. He didn't know what kind of monster his father was, and I'd promised never to tell Gillacoemgain's secret, as much as I wanted to throw it back in Macbeth's face. "No. I stayed here late into my pregnancy while Gillacoemgain was away."

Macbeth nodded, but a frown crossed his face. Clearly, he was not as comfortable wedding his uncle's bride as he professed.

Lulach, however, broke the tension. The little babe woke and cried loudly. From the sound, I knew he was hungry.

"He's hungry," I said softly, hoping Macbeth would excuse himself.

He didn't.

I lifted Lulach, pulling my gown aside to feed the hungry child. He took to my breast at once.

"Hungry little boy," Macbeth said after a moment.

When I looked up, I saw him smiling at Lulach and me.

"Yes," I said, looking down at Lulach.

Macbeth sighed. "He may be Gillacoemgain's son, but he is still my blood."

"That he is. Macbeth, we haven't discussed your plans for the future, but I came to you knowing the consequences. We will wed, and I will secure your hold on the north. Through me, your bid to the crown will strengthen. I care little about these things. Lulach is everything to me, and he is an innocent. What will you do with my son? Will you send him away? I implore you, raise him as your own. He will never know any father save you," I said softly.

Macbeth rose and came to sit on the bed beside us. He gazed down at Lulach. "I'm sorry that after all these years, all those visions, we've found one another in such difficult circumstances. In truth, when I was a boy, I loved my uncle very much. I never understood why my uncle killed my father. Even now, it makes no sense to me," he said then reached out and touched Lulach's foot. "I will raise your child as my own. And when I do, I will remember the uncle I loved. In turn, I will love his child like my own. And his mother too, if she will have me, in more than just name. I know it will be hard at first, with Gillacoemgain just lost and so recently bearing your child, but I cannot help but believe the Lord wanted us together."

"The Lord?"

"Of course. It was the Lord who intervened between us, showed us our true destiny with one another. We are twin souls, meant to be. How else could you explain such miracles?"

"There are more gods than just the White Christ."

Macbeth frowned. "I was told you were fostered in a convent. Aren't you a follower of the White Christ?"

"No. But I have no quarrel with any god."

"Then you believe in the old gods, as your father did?"

"I do, as do many in Moray. You've been at court a long time, Macbeth. The courtly ways are not the ways of the people here. You must learn the values of your people."

Macbeth chuckled. "So Banquo and Thorfinn tell me. I guess there is still room enough in Scotland for all the gods," he said, but there was something in his voice that told me he didn't believe what he said.

The raven eyed him warily.

"I've imposed upon you for too long. You look very

tired. Gruoch… Are you well? There is blood on your dress."

"Just a nosebleed, that's all."

He nodded. "Too much being outside in the cold weather. Let me go. You need some sleep."

"Thank you for checking on me."

"You will be my bride. It is my job to care for you, body and soul. Sleep well, Gruoch."

"Corbie."

"Sorry?"

"People who know me well call me Corbie."

Macbeth smiled. "Goodnight."

"Goodnight, Macbeth," I said gently.

After he'd gone, I lay down with Lulach once more. My whole body ached terribly. I sighed.

"Oh, Andraste. What a mess you've made," I whispered into the darkness just before I was lost to dreams.

What sleep I did get was fitful and full of nightmares. Over and over again, I saw Gillacoemgain burning in the fire. Between the bad dreams and Lulach's hungry cries, I was utterly exhausted.

In the thick of night, I heard Lulach cry out once more. I nearly wept at the sound. I was so tired. Groggily, I reached out for him only to sense someone else in the room with us. Then, I heard a soft voice singing a lullaby. In the dim candlelight, I saw a figure rocking my child.

Startled, I sat bolt upright. Once my eyes cleared, I saw Banquo standing there with Lulach in his arms.

"I brought you a pitcher of fresh water," he whispered. "It's there by your bedside. There is bread in case you are hungry."

Stunned, I stared at him. But a moment later, I realized then how parched I was. I poured myself a glass of water and watched Banquo gently rock my son, lulling Lulach back to sleep.

"Rest your head, my Cerridwen. I'll wake you if he needs to be fed," Banquo told me.

"But..." I began, a thousand protests wanting to tumble out of my mouth.

Banquo, who'd been looking at Lulach, turned to me. "Sleep. I'll watch over you both. Don't worry. I'll be gone before the sun rises. No one will know. Take a few hours of rest. Your son is safe with me."

Exhausted, relieved, conflicted, and desperate, I lay my head back down and closed my eyes. And this time, I slept peacefully.

CHAPTER SEVEN

The following morning, Lulach's cries woke me. I rose groggily to find my baby boy nestled safely beside me in bed, Thora lying protectively at our feet. Our midnight watchman was gone.

"There now, little love. I've got you," I whispered to Lulach. I changed his wet bed clothes then sat down to feed him.

The first light of dawn was just peeking above the horizon. A soft lavender color filled the skyline. I closed my eyes and thought about Banquo. I felt immense gratitude. Unmoored from Gillacoemgain, with Macbeth's nature unclear and Malcolm's plans threatening, I'd felt so alone. How fortune it was that Banquo had appeared in the middle of the mess. There was still something between us. I may have buried my feelings to survive, but they still existed. Only someone who truly loved me would come in the middle of the night to care for me and another man's child.

I sighed heavily. Even before Lulach was sated, Ute slipped into the room and started packing up my belongings.

"We're headed for Inverness this morning," she told me. I couldn't help but hear the excitement in her voice. "Macbeth's father, Findelach has a grand castle along the river Ness. Did you ever see it?"

"No."

"You'll be very comfortable there, my lady. It will be a fresh start. There are too many memories for you here."

Ute sang happily as she worked, trying to cheer me, I suspected. She packed up my belongings then saw to Lulach so I could get myself ready.

"Is it a far ride to Inverness?" I asked.

"We'll be there by midday."

I looked down at my gown. It was spotted with blood and dirty from the road.

"Bring the blue gown," I told her.

"I was going to suggest, my lady, that perhaps you needed some freshening up."

I was still bleeding from childbirth, leaking milk, and covered in blood and mud. I felt like a wild animal who'd been running scared. Once I finally got to Inverness, I'd take a long, hot bath. For now, I stripped off my dirty gown and washed with soap and warm water from a pot sitting by the fire then put on fresh garments. Afterward, I felt much better.

Once I was re-dressed, I left my chamber and went back to Gillacoemgain's room. I took two servants with me. I left them at the door then went inside.

Gillacoemgain had no family save Macbeth. Lulach was not even his own. I opened the wardrobe. Inside, I found some of my dresses. They were gowns I'd worn before Lulach and Crearwy had grown too big. Turning, I opened Gillacoemgain's trunk, which sat at the end of the bed. Inside, I found a chainmail shirt, a shield, a heavy helmet, daggers, and knives. From another chest, I drew out two pairs of leather breeches and a pair of vambraces. I placed everything inside one of the trunks then covered Gillacoemgain's belongings with my gowns. I would keep Gillacoemgain's armaments for Lulach. Taking one last look at the chamber, my heart feeling heavy, I turned and exited the room.

"That trunk," I told the men, pointing. "Please have it loaded onto the wagons headed for Inverness."

"Yes, my lady," they agreed in unison then got to work.

I went back downstairs to get Lulach. Banquo was in my chamber.

"Ah, here you are. Are you ready, my lady?" he asked courteously. There were dark circles under his eyes. Clearly, he hadn't gotten much sleep. "I've arranged a wagon for you, the baby, and your maid."

"Thank you. Where is Macbeth?" I had not seen him at all that morning.

"He rode ahead to ensure everything was ready for you," Banquo replied. I saw him smother an emotion that had fleetingly crossed his face. Jealousy? Anger? I wasn't sure what.

Ute and I followed Banquo to the yard where a large party of soldiers and several carts waited. I noticed that some of Cawdor's household staff was riding along with us. The wagons were laden with Cawdor's treasures: food, wine, ale, and other supplies. The stables were busy as even more soldiers arranged for the livestock to be moved to Inverness. Amongst Macbeth's men, I spotted Standish.

"Ute, please take Lulach and get settled in. Where is Kelpie?"

"Your horse? There. I asked the soldiers to see that he was sent along with the others to Inverness," Banquo said then added under his breath. "I recognized him."

I nodded then motioned for Banquo to come along with me. "I'll only be a moment," I told him then headed over to Standish.

Standish, who'd been with Gillacoemgain for many years, looked tired and annoyed as he eyed Macbeth's men and Cawdor's goods leaving the castle. He softened, however, when he saw me.

"Lady Gruoch. How are you, lady? They said you and your babe arrived here with Macbeth's party. Are you well?" he asked, worry painted all over his face.

"I am. As is my little one," I said.

"May the gods bless you both," Standish replied. "I was sorry to hear about the other child," he said then reached out and gently squeezed my arm.

"Thank you," I replied, my eyes feeling watery. "I'm

glad to see that Macbeth didn't...that Cawdor was unharmed."

Standish nodded sadly. "After we learned that Gillacoemgain had perished, we let Macbeth in without conflict. My lady, I am so sorry for you."

"Thank you. I wanted to ask... I wondered if you knew what happened to...Gillacoemgain's body, if it was brought back to Cawdor."

"I'm sorry, my lady," Standish said, his eyes wet with unshed tears. "They say he was burned beyond all recognition, his men along with him, including Fergus. Many families lost their heads of house alongside him."

I swallowed hard. "Oh," was all I could utter for the moment. Pulling myself together, I added, "Send a rider with names. I will see what I can do to help those families."

"Lord Macbeth may not like—" Standish began then cast a glance toward Banquo.

"I don't give a damn. I am the Lady of Moray. I will care for my people."

Standish smiled. "We're so pleased you've returned, Lady Gruoch, even if it is under the worst conditions. I'm glad Prince Duncan didn't claim you as some rumored."

"As am I. I was wondering, have you seen the lad Eochaid? The others say he went missing."

"No, my lady."

I frowned. "I'll check the mews before we go."

He nodded. "My lady, what did you name our future lord?"

I smiled. "Lulach."

"All hail Lord Lulach," he said with a smile.

"Be well," I said, pulling Standish into a hug.

"You too, my lady," he replied, and when I pulled back, I saw him dash tears from his cheeks.

"Just a moment more?" I whispered to Banquo.

He nodded, and we went together to the mews where Gillacoemgain's falcons had been kept. To my surprise, the pens were open, and the birds were gone.

"What is it?" Banquo asked, catching the startled expression on my face.

I held on to the door of the pen. I closed my eyes then said, "Gillacoemgain's birds… They're not here."

Banquo stepped outside. "There," he said, pointing upward.

I joined him, following his gaze. Overhead, the falcons flew over the field then into the forest.

"Someone set them free," Banquo said.

I turned back to the cage. Inside, I noticed something odd. On one of the ledges was a bright red rose.

I reached in and grabbed it. It was frozen solid, as if someone had brought it freshly bloomed in summer only for it to be frozen by the winter chill.

"A rose," Banquo said, looking at the blossom. "How?"

I lifted the rose to my nose and inhaled. The perfume of summer was still frozen inside. Eochaid had gone back to the realm of the faerie. I was sure of it. And it was he who'd set my love's birds free. It was only fitting. Gillacoemgain's spirit was free. Why shouldn't his birds be as well?

"Fey things," I whispered in reply.

Understanding what was not easy to explain, Banquo nodded then we turned and headed back toward the cart.

"Who will keep watch over the castle?" I asked Banquo.

"Macbeth has assigned another of his generals to stay here."

"He didn't ask me about it."

"Macbeth is the Lord of the North. He doesn't need to ask you," Banquo replied then added, "and it probably never occurred to him that you might have an opinion on the matter."

"Cawdor is Lulach's birthright."

"Yes, and I urge you to remind him of it," Banquo said. "Inverness is Macbeth's home. I think he just wants to go back. He has been Malcolm's ward, a prisoner in truth, for many years. I think he just wants to go back to being… himself. But Macbeth will benefit from your advising. He needs to see you are not a southern court lady. He's used to fine ladies acting like lapdogs. You must show your strength."

"Indeed."

Banquo sighed. "Are you ready?"

"As I ever will be."

Banquo helped me into the cart then left to go rally the rest of the party.

"My lady, I'm surprised to see you're so familiar with the Thane of Lochaber. I didn't know you knew Lord Banquo?" Ute said, her voice thick with unasked questions.

"Yes. I've known him many years," I replied simply, but

said nothing more. Ute took the hint and didn't press me further.

The wagon driver clicked at the horses, and we headed out. I looked back once more at Cawdor. My heart filled with sorrow as I sensed I was leaving both Cawdor and Gillacoemgain's memory behind.

CHAPTER EIGHT

We arrived at Inverness later that afternoon. Kenneth MacAlpin, my ancient ancestor who had united ancient Scotland and ruled over the Kingdom of Alba, kept his seat at Inverness. Despite the fact that I'd grown comfortable and felt safe behind the walls in Cawdor, Inverness belonged to me as much as it belonged to Macbeth. As I passed through the gate, I felt its power. The stones reverberated with the old magic of Scotland. I felt my ancestors around me. And when I closed my eyes, I could hear their voices. It was distracting to suddenly find myself housed in a castle sitting in one of the thin places.

"Do you feel it?" Banquo asked me as he helped me out of the wagon.

I nodded. "I could fall between the worlds here."

"The thinness is useful at times, for those of us who know the path," he said with a wink.

I took his hand and squeezed it gently.

"Gruoch," Macbeth called, crossing the courtyard to meet me.

I let go of Banquo.

"Welcome to Inverness. Please, come inside. Let me show you your new home," Macbeth said, extending his hand to me.

I nodded, took Lulach from Ute, then went with Macbeth.

Banquo turned and walked away from us, Thora alongside him.

"I've had a section of the castle prepared for you and Lulach," he said, leading me inside. "It's winter now, but in the summer there is a small garden in your corridor. Come," he said excitedly, leading me through the winding halls and up a flight of stairs to the second floor. We walked down a rampart that led to a massive door. "This section will be yours."

Pushing open the door, he led me to a comfortable hall which boasted several benches, spinning wheels, a cozy fire, a space suitable for ladies' work. Apparently, I was back to sewing and talking about babies once more.

"There is a room there for your maid here," he said, motioning to a door just off the small hall. I looked back at Ute, who was smiling happily. "And the stairs there lead to the garden below," he added, pointing.

"My lady, may I go have a look?" Ute asked brightly.

I nodded.

"This way," Macbeth said, leading me to another door just off the private hall. "Your bedchamber."

The chamber was vast and nicely appointed. Inside was a large wooden poster bed, a comfortable chair, another spinning wheel, a wardrobe, and several trunks. Someone had lit a fire. The room was warm and nicely adorned.

"This is the best part," he said then led me to the door on the far side of the chamber. He pushed it open to reveal a balcony that looked over the river.

"It's lovely," I said.

"I thought you would like it. My chamber is at the other end of the rampart."

I nodded. So he had not intended for us to sleep together. Was that only until we were married or would we keep separate apartments, as was the fashion at court? It had never occurred to me that I might sleep separately from Gillacoemgain. I had merely assumed we would be together. Perhaps Macbeth had intended a more formal arrangement, or was he just trying to be polite? I hardly knew. I couldn't get a fix on the man. So far, I hadn't seen the person living below the surface of that pale skin and blue eyes. Macbeth was…blocked. What manner of man lived underneath? I wasn't sure.

"I've sent a rider south to Malcolm. We'll need his approval before our nuptials can be formalized, but I promise to take good care of you. You have nothing to fear here. I'll see to your every need."

Can you? the raven questioned with an unseen smirk.

The waspishness of the question surprised me. "Thank you," I replied.

But Macbeth was right. In matters of state, I belonged to King Malcolm. The bloody king who'd masterminded my own father's death would give my hand where he wanted it given. Learning that I was in Macbeth's entourage might influence his decision, but that all depended on whether or not he believed he could rule Macbeth. That was something I wasn't sure about. But Malcolm's plans were not clear. On the surface, it had seemed he had favored Gillacoemgain. But if that was so, how had Macbeth slipped Malcolm's yoke armed well enough to war against Gillacoemgain? Had the king decided, in the end, that Gillacoemgain was not the ruler in the north he'd wanted? I didn't know. But Duncan had been on his way to Aberdeen, and I remembered well that the king had instructed Gillacoemgain to send me there.

"Malcolm... What do you think he will do?" I asked Macbeth.

"I'm not sure," Macbeth said, but I noticed the guarded expression on his face. "Duncan is his favorite and holds his ear. If there is a way to appease Duncan, we should not anticipate any opposition. Much depends on how much Duncan pouts."

"Or on Malcolm's confidence in his ability to bring you to heel. You did, after all, slip his grasp," I replied, seeking to scratch the surface.

"Yes, well..." Macbeth shifted uncomfortably. His averted gaze was all the proof I needed. Malcolm had sent him north. Macbeth had been tasked with taking Moray from Gillacoemgain.

"And, of course, you also did what you were not supposed to do. Claiming me as a war prize wasn't part of the deal you made with Malcolm."

"Deal?" he asked. The muscles under his left eye twitched. "What do you mean?"

"Malcolm sent you north to overthrown Gillacoemgain and subdue Thorfinn of Orkney. Why did you come after me when you knew Malcolm had planned to wed me to Duncan once Gillacoemgain was dead?"

Macbeth stared at me. "How did you know?"

I was right. "Does it matter?"

"Because if I captured the Lady of Moray, Malcolm would have to give you to me or make war to get you back. Either way, I got what I wanted."

"What you wanted?"

"To be free of Malcolm. To come home, back in the halls of my ancestors. You were the key to my freedom. Malcolm cannot make me return to court as his ward now that I am here in Inverness with the Lady of Moray and Gillacoemgain's heir at my side. He cannot war against me now. And he cannot force me to return you without talk that will weaken him. I needed you to win my freedom and my birthright. I will not lick Duncan's boots. I will rule the north as my father did before me, before Gillacoemgain murdered him. I will not give over my birthright to my cousin or anyone else."

I should have run away with Banquo. "I see," I said simply.

"I'm sorry. You were nothing more than a name, a woman with a title everyone was keen to win. Now that I see you—*you*—I would do anything to protect you. Don't you see? We were destined to rule together. How else can you explain those strange visions? The Lord saw fit to show us our destiny."

Once again, the Lord. "But what is the nature of your relationship with Thorfinn of Orkney?"

"He is like a brother to me. I would never raise a hand against him, no matter what I promised Malcolm."

Macbeth had lied to Malcolm in order to make his escape.

There was a knock on the door. "My lady?"

It was Banquo.

A confused look crossed Macbeth's face. He crossed the room and opened the door. "Banquo? What is it?"

Banquo looked equally caught off guard. "Lady Gruoch's belongings," he said, motioning to the men behind him.

"Come," Macbeth said, motioning to servants and pulling on a cheerful mask. "Let's leave those matters behind," he whispered to me. "There is a deer roasting in the hall. The cases of wine are ready. It's a merry return. Let's celebrate," Macbeth said, smiling from Banquo to me, clasping us both on the shoulders. "Here I am with my future bride and one of my dearest friends. What a lucky man I am. I'll see to my devotions then meet you both in the feasting hall this evening?"

Yes, let's celebrate my husband's murder. Sounds festive. Masking my feelings, I nodded.

"At last, I am home. Tonight, we'll rejoice. I'll see you in your finest, Thane of Lochaber."

"Aye, my lord," Banquo replied.

"My lady," Macbeth said, taking my hand and laying a courtly kiss thereon.

I forced myself to smile.

With that, Macbeth left. Banquo and I were alone once more.

"Do you need anything? Are you all right here?" he asked.

"As well as I can be. Seems my embroidery and spinning are waiting for me," I said, motioning to the spinning wheel and baskets of cloth and thread.

Banquo chuckled. "I suppose you're not quite what he was expecting."

"To say the least."

Banquo smiled. "I should go clean up. We've been on the road for weeks. Maybe even shave this beard."

"I don't know. I like it," I said with a smile, reaching out to touch his face. It had been meant as a playful gesture, but the sensation that filled me from head to toe when I touched him rattled me.

Banquo set his hand on mine and pressed my hand against his cheek, leaning into my touch. "Cerridwen," he whispered, soaking in the moment. But then he let go.

I pulled my hand back slowly.

This was going to be impossible.

Banquo shook his head, and without another word, he turned and left.

I set Lulach down to sleep in the beautifully carved cradle beside the bed then went out on the terrace. It was cold and windy outside. A swirl of snowflakes drifting off the roof of the castle spun around me. The cold wind stung my body. I gripped the stone railing, the ice and snow crunching under my hands. I closed my eyes and felt the wind. I could hear the waves on the icy river as the water tripped over the rocks. I gritted my teeth hard and tried to let the cold seep into me, hoping it would freeze the terrible pain racking my heart.

CHAPTER NINE

With Ute's help, I slipped into one of my better gowns, a beautiful red frock with delicate embroidery all along the neck, and got ready to go to the feasting hall.

"My lady, if you took a wet nurse, it would ease your burden. Our little lord will be looking for you in a couple of hours," Ute suggested.

The thought of leaving another of my children to a wet nurse made my stomach turn. An image of Crearwy flashed through my mind. My heart broke at the thought that another woman was mothering her. "No. I'll make do. Just send for me when he's ready."

Ute smiled softly. "Very well."

My mind distracted by thoughts of Crearwy, I headed toward the hall. How was my baby girl? Was she well? Were she and May still getting along all right? Once I'd had some chance to rest and recover, I'd have to send a casting.

When I reached the door of the feasting hall, I heard the sound of rowdy voices inside. I sighed heavily. What kind of hall would Macbeth keep? Like Allister, wild and vulgar? Like Gillacoemgain, quiet and utilitarian? Or like Fife, sweet and festive? In truth, I didn't even want to know. I didn't want any of this. My raven-haired man was on the other side of the door, but I didn't even care. I had dreamed of a life with Banquo, but that hadn't been possible. Instead, that dream had been replaced by my happy life with Gillacoemgain. Now, all I wanted was my dead husband. And since I could not have him, all I really wanted to do was leave.

But there was nowhere to run.

"So, have you decided?" a voice asked from behind me.

I turned to find Banquo standing there. He was freshly washed and neatly dressed, his beard trimmed but not shaved.

"Decided?"

"Whether or not to go in."

"And what about you? You're still standing here."

"Ah, but I had a reason."

"And that was?"

"I was thinking about the daughter of Boite."

Banquo came and stood behind me. We both stared at the feasting hall doors.

"The daughter of Boite," I repeated.

"You should have told me," he whispered in my ear.

"I swore to keep my identity secret."

"If you had told me, I would have convinced you to

abandon the courtly world. And I would have done the same. We could have carried on in our faith, priest and priestess."

"Are you blaming me?" I asked, my voice sounding harsher than I had meant it to. I turned and looked at him.

"No. I am only regretting," he said, and I could see from the expression on his face that he was telling the truth.

I sighed. "Yet here we are."

"Yes. Here we are."

Banquo extended his arm to me.

Without another word, we turned—the Thane of Lochaber and the daughter of Boite—and entered the hall.

By the time dinner was done, I had grown weary of my own name. "Lady Gruoch" this and "My Lady of Moray" that. It seemed silly to become tired of people trying to please you, trying to make you happy, but that was how I felt. I was in no mood to meet Macbeth's loyal servants. Each *Lord this* or *Thane that* who presented himself to me had me wondering which one had set the fire that had killed Gillacoemgain. Which one of these men had burned my husband alive? I knew I should try to open myself to my future, but I could not. All I wanted to do was go back upstairs and hold Lulach.

As I looked around the room, I saw very few familiar faces. Only a couple of the lords who'd served under Gillacoemgain had come for Macbeth's return feast. Had he not extended his hand to the others in peace? Did he not think to make amends with those who had been loyal to Moray? Only Banquo, who sat on my side, felt like someone to trust. Everyone else eyed me like a curiosity. Boite's daughter. Wife of the defeated Gillacoemgain of Moray.

"How do you find the meal, Gruoch? Is it to your liking?" Macbeth, who was sitting beside me, asked. He eyed my plate. I had tried to eat, but my appetite was low. Macbeth had been trying, unsuccessfully, to make small talk with me all night. I had no patience for worthless conversation.

I lifted my goblet and motioned to the crowd of strangers. "In the coming weeks, it would be wise to reach out to Gillacoemgain's supporters and seek peace," I said. "You have your own people here, but you must unite Moray and the entire north behind you."

Macbeth raised an eyebrow at me. "I thought, perhaps, it would be best to wait until I receive word from Malcolm."

He would have us safely married first. He wanted to show Moray that he owned me and Lulach first.

"There will be fear of retribution. Those who were loyal to Gillacoemgain, who fought against you, will be wondering if they should live in fear. You must calm those worries, assure them they will not be punished for coming to the call of their mormaer," I said.

"And should they not be punished? Not removed from power? Perhaps executed for treason?" Macbeth asked.

I turned and stared at Macbeth. "If you wish to rule the

north with tyranny and fear, do what you like. If you wish to rule them in peace, gather them, speak to them."

Macbeth smiled brightly—too brightly. "I only jest. I was planning to do as you said. I hoped our marriage might help to smooth things over."

"If they assume you have taken me by force after murdering their lord, I doubt it."

"I didn't murder anyone," Macbeth retorted sharply. "I'm not like him. He—"

"Gillacoemgain was burned alive. Don't presume to tell me anything," I said, setting down my goblet with a thud. I rose.

Seated on my other side, Banquo stood quickly, startled by the sudden noise and movement. "Lady Gruoch, are you all right?"

"Fine," I said. I realized then that others had noticed the quarrel. I softened my expression. "If you'll excuse me, my lord, I'll go check on my son now," I said, painting on a false smile.

Macbeth rose. "Of… Of course. What a good mother you are, Gruoch. Very well," he said then smiled for the crowed.

I gave a curt nod to the assembled crowd then turned and left the hall.

Behind me, I heard Banquo and Macbeth talking in low tones.

I didn't care what was being said.

I didn't care what anyone thought.

I was halfway up the stairs when I heard footsteps behind me. I turned to find Banquo there.

"Cerridwen," he called lightly.

Annoyed, I stopped.

"May I escort you back to your chambers?"

"Why?"

"Macbeth thought maybe..."

"Macbeth needs to watch his words."

"This situation is difficult for everyone. Macbeth asked me to—"

"Asked you to what?" I said, feeling my fury rise. Unbidden, the raven peeked out from behind my eyes. "Remember who you are, Son of Cernunnos. You are the servant of no one but the gods. This man is not your master."

Banquo stopped. "Yes, my lady," he said, bowing his head.

It was to the raven, not to me, that he offered his deference.

I huffed with frustration at the lot of them, including the Dark Goddess who would not let go, then turned and headed back upstairs and went to my chambers.

"Ah, my lady, I was just about to send for you," Ute said when I entered. She held a fussy Lulach in her arms. When she looked up at me, I saw her expression change. She looked away.

"Very well. You are excused," I told her.

"My lady," she said, handing Lulach to me.

Without another word, Ute turned and left.

I hugged my fussy baby, kissing him on his head, then sat to nurse him. As I did so, I closed my eyes and tried to calm myself. The dark energy of the raven, the sound of raven wings, beat loudly in my ears. Slowly, with each deep breath, I ruled her. Cerridwen fell away, and after a time, I was just Gruoch once more.

When Lulach finally fell asleep, I laid him in the cradle beside my bed then lay down.

I had to make this situation work even if I didn't want it. I had to put my feelings, my love, for Gillacoemgain aside and try my best to get along with Macbeth. War was war. Gillacoemgain had died a soldier.

I had just drifted off to sleep when there was a soft knock on the outer chamber door.

Reluctantly, I rose.

I opened the door, expecting to find Banquo or Macbeth. Who I saw there puzzled me. On the other side of the door stood a holy man of the White Christ. He was just a wisp of a man, shorter than me with dark, beady eyes. He wore the dark robes of his order.

"My lady, I am Father Lawrence. I minister to your future lord. Lord Macbeth asked me to visit you. He was concerned for your well-being. You have endured much of late, my lady. Perhaps prayer—"

"Father Lawrence, I am my father's daughter. You will not offer the words of the White Christ to me ever again. Do you understand?" I said hotly.

The little man swallowed hard then nodded. "We are all God's children, my lady. If you ever change your mind,

I am at your service," he said then bowed and walked away.

Well, at least he had more sense than Macbeth to stop talking while he was ahead.

I closed and locked the door behind him.

I went back to my bedchamber, but stilled when I saw a figure standing over Lulach's cradle. Her braided red hair trailed down her back. The Morrigu.

"Priests," she said with a disgusted snort. "Another problem you must contend with in the future," she said then reached out and gently touched Lulach's cheek. "He is healthy and strong."

"Lady."

She turned and looked at me, "My willful one."

"Lady, how fares Crearwy?"

"Seek the answers for yourself. We have given you that ability."

"You forget what it means to be flesh and blood. I am exhausted."

The Morrigu turned from Lulach and crossed the room. She took hold of my wrists, and looked me deep in the eyes. Her own eyes were so black it was like looking into a starless sky. "Your child is well."

"Thank you."

She looked at my arms. "You have been a mage, and now you are a mother. In the days to come, you must become the warrior once more. Train. Train your body. Remember what Boudicca knew," she said then stepped back into the shadows. "And get your mind clear. You must concern yourself with more than which man's bed you lie in. A new day is coming, and you must be ready."

"Have you no heart? Look where your meddling has gotten me."

The Morrigu laughed. "Heart? My girl, what's fair is foul and foul is fair," she said then disappeared into the aether.

I scanned the room. My trunk was sitting at the foot of my bed. I opened it, tossing the gowns aside, then pulled out Uald's Gift. It had been a long time since I'd trained with Ute. I was out of practice. The Morrigu's words were ominous. Macbeth had just subdued the north. If so, then why was she warning of war? What did the Morrigu know that I did not? But she was right, my body was weak. I still had pain from childbirth, and I had not trained at all since my days in the coven. I needed to train with a man in order to fight men. Once I had recovered a little from childbirth and the rough flight north, I'd start. I would confuse and worry them all, but a man worships a warrior woman because he does not know what else to do with her. Either that or Macbeth's priest would try to exorcise demons out of me. One way or the other, I would do as the red lady asked.

But not tonight.

I set the sword back in the chest and closed the lid.

I lay down on the bed and closed my eyes. Not tonight. A moment later, I was lost to sleep.

CHAPTER TEN

I woke the next morning to the sound of happy laughter and the smell of something sweet. When I opened my eyes, I found Macbeth sitting in the chair beside the small hearth in my bedchamber holding Lulach. He was widening his eyes then leaning forward to kiss Lulach on the forehead. Thora sat beside them, eyeing Macbeth skeptically. In a pan near the fire was a large honey oak cake.

I rose sleepily. I hardly cared that my hair was a mess, my sleeping gown rumpled. What was he doing there?

Both Thora and Macbeth turned when they saw me move.

"Good morning," Macbeth said. "I had them prepare you a honey cake. It's taken all my willpower not to eat it myself. And I suspect your dog was feeling the same," he said then rose, smiling happily. "Oh, and while no flowers are growing, I brought in some winter pine boughs," Macbeth said, motioning to the clutches of winter greens tied to the end bedposts. Their heady scent perfumed the air.

"I… Thank you. That was very…thoughtful."

Holding Lulach gently, cradling his head with care, Macbeth rose and came to sit beside me.

I smiled down at my tiny boy. His eyes looked from Macbeth to me, squinting as he tried to make out shapes. His tiny fingers opened and closed on the air. He lifted his eyebrows, his forehead crinkling.

"He does that a lot," Macbeth said, smiling down at him. "It's as if he's not sure what to make of this world. He has an angel kiss on his brow," he added, touching the mark.

"A blessing from the faerie world."

"Gruoch," Macbeth began, his voice soft. "Things did not go as I planned last night. You have endured so much. I was thoughtless. You deserve better. I just… I don't know what to do. I expected a pious lady who would be frightened and need my guidance. I didn't expect the woman from my visions. And I most certainly did not expect you'd be less like the ladies at Malcolm's court and more like Banquo," he said with a laugh which I couldn't help but join. "I must temper what I imagined with what I find myself blessed with, a wise and strong woman. And a son full of wonder," he said, bending to kiss Lulach.

I raised an eyebrow at Macbeth. His words had a priestly ring to them. Was this what Father Lawrence had advised? Either way, his peace offering was appreciated.

"I was out of sorts last night," I admitted.

Macbeth laughed. "That is to be expected. Look at all you have endured. Now, please tell me that you're hungry so we can eat some cake. Otherwise, I may go mad from waiting."

"Go mad? Well, we wouldn't want that."

Macbeth handed Lulach to me then crossed the room. Fetching the pan, he served the cake into two bowls. I lay Lulach down in his cradle. The baby kicked his legs happily.

Macbeth set the bowls on the small table not far from the fire and motioned for me to join him. He poured us both water then set about eating. I eyed him, feeling amused to see him get completely lost in his bowl. For several moments, it seemed like he forgot I was there. Very soon, the dish was empty.

"Another for you as well?" he asked, rising.

I chuckled. I had not yet taken a bite.

When Macbeth looked at my dish, he grinned sheepishly. "I developed a taste for sweets at court, I'm afraid," he said then went and served himself another piece.

I inhaled the sweet scent of the cake then took a bite. The Morrigu was right. It did not do to dwell. I needed to make the best of things.

I motioned to Thora, who looked like she, like Macbeth, was going to die from waiting. I broke off a piece and handed it to her, patting her on the head. She ate the bite whole then looked at me expecting another.

I chuckled and handed her another piece. "Chew it this time."

"Your dog doesn't seem to care much for me, but at least we have some common ground," Macbeth said as he watched. "I have many matters I must attend to in the coming weeks. I am afraid I will be very busy. What can I arrange for you? I want you to be comfortable. Shall I ask the other lords to bring their ladies to court? Or do you like music? I could try to find—"

"No. Nothing like that," I said, trying not to wince at his suggestions. "I need to rest. When I recover, I will keep myself busy. As Lady of Moray, I will continue my work with my people. I need to make inquiries, check on the welfare of Moray's people. I know you have left a sentinel at Cawdor, but since the castle is Lulach's birthright, I will continue to stay involved in the keep's management."

Macbeth paused, as if he was reminding himself of his own words, then nodded. "If there are matters that need my attention, I'm sure you will seek my counsel."

In other words, don't overstep your boundaries. "Of course."

"Gruoch, if you need anything, please don't hesitate to ask. I want you to be happy," he said. Setting down his spoon, he reached out and tepidly took my hand.

I gazed at him. He was every bit the man I'd seen in my cauldron. My king. He was here in the flesh, yet it was all I could do to bring myself to give him a chance. "I can tell you mean it," I said with small smile.

"Indeed? How?"

"Because this is the first time you've let go of your spoon."

Macbeth laughed.

I couldn't help but join him. And at that moment, some of the sorrow that seemed to own me fled from my heart.

True to his word, Macbeth's manner shifted. I was not a lapdog and would not be treated like one. Macbeth, it seemed, was learning. There were times when I thought his eyebrows might shoot off his forehead when I spoke my mind, but still, he held his tongue.

Within the month, a rider wearing Malcolm's colors and insignia arrived at Inverness. I had been passing from the stable where I'd been checking on Kelpie when I saw a commotion. Macbeth and Banquo stood conversing with the messenger who handed Macbeth a sealed scroll.

Raising the hem of my skirt, I quickly crossed the yard to join them.

By the time I reached Macbeth, he'd already unrolled the parchment and was reading.

Banquo met my gaze as I approached. We both stood and waited as Macbeth read. When he was done, he looked up at me.

"Duncan has been wed to the sister of the Earl of Northumbria."

"An alliance with the south," Banquo said as he thoughtfully stroked his beard.

I felt like a rock was sinking to the bottom of my stomach. I reached out for the scroll. Macbeth paused a moment then handed it to me.

The letter, written in Malcolm's hand, glorified the alliance with Northumbria and bragged about the pageantry of the lavish wedding that had taken place. Then it took a turn.

"I regret that I will not be there to see you wed my brother's daughter, Gruoch. I am very pleased with your success in the north thus far. Please know that your mother sends her blessings and happy tidings for your nuptials. With a strong alliance in the south, and the future of the north firmly in your loyal hands, soon we shall have peace in the realm. I look forward to news of your defeat of Thorfinn the Mighty. With the Lady of Moray as your wife, you have a strong grip on the north and will serve as a valuable and loyal supporter of the crown, now and in the future," I read aloud.

I looked from Macbeth who seemed truly happy, to Banquo who was frowning visibly.

"Well, he has certainly outlined his plans for me. But more immediately, we now have his word on our marriage," Macbeth said. "I shall make arrangements at once."

Banquo sucked in a deep, shuddering breath.

"Banquo?" Macbeth said. "Are you all right?"

"A chill. I... You must excuse me," Banquo said, his voice weak. "I'm suddenly not feeling well. Please, excuse me," he said then turned and headed back into the castle.

Macbeth and I both turned and watched him go. "I'll

send someone to check on him," Macbeth said absently then turned to me. "My father kept a small chapel here on the castle grounds. We'll wed here."

I nodded. Once more, I would be married in the shadow of Findelach's faith. "Very well. And Thorfinn? Malcolm is rather specific on that point."

Macbeth laughed. "Come spring, we *will* go north to meet Thorfinn...so I may introduce my new bride to the brother of my heart. And then, we will begin making plans."

"Plans?"

"For war...against Malcolm."

Macbeth headed to his council chambers, calling his advisers to attend him, while I went after Banquo.

I rapped softly on his chamber door.

"Banquo?" I called. "Can I come in?"

A few moments later, the latch scraped then the door swung open.

Banquo motioned for me to enter. He went to his bed where some packs were sitting out. He'd been packing up his belongings.

"Are you... Are you leaving?" I asked.

Banquo turned and looked at me, tears clinging to his eyes. "I love you, Cerridwen. I love you. I cannot stay and watch you wed to another man. My heart cannot bear it. I'm going to leave for a little while."

I stepped toward him, setting my hand on his cheek. "Where will you go?"

"To the woods. Somewhere quiet, somewhere away from this place." He took my hand and pressed it to his lips. "By the old gods, I swear, you will be mine again in the next life. I don't care what it takes, what promises I must make."

Hot tears welled in my eyes. I nodded. "Be careful what you promise away. But yes, in the next life."

Banquo reached out and touched my lips. His hand shaking, he pulled it away. "There is a place not far from here that's sacred to our people. One day, I will take you there."

Turning my eyes to the floor, I nodded. A tear rolled down my cheek. I brushed it away.

"Cerridwen, I do wish you good fortune and happiness. I truly do. It's just…"

"I know," I whispered. I exited and went to my own section of the castle. Rather than going inside my sleeping chamber, I headed downstairs to the small courtyard Macbeth had told me about. There, I found a small patch of land and a single apple tree, a stone bench underneath. It was snowing lightly. I sat on the bench, leaning my back against the trunk of the tree, then wept until I had no more tears left in me.

CHAPTER ELEVEN

Three days later, I found myself standing beside Macbeth is a small stone chapel attended by strangers. Macbeth shifted nervously. He smelled of soap and incense. He kept giving me sidelong glances, eyeing me uncertainly. I took deep breaths and reminded myself to stay calm. I could not help but compare this wedding with my last. How handsome Gillacoemgain had looked in his tartan. How comical Eochaid and Thora had been. There had been joy there. Love, even. And before that, I'd wed Banquo under the eyes of the gods. I had to suppress a laugh—at least, so I did not cry—that I was not yet thirty and was already on my third marriage.

I cast a quick glance behind me. Aside from Ute and Macbeth, I knew no one. I didn't know what Banquo had told Macbeth about why he'd left, but true to his word, he had disappeared. Wherever Banquo was, I was sure he was feeling far happier than me—well, maybe.

I spent the mass, which was spoken entirely in Latin, feeling very glad my face was hidden from view by the heavy veil that had been part of my wedding trousseau. At least they wouldn't see me rolling my eyes and vacillating from annoyance to sorrow.

I glanced down at my gown. The dress was made of satin, trimmed with white fox fur, and embroidered with small pearls. The elaborate gown had been sent to me by the wife of the Thane of Ross, who was somewhere in attendance. She was an elderly lady, I was told, of good repute.

Father Lawrence said his final prayers. "And may the Lord bless this union."

All gods are one god, and all goddesses one goddess. And together, they are one, Epona used to say. I tried to stay mindful of her words as the priest made the sign of the cross over me again and again. After all, I had no issue with the White Christ, just some of his followers.

"Amen," the priest finally intoned.

"Amen," Macbeth repeated then turned and lifted my veil.

I sucked in a breath then smiled at my new husband.

Macbeth leaned toward me, setting a polite kiss on my lips, then turned to the assembled crowd who clapped.

At that, the wedding party progressed to the feasting hall, where an elaborate winter feast had been laid out. Roasted roots, baked breads, a deer, and a hog had all been roasted to celebrate the nuptials. Musicians played the bagpipes, and the lords and ladies drank wine and chatted merrily. Macbeth and I were seated at a table at the front of the room. An elaborate feast had been spread out before us.

"Lady Macbeth," an elderly man called as he approached.

Lady Macbeth. Lady Macbeth? The title left a sour taste in my mouth.

"Thane," Macbeth called cheerfully. "Let me introduce you to my wife. Gruoch, this is the Thane of Ross."

"My lord," I said with a curtsey.

"Word of your beauty has spread far and wide, my lady. And of your wisdom. I was told you aided in the rule of Moray and ruled well," Ross said.

"I did my best, my lord."

"As one expects from Boite's daughter. May I introduce my wife, Eleanor, Lady Ross."

I curtsied deeply to her. "My lady, I'm told it's you I must thank for this fine gown."

Lady Ross was a wide woman with an even wider smile. She nodded to me. "I had intended it for my granddaughter, who went off and got married wearing some other gown. She had the audacity to tell me no thank you. Can you imagine my shock? The finest dressmaker in Scotland made the gown you're wearing, Lady Macbeth. When I heard you and Lord Macbeth were set to wed, I thought to myself, *the girl has no family and no time to find something proper to wear for a woman of her standing. Why don't I send her the dress?* I can't wait to tell my daughter, who married a lesser lord of a house you've probably never heard of, that the gown she snubbed was good enough for the Lady of

Moray, niece of the king! That will teach that ungrateful girl. Regardless, it fits you well and you look so lovely."

When Lady Ross finally came up for a breath, I took her hand and squeezed it gently. "Many thanks to you. As you said, my family is far from me. It was too difficult for my aunt, Lady Madelaine, to travel so far north in the winter weather. Your generosity means so much to me."

Macbeth shifted. "I am sorry the Thane of Fife and Lady Madelaine were unable to come."

There had actually been no conversation between us about asking Madelaine to come at all. It seemed to me that in his haste to seal his hold on the north, Macbeth had forgotten Madelaine entirely. Now it seemed that the gown, which I thought Macbeth had found for me, had been Lady Ross's idea entirely. Macbeth was certainly no Gillacoemgain.

"Fife is too old and too fat to ride this far north in the snow," The Thane of Ross said with a laugh which Macbeth and his wife both joined.

"Don't they make a handsome couple? Just look at them. Raven-headed, each one. Both with blue eyes—"

"Lady Gruoch's eyes are more lavender colored, actually," Macbeth said, turning to me. "A mix of blue and purple."

"Oh, indeed!" Lady Ross said with a laugh. "Lovers, staring like mooncalves into one another's eyes. Do you remember when we were like that, Ross?" she asked her husband.

The thane shifted, seeming to think. "No. No, I don't."

"Me either," Lady Ross said then laughed loudly. "Come, old man. Let's let these two lovers sit and stare at one another while we go find something else to eat," she said and then curtsied to me.

The thane bowed, and the pair left us.

"Your eyes… I remembered that violet color well. I always thought that if I did not know your face, I would know your eyes," Macbeth said.

I smiled at him. I then took his plate and slid a slice of currant cake, a spoon full of pudding, and two honey oat biscuits thereon. I set the plate in front of my new husband.

Tepidly, Macbeth reached out and touched my hand. "Thank you, wife."

"You're welcome, husband."

Macbeth smiled.

I lifted my goblet of wine and took a sip, hiding the confused feelings that painted my face. I had to try. What else could I do?

Once the revelers had quieted, the bard starting warbling the wedding song, a cue that it was time for the bride and groom to depart for their marriage chamber. Taking my hand, Macbeth led me from the feasting hall to the stairs. The revelers followed, calling to us, cheering and offering their blessings. Hand in hand, we went upstairs.

"Gruoch," Macbeth said carefully as we neared my

chamber door. "Lulach is barely two months old. I was advised that you may not be able to..."

My stomach lurched. The hard ride north in the wake of Gillacoemgain's death had wounded me. In truth, I was not ready to take a man. Neither in body nor in spirit.

"You are advised rightly. I cannot yet consummate the marriage. But...you can come in all the same and...stay." I forced the last words out of my mouth.

Macbeth smiled softly then followed me inside.

Ute and Lulach waited in the outer chamber. Thora lay sleeping in front of the fire.

"Shall I take Lulach to my chamber for a time, my lady?" Ute asked, her eyes downcast. I noticed the red on her cheeks.

"Yes, please."

"Come on, Thora," she said, calling to my dog who followed reluctantly.

Taking Macbeth by the hand, I led him to my inner bedchamber. Ute had lit candles all around the room. I smelled the scent of new, sweet straw. The linens on my bed were fresh. The room was warm, the fire burning cheerfully. A decanter of wine was sitting on the table near the hearth.

"If you're tired..." Macbeth began but stopped when I took his hands.

I gazed into his blue eyes. There was a reason the Goddess had allowed me to walk between the worlds to this man. There was a reason Andraste had shown this man to me in the cauldron. Even if my heart was not yet ready to love him, I had to have faith.

I leaned in and pressed my lips against his.

His lips were soft and warm, the lingering taste of sweets spicing his mouth. At first, he seemed to hesitate, but a moment later, he fell into the kiss. Free of his reservations, Macbeth's passion surprised me. His hands roved everywhere, feeling every curve of my body. Before I was even aware of what was happening, he had loosened the fastens of my dress and was slipping it off. I was rather surprised at his deft hands. It felt like it had taken Ute forever to lace up the gown. He pulled off his shirt, revealing a pale but muscular chest. He then slid off his pants and stood naked before me. He lifted my thin chemise then pulled off my undergarments until I stood naked before him.

He lifted me and lay me on the bed. Crawling into the bed beside me, his hands moved across my breasts. Still full of milk, they were nearly twice their normal size. Macbeth kissed my mouth and neck, his mouth drifting down to my body to my belly button where he stopped. He inhaled deeply, mastering himself, his eyes glancing over my body and down to the downy hair between my legs. I was not ready. I had told him.

Once more, he pressed his mouth to mine.

I touched him gently, feeling his back, his chest. He was breathing hard.

"I know I cannot have you as I wish. That will come in time. But would you... Would you pleasure me?" he whispered, gently taking my hand and placing it on his hard cock.

I nodded.

Macbeth lay back then, touching my hair gently as I lay a trail of kisses down his chest, below his waist, where he waited, hard and erect. I pushed all thoughts from my mind. I focused on the moment. This was my husband now, my life now. It was right that I should try to give pleasure to my new husband.

He quickly found release. Thereafter, I lay in his arms once more while he set soft kisses on my head. My mind was screaming protests, but I closed the door on it, shutting out the hundred versions of me, all of which had a different complaint. I felt like I might go mad if I listened to them all. I lay my head on Macbeth's chest, listening to the beating of his heart. After a few minutes, he rose and poured us both a glass of wine.

He handed a goblet to me.

Standing there in the nude, he drank one goblet of wine then another. He stared off toward the window as if lost in thought. When he polished off the second cup, he picked up his clothes and started getting dressed.

"You can stay if you wish," I said. Perhaps that had not been the way husbands and wives had lived at Malcolm's court, but in my mind, a husband and wife should share a bed. I was about to say so when Macbeth replied.

"No, that's all right. Lulach will need you soon. When you're… recovered, perhaps."

My stomach lurched. Was he angry that I could not give him my body? I had done what I could to please him. I thought he had understood.

"Macbeth?" I said, sitting up. My heart beat hard. I was doing everything I could to bridge the gap between us, but my physical state was not something I could easily fix. He surely understood that, didn't he? He'd said as much.

Macbeth buttoned up his doublet then pulled on his boots. "Rest, Gruoch. When you have recovered from the birth of my uncle's son, we'll work on making a child of our own and truly enjoy one another's bodies. It's not your fault. I'll see you in the morning," he said and then left.

Sitting naked and alone, I stared at the closed door behind him.

My head felt like it was spinning.

What had just happened?

My legs shaking, I rose and dressed in my sleeping gown. I felt too ashamed to go tell Ute to return with Lulach. I lay back down on the bed and stared into the fire. Before long, I felt a tear slide down my cheek. While I was trying to convince myself that it would be okay to love him, Macbeth had been trying to convince himself it was okay to marry the widow of Gillacoemgain. All his life he'd been waiting for me, waiting to marry, and on his wedding night, he couldn't make love to his wife because her body was still recovering from giving birth to another man's child.

I rose, slipped on a heavy robe and a pair of boots. Taking a lantern, I headed out of my chambers and down the halls to Macbeth's wing of the castle. A guard was stationed outside Macbeth's door.

"Is Lord Macbeth within?" I asked the guard.

The man, who I did not know, would not meet my eye. "Sleeping, my lady."

I stood there a moment and waited.

The guard didn't move.

I realized then that the guard had no intentions of moving. He had already given me an answer. Macbeth was sleeping. He would not be disturbed.

"Very well. Goodnight," I said then turned to go.

The man nodded but said nothing.

As I was walking away, I heard a sound from nearby. Somewhere close, I heard the sound of a man's voice and a woman's soft laughter.

I stopped and looked around, my eyes drifting to the courtyard below. There were several people milling about. Everyone below, full of wine and food, seemed merry. Sighing, I cast a glance back at Macbeth's chamber door then returned to my own wing of the castle.

Removing my robe and setting aside the lantern, I knocked on Ute's door.

"My lady," Ute said in surprise.

"I'll take Lulach, now," I said. I reached down and gently picked took Lulach from the cradle Ute kept in her room. "Goodnight."

Ute motioned like she would say something but stopped herself.

Holding Lulach against my chest, I headed back to my own chamber. Thora followed along behind us. I lay Lulach, who was sleeping, in his cradle. I then turned and pulled all the new linens off my freshly-made bed. I bundled the new blankets into a heap then, unlocking the balcony door, went outside and threw the blankets off the balcony. A stiff winter wind tugged at the rich draping, pulling the linens away and into the darkness.

In a tree by the river, silhouetted by the moon, I saw a raven perched on the top branch. It cawed loudly.

My hands shook. Embarrassment, rage, and frustration rolled over me. I felt overwhelmed.

I glanced once more at the landscape. Moonbeams shone down on the countryside. The river's waters shimmered silver in the moonlight. I turned to head back inside but stopped when I saw a figure standing by the water.

The shade of Gillacoemgain stood at the water's edge.

In his specter form, he lifted a hand in greeting, but the expression on his face was pained.

"Gillacoemgain," I whispered.

He turned then disappeared back into the otherworld.

I went back inside. Dropping down on the bare straw, my tears came readily. I wept and wept, my poor soul awash with confused feelings. Thora crept up on the bed beside me, whimpered, then lay her head on my back. Overwhelmed, I cried myself to sleep. Only the soft sound of Lulach's cries woke me late into the night.

Otherwise, I was utterly alone.

CHAPTER TWELVE

It was late the next morning when I woke. Lulach was wide-awake in his crib, gurgling and kicking his legs. The fire in my hearth had been rebuilt. Someone had laid a blanket on me during the night. Ute, I assumed.

I felt hollow. My head hurt. When I sat up, I realized blood had stained the collar and shoulder of my nightgown. Had I had another episode? I thought I'd fallen asleep, but maybe… I couldn't remember.

I rose, picked up my baby, and sat in the chair by the fire.

I held Lulach, gazing lovingly down at him.

"Sweet baby," I cooed at him, and much to my surprise, he smiled, a dimple forming on his left cheek.

I laughed and planted a kiss on his forehead.

"My lady?" Ute called from the other side of the door.

"Come."

Keeping her eyes low, she cast a glance at the bed. Without another word, she opened a trunk and pulled out some blankets and quickly set to work remaking the bed.

"Most of the lords and ladies returned home this morning. Lord Macbeth went out on a hunt," she said, her words seeming to linger at the end.

I said nothing.

"Is there anything you need, my lady? Did you have any plans?"

"No. I'll stay in my chambers with Lulach today. Have my meals sent here."

"Yes, my lady."

After her work was done, Ute disappeared.

Both my head and heart felt heavy. I spent the day playing with Lulach or dozing by the fire. Late in the evening, I opened my trunk and pulled out Uald's Gift, the dagger Gillacoemgain had given me, and my whetstone. I sat sharpening my weapons.

I didn't know what my marriage to Macbeth was. Whatever it was, it looked nothing like my marriage to Gillacoemgain. It was time to stop worrying about it, and do what I was told.

It was time to start training.

Four days passed. While I heard Macbeth's voice in the castle, he had not come to see me. Frustrated, embarrassed, and annoyed, I stayed in my chambers. It was late in the afternoon on the fifth day when I finally heard a knock on the chamber door. My heart clamped at the idea it was Macbeth. Shame and confusion washed over me.

Tepidly, I answered the door.

It was Banquo.

"Merry met," he said, handing me a package. From the overly cheerful tone in his voice, I could tell he was trying to be okay.

"What's this?"

"A gift."

I motioned for him to come in.

Thora rose and went to him, wagging her tail and pawing at his leg. He knelt to pet her. "Bad girl," he told her. "You bored to death inside these walls? Want to come out to the woods and run wild with me?"

"Yes," I answered for both of us.

Banquo chucked. "Open it," he told me, motioning to the package.

I undid the small bundle. Within, I found fresh mistletoe. The bright green leaves smelled of the forest. I inhaled their perfume deeply.

I should have run away with Banquo.

"Thank you," I whispered, fighting back the tears that threatened.

"Cerridwen? What's wrong?"

"Nothing. It's nothing. So, tell me where you were."

Banquo smiled then sat down on the floor by the fire, tousling Thora's ears as she nipped at his bootlaces. "There is a ring of stones about a day's ride from here, a grove of oaks along with it. Like Inverness, it is a thin place. The stones are marked with Pictish designs. Even ravens," he said, reaching out to touch the torcs on my wrists. "It's a quiet place. And the further north you go, the wilder it is. In Moray, how was it?"

"Many keep to the old faith there as well. I hope to see your ring one day," I told him.

Banquo grinned. "When you're ready, I'll show you how to get from here to there," he said with a snap. "The castle and the stones are connected by a line of old magic that rumbles beneath the ground. It runs between all thin places."

"Thin places," I repeated, looking toward the balcony. The specter image of Gillacoemgain came to my mind once more. I shook the image away. "I need your help with something."

Banquo smiled at me. "Of course." Again, I saw the effort behind the smile, the effort to be okay, the effort not to think about whatever he had imagined.

"Uald and I used to spar. I need to train. In fact, I have been told to train."

At that, Banquo paused. "Told? By whom."

"Someone who should be obeyed."

"Why? I mean, why train now?"

I considered whether or not it was wise to share the words of the bloody goddess. Well, she called me willful for a reason. "Blood is coming."

At that, Banquo stiffened. "When?"

"I don't know."

"Then I guess we'd better start training."

"Tomorrow?"

"Tomorrow… Cerridwen, are you well?"

"Well enough."

Banquo frowned but asked no more, much to my great relief.

I smiled at him, more glad that he was back than I could ever say.

Banquo and I had an old hall cleared, and I began to train. Archery targets, daggerboards, and a mass of weapons were collected. I didn't mention the training to Macbeth, not because I wanted to keep it a secret, but because I hadn't seen him at all. When I went to his chamber, he was either sleeping or out. I wasn't sure if he was avoiding me or just busy.

Given the distance he'd put between us, I was surprised when he arrived one day when Banquo and I were in the midst of a duel. Dressed in a man's breeches and a leather jerkin, I was bathed in sweat as Banquo and I fought vigorously. We were testing shields. Though Banquo was much stronger than I was, he allowed me to have at him for as long as I could manage it. I was clearly out of practice, but I was determined to improve.

So involved in the fight, we didn't notice Macbeth at first. When we had both had enough, Banquo disarmed me.

"Good. You're getting better with shields but—"

His words were interrupted by clapping. "Well done!" Macbeth called.

We turned to find him standing at the top of the steps by the door.

Still clapping, he walked downstairs into the chamber.

"My wife fights like a Valkyrie. I hope you haven't ceased the training of my men for the training of my bride," Macbeth told Banquo.

"Of course not," Banquo said. I could hear the irritation in his voice. Was it Macbeth's words or presence that had set him on edge?

"I used to be skilled in arms. I asked Banquo to spar with me," I told Macbeth.

Macbeth smiled icily. "Well, it's good to see you feeling so well." He patted me hard on the shoulder then crossed the room to join Banquo.

"My wife fights better than some of my men," he told Banquo then picked up one of the training swords.

"She does. She had an excellent teacher in her youth."

"Ah, yes. In her youth. Odd. I thought you spent time with the holy sisters in your youth, Lady Gruoch."

"I did spend time with holy sisters and also learned how to wield a sword."

"Unusual training for a lady."

"Not all ladies are the daughter of Boite," Banquo answered for me.

Macbeth gave him a sharp look as he lifted training swords from the rack, measuring the weight and balance of each blade. "Boite. Yes. Malcolm spoke often of your father, Gruoch. Let's see how good you are, wife. If you're feeling well enough for the exertion."

Something in me hardened at his choice of words. Just what did Malcolm say about my father? And what was Macbeth trying to imply about my health?

"If it pleases you."

Macbeth set the training swords aside in favor of a saber lying on the table. "Ah, here is a gentleman's sword."

I raised an eyebrow at Macbeth. Very well. If that was the way he wanted to play, so be it. I lay down my training sword, picked up Uald's Gift, and slid Gillacoemgain's dagger into the top of my boot.

"Remember that you have a free hand," Banquo whispered.

I winked at him and then stood at ready in the center of the room. Macbeth smiled at me and took his position.

Banquo called for us to begin.

I was already weary for the exercise, but there was no way I was going to let Macbeth beat me if I could help it. He was court-trained and fought fancier than Uald or Banquo. His defense was excellent. We moved across the floor, our swords clattering together. Macbeth parried very well.

I decided it was time to play with him. I tossed my sword from hand to hand then feinted again and again. I tried to unsteady and annoy him. The more baits I threw out, the more goading moves I made, the unhappier Macbeth became. His brow furrowed heavily. His frustration unbalanced him, and his attacks became clumsy. If I wanted to beat him, I knew all I had to do was cause an unexpected diversion.

We moved back and forth across the room. Soon his sweaty brow matched my own. I grew tired of his excellent parries, so I lured him in close to me. I saw his eyes gleam as he perceived a win coming and then, reaching out with my free hand, I shoved him hard and quickly spun around behind him. When I turned, however, I found myself looking down the length of his blade.

I cast a glance up at his blue eyes, which glimmered wildly.

"Thought you could trick me?" he asked.

I grinned then tapped the blade of my dagger against his side. I'd anticipated his move. Had we really been on the battlefield, he'd have my dagger sticking out of his gut.

He lowered his sword then looked down at the dagger. His cheeks flushed an angry red, his features hardening. "If any dagger ever kills me, I'm sure it will be this one," he said then glared at me. "What are you playing at?"

"Only the game you started."

Macbeth sneered at the dagger. His eyes met mine, and he lowered his voice. "Bloody, murdering dagger. But what can I say? I knew whose bride you were."

"I…" I began, but I wasn't sure what to say. I knew what Macbeth thought, that it was the blade Gillacoemgain had used to… But I didn't know that, hadn't even thought of it. And I hadn't meant anything by it.

Macbeth stepped back then and smiled brightly. The

shift in expressions, from rage to happiness, was sudden and unexpected. "You fight excellently," Macbeth said, his face looking overly cheerful. He smiled wide, his eyes even wider. "It's good to see you out of your chamber, wife. I wondered where you've been. And here I find you with Banquo, of all people. My dear, I've hardly laid eyes on you these many days. Why are you avoiding me?"

"I'm not. I've been by to look for you many times. You're always either out or busy."

"Really? That hardly seems possible. I'm usually at work in my chamber or in the hall. Are you certain you were by? Either way. I doesn't matter. Do all these physical exertions mean you're…recovered?"

"Somewhat. Yes."

Macbeth leaned in and set a quick kiss on my lips. "Stop avoiding me," he whispered in my ear then slapped my bottom. "What do you say, Banquo? She had me, didn't she?" he said, turning to Banquo, a smile on his face.

"Indeed she did," Banquo replied.

"I dare say, had it been a real fight, we might have killed each other."

"That's the risk of the dance," Banquo answered.

Macbeth nodded then set the sword back on the table. "Do make sure my soldiers are getting the same training as my wife, old friend."

Banquo smiled awkwardly then nodded to Macbeth.

"Lord Macbeth," a footman called from the door. He was holding a scroll. Macbeth crossed the room and took the message. After he read it, he turned back to us. "You must forgive me. Duty calls," he said then turned and headed away from the hall.

I took a deep breath, went to the table, and poured myself some water.

"What did he say? You're upset," Banquo said.

I shook my head. Did Macbeth really think I had been avoiding him? Why would he think that?

"I…nothing. Just the troubles of learning one another's ways, I guess."

Banquo nodded thoughtfully.

I suddenly laughed aloud, the ridiculousness of the situation unmooring me.

"Cerridwen?"

"Has there ever been a more preposterous situation? So, husband, my other husband is not what I expected, and I cannot decide what to make of him, especially considering he's not anything like that other husband I had—the one everyone thinks was very evil but who was very good to me—in the interim."

At that, Banquo chuckled. "Indeed. Absurd."

I shook my head.

Banquo sighed. "I can try to talk to him."

"Yes, husband, please talk to my husband."

Banquo groaned. "I think I need a strong drink."

"Me too. Most certainly, me too."

CHAPTER THIRTEEN

Despite the awkward conversation between Macbeth and myself, I did not see him again that day. He was not in his council chambers, his sleeping chamber, nor anywhere else that I could easily discover. It wasn't until I found my way to the stables that I realized his horse was missing.

"Has Lord Macbeth gone hunting?" I asked the stablemaster.

"No, my lady. He's gone to the village."

"The village? Is anything the matter?"

"I wouldn't know, my lady."

I smiled at the man. "Your name, sir?"

"Samuel, my lady."

"Samuel, as far as common knowledge is concerned, are there any problems in the village? Illness or strife?"

"No, not that I know of."

I nodded. "Very well."

Perplexed, I went to Kelpie's stall where I found someone inside brushing my horse. To my great surprise, it was a young girl about sixteen years of age. She had very black hair, just like mine.

"So, you've managed to sweet talk a pretty girl," I said, reaching out to pat Kelpie's neck.

At the sound of my voice, the girl turned. She jumped a little. "My lady," she said then gave me an awkward curtsey.

"And how is my boy behaving?"

"I can tell someone has spoiled him, if that's what you mean. He seems to think he's the only beast in the barn, always nickering for my attention."

"Cheating louse," I told Kelpie, kissing him on his nose.

"Your name, miss?"

"Elspeth, my lady. My father is the stablemaster."

"Thank you for taking good care of my horse."

"They told me his name is Kelpie."

"It is."

The girl giggled. "I'll keep an eye on him then, see if he shifts shapes at night into a handsome lad."

I laughed. "And no doubt, he'd still be nickering behind you."

The girl laughed.

"If he needs anything, please let me know?"

The girl nodded. "Of course, my lady. It's good to see you here in the stables. Do you like horses?"

"I do."

"As do I. Love them, actually. May I show you something?"

I nodded.

"I'll be back," she told Kelpie, giving him a pat on the back. She set the brush down then closed the stall door behind her. Waving me along, she led me through the stables and out to the small pasture.

"Since it's winter, we mostly keep the horses inside, but I like to let them out a bit so they can breathe in clean air. Now, have a look," she said then pointed to a beautiful white mare who was nosing through some tufts of grass sticking out of the snow.

"Beautiful animal. She's as white as snow."

The girl nodded. "I'm hoping to get her and Kelpie acquainted this spring. Maybe by the time you return from Thurso, I'll have sparked a romance between the two. You have such a fine horse, my lady. I hope to get his stock intermixed."

"That all sounds very good. Did you say to Thurso?"

"Of course. Once the thaw comes, of course, and you leave to join Lord Thorfinn in Thurso. Lord Macbeth told me he was going to leave the horses here."

I nodded. "Indeed."

"They don't take to the ships well anyway. Thoughtful of Macbeth. He's a good lord," she said with a soft smile.

I raised an eyebrow at her. Of course, she would admire him. That was only natural. "Very good. She's a beautiful mare. I hope you can get a spark between her and my grumpy old warhorse."

The girl giggled. "He still has some fire left in him. He's already nickered hello to her a few times. I don't think they'll need much convincing."

I grinned then cast a glance up at the sky. It was getting late. Lulach would be looking for me. "I must go. It was nice to meet you, Elspeth."

"And you, my lady."

With that, I returned to the castle. Since Macbeth was out, and Banquo was busy with his men, I decided on a quiet dinner in my chambers with Lulach and Ute. The night passed quietly. After I finally got Lulach to sleep, I lay down. After the morning's exertions with Banquo, I was exhausted. I fell asleep immediately.

I woke with a start, however, late into the night when I felt someone slip into bed with me. For half a moment, in my sleepy state, I thought it was Gillacoemgain. But the thought was short lived when I remembered Gillacoemgain was gone.

Startled, I sat bolt upright.

"My shieldmaiden sleeps," Macbeth said, pulling me beside him.

"You scared me."

"Sorry. You were sleeping so soundly, I didn't think you would wake up."

"You men have worn me out today."

"Which of us is the worst?"

"Lulach."

Macbeth laughed. "I must confess that it was you who startled me today. "

"How so?"

"Your sparring session."

"I needed the practice."

"I have a master of arms who can work with you."

"I'm at a disadvantage. I know few here save the servants who came from Cawdor and Banquo and Ute."

"Then, perhaps, you should make more of an effort to make yourself at home here. You are the Lady of Inverness now, as my mother was before you."

"I did meet the stablemaster and his daughter today."

"Yes, Samuel. Good man. He served under my father."

"His daughter is very knowledgeable about horses."

"Who now?"

"Elspeth."

"I don't recall her," he said then rolled over and looked deeply at me, his hand resting on my stomach. "I was glad to see that you were feeling well. I was surprised you didn't let me know you were ready."

"Ready? I've hardly seen you."

"We already talked about that," he said, his hand drifting up to the tie on my dress.

My mind drifted back to our wedding night. Things certainly had not gone as planned, and in a way, our marriage was not yet consummated. Maybe Macbeth was right to come. Maybe I had avoided telling him. Now I wasn't sure. I guess I wanted a couple more weeks to heal, but I could manage now, I supposed.

"You'll need to go gently," I whispered. My stomach

churned. Nothing had been going right in this marriage so far. Now, at least, maybe we could get things on track.

Macbeth set his lips on mine, giving me the sweetest, softest kiss. I fell into the kindness of it, recalling the visions I'd had of him, the feelings I had harbored for him before we'd met. My king. He could still be that. I just needed to let him into my heart. Setting aside my awkward feelings, I pulled off my nightdress then helped Macbeth slip off his clothes.

I kissed him sweetly, opening my heart and mind to him. My hands slipped across his smooth back, feeling his muscles, allowing myself to enjoy his flesh. I closed my eyes and tried to relish the taste of his skin, ignoring the heady scent of incense in his hair. Andraste had shown him to me for a reason. He was my future. I had to try.

Macbeth crawled between my legs. "I'll go slowly. Tell me if you feel any pain."

I nodded.

True to his word, Macbeth made love to me carefully. Tenderly. He rocked in and out of me slowly, kissing my lips, moving with great skill and care. But he didn't linger long. When he finally found release, Macbeth gently pulled back then lay his head on my chest.

"Now, finally, we are wed," he said, entwining his fingers in mine.

"Yes."

"I hope you're happy here," he whispered.

"I am. I'm still finding my way."

"But Banquo is helping. Odd that he never mentioned he knew you."

"Our meeting was brief, and I was a young, silly girl. Perhaps he didn't like me."

Macbeth laughed. "I find that hard to believe. The way he looks at you, it is certain that he liked you. Maybe he wanted to keep his fond memories to himself."

I bit the inside of my lip. Macbeth was circling the truth but was missing pieces of the puzzle. Guilt nagged at me.

"I understand we are making plans to go to Thurso?" I said, hoping my change of subject was not too apparent.

"When the weather clears."

"The north will be busy in spring. The farmers, your people, may need your help here."

"With what?"

"It sometimes floods in the spring. At Cawdor—"

"The commoners have their local thanes. We need not be worried about such small matters."

I chewed my lip. Gillacoemgain had not seen such troubles as too far below his concern. "If we will not be directly involved in the management of the north, what will we be busy with?"

"Planning."

"Planning for what?"

"Well, I hope *you* will be planning for my heir."

His comment made my stomach quake. "I shall do my best. We have taken the first step," I said lightly, trying to hide my unsettled feelings.

"You must take care that you don't exert yourself too much to prevent it."

"Exert myself?"

"Yes. Your play with Banquo. Don't you think it would be wise to restrain yourself a bit? You are a new mother, after all. And a lady. It's not proper. And when you conceive our child, you will want to take care to ensure his safety. We cannot afford any missteps or accidents."

"Proper is a matter of perspective. But I'll keep it in mind, my lord," I said, the flower of hope within me fading.

Macbeth unlaced his hand from mine then rose. Without another word, he redressed. "Get some rest before my uncle's son disturbs your slumber," he said then left.

CHAPTER FOURTEEN

The journey north came within the month. Dispatches were sent to Lord Thorfinn, and three ships arrived to carry Macbeth's household by sea to Caithness.

The Northmen's longships were similar to the ships in Ynes Verleath. I tried to learn what I could about how the ship actually functions, but was eventually escorted by a well-meaning sailor to a safe spot where I wouldn't be able to put myself in danger. I bit my tongue. Since I'd come into Macbeth's company, I'd returned to the same attitude that ruled Allister's household: women were property, not people.

I should have run away with Banquo.

Thora, however, had the run of the ship. The men seemed to think she was good luck. And from the looks she was giving me, it amused Thora that I was told to go sit while she got to do as she liked. Annoying, willful, magical dog.

So, instead of learning how to do anything, I sat and held Lulach while the North Sea passed me by. The sight of the water made me feel lonely for Ynes Verleath. There was so much Andraste hadn't taught me. My mind went back to the moment in the chamber of the Lord of the Hollow Hills. What I'd seen there was nothing short of wizardry. Now I was forced to sit in a corner and stay out of the way. In Ynes Verleath, I'd learned how to raise the dead. But I should have expected as much. My husband's brief, nightly visits had become a clear indication that my new purpose in life was to provide him with an heir. Since the first encounter, Macbeth had come again and again. Macbeth's visits were always brief. He never stayed afterward, never seemed to realize that I might actually want or need pleasure. He pleased himself, filled me with his seed, then left. I knew this was the way most lords and ladies lived, but it was not how I wanted to live. And it was not how I had lived with Gillacoemgain. Maybe Macbeth just didn't know any better. I was at a loss for what to do. If I did give him a child, maybe things would be different, better.

My hand drifted to my stomach. My courses had not yet started again, but I was still nursing Lulach. There was no way to be sure yet if I was pregnant. I didn't feel life inside me. My mind drifted to Crearwy. I ached desperately for my child, but this was no life for her—not for any woman. The priests of the White Christ preached submission of women. Macbeth had grown up on the doctrine, and, it seemed, believed it.

I hoped things would be better in Thurso. Otherwise, I was about to spin myself a noose. Surely, those who lived so far in the north knew and honored the old ways—and their women.

When the port of Thurso became visible, my heart leaped with excitement.

"Is that it, my lady?" Ute asked.

"I think so."

"What an adventure," she said wistfully. "Ah! There is Macbeth," she said, pointing happily to another ship that was already in port. I scanned the dock for Banquo but didn't see him.

At last, our ship finally joined the others. Once our ship was safely moored, Macbeth boarded to see me safely debarked.

"I love Thurso," he told me. "Come. You'll see. It is a wonder."

With his arm wrapped around me, we made our way up the pier toward a hulking blond-haired man. He had long blonde hair with an equally long beard. Braids had been woven through his hair and beard.

Ute followed behind us carrying Lulach.

"Brother!" the man called to Macbeth.

I recognized the blond giant from my visions in the cauldron. This was Thorfinn the Mighty, a man whom Gillacoemgain had vehemently detested. Macbeth embraced him.

"My wife, Gruoch," Macbeth said, turning to me.

"Lord Thorfinn," I said with a curtsey.

The huge man smiled down at me. "Pretty, very pretty," Thorfinn said, looking at me assessing. He smirked at Macbeth. "Hard to tell what you're going to get with a royal lady."

Macbeth laughed. "There is no lovelier creature on Earth," he said, eyeing me with such unexpected devotion that I felt confused. Who was this man? Where had this kind creature been all these months?

I turned back to Thorfinn. "Pleased to meet you, my lord. And what about you? Are you married, sir?"

"Not yet. But if I can get these ridiculous Norwegians to hand over Ingibjorg before I am compelled to take her by force, I will be."

I laughed. "Is she such a beauty that you would risk war just to claim her?"

"I would risk the whole of England for her!"

The three of us laughed then turned and headed down the pier. Thora raced ahead of us to Banquo, who was waiting alongside a dark-haired woman I'd seen—as the raven—once before. The woman was holding onto a small boy who was wiggling to get down.

"Ah, your playmate awaits you," Macbeth commented lightly, speaking only loud enough for me to hear.

His words startled me. I searched Macbeth's face, but he quickly covered his expression with a smile.

"My Lady of Moray, may I present my wife, Merna, and my boy, Fleance," Banquo said. He would not meet my eye.

Merna smiled. "My lady."

I felt like someone had struck me with a dagger. Was this how Banquo had felt all this time? I stared at Merna in disbelief. How was she his wife?

Pulling myself together, I said, "Merry met." I turned my attention to their child. "Fleance, eh? Well, come to me, little lad, so I can get a better look at you," I said, reaching out to the child.

The boy, who was about two years old with curly brown hair like his father, reached for me. I held him on my hip then gazed into his mischievous brown eyes. How like his father he looked. If Banquo and I had our own son, would he have looked like this?

"Aren't you a handsome one? Strong too," I said, feeling the muscles in his little arms.

Merna laughed. "Now, that's a sight. That boy won't even go to his own kin. He took right to you, my lady. Can you believe it, Banquo?"

"I can," Banquo answered softly, which earned him a questioning look from his wife.

"Hello, Fleance," I told him. "I'm Gruoch."

"Gru...Gruc...Gorch," he said with a laugh then reached out to touch the torc hanging around my neck.

"Gruoch is such a dreadful name. I never understood why my father gave it to me. How about Corbie? Can you say Corbie?" I asked, tickling him.

The boy laughed. "Cor-bee!"

I hugged the boy tightly, closing my eyes. This was

supposed to be my child. I kissed him on the head. Sweet piece of life.

When I opened my eyes again, I caught Banquo's gaze. I glanced away before the others saw. I could not rest my eyes on him now. If I did, they would all see. They would all see how much I still loved him.

A sharp pain crashed across my skull. My knees nearly buckled.

"Oh," I gasped. Moving carefully, I handed Fleance to his father.

"Gruoch?" Macbeth said, taking me by the arm. "Are you ill?"

"It's nothing," I lied. "Just a wee bit seasick." Waves of pain rolled across my head, shooting toward my temples and the backs of my eyes. I bit the inside of my mouth, forcing away the pain that wanted to take over me. My hands shook.

No.

Not now.

"Come," Thorfinn said, his voice sounding serious. He studied my face carefully. "Your wife needs rest, Macbeth."

His arm wrapped around me, Macbeth led me to a fortress that sat high above the water. When I entered the space, I was surprised to find that I recognized it. Every detail of the longhouse was clear in my memory. Many years ago, with Sid's guidance, I'd sent a casting to Banquo. This is where he'd been.

The memory was further driven home when a black-robed

man stood to greet us. He had long black hair and an equally long beard which was streaked with white hair. Around his neck, he wore the amulet of a skald. He bowed to his lord then looked over the rest of us, pausing when his eyes met mine.

"You," he whispered, narrowing his eyes as he looked at me.

"This is Lady Macbeth, Anor," Thorfinn said, his voice sounding sharp.

"I've seen this lady before."

"That is not possible," Macbeth said with a frown.

Anor stared at me.

I turned to Banquo. His eyes met mine, and I could see that he remembered. What had Banquo and I said to one another all those years ago? What had the skald heard?

My thoughts were distracted when a wave of pain washed over me once more. My body jerked in response.

"Come, Gruoch. How pale she looks. Come sit," Thorfinn said, leading me to the massive center fire. "My skald, Anor. He sings well, but he's meddlesome," Thorfinn complained. "I half suspect he's my cousin, Rognevald's spy."

"I am no spy," Anor retorted.

"I'm sorry, sir. I think you have mistaken me," I told the skald, my voice shaky.

"Indeed. That must be the case. My apologies, Lady Macbeth," Anor said.

"He's full of superstitions, that one. But he won't wag his tongue about you, or I'll have it cut out of his mouth. You hear me, Anor?"

"Yes, my lord."

"Red," Thorfinn called to a buxom woman with a long red braid trailing down her back, "bring Lady Macbeth some wine."

"Maybe you should lie down," Macbeth said, hovering nervously.

"No, I'll be okay," I said.

The red-haired woman hurried back with a goblet of wine. "M'lady," she said with an awkward curtsey.

Thorfinn frowned as he looked me over. "You're right, Macbeth. Forgive me, my lady, but you look pale as milk," he said then turned to Macbeth. "Let's go make sure your longhouse is ready then we'll get her settled. Banquo and Merna will watch over her until we return," Thorfinn said then led Macbeth outside. As they exited, I heard Thorfinn ask, "Hasn't she ever been on a ship before? Didn't you advise her on how to keep her stomach calm at sea? Why didn't you sail with her?"

I heard Macbeth stammer a reply as the two exited, leaving me behind with Banquo and his family.

"Gruoch, are you all right?" Banquo asked. He reached out to touch me then pulled his hand back.

I inhaled deeply then exhaled. "I'll be okay. It...will pass."

"My lady," Ute said, settling in on the other side of me.

"I'm okay," I whispered.

"Merna, this is Gruoch's son, Lulach," Banquo told his wife. Moving carefully, Ute handed Lulach to Banquo.

Merna gasped. "My lady! He's such a wee thing. How old is he?"

"Four months," I said then took a sip of wine.

"Oh, but I thought—" she began but left off, her brows furrowing when she could not make sense of the matter.

"Lulach is the son of Gillacoemgain of Moray," Banquo explained.

Merna's brows raised in surprise then she nodded. "Difficult times for you then," she said, looking at me tenderly.

I smiled softly at her, studying her face which had a sprinkle of freckles over her nose, her cheeks dimpling when she smiled. She had a full bosom, round hips, and long, curly dark hair. She was a sweet, pleasing woman. But more, goodness exuded from her, as did the glow of the otherworld. She was one of us. I suddenly felt annoyed with myself for the jealously I'd felt. It was petty of me.

"My husband told me he knew you in his youth, that you met when he traveled with Balor," Merna said.

I nodded. "Yes."

"I'm so glad to have you here amongst us. You'll find Thurso very welcoming to people of our beliefs."

"And when you have time, I have a little treasure to show you," Banquo told me.

"Treasure?" I raised an eyebrow at him.

"You'll see," Banquo said teasingly. He was trying to lift my spirits, distract me from whatever was ailing me. "She'll see, won't she?" he said, looking down at Lulach who giggled and reached out to grab his nose. "She'll be surprised. Won't that be fun?"

I chuckled, feeling some of the pain recede.

"Welcome, dear sister," Merna said, reaching out to squeeze my hand.

I stared at her. In that moment, my heart softened. It was no more Merna's fault that Banquo and I had loved than it was Gillacoemgain's. I would not hold any resentment toward her.

"Fleance," Merna called as the boy dawdled to the door, laughing mischievously as he went. She rose and went after the boy, who took off like an arrow when he saw his mother coming for him, racing out the door as fast as his little legs could carry him. Ute rose to help Merna before the child fell into the sea.

Banquo shook his head then turned to me. "Are you all right now?"

"I will be. I've always been prone to these kind of fits."

"Have you talked to a healer?"

"I'll speak to Epona," I said absently as I watched through the open door as Merna picked up Fleance who was grinning wickedly. She kissed his face while she chided his recklessness. "He's a handsome child," I said.

Banquo gazed down at Lulach. "As is Lulach."

We turned then toward each other, our eyes meeting. A million words went unspoken.

How had everything turned out like this?

CHAPTER FIFTEEN

Macbeth and Thorfinn returned a short while later.

"Our home is ready, the fire lit, the rooms warm. Come, my dear. You need some rest. Ute," Macbeth said, indicating to my maid to take Lulach. She lifted the boy gently from Banquo's arms then followed along behind us. We moved away from the great longhouse at the top of the hill to a smaller, similar structure not far away. A dozen such places dotted the landscape.

"Thorfinn had this place built for me," Macbeth said with a smile. "My home in the north," he said then pulled open the heavy wooden door.

A wave of heat wafted from the room.

The house, true to its name, was long and narrow and built with a rustic design. The roof was made of thatch supported by wide timbers. The walls made of stone, wood, and clay. The floor was made of stone and covered with fresh straw to retain the warmth. The house was divided into sections. It opened to an open room with a hearth. To the right was a partitioned section which appeared to be the sleeping space for Ute. There was another closed space behind that. On the left end of the house was a more substantial sleeping space for Macbeth and me.

"It's lovely," I said.

"Lady Macbeth will take her rest now," Macbeth told Ute. "Only disturb her if you must."

"Yes, my lord," Ute said, her voice uncertain. She was not used to taking directions from anyone but me.

Macbeth led me by the arm to our bedchamber. A large wooden bed covered in heavy furs waited. A stone fireplace was built into the corner. It filled the space with a cheery orange glow. There was a tall wardrobe engraved with images of cats and dragons.

"The journey was too hard for you. I forget that the sea is rough, especially if you're not used to it. Lie down a while. I'll send someone to fetch you when the feast begins tonight."

I wanted to protest. The sea had not made me ill, but I was still fighting off the shaking in my hands. "All right."

"Do you need anything? Ute can fetch you wine or water. We have a large storage area and a cooking space at the other end of the longhouse."

I looked around the room. "There is no cradle for Lulach."

"It is in Ute's sleeping space. I…had hoped that maybe we could…that maybe I could stay with you. Lulach will be close at hand if you're needed. We haven't had much of a chance to live as husband and wife. I've been keen to come to Thurso, away from rules of propriety in Inverness."

Was that what he had worried about? Was he trying to keep the ways of Malcolm's court in Inverness? No wonder he'd seemed so uneven. Something that had hardened inside of me relaxed.

"I'd like that," I said.

Macbeth kissed my forehead. "Take your rest, and tonight, dress in your finest. You will dazzle them all and put Lochaber's milkmaid of a wife to shame," he said then laughed.

Frowning at Macbeth's rude comment, I lay down on the large bed. The furs were soft, but I felt a sharp pain poke me. Sitting up, I realized Gillacoemgain's dagger had poked a hole through the bottom of her sheath. To my surprise, the blade had broken through, penetrated my long skirt, and pierced my leg. A tiny spot of blood appeared on the fabric of my dress. I unbelted the dagger and set it on the table beside me.

As I lay down, a thought crossed my mind. I had not named the dagger. My sword had taken the name Uald's Gift quite by accident—I'd called the blade that so many times, it had become her name. The dagger, as far as I knew, had none. I picked up the dagger once more, pulling it from the sheath. "Scáthach," I said. "Are you trying to tell me something?" I asked the blade. I turned it over in my hands. It reflected the orange light of the fire. I turned it over and over, the orange flames of the firelight reflecting on the blade. "Scáthach."

My eyes grew drowsy, but still, I turned the blade.

On the next turn, a vision appeared on the length of the glowing metal. Before my eyes, I saw a field of battle. Banquo rallied a massive force. Torches burned brightly, shimmering orange against the skyline. Banquo rode down the line. Reining in his horse, he paused and inclined his head to me. I looked down to see Kelpie beneath me, my sword and dagger armed and ready.

I gasped, gripping the blade by the handle as it nearly slipped from my hand.

"Trying to stab me again, Scáthach?" I said with a smile then set the weapon aside.

War was coming. And I would be in the midst of it.

CHAPTER SIXTEEN

I fell asleep thereafter, not waking until Ute shook my shoulder.

"My lady," she said gently.

I opened my eyes.

At first, I was disoriented. The unusual smells of the longhouse and sea were unfamiliar. It took me a moment to realize where I was.

"They'll begin the feast soon, and our little lord is hungry," Ute said.

Nodding, I sat up sleepily and took Lulach.

"They've brought some of the trunks from the ship. I've been putting things away. I'll go get one of your gowns ready."

I settled in with Lulach. "Well, wee boy," I said with a smile. "You've traveled almost the entire length of Scotland in your short life. What a strong boy you are."

Lulach treated me with a smile, his eyes watching my

mouth carefully as I spoke, his hand opening and closing as he ate. I closed my eyes and thought of Crearwy. I would never have been able to manage all this with two tiny babies. It was better this way. She was safe and away from all this...mess. While my thoughts were correct, my heart still hurt, and I longed for my daughter regardless. Who had earned her first smile? I hoped it was Sid. In fact, I was almost sure it would be Sid.

After Lulach was sated, I rose and got dressed. All my muscles ached.

"Where is Thora?" I asked Ute as I pulled on an elegant red gown trimmed with fur around the neck and wrists. Ute brushed out my hair then braided it from the temples, fixing it at the back.

"She was here. She nosed through everything then went back outside. There are other dogs around. Last I saw her, she was running off with a pack."

Typical.

Once I was dressed, I slipped on my raven amulet and torcs. Ute, I noticed, was still in a house gown.

"Aren't you coming?"

She smiled nervously. "Lord Macbeth asked me to stay back and look after Lulach."

"He did?" I asked, feeling annoyed with Macbeth for ordering my maid—and my child—about.

"It's all right. I don't mind," she said then added, "It's just... It's a wild place, and I don't know the manners of the gentlemen here."

I nodded. "I'll see to it you and Lulach have a guard."

She exhaled deeply. "Thank you, my lady."

I nodded, pulled on my heavy fur cape, and then turned to exit. "If you or Lulach need anything, please come right away." I eyed Lulach who was now lying in the crib. Suddenly the same anxiety that had Ute jittery washed over me. I turned then and left.

The noise coming from the longhouse was very rowdy. Loud voices, music, and light seeped from the house.

"Corbie," a voice called.

Banquo, who had come from the docks, made his way toward me.

"Are you feeling better?" he asked, extending his hand to me.

I nodded. "Do you... Are there some of your men here? Loyal men of Lochaber?"

Banquo paused. "Yes. Why?"

"Macbeth suggested that Ute and Lulach stay behind tonight. I want a guard on my son. Someone I can trust."

"And you're asking me, not Macbeth?"

I stared into Banquo's chestnut-colored eyes. "I am."

Banquo stiffened.

"Lulach is the heir of Moray, a fact that, despite his pretty words, does not seem to sit well with Macbeth. Macbeth is so... I don't know."

Banquo stroked his beard. "It troubles me that your instincts bid you be wary."

"As it does me. Believe me. Macbeth is difficult to read."

Banquo nodded. "He's been more erratic of late. I've also felt a frost from him that was not there before. I don't think he likes our friendship. And he certainly didn't take well to my brotherly advice on how to make you more comfortable."

"Brotherly advice?"

"I see you are unhappy. I tried to tell Macbeth that you are not like the southern ladies he is used to. He was not interested in my counsel on the matter."

"I see."

"Merna's maid, Morag, is watching Fleance tonight. I'll ask her to join Ute and send a guard to them both so not to raise questions. Our sons will grow up together. We shall raise them to be the best of friends," he said then took my hand, kissing it gently.

"Banquo," I whispered.

"I'll see to it and meet you later. You look very beautiful, Lady of Moray."

"And you look very handsome, Thane."

He laughed. "I haven't even changed out of my traveling wear yet."

I grinned. "I know."

Banquo smiled, pleased with the comment, then headed toward one of the smaller longhouses nearby.

My nerves calmed, I joined the others in the feasting hall. The place was a wild scene. Its drunken revelry reminded me of Allister's hall. But here, everyone was merry—not just the lord. The other thing I noticed was how much larger the ale tankards were. One could practically bathe in them.

"Lady Macbeth!" a loud voice called.

I looked across the room to Thorfinn who was standing —more swaying—his tankard lifted, a smile on his face.

"My friends, let us all properly welcome Lady Macbeth, wife of the Lord of the North, and queen hereafter!"

The assembled crowd broke into raucous cheers. I couldn't help but chuckle, feeling my worries dissipate. The room was full of drunken Northmen, not cutthroats. I was over-zealous in my care of Lulach, but I was a mother.

Macbeth rose. I was surprised to see his steps were also unsteady. From what I'd seen of him in our marriage thus far—little as it was—he was usually careful to be very correct in his manner. His cheerful smile and red cheeks, rouged from drink, were unguarded.

"Come, Gruoch," he said, taking me by the arm. "Glad to see you feeling better. How lovely you look. Like a queen, a true queen. Come," he said, pulling me toward the head of the table where Thorfinn sat.

"Sit here by me. I've heard enough of your war mongering for the night," Thorfinn told Macbeth, pulling out a chair beside him. He patted the seat.

Chuckling, I sat beside Thorfinn.

"How are you feeling?" he asked.

"Well, my lord."

Thorfinn leaned toward me. "Ah, she smells as pretty as she looks," he said then looked me over with such intensity that I blushed. "She's a beauty. Not pretty…more than that. You have a glow to you, girl."

"Do I? Or all that ale you've drunk doubled your vision," I said, tapping on the side of his tankard.

He laughed. "That's true. All women look beautiful once I've found the bottom of my cup," he said with a laugh, slapping the bottom of a girl passing with a basket of bread.

The girl laughed. "My lord," she said, then pinched his cheek playfully.

"Now," Thorfinn said, leaning in toward me. This time I got a good look at his green eyes. They were a mix of spring green with flecks of gold. He had playful, but honest eyes. "Now, tell me, how do you like Macbeth? Does he treat you well?"

I looked over my shoulder at Macbeth. He was grinning at Thorfinn.

I struggled to find a good answer. "He treats me like a lady." *That, at least, was honest.*

Thorfinn laughed. "I hope better than that."

"Of course she's well treated," Macbeth interjected. "Her and her boy, little Lulach. I'm so proud of them both," Macbeth said, gently stroking my hair and pulling me close to him, planting a wet kiss on my cheek.

What the hell? I looked at Macbeth, who was smiling at me in complete adoration. Who was this man? Where had he been all this time?

The door opened again, and Banquo and Merna entered. Banquo made quick eye contact with me, his gaze reassuring me that he'd done as I asked and all was well.

Some of my tension left me.

"Thane of Lochaber!" Thorfinn called, the others in attendance cheering.

"My lord," Banquo said, joining us at the front, taking a seat on the other side of Thorfinn.

"Come, Merna. Kiss me. How sweet you look," Thorfinn said, claiming a kiss on the cheek from Banquo's wife, who smiled at me in greeting. "I was just getting acquainted with Lady Macbeth," Thorfinn told them.

"Did you know that Banquo had already known my wife? Only after I made war to win her did Banquo bother to tell me they were childhood friends," Macbeth said, his voice slurring.

"Is that right?" Thorfinn asked, his eyebrows raising. "You knew one another?"

"In passing. When I traveled with Balor," Banquo explained.

"Ahh," Thorfinn said thoughtfully. "Is that so?"

Banquo nodded, and a look passed between them.

Thorfinn smirked knowingly then winked at me. After, he turned his attention back to Macbeth.

"Macbeth, you look for reasons to complain. How is Banquo supposed to remember every pretty girl he met in his youth? I can't even remember the names of all the ones I've tumbled this week. Hell, sometimes I forget their name before I get their knickers off," he said then laughed.

"My lord," Merna scolded him. "Lady Macbeth is not used to such rowdy talk."

"Oh, isn't she?" he asked, lifting an eyebrow at me. "Those eyes tell me differently. Macbeth, go easy on Banquo. God knows, I'm sure you can't remember all the ladies you've *met* in your travels. Don't pick on poor Banquo."

Macbeth stiffened a bit but smiled all the same. "Of course, brother. You're right."

"He's just jealous," Thorfinn said, patting Banquo good-naturedly on the shoulder. "He's afraid you tumbled her first. Not like he's one to talk. Do you remember when we were in port at the Isles? How many girls did Macbeth have that one night? Lord, there must have been at least four—no, five—or was it more? I've never known him to—"

"My lord," Banquo interrupted, casting a glance at me.

Thorfinn passed me a quick look then stopped talking. "No matter. Let's have some ale, wench! We're thirsty," he called to one of the women passing through.

I inhaled then exhaled slowly. So, Macbeth had enjoyed his share of women. It was no matter, of course. Many young men were prone to indulging. Gillacoemgain had not been of that mind. Nor was Banquo, from what I could tell. But it didn't matter. I looked down at my hands in my lap and smirked. With all his practice, one would think he'd be a bit more polished in the bedchamber. Perhaps it hadn't occurred to him that the exchange was usually two-sided. Given he was an heir to the throne, no doubt court ladies were very eager to please him any way he liked.

"My lady," one of the serving girls said, pausing to pour me a drink.

Against my better judgment, I picked up the tankard and drank. The sooner I stopped thinking about it, the better all of this would go.

After that, Merna deftly shifted the conversation to Thorfinn's ships. Soon, Banquo, Macbeth, and Thorfinn were lost to the conversation. I scanned the room. The men of Caithness and the Orkneys filled the place. The dress of some of the men there told me they'd come abroad from Norway and other northern kingdoms.

King Malcolm had a good reason to be worried. Thorfinn had men and alliances that exceeded Malcolm's grasp. It was this force Gillacoemgain had feared. Now I could see why. But Thorfinn was not what I expected. He was a merry and honest man. I liked his frank nature, even if the raw truth was not always easy to hear.

In truth, Macbeth had done very well for himself by aligning with Lord Thorfinn. Together, the two of them held sway over all of the north of Scotland and the isles. This was a mighty force. If King Malcolm could not broker peace, he would have a massive enemy at his backdoor very soon.

But then I remembered the Morrigu's words. There would not be peace. Once more, war was coming.

Regardless, the night passed cheerfully. Thorfinn was perpetually smiling, and I found that I liked him very much. His hall was a happy place. The wild drumming and pipe players had us all dancing. Switching dancing partners from Macbeth to Banquo to Thorfinn, my feet were exhausted by the end of the night. As the evening waned on, the revelers either fell asleep near the fire or returned to their lodgings. At some point, I realized I could barely understand Macbeth's slurred words, and his head bobbed drunkenly. I had never seen him in such a state before.

"I think my lord needs to find his bed," I told Macbeth whose eyes fluttered drowsily. He might be drunk, but he was also happy, which was a good change of pace.

"Yes. Gruoch. You're right," he said then tried to stand but swayed and sat back down.

"Good night, my lord," I told Thorfinn.

"Lady Macbeth," he said, raising his tankard.

I chuckled. It was a miracle Thorfinn was still upright. His blood must have been half ale.

"Merna and I shall go now as well," Banquo said, taking Merna's hand.

I had kept an eye on Banquo that night, watching his practiced hands and eyes. Druid-taught, he melded into the cheer without drinking too much or forgetting himself. Long ago, druids were the chief advisers to kings. They needed to keep their wits about them at all times. It seems this was a skill Balor had instilled in his student.

Macbeth, on the other hand, had grown up at Malcolm's court, and he was dead drunk. "Come along, my lord," I said, practically lifting Macbeth.

Macbeth stumbled to his feet. "Brother," he told Thorfinn. Then leaning heavily on me, we exited the hall.

Banquo chuckled. "You're swimming home, Macbeth."

"No, you are," Macbeth retorted stupidly, which made us all laugh.

We walked to our longhouse where Merna and Banquo collected Fleance and their maid. When Banquo's man who'd been standing guard saw us approach, he nodded to his lord then turned and left.

"Morag, this is Lady Macbeth," Merna said, introducing me to the woman. She was an older woman about Madelaine's age with silver in her dark hair and lines on her brow. She dropped me a tired curtsey.

"My lady," she said. "A fine boy you have, my lady. Sweet-tempered and easy to soothe."

"You almost sound jealous," Merna exclaimed good-naturedly.

"I am! Fleance is a wee devil. In three hours' time, he nearly fell into the sea twice, the fireplace three times, upset the Macbeth's bed and food stores, and almost had the wardrobe pulled down on himself."

Banquo took the sleeping child from Morag's arms. "Morag, you'd be far too bored with a babe like Lulach."

"Would I? I spent the entire night wondering if Lady Macbeth would have me! My old bones… Ute is young. Perhaps a trade?"

"We could never give you up, Morag," Banquo exclaimed.

The woman shook her head sadly. "So I was afraid you'd say, my lord."

We all chuckled.

"Goodnight, Gruoch," Merna said, kissing me on both my cheeks. "Sleep well."

"And you."

Banquo, hands full of his wee devil, inclined his head to me then they headed back to their own house.

I smiled at Morag who winked at me.

Ute, who had stepped outside, waited for me. "Lulach is sleeping, my lady," she said.

"Thank you, Ute. Come, my lord," I said, leading Macbeth to the bed. He swerved as he walked. "Watch your step here," I said, guiding him across the threshold.

Ute chuckled at the sight.

Moving carefully, I helped Macbeth to bed then pulled off his boots.

"Prettiest wife in the hall," he said, reaching for me.

I shook my head then sat on the side of the bed beside him.

He reached out and touched the amulet I wore. "Where'd ya get this?" he asked, his voice slurring.

"My father," I lied.

"So, did he tumble you?"

"What?"

"Banquo. Like Thorfinn said, has he had you?"

My stomach knotted. "No," I lied again, feeling guilty for it.

"I see the way he looks at you."

"There is nothing to see."

Macbeth laughed. "You're a liar, Gruoch. I see the way you look at him too. Did you look at Gillacoemgain like that? God knows that's not how you look at me. By Christ, I think I drank too much."

"Oh? You think?"

Macbeth laughed, rolled over, and then fell asleep.

I sat there a moment longer. I hated lying, and in the

span of a single moment, I'd lied twice. I dwelled for a moment on Macbeth's words. How did I look at Banquo? Was my love so obvious? And Gillacoemgain? A light smile crossed my face. Yes, I had looked at him with love. I glanced down at Macbeth and sighed. He was drunk, but he was also right. I didn't look at him like I'd looked at Gillacoemgain or Banquo. It's just…nothing was working. I wanted to love Macbeth. I really did. He was just so damned difficult to deal with.

A cry pulled my attention away. Lulach.

Sighing once more, I rose and joined Ute by the fire.

"There now, wee boy," I said, lifting the child from his bed. "Ute, why don't you get some rest? I'll be awake for a while."

"Thank you, my lady. And thank you for sending someone. Morag was good company. And it was kind of Lord Banquo to have a man keep watch."

I nodded.

"Goodnight, my lady."

"Goodnight, Ute."

I sat there in the silence, listening to the crackling of the fire, and staring down at my sleepy boy. Lulach got his fill then slept. I stayed with him, holding him a bit more, staring down at him. He smiled in his sleep, his left cheek dimpling. I kissed the baby on his forehead then lay him back down in the wooden cradle near Ute. I still didn't like having him so far from me.

I turned and headed back to the other end of the house

when I heard a distinctive scratch on the door. I unbolted it only to find a shivering dog on the other side.

"Well, do they know you're the alpha yet?" I asked Thora.

Thora wagged her tail then trotted inside, heading directly toward the hearth where she flopped down.

Bolting the door once more, I headed toward our partition. There, I found Macbeth snoring loudly and reeking of ale.

Sighing, I pulled off my boots and slipped into bed beside him, pulling the heavy furs over me. For the first time in our marriage, my husband slept by my side, passed out cold from drink.

CHAPTER SEVENTEEN

A few weeks later, Banquo and I rode out to see what he called "the treasure of Caithness." We'd left early that morning. Having had success getting Lulach to eat a few bites of porridge in the past weeks, we would be able to make the trip and back before my wee lad got too fussy. Ute, Morag, and Fleance would, no doubt, keep Lulach distracted. It warmed my heart to see Fleance hopping around my own son, making Lulach laugh and smile.

Things had improved with Macbeth—a little. He was much more relaxed in Thorfinn's company than I'd ever seen him at Inverness. He'd taken to drink, but it cheered his mood significantly but also unevenly. He came to my bed each night. Thus far, however, only for sleep, which I found peculiar. I couldn't tell if the man wanted me or not. Did he love me or not? The whole thing was so confusing, at times I felt like I was going mad. The trip into the countryside with Banquo was a much-needed respite from the confusion.

"So, you won't tell me where we're going?" I asked as we rode toward a glen.

"No," he answered with a smile.

"Is it somewhere...old?"

"No."

"Somewhere picturesque?"

"Not exactly."

"Did you ever bring Macbeth here?"

Banquo laughed. "No."

"Or Merna?"

"No."

"I hate it when you're mysterious."

"Liar," Banquo said, playfully pinching my cheek.

We passed Loch Calder and followed one of the tributaries upstream where we eventually met with a farm.

Banquo grinned at me but said nothing. He guided his horse toward the house.

Outside the small roundhouse, I spotted a red-haired child playing in the vegetable garden. Upon spying us, the child raced toward the house. "Mama, mama, riders!"

The child's alarm brought a striking blonde-haired woman to the door. She wiped her hands on her apron as she crossed the lawn to meet us.

Banquo grinned happily.

Once she was in plain sight, I recognized her. "Gwendelofar?"

"Cerridwen? Is that you?"

I couldn't believe my eyes. How long had it been since she'd left Epona's care after her handfasting to Sigurd?

Dismounting, I rushed across the grass and hugged her tightly. Well, not too tightly when I realized she was with child. I leaned back and looked at her.

"Sister, why are you here? Has something happened?" she asked.

"Our sister is Lady Macbeth," Banquo explained. "We are at court with Lord Thorfinn."

Gwendelofar gasped. "Lady Macbeth. I did hear Lord Macbeth and his wife had come. I always knew you were someone of importance, you and your aunt. Oh, how wonderful to see you!"

The sound of jingling rigging caught all of our attention as a team of shaggy oxen were driven around the side of the house. An equally shaggy man with red hair followed behind them. Sigurd.

The hulking Northman left his yoke and joined his wife.

"Cerridwen? And Banquo," he said, clapping Banquo's shoulder. "Now, this is a surprise."

"Cerridwen is Lady Macbeth," Gwendelofar explained.

"Oh, aye? M'lady," he said, dropping me a courtly bow, chuckling all the while.

"Oh, stop," I said with a laugh, reaching out to embrace him.

"Come inside. Let's see where Neda has gone to hide. Neda?" Gwendelofar called. She led us into her little house. Scanning all around, she pointed to a trunk in the corner. A tuft of red hair and the hem of a dress was plainly visible.

"I'm sorry, Lady Macbeth. I guess my daughter doesn't want to meet the Lady of Moray."

"Mama!" the child exclaimed angrily, stepping out from behind the trunk. She glared at her mother with such fury that we all laughed.

I approached the child, bending down to greet her. "Hello, Neda."

"I'm very pleased to meet you, my lady," she said then curtsied.

What a beautiful thing she was. Striking red hair, blue eyes, and porcelain skin, she looked every bit like her mother with a mop of her father's hair.

"Such a beauty," I said, reaching out to gently stroke her cheek. "And how old are you now, Neda?"

"Seven," she told me.

Seven. My stay in Ynes Verleath had seen the world move on without me.

"She's beautiful," I told Gwendelofar and Sigurd.

They smiled at me.

"And another on the way?"

Gwendelofar nodded. "Coming July or August, I think."

"I'll still be here in Thurso, I believe. Send word when you're close to your lying in."

Gwendelofar smiled brightly. "That will be a comfort. And you? Do you have any children?"

"I have a son. Lulach."

"You'll need to bring him next time. Now, sit down and let us bring you something to drink."

Banquo and I spent the morning there, talking about

Gwendelofar and Sigurd's life since they'd left the service of the gods. They lived simply but were very content. And from what I could see, they were still very much in love. Sigurd cut wood and sold it to the shipbuilders. Gwendelofar had made a reputation as a local healer. Their lives seemed very content.

The morning stretched on, and eventually, Banquo and I had to take our leave.

"I made this for my little one. Will it fit your boy?" Gwendelofar asked, handing me a beautifully embroidered shirt. The neckline was decorated with leaves and acorns.

"It's so beautiful. I can't accept this," I said.

Gwendelofar laughed. "Cerridwen, if it were not for you, I wouldn't have this happy life. Please."

I took the gift, kissed her on the cheek, then pulled her into an embrace. "Thank you. And take care. If you need anything, I will be with Jarl Thorfinn. Please, just send word."

Gwendelofar leaned back and looked at me. "And if *you* need anything, you know where to find us."

I smiled at her then hugged her again. Once more, I turned my attention to little Neda, the merry-begot babe whose parents I'd encouraged to marry. How glad it made me to see their family so happy. "What can I bring you when I come next?"

"Cerridwen—" Gwendelofar began, but I hushed her with the wave of a hand.

"My lady, I have no right to ask you for a gift."

"Now, you must understand, Lord Banquo brought me here as a surprise. If he had told me where we were going, I would have brought something. It is his fault I don't have something special for you," I said, shooting Banquo a playful scolding glance. "Tell me what you'd like, lass."

Neda looked up at her mother, who nodded in assent.

"My lady, if it's not too much to ask, would you bring me a harp?"

Be still my heart. "I will do my very best to get one for you."

"She's got a lovely voice," Sigurd said. "Blessed by the gods."

"Then a harp you shall have."

I kissed the child on the forehead then mounted my horse. Banquo gave his farewells, and soon we were ready to go. We waved goodbye then headed back to Thurso.

We rode in silence for a long time.

Too long.

I could tell Banquo's mind was busy.

"Not going to tell me what you're thinking?" I asked.

He sighed. "We had the same training, worship the same gods, but look how content they are whereas we must play Thane and Lady."

"We had no say in the matter."

Banquo reached out to take my hand. "Cerridwen," he whispered.

In truth, the same thoughts had plagued me. "Banquo, I—"

"How many children do you think we would have had by now?"

I stared at him. We were alone. For the first time in so long, we were alone. It would not hurt to play pretend here…at least, it would not hurt anyone other than ourselves. "Seven years… Let's say four or five."

"And would we be farmers?"

"No. We'd have our own place, just like Epona, and we would raise and train people in the ways of our ancestors, men and women alike, side by side."

"And we would be happy?"

"Perfectly."

"Every day? Never quarreling?"

"Never."

Banquo pulled on his reins, stopping his horse. Mine stopped as well. He reached out and touched my cheek. "And we would make love?"

"Every night."

He pulled off my glove then stroked the scar on my palm. He pressed his hand to mine.

I shivered.

"Cerridwen," he whispered.

It was just him and me. We'd stopped in the middle of a thick forest. Only the eyes of the gods were on us.

"You are my wife," he whispered.

"I was your wife. Merna is your wife now."

"You will always be my wife. Feel the spirit world around us. Don't you feel the Lord of the Wild Hunt? The

Great Lady? We are their children, and under their watch, we are man and wife."

"Banquo," I whispered. His words spoke to my heart.

Banquo exhaled a shuddering breath. "There are standing stones on the other side of that rise, a sacred space. Do you have time to see them, just for a moment?"

I looked around me. The forest floor was covered in thick green moss. Shafts of golden sunlight slanted through the green canopy overhead. Motes made the air sparkle. Trained in Ynes Verleath, the goddesses of death and darkness called me. I was not a druid and knew only what Epona had taught me of the Stag God and the Great Mother, but I did feel the woodsy energy around me. It called to me.

I nodded.

We dismounted and led the horses through a thicket of tall ferns to a small, secluded valley. Leaving the horses to graze, we walked into the green space. At its heart was a small ring of stones. Golden sunlight shimmered on them, illuminating the swirling symbols carved thereon. A ring of oaks surrounded the stone, their tall branches reaching toward the sky. It was a beautiful place. Magic filled the air.

"When I found you in that dark place, this was the passage I used to enter the otherworld. This place is a gateway. The worlds are thin here, and these stones are very, very old. They are different. See their color, texture," Banquo said, setting my hand on the stone. "This stone isn't from our island. It's from a lost land. Even the symbols are not Pictish. The faces, the designs, these are not the engravings of druids. Balor taught me how to move between the worlds, to use the thin places," Banquo said, touching the stag tattoo on his brow. "I searched everywhere for you. But then it occurred to me that you were not in the places known to the druids. You were somewhere far older, darker. That place… It was so strange."

"Yes," I said in a whisper.

"An ancient place," Banquo said.

"An island lost in the mist," I said, staring up at the monolith.

"Were you alone there?"

"No. I was with the Wyrds."

"The Wyrds," Banquo said aghast. "The earth has bubbles, and they are of them. And what did the three dark ladies teach you?"

"Two."

"Two?"

"There were but two there…until I came."

Banquo stared at me, understanding washing over him. "The gods are at work."

"Yes."

My hand still lying on the stone, Banquo set his hand over mine. I could feel his body beside me, feel how I fit into the curve of his shape. I could feel his warmth and breath on my neck. And more than anything, I wanted to turn around and take him into my arms and make love to him there in the eyes of the gods. But I couldn't.

"It is agony to be this close to you," he whispered in my ear.

"It is a pain we must endure."

"Must we? We are alone here."

"Please don't ask me such questions."

"Do you still love me?"

"More than anything," I said then turned and looked at him. "But we cannot. We cannot. I love you, but we cannot. We must wait until the time is right again."

"And what if that time never comes?"

"Then I shall meet you in the next life."

"Promise me here, before the old gods, that in the next life we will overcome any obstacles and be together. We will forsake any blood or creed to be together. Promise me. Promise me that we will be together in the next life. Promise me, then I can bear it." Banquo's brown eyes shimmered with tears. In them, I saw the druid I had fallen in love with. And through his eyes, I saw the echo of Prasutagus.

The wind shifted, and I felt buzzing in the air. The gods were listening.

"I promise."

"As do I," Banquo said.

Banquo pulled me into his arms. I closed my eyes, lost in his embrace. When I opened them once more, I discovered that the world around us had changed. It was very dark, and I smelled the sweet scent of wisteria. Slowly, the world came into focus. Ynes Verleath.

"Banquo," I whispered, pulling back.

Banquo turned, his eyes wide as he took in the sight.

We were on the cauldron terrace.

Nimue stood there in her purple robe.

"Hail, Banquo!" Nimue called.

Banquo stared at her.

"Hail, Banquo. Lesser than Macbeth but greater. Thane of Lochaber, thou shalt get kings, though be none. Thou shall have the love of a queen, though wear no crown. Hail, Banquo and his queen hereafter. Old blood, may your vows carry on the winds of time, and your love last forever," she whispered then waved her hand, closing the veil between our world and hers.

Ynes Verleath, the terrace, and Nimue disappeared.

Once more, we stood in the grove of standing stones.

Banquo stared into the space where Nimue had appeared then looked at me.

"Come, my druid, it's time to go," I said. Taking Banquo's hand, I led him back to the horses.

"What is the name of that dark place?" Banquo asked.

I smirked, remembering how I'd asked Andraste the same question. I shook my head then mounted my horse once more.

"One day, you will tell me," I said.

Banquo raised an eyebrow at me. "I will tell you?"

"Yes."

"How?"

"You will remember," I said with a smirk.

"Remember?"

I nodded.

Banquo shook his head. "Was there ever a pair like us before?"

"Yes," I replied with a laugh, "life, after life, after life, which is precisely our problem."

At that, Banquo laughed, his strong voice filling the enchanted woods.

CHAPTER EIGHTEEN

When we returned, Banquo and I reluctantly parted ways. Morag and Fleance were with Merna at the great hall. Lulach was sleeping at the longhouse. Ute looked exhausted, her eyes having an odd, wild gleam. Lulach must have been hard on her. I didn't remember her ever looking so frazzled before. Suddenly I felt sorry for taking so long. Ute appeared to be in desperate need of a break.

Macbeth, much to my surprise, was also at our longhouse. He was drinking wine and looking over dispatches.

"Ah, so my wife returns from the wild. Now that your lady is back, Ute, why don't you go out," Macbeth said absently as he looked over a letter.

"Yes, my lord," Ute said then rushed out of the house leaving the door open behind her.

There was a strange tension in the air. Had Ute and

Macbeth quarreled? I turned and watched Ute go. She headed down the hill toward the shore.

"Is everything all right?" I asked, closing the door.

"Hmm? Yes. Why do you ask?" he asked as he sipped his wine, a light smile dancing on his lips.

"It's just... No reason. Anyt news of importance?" I asked, glancing down at the scrolls.

"Nothing interesting. Duncan is Duncan. Malcolm plays games. All is the same."

Somehow that seemed like a less than specific answer.

"Is Malcolm aware you are in Thurso?"

"Apparently," Macbeth said, tapping one of the scrolls.

"And?"

"Questions, veiled threats, boasts of power, lots of wind, but nothing to worry yourself over. I've already written to him, told him I'm here spying," Macbeth said with a laugh. "Thorfinn and I are watching and waiting. We will make our plans carefully. Now, tell me, where did you and your playmate run off to?"

His choice of words stung. I bit back my annoyance then said, "There is a family living not far from here. The lady of the house is an old friend."

"From court?"

"No."

"From the *convent*?"

I paused. Already there was too much mistruth between Macbeth and me. Perhaps I was partly to blame for the difficulties between us.

"In truth, I was never at a convent. It was a lie we

spread to hide the fact that I was, in fact, sent to study amongst some holy women of the old faith. You know Banquo studied under a druid. So did I. That is how we met."

Macbeth lowered his paper then looked up at me. For a long moment, he said nothing.

"Macbeth?"

"Malcolm always said your father was a heathen."

"Malcolm should not breathe a word about my father. My father's blood is on Malcolm's hands. Half this kingdom is *heathen*. And most of the north. You've been away from the north for a very long time."

"As if that was my fault," Macbeth growled. "It was only after your husband murdered my father that I was sent away."

"That was long before I had anything to do with Gilla—"

"Don't speak his name in my presence."

"So much for your pretty words about that matter."

"And so much for your honesty, Lady of Moray. So, you spent the morning playing druid while I sat here keeping an eye on my murdering uncle's son. Very good, Gruoch. Well done."

"No one asked you to stay with Lulach. Ute was here, and Merna and Morag are close by. Why do you even bother to play father to Lulach when you've made it so clear to me how much you despise him? I went with Banquo with your blessing. God knows I don't dare give Banquo a passing glance without being accused of tumbling him."

Macbeth rose. Red flashed in his cheeks. "Do not take the Lord's name in vain."

"Are you joking? You, who stand there speaking nonsense, mean to lecture me about God?"

"You are the one speaking nonsense. What are you talking about? I've never accused you of anything."

"Yes, you have. When you were drunk, of course, but that seems to be your usual state since we got here."

"And did you?"

"Did I what?"

"Enjoy a tumble with the good Thane today?"

"Macbeth! He is your friend, and I am your wife."

"Yes, you are," Macbeth said sharply. "Don't you think it's about time you started acting like one?"

"What?" I stared at Macbeth. His eyes were bulging, and he was breathing hard.

"Do you love me?" he asked coldly.

"Of… Of course."

"God gave you to me. He showed you to me in a vision. You are my wife, aren't you?"

"I am."

"Then come," he said then grabbed my arm.

I stared at him. "Come where?"

"Come to your bed and do the duty of a wife." Pulling me along behind him, he led me to our bed.

"Macbeth, this is hardly the right moment," I protested, but still, he took me to the bedchamber.

Turning, he started untying the laces on my dress.

"Macbeth."

"If you are my wife, be my wife."

"Macbeth."

He yanked on my dress, pulling the bodice down to reveal my breasts. When the fabric did not bend to his satisfaction, he yanked it hard. I heard the material rip.

"Macbeth," I whispered, my hands shaking. What was happening?

"Have your courses come on you since we've arrived?" he asked, moving me onto the bed. Moving, however, was more like pushing. Underneath my gown, I wore simple linen riding breeches. He untied those and pulled them and my boots off at once.

"No," I whispered, feeling tears prick the corners of my eyes.

Macbeth's hot mouth closed on my nipples, and he sucked hard. I struggled to move away. My breasts still ready with milk, the sensation confused my mind.

Macbeth stepped back then undid his pants. "No courses. Are you with child?"

"I...I don't think so. My courses won't be regular until Lulach is weaned."

"Then wean him," he said then grabbed my legs and pulled me toward him.

He put himself inside me and pumped hard, beating himself into me as I lay staring at the ceiling.

My mind flashed back to Duncan who had forced me facedown in the mud, pleasing himself as he liked. But this was not the same, was it? Macbeth was my husband. That made this different, didn't it? But if it did, why did it feel the same as before?

"Macbeth," I whispered.

"I love you too," he whispered between breaths.

He rode me hard, and when he had pleased himself to satisfaction, he let me go.

I lay still on the bed, my legs bare and open, staring up at the ceiling. I heard Macbeth refastening his clothes. As I lay there, half-naked and feeling terribly confused, Lulach started crying.

Macbeth leaned over and kissed my cheek. "Our son needs you. Do you want me to bring him?"

"N-no. I'll get him."

Macbeth stroked the stray hairs away from my face. "You won't go out alone with Banquo again, do you understand?"

"What?"

"You heard me. Now get up and see to that babe," he said then a moment later, I heard the longhouse bang shut.

Lulach, his needs unmet, began crying in earnest.

My knees and legs shaking, I rose and pushed down my skirts. Crossing the house, I went to Ute's bedchamber where Lulach lay in his crib, his face red, a pouty expression on his face.

"Oh, my little one, I'm so sorry," I said, picking him up and pressing him against me.

As I turned from the little space, I noticed that Ute's bed was unmade, the furs and blankets thereon a tangle.

Lulach squirmed in frustration. "All right," I whispered,

then went back to the fire and sat down. I set Lulach to breast then leaned back and closed my eyes. My head was spinning. Did Macbeth just not know how to be gentle with a woman? Had he been raised to believe it was all right to behave just like Allister? Thorfinn's words told me my husband was experienced with women, but he was decidedly inexperienced with how to please a lady. He most certainly did not know how to be carnal in a way that felt like love.

I closed my eyes.

Tears streamed down my cheeks.

No. Nothing about this felt like love.

CHAPTER NINETEEN

That night at the feasting hall, Macbeth was smiles and cheer, petting my hair and kissing my cheeks, the picture of perfect happiness. In fact, his effusive displays of affection seemed to grate on Banquo's nerves. It was early in the night when Banquo claimed a headache and left. I could hardly blame him. The moment in the forest and the echo of the life that could have been lingered in my heart as well. That, coupled with what had happened with Macbeth, left me feeling desperately confused. I couldn't handle any more of his excessive affection. Taken alongside his rough treatment, it made my soul feel sick.

"If my lord will excuse me, I think I'll return to our lodgings," I said sweetly, hoping desperately to not incite his unsteady nature.

"Goodnight, lady," Thorfinn called happily, raising his drink to me.

"I'll walk with you," Macbeth said. Taking my arm, he led me outside. Given the sway of his step, I wasn't sure who was walking whom. I didn't want to be with him. I wished he'd let me go alone. I didn't understand his moods, wavering from sweetness to darkness one moment to the next. I had heard of some people who had a mad streak to them, and from what Gillacoemgain had told me, Findelach was certainly a sick man. Perhaps, after all, the son did resemble the father. It had never occurred to me that Macbeth might be like Findelach—and Duncan. I was so fixed on escaping Duncan, I had never considered that Macbeth could be worse.

I should have run away with Banquo.

When we got to the door of the longhouse, Macbeth set a soft but clumsy kiss on my lips. "I need to go back. Will you be all right on your own?"

"Yes, thank you."

"I had word amongst the dispatches that Malcolm has taken a bad fever. It's rumored he may die. Thorfinn and I have much to discuss."

"A fever? Why didn't you tell me earlier?"

"You looked so happy about discovering your old friend, I didn't want to upset you."

I stared at Macbeth. Was he joking?"

"Goodnight, wife," he said, kissing me once more. He turned and headed back to the hall.

I stood outside the door and watched him go. What in the world? Sighing, I turned from the house and walked to the cliff overlooking the sea. The view of the water brought

Ynes Verleath to mind. One day, I would return. I felt sure of it. And right now, the idea of escaping to that dark place sounded wonderful.

"My lady," said a voice.

I turned to see Anor, Thorfinn's skald, walking toward me. I had seen the man around the hall since that first day but had never spoken to him again. Part of me hoped that if I avoided him that he would forget he'd ever seen me during the casting. As I looked into his dark eyes, it was clear to me he had not forgotten.

"Anor," I said, painting on a smile.

"It's a beautiful view," he said, looking out at the harbor. He pulled his dark robes close around him. "But in the winter, when the wind whips off the sea, you'd think your very blood could freeze."

I laughed lightly. "I believe it."

"But when the full moon falls on the dark waters, casting her beams against the wave caps, one would almost think they were living in another time, another place, so different and far from here."

And there it was. "I'm told you are schooled in such matters."

"I'm told nothing about you, lady, save you are the daughter of a man who would have been king and the widow of a murdered soldier. But you are, of course, aware that I know aught of you."

"Do you?"

"Long ago, I saw you appear to Lord Banquo. I never

forgot your face. I had thought...I *had* thought you were one of the dark ladies, one of the Wyrds."

I stared out at the water, debating what would serve me better, lies or truth.

"I am of the old ways, like yourself," I said simply.

"Then it is good you will be queen alongside such a Christian man."

"Malcolm is king. And Duncan will follow him. We are the Lord and Lady of the North, no more."

Anor chuckled. "Lady Macbeth, I am a skald, not a fool. May Odin and Freya guide you to the throne, and may you bend your husband's ear to your wisdom," he said then bowed. "My lady," he added then walked away.

I took a deep breath, inhaling the scene, letting the crisp sea air refresh my wounded spirit, then turned and went inside.

CHAPTER TWENTY

The next morning, I left before Macbeth woke. It was just after sunup when Thora, Lulach, and I headed out. I had overheard Morag and Ute speak of a waterfall on the cliffs near Thurso. Headed in that direction, I set out, Uald's Gift and the dagger Scáthach at my side. After an hour's walk, I finally found the spot. A stream ran across the grassy land then tumbled over the cliff to the sea below. I settled into a spot nearby.

At once, Thora waded into the water, turning over stones with her feet and snapping at fish.

"Don't let the current catch you. I'll be picking up your bones at the bottom of the cliff," I told her.

She lifted her head, cocked it sideways to look at me as if she were saying she knew better, then went back to work hunting the perfect rock.

I lifted Lulach, bouncing him up and down. He giggled. "When are you going to start talking, my big boy? Look how strong you are! Look at those legs. I wish your father could see you," I said, kissing Lulach's cheek.

The boy giggled, his cheek dimpling. His smile was so much like Gillacoemgain's, but that was impossible. I only saw what I wanted to be there.

"I spot a troll and her ilk atop a hill," a voice called from behind me.

I turned around to find Sid standing there. Not just in spirit form either. She was really there.

I gasped then rose. "Sid?"

"How fare you, sister?"

I rushed to her, pulling her into my arms, Lulach laughing as he was squished between us. "Sid! Blessed, Sid. What are you doing here? How?"

"Oh, the fey are full of tricks today. Look there," she said, pointing back upstream where the forest grew thick. "I was headed one place then popped out in that glen. I followed the stream hoping it would lead somewhere when I saw a woman sitting by the water. And look who I found."

"The fey brought you here. Why? Is anything the matter? Come sit. Eat. I have bread and cheese."

"Where am I, anyway?"

"Thurso."

"No wonder it's so cold."

"And Nadia?"

"There." Sid pointed to Thora, who was watching what appeared to be a glimmer of light circling all around her.

Taking her by the hand, I led Sid to the spot where

Lulach and I had been lounging. I eyed her over. I could not believe she was really there. She was really there. But she was also terribly thin and as disheveled as ever. I handed her my water pouch while I put some bread and cheese into a bundle which I also gave to her.

She drank and ate hungrily, eating so quickly she became a crumbly mess. She turned to Lulach, her arms outstretched.

"Now, let me see the little lad. Well, wee one, how are you? What do you think of this world?"

Lulach blew bubbles and reached out for Sid's hair.

She laughed. "He and his sister are just alike. She's still feisty though."

"Is May having trouble with her?" I asked, feeling my heartbeat quicken.

"Oh, no. Crearwy just seems like she's mad at the world," Sid said with a laugh. "I've never seen a baby scowl so much," Sid said, scrunching up her face.

"Oh," I said sadly.

"Not like that, raven beak. She's happy, I promise you. She's just got a sour disposition, like her mother. She's doted on. Epona hardly lets her out of her sight. We love your little lass. She caught a cold a bit back, and Druanne worked night and day looking after her. I don't think I've ever seen Druanne be so nice before. It was remarkable, considering how much she hates you."

I chuckled.

"And how are you? Epona said that hulking beast you

were married to was murdered and that you married his killer."

I frowned at Sid. "It was war."

"Oh? Indeed. And?"

"And, I am sorry to have lost Gillacoemgain."

"He was pretty. And this Macbeth? Is he just as pretty?"

"Pretty is not the word I would use. His looks are fetching, but his manner is…troublesome."

At that, Sid turned serious. "I don't like that word, troublesome."

"Nor do I. But there is some bright light. Banquo is here."

Sid took a huge bite of bread. "No wonder this Macbeth is troublesome. He's in the way," she said between chews.

"Banquo is married. His wife is here as well. She's one of us."

"Why don't you just grab that druid of yours, bring your wee one, and come home?" Sid suggested.

I kissed Lulach on his brow. "Lulach will be Lord of Moray. And if Duncan produces no heir, he will inherit Scotland."

"Future king, eh?" Sid said then turned her attention o Lulach once more. "How about I introduce you to a faerie princess, Your Majesty? We could mix the old blood with human blood again, see what kind of mischief we can cause."

At that, Lulach laughed once more then his eyes went wide as a blob of bright light zipped all around him.

Sid rolled her eyes. "I was just joking," she told Nadia in

an exasperated tone but then leaned toward Lulach and added, "I wasn't joking. You should see the lovely Eolande, daughter of the Seelie king. By the time you're a grown man, she'll be of marrying age."

"Sid," I complained, and at the same time, it seemed that Nadia also pulled her hair in protest.

"All right, all right," Sid assented with a laugh.

"I'll not sacrifice my happiness for Lulach's just to get my boy abducted to the faerie realm," I said, then felt a sharp tug on my own hair. "Nadia, be reasonable. There are dozens of tales of humans disappearing into the faerie realm," I said with a laugh.

"Indeed! Including mine," Sid said with a laugh. She gazed at the waterfall and across the landscape. "I'm surprised to see you here without a ring of guards, Lady of Moray. Doesn't your new husband care what happens to you?"

"I snuck off on my own. I'm sick of the things my new husband cares about."

"Troublesome indeed," she said then set her hand on mine. "I should go back. I don't want to be found in this place."

"Then why don't you stay with me for a while? It would be good to have you here."

Sid scrunched up her face. "It's too cold."

I nodded. I knew I should not press. Sid was not suited for court life, not even Thorfinn's court. She would not survive here.

"I do have one sad piece of news to share," Sid said. "Bride has passed."

I frowned. I was sorry to learn it, but not unexpected. "I knew her time was close."

"Well, at least maybe we'll see Tully again," Sid said, standing once more. "She'll need to bring in our new girls."

I glanced from Sid back to the forest.

"Thora," I called to the dog. I rose then motioned for Thora to come to me. "Go with Sid. Stay until close to her until she…leaves."

Thora tilted her head then turned to Sid and wagged her tail.

"You need to be more careful. You can't just wander about the country like this. What if you pop out somewhere bad?" I told Sid.

Sid shrugged. "What's the worst that can be done to me that hasn't already been done?"

I frowned.

Sid embraced me once more. "Love you, raven beak."

"I love you too. Send my love to Crearwy."

Sid nodded then turned to go. On second thought, she snatched up my water pouch then took off in a run, Thora racing after her.

Sighing, I looked at Lulach. "Don't fall in love with a faerie princess."

Lulach laughed then blew spit bubbles at me.

"Very funny," I said then kissed his cheek. "Time to go."

Gathering up my things, I turned and headed back toward the village.

By the time I returned, everyone was awake and moving about. I slipped quietly back into my house, where I found Macbeth still sleeping. I fed Lulach then lay him down for a nap. By the time I was done, Macbeth was awake.

"You're up early," Macbeth said, rubbing his head as he came and sat down by the fire.

I eyed him warily then poured him a glass of water.

"I went for a walk."

"Alone?"

Something inside me stiffened. "I took Thora."

Macbeth frowned hard. "Take a guard with you next time. You could be kidnapped."

"Things are that bad?"

"We are far north. Norway is an issue."

"And what is the problem with Norway?"

"The problem with Norway is England. Now that King Cnut has declared himself King of Norway, there is strife. Magnus, the rightful ruler, is all of eleven years old. Cnut says he is king. Norway says Magnus is king. King Magnus has Thorfinn's support, which does not please Cnut. And Magnus has what Thorfinn wants."

"Which is?"

"Ingibjorg's hand, which he will only grant once Thorfinn helps him settle this dispute."

"Magnus is looking for strong allies."

"Malcolm has not lifted a hand to stop Cnut. With Malcolm's new alliance to the south, he has no reason to interfere. Keeping Norway in check keeps power out of Thorfinn's hands. When Malcolm passes, from Moray north, we will handle things differently, including recapturing Norway from Cnut for Magnus."

"Who will then ally with you when you and Thorfinn seek to unseat Duncan?"

"All for Ingibjorg," Macbeth said with a laugh then cringed. "Ow, my head aches."

I went to my trunk and pulled out my box with medical supplies. Returning, I opened up the boxes and began putting together a concoction of herbs.

Macbeth watched me carefully.

I ground the herbs down to a fine powder then mixed them with warm water, preparing a healing draft which I handed to Macbeth. "Drink," I said.

"What's this?" he asked.

"It will ease your headache."

Macbeth drank the concoction, frowning at the flavor. "Tastes awful."

I chuckled. "Yes, but you'll feel better within the hour."

"I heard people talk about you at Inverness. They said you were a healer, that you prevented an illness from spreading in Moray."

"Not all of my heathen ways will damn me forever. I suppose I could have gone to the convent and learned to sing. Instead, I learned to heal. Which is better?"

"That depends. How well do you sing?"

"Terribly."

"Show me."

"Dogs will bark. Crows will caw. Night will become day.

And worse than all that, Lulach, who just fell asleep, will wake up."

Macbeth smiled. "Clever wife."

I stared at him, unsure what to think. The expression on his face was so open and honest that I softened. Maybe, one day, things could be better.

Maybe.

CHAPTER TWENTY-ONE

Things improved between Macbeth and myself. I trained myself to worry less over his moods and keep my mind more on my own concerns. Against all odds, I'd gotten lucky with Gillacoemgain. We'd found our way from the start. Even those who married for love struggled the first year of marriage to find their way together. The summer passed peacefully. As time passed, Lulach grew into a strong boy with a mop of dark hair and twinkling blue eyes. Everyone remarked how much he favored me.

It was nearly August when I realized that not only had my courses not come on me again, but my dress was fitting snuggly around my waist. This time, I had no visions of my child as I'd had with Lulach and Crearwy, but from the quickening feelings in my womb, I knew I was with child once more.

Merna was the first to notice. We were sitting outside, and I was busy embroidering a dressing gown for Gwendelofar's babe who would arrive soon when I noticed Merna eyeing me carefully.

"Gruoch," she began, her voice light. "How has Lulach taken to eating solid foods?"

In that single moment, I realized I was sitting around embroidering and talking about babies. Wasn't this precisely what I didn't want?

"Well. He's taken to bread, cheese, and porridge. And he liked the summer fruits and vegetables. Macbeth tried to get him to eat mashed fish, but he wouldn't have it."

"Hmm," Merna said. "Then you've been able to wean him some."

"Y-yes."

"Gruoch," she said then leaned toward me, "Are you with child?"

I set down my embroidery and took a deep breath. "I… I'm uncertain. My courses were not regular yet. But this," I said, my hand drifting down to my bulging midsection, "seems to suggest there is something to that question."

Merna reached out and squeezed my hand. "I'm so pleased for you. Macbeth dotes on you so. I cannot imagine his joy when he learns. And Banquo—you're like a sister to him—will be so pleased for you," she added, her voice falling a bit flat at the end, her expression darkening for just a moment. She quickly covered it with a smile then pulled her hand back.

Did Merna suspect something between Banquo and me? Or had Banquo told her something?

"Look at Fleance and Lulach," she said, pointing to her

son who was rolling a ball to Lulach. Ute held Lulach's hands as he walked, but very soon, he would be able to get around on his own. Lulach gave the ball a kick, laughing wildly when he did so. "I hope you have a girl."

My stomach knotted. I did have a girl. A feisty, sour, but a much-loved girl. "And why do you say that?"

"Our boys will be close. But a girl would give us a way to link our houses."

Merna had never struck me as the ambitious sort. I eyed her as she gazed happily out at Lulach and Fleance. No. Her words had been spoken out of love. "I hope so too," I said, setting my hand gently on her arm.

It was late in the evening when Macbeth returned from the longhouse looking overly tired, but not over-worn with drink, for once. I had laid all the dressing gowns I'd made for Gwendelofar into a pile. I wanted to have everything ready by the time her lying in began.

"What's this?" Macbeth asked, pausing to look.

"My friend will deliver her baby soon. I'll go stay with her then, make sure she has someone learned in medicine watching over her. I made these for her little one."

Macbeth looked down at the tiny garments. His thoughts hung unspoken like a dense fog in the air. In that denseness, I felt his despair. My heart felt glad that, for once, I could do something that would make him pleased with me.

"And after I finish these, I'd best begin a new set."

"For whom? Merna? She always looks plump to me. I can't tell if she's—"

"For me."

Macbeth stilled. "For…you?"

I nodded then looked up at him.

"Gruoch, are you certain?"

"Yes," I said, taking his hand and setting it on my stomach.

Laughing, he stroked his hand across my stomach. "Bless you," he said, kissing me on the cheek. "And bless you," he said, bending to kiss my stomach.

I laughed.

"Do you know how far along you are?"

I shook my head. "Not for certain. I'm guessing maybe ten or fifteen weeks." Last time I'd grown so large due to the twins, I showed far earlier, but I didn't want to bring any of that to Macbeth's mind. The sooner everyone forgot there had ever been two children, the safer for Crearwy.

To my surprise, Macbeth scooped me up then and carried me to the bed. He planted kisses all over my face then touched my stomach. "A boy or a girl?"

"I don't know."

"If a boy, we'll name him after my father. And if a girl, we'll name her after my aunt Crearwy. Poor lass, she died young. Did Gil—did anyone ever tell you about her?"

My heart skipped a beat. "Perhaps if it's a girl, you'd consider my mother's name?"

"Your mother?" Macbeth said then paused. "Gruoch, I don't even know who your mother was.

I smiled. "Few remember her. She was Emer."

"Emer. Emer of House..."

"I don't know, really. I've had no contact with my mother's family. But Allister, my aunt Madelaine's first husband, once mentioned that my father went to war against Máel Sechnaill of Ireland, making treaty thereafter which included one of his daughters, my mother."

Macbeth stared at me. "Máel Sechnaill?"

"I believe that was the name."

"You've never studied the Irish families?"

"No. I've heard since before I could remember that I was of Kenneth MacAlpin's line. I gave little thought to my other family, considering Emer was one of six daughters."

"Malcolm taught Duncan and me about the wars, the feuds. The blood of the Irish kings is mixed with the old kingdom of Dal Riata. Gruoch, Máel Sechnaill was of the Uí Néill."

My brow furrowed. "The Uí Néill?"

"The kings of Tara... Gruoch, your mother was an Irish princess."

"But that's—"

"No wonder Malcolm keeps you chained to one man or another. As his brother's daughter and the granddaughter of a foreign king, your claim to the throne outweighs Duncan's or mine."

"My mother's family has forgotten me. My mother died very young, wed off to a foreign prince who died. None of the Uí Néill will remember I exist. It hardly matters."

"What matters is that *you* know. And if the need ever arises, *we* know. But for now, little one, what do you say? What name can we claim for you?" he asked my stomach, laying a gentle kiss thereon. Macbeth stared at me, his eyes swimming with emotion. "I love you, Gruoch."

"And I you," I said, but there was hesitation in my heart. Did I love him?

CHAPTER TWENTY-TWO

I had never seen Macbeth so happy. It was as if all our old troubles had been erased, wholly forgotten in the wake of the happy news. That night at the feasting hall, everyone toasted in cheer at the good news.

"He'll be a fine, strapping lad," Thorfinn said. "We'll make sacrifices to Thor and Odin to celebrate."

Macbeth smiled at his friend. "Your cheer is all that's needed."

Thorfinn rolled his eyes and leaned forward to look at Banquo, who'd said little throughout the night. "You hear that, Lochaber? We've failed miserably to turn Macbeth to the old ways. Odin, forgive him."

"Aye," Banquo said then picked up his tankard. He finished it off in one long drink then waved to one of the serving maids to bring him another. Merna was not in attendance this night.

"Aye, aye, aye. That's all you have to say tonight, Lochaber. Aye, indeed. Maybe Lady Macbeth will have more luck getting you to speak up," he said clasping my shoulder.

"Are you well, Banquo?" I asked, suddenly feeling all eyes on me.

Banquo smirked then nodded. "Aye," he said then took a long drink of his freshly-filled tankard.

Thorfinn laughed.

I stared at Banquo who wouldn't meet my eye.

While there was much merriment to be had that night, the growing life inside of me drained my energy. Soon, I found I was overly tired.

"I'll retire for the night," I told Macbeth and Thorfinn. "I'm feeling weary."

Macbeth kissed my cheek. "Sleep, my dear wife. I'll check on you later."

Banquo rose. "I'll also retire. I'll walk with you, lady," he told me.

"Aye," Thorfinn said cheerfully then waved farewell to us.

With that, Banquo and I departed. We walked in silence for a time. The air between us was charged. After a bit, he said, "I do wish you congratulations."

I linked my arm with his. "Banquo, I know that—"

"I've meant to tell you that I must return to Lochaber when we travel south."

"Oh? You will not be gone for too long, I hope."

Banquo stiffened then stopped. "What do you expect me to do? How would you feel watching Merna grow ripe with my child? I'll be gone as long as I need to. Goodnight, *Gruoch*, daughter of Boite," he said then let me go. Turning, he headed toward the beach.

"Banquo?"

He did not look back.

"Banquo, please."

He disappeared over the rise and into the dark of night.

Sighing, I turned and went to my house. There was a strange shiver in the air and a cold wind whipped around. When I pushed open the door, I was met with the sharp scent of flowers. I was standing on the cauldron terrace of Ynes Verleath.

"How now, daughter?" a familiar, crackling voice asked.

"Andraste?" I had walked between the worlds.

"I come as the raven," Andraste said.

"And what do you herald?"

"A royal death. "

"A royal death?"

"Your father will be avenged," Nimue said.

"Malcolm. When?"

"When the mother sleeps, so shall he," Andraste replied.

"And after?"

"Strife," Nimue said.

"And blood," Andraste added.

"And crowns for kings," Nimue said. "And queens."

"Make yourself ready," Andraste added then waved her hand before her.

The cold wind blew once more. I rocked a little as I reappeared in the longhouse, standing just outside the open door.

"Oh, my lady, you startled me," Ute said, turning. She was kneeling before the fire, banking up the logs.

I entered slowly, my hands and knees quaking. "Sorry. Is Lulach sleeping?"

"Yes, my lady."

I nodded absently.

"My lady, you should take your rest. I…was so pleased to hear your news," she said, her voice wavering a bit.

"Thank you, Ute. Ute, are you well?" In truth, she had been acting odd since we arrived in Thurso. I had thought it was the strain of the travel and the foreignness of the place, but perhaps there was more to it. Of late, she seemed…nervous.

Ute gingerly set another log on the fire. "I'm well."

I was keenly aware that she was not meeting my eyes.

"Are you certain?"

She rose, clapping her hands. "Yes, my lady," she said with a forced smile.

"Very well," I said, eyeing her carefully. "Goodnight then."

She nodded. "Goodnight."

When I finally lay down, I thought about Andraste's words. A royal death was coming in the winter. Did I dare warn Macbeth? Would he trust my sources? Word had come that Malcolm's spring illness had left him weak, but had not killed him. Yet Andraste's word was to be trusted. She knew what would be.

I would say nothing…yet.

CHAPTER TWENTY-THREE

Two days later, I was wandering along the seashore with Lulach, tossing stones into the water, when Banquo and a man I did not know approached. The man wore the garments of a humble farmer.

Banquo had not spoken to me since we'd quarreled. And he hadn't come out of his house. Merna told me he was not feeling well, but her eyes held a different tale. When I offered to check on him, she dissuaded me.

"Oh no, I've got the matter in hand. It's nothing serious," she had said then changed the subject.

I had no idea what was going on, but I was pleased to see him up and about once more.

As he approached, he only fleetingly glanced at me. I noticed he had dark rings under his eyes and looked very pale.

"Banquo? Is anything the matter?"

"This is Master Young. He's a neighbor to Sigurd and Gwendelofar."

"One of my lads helps Sigurd on their farm. Gwendelofar asked us to send for you. She expects her little one soon," the man said.

I nodded. "Thank you for coming. I'll get ready at once."

"Shall I wait and take you, my lady?" Master Young asked.

"No, I'll take her. Thank you, Master Young. Please have your horse refreshed at the stables. Tell them I sent you."

"Thank you, Thane."

Banquo nodded.

The farmer turned and headed back toward the village.

"Dat, dat," Lulach babbled. "Dat, mum, dat," he said, tugging on my skirt.

Following his gaze, I looked out at the water. Not far away, a pod of dolphins swam, their fins breaking the surface of the water.

"Dolphins. They're hunting fish," Banquo said, kneeling beside Lulach. "The fish swim near the shore, so they've come to eat them up. There are many dolphins in the Moray Firth which you will rule over when you are mormaer," he told my boy.

Lulach's blue eyes widened as he looked out at the water. Banquo picked him up. "Here, lad. Have a better look. There," Banquo said, pointing.

As Lulach studied the water, Banquo studied Lulach. "His eyes and hair are like yours, but not his brow nor that chin…or dimple," he said, squeezing Lulach's cheek. "I met Gillacoemgain once. You were married to him at the time. He came to Lochaber to check my allegiance. He was guarded and suspicious of me, but he spoke plainly and fairly. In truth, his manner surprised me. He did not seem like the man he was rumored to me. Lulach does look like him."

My stomach clenched. The truth would help nothing here.

"Merna said you've been unwell."

"I'll be fine," Banquo said dismissively. "Look, Lulach. You see? Watch them. They may jump."

"Banquo," I said then moved closer to him.

"I'm fine," he said stiffly. "Shall we go back and provision? We'll want to leave soon."

"I must speak to Macbeth."

"Of course," Banquo retorted, his voice sharp.

I made no comment.

"Can you say goodbye to the dolphins?" Banquo asked Lulach.

My little boy waved, watching and waving even after the creatures were out of sight. Banquo followed Lulach's gaze. Banquo narrowed his own glance, and I felt the air around us shift.

"Dat. Dat. Banc, Banc, look. Dat," Lulach said, pointing.

I followed both their gazes. There was a shimmer on the waves, and the water moved as if something had been there, but I couldn't see anything.

"Yes, I see," Banquo told Lulach then kissed his cheek.

"But they are very naughty. You must stay away. Do you understand?"

"Dat. Dat," Lulach said pointing.

"What do you see?" I asked.

"Your child has eyes for the otherworld," Banquo said.

Frowning, I looked again. "As do I, but I see nothing."

Banquo smiled. "Men's eyes are different, Cerridwen."

"Indeed?"

"Indeed. Those who sing from the waves call to men, not women."

I stopped and looked back. How oddly the sun shimmered on the water, making it sparkle and come alive with light. There was something there, but I could not see it. "Selkies?"

"You're the one who named your horse Kelpie," Banquo said with a soft smile. I was glad to see him relax.

I took Lulach's hand and kissed it. "No selkies for you. And no faerie princesses either."

"Faerie princesses?"

"Sid... She told Lulach he should marry the princess of the Seelies."

"Sid was here? When?"

"But a brief moment in the early summer then gone again, as is her way."

"Cerridwen, I'm sorry for my tone the other night. You know I wish you well, I just..."

"You don't need to say anything."

"I do. I was less than kind. I was jealous. And angry. It was wrong. I'm having a hard time—"

"You are only human. And you are forgiven. I did not think I would be able to bear a child again. And things with Macbeth have not been easy."

"You don't have to explain. You are the lawful wife of Macbeth. Please, let's speak of this no more."

"Very well."

We walked back to the village. Banquo handed Lulach back to me. "I'll be in the stables when you're ready. I'll have them prepare a cart."

I nodded then turned and went to the hall. It was still early in the day. Macbeth and Thorfinn sat together looking over dispatches. Their conversation was low and dark.

"My lords," I called as cheerfully as possible.

Macbeth stood.

Thorfinn smiled at me. "Ah, the Lord of Moray has come to hear the news. Come, Lord Lulach. See what we are scheming." Thorfinn rose and reached out to Lulach who went readily to him.

I felt a brush against my leg as Thora suddenly appeared.

"Now, where have you been?" I scolded her then turned to Macbeth. "Word has come, my lord. My dear friend's lying in has begun. With your blessing, I will go attend her."

Macbeth smiled kindly. "Of course. Banquo will escort you. Ask him to prepare a cart," he said then turned to Lulach. "What say you, my boy? What shall we men do while your mother is gone?"

"Is there news?" I asked, looking down at the papers scattered on the table.

Thorfinn groaned. "Cnut posturing in Norway. Malcolm unusually quiet."

I chewed my lip. No. This was not the time.

"Anything from Madelaine?"

Macbeth shook his head.

I frowned. It had been some time since I'd heard from her. I had not yet sent news south of my pregnancy in case one of Malcolm's spies intervened. If Macbeth and I had a son—before Duncan—it would further add to our claim. It was best that no word was sent until the child was delivered.

"I'll go make ready then?" I said, letting the question linger, well aware of Macbeth's reaction the last time I'd gone out with Banquo.

Thorfinn kissed Lulach and handed him back to me. "Safe travels, lady. You're a lucky man, Macbeth. Your wife is wise, beautiful, and has a healer's touch. One day, she and my Ingibjorg will be quite the pair."

I chuckled. "And your Ingibjorg, what is she like?"

"She has the sweetest heart, tits big as melons, and a blonde braid thick as a horse's tail down to her round ass."

Macbeth laughed.

"So, many good qualities then," I said with a laugh. "Anything else?"

"Does a man need anything else?" Thorfinn replied.

"Perhaps not."

Thorfinn smiled. "Be safe, Lady Macbeth."

"No worries there, Thane," Macbeth said. "Banquo watches over her like she was his sister."

"So he does," Thorfinn said with a nod then turned back to his papers, smothering a look that had only briefly crossed his face.

"Come back soon," Macbeth said, kissing me once more. "And stay safe."

"And you," I said then turned to go. My heart felt much at ease. Perhaps the last time too much drink had provoked his jealousies. Whatever worries had nagged Macbeth, they were gone. He was not the man he had been some months ago, thank the Goddess.

It took me about an hour to prepare, but soon Banquo and I had the wagon loaded and were ready to go.

Merna chatted quietly to Banquo, who nodded and replied to her in whispered words. From the expression on her face, I could tell she was worried about him. In truth, I was not sure if he had been truly ill or merely melancholy.

"I'll be all right," he finally told her, his voice sounding a bit exasperated, then he kissed her on the forehead. He turned to Fleance. "Mind your mother," Banquo told him.

"Yes, sir," he said in his sweet, earnest, child's voice. But the fact that he was lying was so plain, it made me chuckle.

"And don't get into any trouble," Banquo added.

"No, sir," he said then giggled knowing that his lie was too bold.

Banquo smiled then shook his head.

"Are you sure you don't want me to come, my lady," Ute asked me for the hundredth time. "I'll be on hand in case you need help. And I can help your friend with her little ones. Are you sure, my lady? It won't be any bother."

I looked at Ute realizing then that she wanted to come but didn't have the courage to break protocol and just ask. I eyed her over. She was very pale and worked her hands nervously. "Ute, is everything all right?"

"Oh, of course. I just worry about Lulach. I know you've got him almost weaned, but I hate to have him far from you, especially since you might be gone a couple of days. I worry," she said then looked down. "And you might need help. I could help you."

She was lying. Something was wrong. "Ute?"

"Are you sure you don't want me and Lulach to come? I got him ready just in case. I have everything packed for him and me, in case you changed your mind."

I stared at her. There was something going on here that I could not see.

"You will need to keep Lulach out from underfoot," I said.

"Of course, my lady. I'll go get our things now," she said then turned and rushed to the house.

I turned to Banquo who looked like he'd just caught the tail end of our conversation.

"Ute and Lulach will join us," I told him.

Banquo nodded. "Very well. And where is Thora?"

I spotted her in the distance running around with her pack of mongrels. "There," I said, pointing.

Banquo whistled loudly. The sound grabbed Thora's attention. Leaving her pack behind, she raced across the village and hopped into the wagon.

"Merna, will you be so kind to let Macbeth know Lulach and Ute decided to join us?"

"Of course," she said with a smile.

I exhaled deeply. Surely, Macbeth would take no issue with it. After all, it would free him from being troubled with Lulach while I was gone.

Ute raced in and out of the house, first depositing bags and then returning with Lulach who was bundled up. I climbed into the wagon then she handed my boy to me. After, she crawled into the back of the wagon with Thora, wrapping her arm around the dog. I didn't miss the look of relief on her face.

"Safe journeys," Merna called. Fleance, Morag, and Merna waved to us as we set out.

Banquo and I waved farewell then headed off.

"No talking to the good neighbors when we go into the forest, my pretty boy. They'll take you and leave me a changeling," I whispered to Lulach.

Banquo laughed. "They'll never touch him. Don't worry."

"And why do you say that?"

Banquo pointed to the red dart on Lulach's brow. "He comes by his protection naturally."

"It was a blessing gifted to him."

Banquo nodded. "Have you noticed the shape of it? It's changing as he gets bigger."

I stared at my son. Banquo was right. The red dart had the subtle shape of a stag's head.

"What does it mean?"

Banquo smiled. "As you said, he's blessed."

I thought back to that morning by the water and how Lulach had been able to see the selkies. And when Sid had come for that brief moment, Lulach had noticed Nadia. I had always assumed Crearwy would be the one gifted with the old magic, but Lulach truly had been touched.

I exhaled deeply and looked at my little boy who was snuggled against me. In protecting his claim to Moray and to the crown, I had never considered what might happen if Lulach's spirit was more suited for a different life. A terrible feeling of dread washed over me. What if he was more like his father? Gillacoemgain had much preferred the woods, the animals, birds, and sunny fields to statecraft. But I tripped over my own thoughts. Gillacoemgain was not his father.

I'd told the Morrigu that Lulach's fate was beholden to none. It was his own to decide. But what if I had already steered him down a path ill-suited for him?

"Little Lulach," I whispered then kissed my child on his brow. My hand drifted to my stomach, to the life growing so unexpectedly inside my womb. Soon, I'd have another's future in my hands. I hope the fates would be easier to the child of Macbeth.

CHAPTER TWENTY-FOUR

We reached the small farm just before nightfall. Sigurd met us at the door.

"Ah, here is Cerr—"

"Lady Gruoch," Banquo interrupted. "And her maid, Ute."

"Ah, yes. Lady Gruoch. Just in time. Gwendelofar started swearing in Rus about an hour ago," he said then laughed.

I chuckled. "My maid kindly offered to come along. We thought she could help keep Neda occupied. And here is my little Lulach."

"Oh, aye. Let me see him," Sigurd said, reaching out to Lulach who grinned at him. "He looks much like you."

I smiled. "Thank you."

Banquo handed me my medicine kit. "We'll see to Lulach. Why don't you check on Gwen?"

"Come along, Lord Lulach. Neda is hiding in the barn. Let's see if you can talk her out," Sigurd told my boy.

I headed inside.

Before I even reached the door, I heard Gwendelofar muttering in her mother tongue.

"Gwen?" I called.

"Cerridwen, thank goodness. Took you long enough."

I bit my tongue then grinned at her. "Very sorry. My maid came with me, so it will be Gruoch or Corbie."

Gwendelofar nodded like she couldn't care less. "I think this baby is trying to break my back," she said, pressing her fists into the small of her back.

"And your labor pains?"

"I knew it was starting. That's why we sent our neighbor to you. My water broke soon after. The pains are not too close yet, but getting worse."

"Let me prepare you something to ease the aches," I said then opened my box.

Gwen didn't argue.

I mixed a concoction, which she drank readily. Then we prepared for a long night.

Gwen paced most of the evening, but with mine and Sigurd's firm but loving suggestions, and just a little bit of muttered cursing, she finally lay down. To my great relief, she fell asleep. Before Neda fell asleep, I made good on my promise to her.

"Neda," I called to the girl. Bending down, I opened the trunk I'd brought with me. I smiled at Neda, her long red hair flowing down her back. Her locks put me in mind of

Madelaine. "I have something for you," I said handing her a package.

Sigurd watched, a smile on his face.

The girl unwrapped the parcel carefully, revealing the small harp therein. "Oh, how beautiful!" Setting the harp down carefully, she threw her arms around my neck and hugged me.

I chuckled. "I'm glad you like it."

Sigurd smiled. "It's beautiful. Thank you."

Neda beamed up at her father then snatched the harp and ran outside. Not long after that, we heard the strings jangle discordantly. Sigurd let the girl play for awhile before he finally ushered her into bed. She passed out with the harp clutched to her chest. Sigurd made up a pallet for Ute and Lulach as well. And as the night wore on, they both finally fell asleep.

Sigurd and Banquo spent most of the night outside by the fire. I had stayed inside beside Gwendelofar who mostly dozed, but finally, I had gotten weary as well. I joined the men only to find they had both been overzealous in toasting the coming babe. They had both drunk themselves half blind which was unusual for Banquo. The sight of them sitting by the fire took me back to nights long ago.

"Cerridwen," Sigurd called. "Is everything all right?"

"Thank the gods she is sleeping. She'll need her rest before the hard work begins."

I sat down beside Banquo, who handed his ale horn to me. I waved it away.

Banquo laughed. "You know, I don't think I've ever seen you lost in your cups before."

"I don't think I ever have been. And tonight, alas, is not the night."

"Cerridwen is far too serious for that," Sigurd said.

"I am not."

"I'm not saying it's your fault," Sigurd said. "You just spent too much time with Uald."

"Uald is not serious. She just doesn't like people," I said with a laugh.

"And you?"

"Maybe I'm a little serious, and I don't like *most* people."

Sigurd chuckled.

"Cerridwen knows how to have fun. And she's very serious about it when she puts her mind to it," Banquo said then smirked at me. There was heat in his eyes which he never showed in public. I was surprised to see his expression so open.

Sigurd caught the glance. "Indeed. Druid?" he said to Banquo then turned to me. "Is that true?"

"What better time to be serious than when you're having fun?" I asked.

Sigurd laughed. "I hear many a man and woman are serious on Beltane."

"As Neda can prove," I said.

Sigurd chuckled then rose. He was wobbly on his feet. "Every day is Beltane when you're with your beloved. Speaking of, I'll go check on my wife."

"For the love of all the gods, do not wake her," I called.

"I'll do my best," Sigurd said then headed inside.

Banquo filled his ale horn once more. "Don't know how you can handle it without drink. When Fleance came into the world, I thought my hair was going to turn white."

I laughed.

The fire crackled and popped sending sparks into the sky.

"The old ones are speaking," Banquo said, motioning to the fire.

"And what are they saying?"

"They're dreaming of Beltane."

"Them or you?"

Banquo chuckled. "Both of us."

"Banquo, are you well?" I asked, looking him over carefully.

"I...I'm fine. In fact, at this moment, there isn't a thing more I could ever need," he said then set his hand on the back of my head, gently stroking my hair. "My Cerridwen."

I gazed into his eyes. He had drunk too much, and it had loosened his tongue.

Why would the Goddess do this to me? Why would she give me someone to love, take him from me, then throw them back in front of me in a place and time where we could not be together?

But what was standing in my way? A promise I'd made to Macbeth, fidelity promised to please a god I did not honor. Didn't my vows to Banquo mean more than that? In truth, Macbeth was difficult to love. No amount of visions and dreams could change that truth. My honor held me back from taking what I really wanted. But should it?

As if reading my thoughts, Banquo took my hand. "There is a glade not far from here where the moonbeams fall on a stream, and a wide oak grows. Maybe we should have a look. We wouldn't be far away. If Sigurd called, we would hear. Cerridwen, I *need* you."

I stared into the fire. Could I? I carried another man's child. It was not right. But still.

"Banquo," I whispered, squeezing his hand.

Banquo rose. Taking my hand, he gently pulled me to my feet.

The door to the house opened, and Ute stepped out.

"My lady?" Ute called, her voice wavering.

"Is something the matter?" I asked, trying to kill the resentment in my voice. By all the gods, why had she come?

"Um, no. Lady Gwendelofar and Lulach are fine. I... Can I have a moment, Gruoch?"

Her use of my common name stamped out the fire in me at once. Something was very wrong. I turned to Banquo. From the look on his face, I could see he had also heard the plea. He nodded to me then dug into his coat where he pulled out a pipe and lit it. He refilled his ale horn once more and sat back down, staring into the fire.

I crossed the lawn to meet Ute.

"What is it?" I whispered, looking closely at her.

She cast a glance back at Banquo, seemed to steel her nerve, but then a small sob escaped her lips.

"I... I am with child," she whispered.

When I opened my mouth to tell her it was no matter for me, she tapped me on the arm gently to stop me.

"You're skilled with herbcraft. I want to be rid of the babe," she said.

"Oh, Ute. Are you certain? You know I follow the old ways. A child born out of wedlock is not a probl—"

"No! I want to be rid of it. Will you please help me? I trust you, my lady. You're such a good woman. You deserve a good life," she said then broke out into a sob. She sucked her tears back. "You've been so good to me. Please, will you help me?"

"Maybe if you told the father," I began then stopped cold when her eyes, wet with tears, met mine.

"No," she said with a shaking gasp.

It was not my business to press her for details. If she wanted to tell me, she would. "It's not without risk," I told her.

"I know."

"I… I will have difficulty attending both you and Gwen. But Lord Banquo was druid-trained. He can watch over you."

"Do you trust him to keep my secret?"

"I'd trust him with my very soul."

Ute paused then nodded. "Go ahead and make the draft. I'll go sit by the fire."

"Very well." My head was reeling. Poor Ute. This was not what I wanted for her. She knew the cost. This would be painful, and there was a risk she may not have a child again. And it was ill-timed with Gwen's baby coming. But at least now I knew why she had come, knew what had been troubling her. She'd wanted to get away from the village to take care of this problem and do so in secret.

I motioned to Banquo to join me at the wagon.

Still weeping, Ute sat down by the fire.

"I need your gloves," I told Banquo.

"What's happening?" Banquo asked quietly.

"Ute has asked me for a tonic to rid her of a child. Will you help me watch over her?"

Banquo paled. "Whose child?"

"I don't know. She didn't say."

Banquo frowned hard then pulled out his gloves and handed them to me. I slipped them on.

"You must be very careful with the mixture in your state," he cautioned.

"Yes, you're right. I will be."

Banquo put his hand on my arm, his eyes meeting mine. "Do you ever get the feeling it's just not meant to be between us. Maybe never again?"

Tears pricked at the corners of my eyes. "Speak on it no more."

Banquo squeezed my arm then let me go.

My medicines were inside. "Give Ute an ale. I'll be back soon," I said then headed within. There I found Lulach and Thora sleeping together. Sigurd had lain down beside Gwen. Both were sleeping, but Gwen winced in her sleep. She wouldn't rest for long.

I opened my box of medicines and pulled out what I needed. Epona had taught me the mixture. Working carefully with my gloves on, I ground the herbs and mushrooms into a fine powder. It had a sharp smell that made my nose burn. When I was done, I used a simple wooden cup to prepare the drink. It would need to be burnt afterward, as would the tools I'd used to make it. Working carefully, I made the concoction. If prepared it wrong, it could kill her. She could bleed to death. If it was not strong enough, the child would still be born but deformed. Epona had warned of the use of such heavy hearth magic. I would have advised Ute against it once more if not for the look on her face. She was desperate to be rid of the babe.

While Ute was my maid, I did not own her. I could not force her to tell me what had happened, or who the father was. Perhaps the man was married. Or maybe she did not want to ruin her future prospects by having a child out of wedlock. No matter the reason, it was her reason alone. I would not press her.

My work done, I set the tools and the drink on a tray then carried them outside.

Banquo and Ute sat together.

Banquo was speaking kindly to her. She nodded mutely, dashing tears from her cheeks. When she saw me walking toward her, she paled then rose to meet me.

"Are you certain?" I asked her once more.

She nodded then took the drink.

"Drink it all at once then lie down. You'll have pain like you do during your monthly cycles, but it will be worse."

"How long?"

"A day. No more."

"I am sorry. I know that I suggested you bring Lulach, but I might not be able to watch over him as I intended."

"No matter," Banquo said. "I'll take care of him."

Blessed Banquo.

Ute returned to the fire where she sat and drained the drink, wincing at the taste. She threw the empty cup into the flames.

I handed the tray to Banquo who carefully pulled off my gloves. He took the materials and disappeared into the night with them. I sat down beside Ute and took her hand.

"Whatever went wrong, I am very sorry," I said softly.

"Thank you, Gruoch."

"Is there anything I can do to help?"

"No," she said with a soft sob.

I wrapped my arm around her and pulled her close.

Banquo returned once more, his hands empty, and sat down beside us.

It was late in the night when Sigurd called for me. I woke to discover that sometime during the night, I'd fallen asleep by the fire leaning against Banquo, his arm wrapped around me, my head on his chest. Ute slept on the ground nearby. She shook in her sleep, looked very pale, and was sweating.

"She doesn't have any fever. I checked on her. I'll watch over her," Banquo whispered. "But we should tell Sigurd what's happening."

"Discreetly," I said.

Banquo nodded.

I rose and went to Gwendelofar who was sitting on her bed, gripping handfuls of straw as she gritted her teeth.

"Well, your little one about ready?" I asked her, helping her lie down once more so I could have a look. After a quick examination, I saw she was very close.

I stayed with Gwen the rest of the night. It was mid-morning when, at last, Gwen's baby arrived. After a good hour of pushing, along with a lot of swearing in Rus which I was glad I did not understand, a little boy was finally born. His hair was as red as his face, and he squalled loudly.

On hearing his son's cry, Sigurd appeared at the door.

I cleaned the child off then handed him to his mother. Gwen's labor had been hard, but she'd delivered cleanly, unlike my own birth which had left me torn and in pain.

Sigurd rushed to his wife, kissing her and his newborn child. They were all smiles and love.

"Have you decided on a name?" I asked.

"Uffe," Sigurd said.

Rising, I washed off my hands and removed my apron. I headed back outside. Banquo had already given the children their breakfast and was playing a game with Neda, Lulach, and Thora. Ute was nowhere to be seen.

"Neda, you have a little brother," I told the little girl, who stopped and looked up at me.

"Can I see him?"

I nodded.

The girl ran off to join her family.

"Ute?" I asked Banquo as I stretch my back. My whole

body ached, my muscles feeling like I had carried a thousand Gwendelofars to Edinburgh and back.

Banquo exhaled deeply then nodded. "It's done. She's all right. She was sitting by the stream when I saw her last," he said, motioning across the field.

"Thank you," I said, taking his hand.

"She wept a lot, and there was some pain. I eased her struggle as best I could," he said, setting his hand to his brow.

Druid magic.

I squeezed his hand. "Thank you. We'll let her rest today then go back tomorrow morning."

Banquo nodded then looked toward the house. "Let me go greet the little one."

I took Lulach from Banquo.

"He's getting pretty good on those little legs of his. You'll be in trouble soon," he said, grinning at Lulach.

I smiled and kissed my boy. "Come, let's check on Ute," I told Lulach.

Banquo headed inside while I went in the direction of the stream. It took me a bit, but finally, I found Ute sitting beside what I guessed to be the same wide oak tree Banquo had mentioned the night before.

She sat with her knees drawn to her chest, her face wet with tears. She looked terribly pale.

"Uuuute," Lulach called to her.

She smiled at him, wiping the tears from her cheeks.

I settled on the ground beside her, holding Lulach in my lap.

"How is Gwendelofar? The baby?" she asked.

"Both are well. It was a boy. They've named him Uffe."

"Wolf," Ute said. "The name means wolf."

I laid my arm across her shoulders and pulled her close to me.

"Are you all right?" I asked softly.

"I will be. Lord Banquo… He is a very good man."

I kissed her on her forehead and said no more, only sat with her watching the water tumble over the rocks.

Sigurd, Gwen, and Neda were lost in their new little one. Ute rested. As the day wore on, my back ached more and more. I had been under a heavy strain of tension all night. Every muscle hurt. Later that day, I'd prepared dinner for everyone then went and sat down at the table, watching pretty little Neda eat with one hand while she held her harp with the other. My mind drifted to Crearwy. Would she like a harp too? I remembered the story the Lord of Mar had told me about my mother, about how she'd played the harp. What was Crearwy even like? My own daughter was a stranger to me. I began to feel drowsy. I was surprised when Banquo shook my shoulder. I had fallen asleep at the table. It was already dark outside once more.

"There's no room left in the house. If you'll consent to sleeping in the barn, your bed is ready," he said playfully.

I yawned tiredly. "I'd sleep in the mud at this point." I rose and looked around to find Gwen and Sigurd asleep with their little one and Neda on her own bed with her harp.

"How long have I been sleeping?"

"An hour or so. I say, I never knew you could snore as loud as Thorfinn," he said with a laugh.

"I did not."

I cast a glance at Ute who also lay sleeping, Lulach at her side. I stopped and checked her for fever. She was fine. I lifted Lulach. Thora, who had been sleeping at their feet, lifted her head to see what was going on. She rose and followed Banquo, Lulach and me outside. In the barn, the horses nickered at us. Banquo lifted a lantern and led me to a stall where he'd laid some furs and blankets over a heap of straw. Exhausted, I lay Lulach down then settled in beside him.

Banquo lay down on Lulach's other side.

Thora stomped around until she finally found a spot at our feet.

Banquo and I giggled then lay looking at one another, staring into one another's eyes. I smiled gently at him. The moment was a rare bliss. There was no one here who could ruin this.

Banquo reached out and brushed a strand of hair away from my face. His finger stroked my bottom lip.

"Sleep, Cerridwen," he whispered. "You look very tired."

My eyes closed as if he'd cast a spell on me. In truth, my whole body ached. My back and hips hurt the most. I wanted nothing more than sleep.

"I love you," Banquo whispered.

"I love you too," I replied as I drifted off to sleep. A strange pain racked my stomach. Macbeth's seed seemed to protest my love on his father's behalf.

"Shush," I whispered, my hand drifting to my stomach. And then I was lost to dreams.

CHAPTER TWENTY-FIVE

When I woke the next morning, Banquo was gone, and Lulach was laying handfuls of straw on me as if to cover me.

I laughed then sat up. Nausea swept over me, and unable to control myself, I rose and vomited.

Lulach went still. "Mum?"

"I'm all right," I said. My body still ached, my back feeling stiff. "I'm all right."

Once I got myself steady and cleaned up, Lulach and I headed to the house. The smells of bread and pork filled the air. My stomach growled hungrily but also heaved with nausea. Such was the way with pregnancies.

The others gathered at the table. Even Gwen was up and looking cheerful.

"How are we this morning?" I asked, taking a seat beside Banquo, who took Lulach so I could prepare some food for the boy and myself.

"He's full of fire," Gwen said, smiling down at her little one. "He's a good eater."

"Are you feeling all right?" I asked her.

She nodded. "As well as can be expected. Many thanks to you, sister."

"I'm glad I could come."

Ute was very silent. She picked at her food, but her color was improving.

"Will my ladies be ready to return this morning?" Banquo asked, casting a glance at Ute.

"Aye, my lord," Ute answered absently, knowing the question was more for her than me.

I smiled and nodded. "Back to Thurso for now, but we'll return south soon," I told Sigurd and Gwen. "Within the month."

Gwen smiled sadly. "We'll miss you."

"And I shall miss seeing little Uffe grow. And little Neda," I said, reaching out to pat the child's head.

She smiled at me. With her father's red hair and her mother's face, she was going to be a startlingly beautiful young woman.

With Gwen and the baby in good health and good spirits, we prepared to depart. My stomach rocked all day, and I barely kept down the breakfast. I hated that my pregnancy sickness was returning. Lulach and Crearwy had not been easy on me while in the womb. I had hoped Macbeth's child would be calmer. But it seemed that would not be the case. With a promise from Ute that she was okay to travel, we headed out for Thurso.

As we rode across the countryside, the rocking of the cart made me increasingly more nauseous. I started to sweat, and more than once, I had to steady myself when black spots appeared before my eyes. The village was in sight when I swooned dizzily.

Banquo pulled the cart to a stop. "Gruoch, are you sick?"

I nodded and got out, retching at once.

"My lady," Ute called, but she was hardly in a better state than myself.

Banquo rushed to my side, his waterskin ready for when the worst of it had passed.

"It's just… The wee one doesn't like the cart, I think," I said.

Banquo rubbed my back then handed me the water.

Once I'd caught my breath, I climbed back in, and we headed off once more.

"I'll ask Morag to come and look after you and Ute. Ute should be off her feet for few days, and you are not well."

"Merna won't mind?"

Banquo smiled gently. "No."

His expression distracted me from my illness. Would she not mind because she was so kind or because she was so obedient? In truth, a man's manner with his wife is only truly shown in private. No one knew how tough Macbeth was. Did Banquo place such demands on Merna? Was he taken to moods in private?

I chided myself. No one knew Banquo better than myself. He was nothing like Macbeth.

When we finally arrived, Banquo helped Ute out of the wagon. I followed behind with Lulach. Thora was already running off to find her pack. Once inside, I poured water for Ute and myself. Ute had already gone to lie down.

"Are you all right?" I asked, setting a glass of water on the table beside her bed. She lay with her knees pulled up tight against her chest.

"Yes," she said tiredly.

"Do you want anything for the pain?"

"No," she said. "The worst is past. I…am sorry to trouble you with such things. I am indebted to you."

I smiled down fondly at her, chiding myself for my earlier annoyance with her. Ute had been good to me and had endured a lot on my behalf. She deserved better from me.

"As I am to you. If you need anything, please don't hesitate to ask. Now or ever in the future."

Ute's eyes watered, a tear slipping down her cheek. "Thank you."

I left her. My body ached as well, and I'd started to feel twisting cramps. I knew this was normal, that my body was just making ready for the baby, but I didn't feel well.

A short while later, there was a knock on the door. Morag and Banquo appeared.

Morag nodded to me. "My lady."

"Reinforcements," Banquo said.

"Now, come along, Lord Lulach," Morag said, picking up the boy.

"Gruoch, you should lie down," Banquo told me then set a hand to my forehead. "You're warm."

"Ah, my wife has returned!" Macbeth called happily as walked toward us. His smile dimmed when he took us all in. "Is everything well?"

"Ute took ill on the trip. She's resting," I said.

"Morag will attend Lady Gruoch until Ute is better," Banquo added.

Disinterested, Macbeth gave a slight nod. "And you, lady?" he asked, looking at me.

"Just the normal troubles," I said, setting my hand on my stomach.

"And your friend?"

"Safely delivered a son."

Macbeth smiled. "Would we were so lucky, Gruoch."

"I think Lady Gruoch should lie down," Banquo said, his face scrunched with worry.

"Indeed, you're not looking well, my lady," Morag said, taking me gently by the arm. "Sons, sons, sons, that's all some men care about. Can't he see you're aswoon on your feet," she added under her breath.

Settling me into bed, Morag patted my arm. "Don't worry about your boy, Lady Gruoch. Merna and I will watch him like he was our own blood. Get some rest."

Grateful to her, I slipped under my blankets.

"Gruoch, are you all right?" Macbeth, who was standing in the doorframe, asked.

"Just weary. I didn't sleep much. I just need some rest, that's all."

"Oh. All right. Very well."

"I'll be fine by morning. Nothing to worry about."

He nodded then turned and left.

Afterward, I fell asleep. I saw a terrible dream. Gillacoemgain standing in the roundhouse as fire burned all around him. I heard him calling my name. I watched as if through a window and could do nothing, could not move, could not speak. The fire burned so hot. I stood frozen, watching as the flames took him. All the while, he screamed my name. The image startled me so that it shook me awake. I woke with a scream.

"Gruoch?" Macbeth said, sitting up.

When had he come to bed?

"Macbeth. I…" I began then a sharp pain rocked my groin. Grunting in pain, I strangled back a scream.

"My lady," Morag called. Without waiting for permission, she entered the room. "What's the matter?"

"She had a dream," Macbeth said.

Morag frowned at him then set her hand on my forehead. "Burning with fever. We need to get you out from under the blankets," she said then pushed the cover aside to reveal the puddle of blood all around me.

Macbeth gasped.

"Go get Lady Merna. Now," Morag told Macbeth.

"Morag," I whispered.

Macbeth rose and ran out of the house.

"Lie back, Gruoch," she said.

Another sharp pain crashed across my back and waist.

Morag adjusted my legs and lifted my skirts to examine

me. After a moment, I heard her suck in a deep breath then let it out slowly.

"Morag?"

She lowered my dress. "Lay on your side. It will ease the pain. Gruoch… I'm sorry."

I closed my eyes. The pain hadn't felt right. I should have known. I should have known. My back ached miserably, and hard cramps shook me. Black spots appeared before my eyes.

"The pain will pass by morning," Morag said. "But then it will be over."

No, no, no, no. This can't be happening.

"My lady?" Ute called from the door.

"Lady Gruoch has had a misfortune," Morag whispered.

Ute gasped.

"It happens to many ladies, most of whom go on to have children later. I'll watch over her. Get your rest," Morag said.

A few moments later, the door opened once more.

I heard Merna, Banquo, and Macbeth. I could not make out their words, but Macbeth seemed to be in a panic. Merna was the first to enter the bedchamber. Morag spoke quietly to her. I did not hear all their words, but a few moments later, Merna sat beside me on the bed.

"Morag will bring you something for the pain," she said, gently taking my hand.

I kept my eyes closed. Terrible cramps racked my body.

The outside door opened and closed once more. From outside the longhouse, I could hear Banquo's and

Macbeth's voices. Their conversation was heated. Macbeth's voice was low and angry. I heard a hard edge to Banquo's voice I'd never heard before. Their words were muffled, but I guessed the nature of the quarrel. Macbeth would blame Banquo. And me. He would place the burden of this on our shoulders.

As I listened, their voices grew louder.

Macbeth screamed at Banquo. "This is your fault. You, who are so free with my wife. What have you done? My son!"

"Macbeth, please," I heard Banquo try to reason, but soon I heard a scuffle.

"Oh, my gods. These men," Merna said glaring at the door.

"What's happening here? What in Odin's name are you two doing? Get off him, Macbeth," Thorfinn said.

There was another muffled, angry exchange when finally Thorfinn, it seemed, had enough.

"Don't you know your wife could die?" Thorfinn shouted. "Stop blaming Banquo, and go to her."

A few moments later, Morag returned. "Men. Always looking for someone to blame. Sometimes it's just not the will of the gods. Drink," she told me, handing me a cup.

I sat up slowly, drinking the warm tonic. I recognized the herbs therein. They were strong. I knew they would loosen my mind and numb the pain.

Outside, the shouting continued, and I heard Macbeth's voice recede into the night, Thorfinn following him.

A moment later, the door opened. Banquo appeared at

the entrance to the bedchamber. His face was shadowed in the darkness, but I could see there was a fresh cut above his eye.

Merna flicked her eyes toward her husband. She shook her head but said nothing. Instead, she turned back and smiled down at me, gently pushing my hair behind my ear.

"I'm sorry this happened. I truly am. Please don't worry about Lulach. I'll take him to my home and put him down with Fleance. I'll look after them. Morag will stay with you."

"Thank you," I whispered.

Merna squeezed my hand, nodded, then rose. Passing a few low words to her husband, she left.

"I'll make a hot compress for your back," Morag said then went back out to the main room.

Banquo sat down beside me.

"You're bleeding," I whispered, reaching out toward his broken face.

Banquo shook his head, dismissing it. He gently touched my cheek. "Do you think it was the tonic you made for Ute?" he whispered.

"No. I was careful. Epona taught me well."

"The wagon?"

"It started before that. I just didn't realize. It was just not meant to be."

A look of guilt crossed Banquo's face.

"It is not your fault, no matter what Macbeth said."

"You heard?"

"I heard enough."

Banquo exhaled. "He's so damned difficult. I hoped you would never know that side of him."

"It's the side I know best."

"Then I am truly sorry."

Banquo gazed at me. He sighed heavily then took my hand in his. He closed his eyes and began whispering softly. From the cadence of his words, I knew he was casting an incantation. He pulled out his dagger and opened his palm. He made a small cut, following the scar on his palm from our handfasting. He then wet one finger with his own blood. Opening my hand where I had a similar scar, he drew a rune in blood. He whispered as he spoke, and I felt magic in the air around us. When he was done, he whispered, "So mote it be" then closed my hand.

Banquo leaned over me and kissed me on my brow.

"Banquo?"

"Rest. I'll stay nearby. When Macbeth returns, he can either murder me or have Thorfinn force me to leave. But I'm not going until you are out of danger."

"Ah, here we go," Morag said, returning once more. She carried a mug of something and a bundle of steaming cloth. A strong, heady herb smell filled the air.

"Banquo, will you please check on Ute," I whispered.

He nodded then left.

Morag smiled after him then turned me so she could apply the hot compress to my back. "A good man, the Thane. I was a maid for his mother. I have always served the house of Lochaber. I was with him when he was just a boy. Banquo cares deeply for you." There was no accusation there, only understanding. But the comment led me to wonder just how much Morag knew.

I closed my eyes. Everything was going wrong.

I should have listened to Banquo that night in Gillacoemgain's chamber. We should have walked between the worlds and disappeared forever. Now it was too late.

As I drifted off the sleep, I dreamed once more.

This time, I was walking through the ruins of Ynes Verleath to the temple of the goddess. The place was the same as it had always been. But *I* felt different.

"Cerridwen?"

I smiled at the sound of my name. My heart filled with joy when I looked up to see Banquo at the top of the temple stairs. His dark hair had faded to silver. He wore it long. He smiled and beckoned to me.

Leaning against my tall staff, my steps slow, I went to him, my heart filled with love.

CHAPTER TWENTY-SIX

I rested for the next several days, Morag and Merna attending me, Banquo making regular visits. But I had not once seen Macbeth. My child was gone. Once more, it was only Macbeth and me in the marriage. His absence clearly denoted his thoughts on the state of affairs.

On the third day, I was up once more, sitting by the fire when Banquo came in. He had a frustrated expression on his face.

"What is it?"

"Macbeth has arranged for the return south. I had asked him to delay a few more days, but he will not have it. We sail tomorrow."

"Tomorrow?"

Banquo sat down then shook his head. "He's…unreasonable right now, despite Thorfinn's best efforts. And he will not hear from me. At all. I will sail back to Lochaber.

Ask Macbeth to send you to Madelaine. It would do you well to be with your sisters at this time."

I nodded then stared into the fire.

"He blames me," Banquo whispered.

"How could this possibly be your fault?"

Banquo sighed.

"I need to get my house ready," Banquo said. "Is there anything I can do for you?"

I shook my head. "I'll be all right."

Banquo set his hand on my shoulder then left.

I didn't see Macbeth at all that day, but he sent men to begin stowing our belongings for the trip south. The idea that Macbeth was brooding vexed me. I was enduring the hardship alone. Ute, who had lost her own child in secret, carried her own burden. Why was Macbeth acting like this? And where was he? Didn't he care at all how I was? Did he really have no love for me? Was I truly just a tool, a name, a womb to bolster his legacy? Every time I thought it, anger rocked me.

By the time Macbeth finally arrived, I had worked myself up into a fury. The raven had choice words for this puppet of the White Christ who would use my body to make himself king.

"Gruoch, we'll set to sail in the morning. Thorfinn will feast us tonight, and we'll sail at dawn," he said, looking everywhere but at me.

"How nice of you to inform me."

Macbeth stiffened. "I am trying to get you home as quickly as possible."

"Why? To stuff another child inside me right away?"

"I... Gruoch, have you lost your mind? I'm trying to get you home so you can recover in comfort."

The raven laughed. "Liar," I spat out. "Where have you been, Macbeth? You left me all alone in this house, not even bothering to comfort me, to see if I would live or die. Where have you been? And now you're packing me up to send me south like some damned animal."

"I was praying to God for your life, Gruoch! What good would it serve to sit at your bedside and pet your head? I was praying to God to save you."

"Well, tell your god thank you. I'm alive."

"But my child—"

"*Our* child. We *both* lost a child."

"I told you not to go running about the countryside again. I warned you. But you are so reckless, so willful. Banquo is too bold in his handling of you. One would think he believes he's your husband, not me."

"So I am to blame? Banquo is to blame? Sometimes it is not meant to be, Macbeth, and that is all. I was surprised I could conceive at all."

Macbeth made a grunting sound that sounded almost like a growl. He ran his fingers through his hair so forcefully I thought he'd rip his hair from his scalp.

"Tomorrow, we'll go home," he said then turned and left, slamming the door behind him.

I sat staring into the fire. I was not to blame. Neither was Banquo. But Macbeth's words had cut close to the heart. Macbeth did not know how true his words were. Perhaps he could feel the secret just under the surface, an itch he could not scratch. I set my hand on my now empty womb. I had not thought much of the little one who had lived and died there. It had not felt like a real thing to me, not in the way Lulach and Crearwy had. In truth, I had felt indifferent toward the child. How strange. Lulach and Crearwy had come to me unwanted, unbidden, but I had loved them both fiercely. I'd wanted a child with Macbeth, or so I'd thought. If so, why did I feel so empty about it?

Frowning, I rose. Working slowly, I packed my things and got ready to travel south.

That night, we feasted with Thorfinn and the others in the hall. Macbeth neither spoke nor looked at Banquo. Thorfinn tried to keep up the cheer, but the room seemed more subdued than usual. Merna and Banquo departed as soon as they had eaten. Not long after, I also said my farewells, leaving Macbeth, who'd seemed not to notice, behind.

I was walking back to my house when the skald Anor joined me.

"Lady, I am sorry to see you depart. And I'm even more sorry to hear of your woes."

"Thank you, Anor."

"You must not trouble yourself with worries of legacy, my lady. Lord Lulach is a fine boy and will grow into a strong and wise man. And a man of our faith, I think."

I paused then looked at him. "What have you seen?"

Anor cast a glance over his shoulder.

"It's all right," I said.

"Lord Macbeth will have no rightful heir save Lulach. You must not trouble yourself, my lady, if you cannot conceive his child. The gods have willed it."

"And my son?"

"In my visions, I have seen him on a throne. But around his head, I see a crown of mistletoe. More I cannot see."

A druid king. My heart lurched. But druid kings were often year kings, sacrificed to the slaughter when the year ended. There was no way to know what the skald had seen. I would press Andraste on the issue.

"Thank you, Anor."

He bowed to me. "Jarl Thorfinn thinks I know things before they pass because I am a spy. It is merely Odin speaking through me."

"Bring him news of Ingibjorg. That, no doubt, will win you some favor."

Anor laughed. "You are right, my lady. The only time Lord Thorfinn was ever pleased with me was when I told him he would win his bride."

"Indeed? And when will that come to pass?"

"When Macbeth becomes king."

"When?"

"Ask your red lady," he said with a smile. "I wish you safe journeys south, Lady Gruoch."

"Thank you. May the gods bless you."

"And you."

We sailed the following morning. Thorfinn and Macbeth stood on the dock beside me as Banquo and Merna prepared to board their ship.

"I hope to see you again soon," Merna said, hugging me in farewell. Lulach, whom I was holding, giggled at being squished between us.

When she let me go, Morag embraced me. "My lady, take care."

I smiled at them. "I shall miss you both. And you, little Fleance," I told the boy who made a silly face at me, making me laugh. Slipping from Merna's grasp, he rushed off. Merna turned and raced after him.

"Lady Macbeth," Banquo said, giving me a formal bow.

Lady Macbeth. What a cursed name. "Thane," I said, nodding to him. "Safe voyage to you and yours. We will see you soon, I hope."

If things remained cold between Macbeth and Banquo, it might be a long time.

With a nod, Banquo turned to go.

"Baaaannccc," Lulach screamed at him.

Taking a step back, Banquo leaned in and kissed Lulach on the cheek. "Be a good boy. Watch over your mother," he said, his eyes resting on mine for a moment before he turned once more.

I love you. I love you. I love you. I willed him to hear the words that hung unspoken in the air.

Snatching Fleance from Merna's grasp, Banquo turned to go. Merna, Fleance, Banquo, and Morag boarded their ship.

"Lady Macbeth," Thorfinn said, wrapping an arm around me. "We shall see you next spring, I hope."

"Thank you for your hospitality."

He nodded kindly, but there was sadness behind his eyes.

I whistled to Thora, who bounded down the dock toward me. "No more playing wolf pack. Let's go," I said, turning to look at Ute who stood staring glassy-eyed behind me. With a nod to Thorfinn, we boarded our own ship.

Thorfinn and Macbeth stayed behind a few moments more. Thorfinn was telling Macbeth something. My husband, such as he was, stood listening, his arms crossed, nodding on occasion. When Thorfinn finished speaking, they both looked up at me.

I frowned and took a spot along the rail out of the way. Not long after, Macbeth boarded the ship.

We headed out to sea, sailing once more to Inverness.

And not once did my husband either speak to or look at me.

And I was glad.

CHAPTER TWENTY-SEVEN

We returned to Inverness with little fanfare. At once, I sent a rider south to Madelaine asking to make a visit. Within the week, a rider returned with an invitation and a bubbly letter from Madelaine who was brimming with excitement at the prospect of seeing me.

I had not seen Macbeth more than in passing since we'd returned. When word came from Madelaine, I sought him out for the first time. Not finding him in this chambers or the hall, I headed to the stables. I had neglected Kelpie all this time and had missed him during my time away.

The stables were quiet. Some of the horses were out. Either Samuel had them out exercising or Macbeth had everyone on a hunt.

That would be a very courtly thing to do.

I set my husband from my mind and chatted with the horses as I made my way through the stable. Finally catching the sound of my voice, Kelpie started nickering and kicked his gate. Along with his noisy hello, I also caught the sound of whispering and a few moments later, Elspeth climbed down from the hayloft above. Her cheeks were flushed red and she had an odd air about her. The boards overhead creaked. *Ahh.* Pretending I didn't notice she had a lover stashed away, I smiled nicely at her.

"Lady Gruoch," she said politely, pushing her hair back. "Someone is excited to see you," she said, motioning to Kelpie who was neighing loudly.

I chuckled. "So it seems."

"I've kept him exercised. Had him out almost every day. He's such a strong beast," she said then smiled.

I went to Kelpie, patting him on his nose. "How about a ride, old friend?" I said, hugging his neck.

"I've got something to show you," Elspeth said, waving me along behind her. We headed out to the pasture where some of the other horses were grazing. "Look there, the white mare. See how round she is?"

"Kelpie's?"

She nodded. "I think so, at least. He wouldn't let any of the other horses near her. I put him in his pen this morning because he's been picking at the other stallions. He is trying to keep his herd in line, I think."

"Grumpy old man," I said with a laugh, looking back at him.

When I did, I caught just the flash of a coattail turning the corner out of the barn.

I coughed lightly and pretended I had not seen Elspeth's lover making a hasty escape.

"I'll be heading south soon. He'll get his exercise then."

"Indeed? I didn't know."

"Word has just come," I said, tapping the scroll on my hand. "I still need to make the arrangements. Have you seen Lord Macbeth?"

"No, my lady," she said softly, turning to pick up some grain buckets.

"Very well. Thank you for taking such good care of my horse."

"Of course," she said. Her eyes downcast, she gave me a little curtsey.

Turning, I headed back inside.

I was surprised to find Macbeth in the great hall. He was pouring himself a mug of ale.

"Gruoch," he said as I approached. He ran his fingers through his hair.

I handed the scroll to him. "I'll ride south, and stay south, until the weather turns," I said then turned and walked away.

"Maybe we should discuss—"

The raven sneered at him. "There is nothing to discuss. I will ride south and stay south until the weather turns," I said then turned on my heel and stormed out of the hall.

When I returned to my chambers, I found Ute and Lulach playing with a wooden top. Ute's face looked drawn, a sad expression thereon.

"I've had word from Madelaine. I will ride south. Are you well enough to travel?" I asked Ute.

A look of relief washed over her face. "Oh yes, my lady."

"Very good. We'll leave in the morning," I said then set about getting ready. I sent footmen to the kitchens, stables, and asked Macbeth's guard to speak to his lord about assigning me four men to accompany me on the trip. By the time I was done, I had everything ready and it was time for bed.

I lay down that night with Lulach beside me, a small hope in my heart that Macbeth would come to me and ask my forgiveness. Would say something. Would make some gesture.

But that night, I slept alone.

I woke early the next morning. Ute, Lulach, and I dressed for the road. Thora trotted around excitedly. Kelpie had been saddled, as had a horse for Ute. A mule carried what small supplies I had requested to take with me south. A small group of guards had been assembled to ride with us. It was an unusually warm morning.

A footman rushed out of the castle. He handed me a letter. "A scroll for Fife. Lord Macbeth wishes you a safe trip, my lady."

"Does he?"

I looked back at the castle. Macbeth was nowhere to be seen.

Angry, I clicked to Kelpie. Lulach seated on the saddle in front of me, and lashed to me for safe keeping, I turned and headed south, swearing I would never speak another word to Macbeth again.

CHAPTER TWENTY-EIGHT

The ride was long but without consequence. When we finally arrived at Madelaine's castle, I discovered Fife was away.

"He's in Edinburgh," Madelaine said, taking Lulach from my arms as I dismounted. "There's trouble with Norway," she added in a low tone. "But no matter. Let's get Macbeth's men provisioned and back on their way. How big you are, Lulach," Madelaine chirped happily, kissing a very sleepy Lulach. "And how much he looks like you, Cerridwen. Ah! I see Gillacoemgain in his brow and chin," she said, tickling Lulach's chin to make him smile.

I smiled lightly. What could I say? It was lucky that Lulach had some features that resembled Gillacoemgain. It made the deception easier.

"Gruoch," Tavis called happily, crossing the lawn to embrace me. "Good to have you home."

"If just for a day. We'll be off again tomorrow. Will you see to the preparations?" Madelaine said.

Tavis nodded. "Of course."

"Off? Off where?" Ute asked, her voice sounding nervous.

"To our holy sisters," Madelaine answered.

"Oh," Ute said softly.

"I think you'll be comfortable here with Madelaine's household. Madelaine and I will take Lulach with us. You can get some rest," I told her. "Will that be all right?"

"Yes, my lady. I would like that."

"You will be safe here," I said softly. As I'd reflected on Ute's behavior, it had occurred to me that maybe she had rid herself of her child because some mischief had been done to her. Her sadness reminded me of myself when I was so misused. I cared deeply for Ute, but I didn't know how to ask. And if I was wrong, it could cause her terrible embarrassment. It was better if I just let the matter lie until Ute was ready.

She nodded. "Thank you, my lady."

We rested that night, and in the morning, Lulach, Madelaine, Tavis and I journeyed to the coven. Thora pranced around excitedly, racing ahead at every chance, rushing back time and time again as if to hurry us along. We rode until we reached Tavis's usual camp spot.

"You sure you'll be all right?" Madelaine asked him.

"I'll be hunting. Maybe…Uald will come join me."

Madelaine smiled. "I'll let her know," she said then leaned in and kissed him.

Tavis cupped Madelaine's cheek then kissed her once more. "Be safe," he whispered.

"You too."

I waved farewell to Tavis, then Madelaine, Lulach, and I —and an impatient Thora—made our way deeper into the forest.

"He should just join us," I said. "After all these years, the coven is no secret to him. Ask Epona. I am sure she will consent."

Madelaine nodded then sighed. "Epona is not the problem. In fact, Tavis and Uald are old friends at this point. It is Tavis who will not agree to it."

"Why not?"

"Holy ground. Sacred space. He says he is no druid, so he stays away."

"His stubbornness is going to earn him frostbite one of these times."

Madelaine laughed. "I'll be sure to tell him you said that."

I grinned.

As we rode through the hidden pass into the coven, all concerns about Macbeth fell away as I focused on a single thought: Crearwy.

At last, I would have both my children with me.

Anticipating our arrival, Epona and Uald met us in the square.

"Sisters," Epona called and came forward. Madelaine's face flashed with the same surprise as mine. Epona looked older. Around her eyes, little wrinkles reached out with spiderweb hands. Her mouth showed all her years of smiling, her laugh lines deep, as were the grooves on her forehead. Epona was aging. All this time she had seemed to be frozen around the age of thirty. Now she looked nearly twice that. It was chilling to consider why.

Uald helped Madelaine dismount then embraced her.

"Well met," Epona told me then kissed Lulach on his forehead. "How much he's grown. And how like his sister!"

"Corbie," Uald said, smiling at me. "And Lulach."

Kelpie nickered at her.

"Yes, you old goat, I haven't forgotten you," she said, patting Kelpie on his nose. "Come along, you grumpy old beast. You too, Thora. I have a bone for you somewhere," Uald said then took Kelpie's reins from my hands.

Madelaine gave me a little wave then went with Uald. Thora trotted along behind her.

My eyes scanned the coven very quickly. No one else was up and about. The windows of Sid's house were dark. I hoped the faerie would tell her I was there. I cast a look toward Bride's house, feeling sad that I had not had a chance to say goodbye. I was surprised to see puffs of smoke coming from her chimney.

"You will be anxious to see Crearwy," Epona said.

I nodded.

"May has gone to the stream to bathe. She took Crearwy with her. They will be back directly. "

"Sid told me that Bride passed away," I said.

Epona nodded. "We were very sorry to lose her, but the Crone called. She went peacefully. Tully was here. She brought a young woman who has taken the name Juno. You will like her. She also belongs to the Dark Goddesses. We expect Tully to return soon with two more girls. It is getting more difficult to find families willing to send their daughters for training. The world is changing," Epona said sadly then looked at Lulach once more. "Come, let's get you inside. Lulach looks like he could use a biscuit."

"Eat," Lulach said. "Me eat."

Epona chuckled. "Clever boy."

"And how are Inverness and Macbeth? My, it's chilly," Epona said, pulling her shawl around her. Once inside, she rummaged through her cabinet, returning with a biscuit for Lulach.

I studied Epona closely. There was no chill in the air, and Epona's house was overly warm.

"I confess, I don't know what to say. I started the marriage hopeful, but..."

"But?"

"But Macbeth is not Gillacoemgain. I had visions of Macbeth long before I even knew who he was. And Andraste, that old riddler, had once called him my king. But he's not what I expected."

Epona poured us both a goblet of wine then sat back in her seat and looked thoughtful. "You saw Macbeth in the cauldron?"

"Yes."

Epona frowned heavily, drank her goblet of wine, then rose and stood by the fire. "It is no secret that Andraste and I do not see eye-to-eye on many matters, including her over-involvement in things—including conjuring visions. But the Wyrds are kingmakers."

I stared at Epona. "What do you mean?"

"Do you like Macbeth? Is he a good man?"

I clutched Lulach tighter and pressed my cheek against his head. Epona always had a way of putting things that made the truth clear. "No," I whispered.

Epona nodded. "But you gave him a chance?"

"Yes."

"Why?"

"Because…"

"Because Andraste told you he was your king and because you saw him in your cauldron."

"Are you saying—"

"You know what I am saying."

I frowned heavily. "Epona, what should I—"

But my words were cut short when the door to Epona's cabin opened. A little hand held onto the doorframe as the little body that went with it struggled to pull herself up and into the room. I stared as my baby entered then rose slowly.

Epona lifted Lulach from my arms. "Come, let's get you another biscuit, Lulach."

Taking her other hand to help her along, May assisted Crearwy into the room. The girl had very dark hair, dark blue eyes, and pale skin. She looked just like Lulach and me. Yet in her brow, her chin, I saw Gillacoemgain. I gaped as I looked at her. She was a miniature doppelganger of Crearwy, Gillacoemgain's sister, for whom she was named. I tried to hold all of the emotions in, but tears welled in my eyes. I kneeled down and held out my hands to her. "Hello, Crearwy," I whispered.

She looked uncertain, casting a glance to May for reassurance. The idea that she needed the approval of a stranger to come to her mother startled and saddened me. May nodded to her, and tepidly, the girl came to me.

"Dat one? Mum. Mum? Mum! Dat one?" Lulach called.

I cast a glance back to see Lulach straining to see his sister.

Keeping in mind that while I was her mother, I was also a stranger, I gently picked Crearwy up. She smelled of soap, her hair wet from being freshly washed. She wore a green woolen dress. Her hair curled around her ears.

"Sweet baby," I whispered then hugged her. "My sweet Crearwy."

She squirmed a little.

I pulled back a little then eyed her carefully. She gave me a look so full of suspicion that everyone in the room laughed.

"Really, Crearwy. Won't you smile for your mother?" Epona told her good-naturedly.

I stroked her cheek, and she gave me a soft, shy smile.

"Dat, dat, dat! Mum," Lulach screamed, annoyed with being ignored.

Once more, everyone chuckled.

"Yes, Lulach. I hear you," I said then moved toward him. "Lulach, this is Crearwy."

Crearwy perked up then and looked at Lulach. Her brow furrowed like she was trying to figure out a puzzle.

"Dat, Dat," Lulach said, pointing at her.

"Crearwy," I told him.

"Crw, Crw," he tried.

"Crearwy, this is Lulach. He is your brother," I said.

She stared at him. "Lulu," she said, pointing.

"Yes, Lulu," I said with a laugh.

Crearwy gave me a sour look as if she took my laughter as mocking.

Oh my goodness, Sid was right. What a personality.

The door opened once more, and Madelaine and Ute entered.

"Oh, I missed it!" Madelaine lamented, joining Epona and me. "Well, Crearwy, here are your mother and brother."

"Lulu," Crearwy explained to Madelaine, pointing to Lulach.

"This is Lulu?" Madelaine asked her. "Oh, all right then," Madelaine said then smiled, kissing the girl on her forehead.

Crearwy favored her with that same soft half-smile.

"She looks very well, very healthy. Thank you for your care," I told May.

May smiled. "Of course. I love her very much."

My stomach felt queasy.

I sat down then, Crearwy in my lap. I dug into my pocket and pulled out the small wooden top Lulach always played with and handed it to Crearwy. Lulach, distracted by yet another biscuit, didn't notice.

"Would you like to see this?" I asked Crearwy. "It's Lulach's toy."

"Lulu," she said then pointed to Lulach once more.

"Yes, Lulu."

The door opened once more, and Aridmis, Druanne, and a stranger entered. I assumed this to be Juno, the girl Epona had mentioned. She had a head full of curly black hair that fell down her back. Her nose and cheeks covered with freckles. She smiled at me.

"Well met, Cerridwen," Druanne said stiffly.

"Druanne."

"Cerridwen," Aridmis said happily then embraced me, pausing to kiss Crearwy, who seemed not to mind. "Welcome home."

"Thank you, sister."

"Cerridwen, this is Juno," Epona said, introducing the girl.

I moved to rise, but she motioned for me to stay seated.

"I'm pleased to meet you, sister," Juno said with a smile. She then went to Epona's cupboards, pulled out cups and started pouring everyone some wine.

"And where is Sid?" Madelaine asked.

"Wherever the wind blows," Uald said. "She'll be back soon, I suspect."

Everyone sat and Juno handed out goblets while Epona served small cakes and sweets to the assembled crowd.

I smiled at my sisters. I was home. I was safe. I grinned at everyone even Druanne whose chilly—but consistently chilly—nature felt comforting and familiar. I was with my family. Madelaine eased back into her seat, sipping her cup of wine. Finally, I felt at ease. Finally, I felt like myself again. I squeezed Crearwy close to me.

"My little lass," I whispered in her ear. "I'm your mum."

Crearwy looked up at me from under her long, dark lashes. "Mum?"

I nodded.

She smiled then turned her attention back to the top, turning it around and around in her hands, a slight smile on her lips.

I kissed the back of her head. Closing my eyes, I inhaled the scent of her hair. I never wanted this moment to end.

CHAPTER TWENTY-NINE

It was several days before Sid finally arrived.

"Sorry for the delay, love. The Seelie queen had another baby, and there was much ado regarding the matter. We had to call some of the fey healers in because her delivery wasn't going well. In the end, her little baby came forth without any problems."

I'd taken up residence in Sid's house in her absence. She'd found me there resting with my children. Lulach and Crearwy had taken to one another at once. It seemed that Crearwy's sourness and apprehensions did not extend to her brother, with whom she played very happily. Having tired themselves out, the pair was sleeping in Sid's bed.

Crearwy stirred a little at the sound of Sid's voice but did not wake.

"She's such a bright girl, interested in all the world. Epona spends a lot of time with her," Sid said, bending down to kiss Crearwy. "How alike they are," she said, looking from Lulach to Crearwy.

"Sid, what's happening to Epona?"

"That's a common question here, but none speak of it. All this time she has held the charm of youth. Now she begins to age. You must understand, given her true age, if she lets go completely, she will die. I believe she is letting go a little at a time."

"Why?"

"To give Crearwy time to grow up."

"Crearwy?"

"Crearwy is her chosen successor."

I stared at Sid. A memory of Andraste's prophetic words rang through my mind. I was suddenly feeling very sour with Andraste and planned on given her my most Crearwy-like glare when I saw her next. Meddlesome creature. "So she is."

Sid sighed heavily then started pulling off her tattered and muddy clothes. I watched her as she undressed. Once more, that strange longing filled me, a sensation I didn't know what to do with. My eyes drifted over her breasts, and my mind went back to pleasant memories.

Sid paused then looked up at me.

She smirked. "Dirty as I am, glad to know I can still put that look on your face."

"Sid," I chided her then looked away, my cheeks reddening.

Sid moved behind me then, pushed my hair to one side, and set some soft kisses on my neck, her hands reaching around to cup my breasts. My heart beat hard in my chest. "Raven beak," she whispered then pulled away. Grabbing a cloak from near the door, she pulled it on then headed outside half-naked.

"Want a bath?" she asked.

I shook my head.

She slipped open her robe so I had a full view of her naked self. "You sure?"

"Sid!"

She giggled then turned and rushed off.

Shaking my head, I closed the door behind her. Was there ever anyone else in the world like my old friend?

Madelaine and I spent the next several weeks at the coven, but as Lughnassadh neared, we knew we must go. Soon, others would arrive for the festival. I could not let outsiders see Crearwy and me together. It would be dangerous if people discovered her maternity.

I spent my last day at the coven with Crearwy and Lulach. I took them for a walk to the stream. We stopped to look at every stick and leaf they found interesting. Thora dodged between them, making them both laugh—and, often, fall down. They had both just started walking. Their dawdling steps were adorable.

Afterward, I went back to Epona's house and fed my

children their lunch. They sat side by side fingering through their plates and giggling at one another.

"You're a good mother. I feel very guilty for having taken your child. Sometimes the Goddess asks us to do things that are difficult, but I want you to know I'm sorry," Epona told me.

"Crearwy is happy and well taken care of," I said.

"But she is not in your care, nor with her brother, and I apologize for that."

I was silent as I digested her words. "Thank you," I finally said in reply. "But it's better this way. I would not wish the court life on her." After a few moments, I turned and looked at Epona. Her hands, which had always looked so smooth, were wrinkled and covered in spots. "You're aging," I said simply.

Epona nodded. "My time is coming to an end."

"How soon?"

"I will wait until Crearwy is ready. You can measure time with that knowledge."

"You riddle like Andraste."

Epona laughed. "Someday you too will riddle."

"If I live that long."

"What a thing to say."

She was right. What a thing to say. Why had I said that?

Outside, I heard Uald and Madelaine talking. The jingle of rigging told me that the horses had already been saddled.

"I fear it will be awhile before I can return," I told Epona.

She nodded. "Change is in the wind. "

We sat in silence until the children finished eating. Once they were done, Epona and I washed their hands and faces. I picked up Crearwy while Epona held Lulach.

"Lulach, you must say goodbye to Crearwy. We have to leave now," I told him. "Can you give her a kiss?" Epona brought him close, and Lulach pressed his face—more smashing than kissing—against his sister's cheek.

Crearwy let out the softest of giggles.

"Well, that's a first," Epona said.

I looked at my daughter. "I'll be back as soon as I can. Be a good girl, Crearwy. Listen to Epona," I said.

The little girl stared at me, her dark blue eyes meeting mine.

A tear rolled down my cheek.

Crearwy scowled when she saw it, her lower lip trembling. She reached out and wiped it off.

"Sweet baby," I whispered, pressing her against me.

"Mum," she said.

Swallowing hard, I kissed my daughter then went back outside where the others waited.

"Come to me," Sid told Crearwy, taking her from my arms.

I leaned in and kissed Sid on the cheek. "I'll miss you."

"No, you'll forget me. Like always."

"Sid!"

She laughed. "I'll miss you too."

I kissed Crearwy once more then turned to go.

Druanne nodded to me, Juno smiling in farewell. Uald

and Aridmis both embraced me, then Uald helped me mount then lashed Lulach securely onto the saddle and against me.

"I'll have to find him a pony. When you come next time, we'll teach him how to ride," she said.

I smiled at her. Though tears threatened, I held them back.

Madelaine was already ahorse, and Thora was waiting by the exit.

"Until next time," Epona called, lifting her hand in farewell.

I inclined my head to her then turned and looked at Crearwy once more. I waved goodbye and turned Kelpie toward the exit.

I had no words.

"Lulu!" Crearwy called.

I turned Kelpie once more so we could look back.

"Wave goodbye," I told Lulach who waved.

Sid held Crearwy, bouncing her in her arms, but Crearwy simply stared at us.

Waving goodbye once more, I turned, and we rode away from the coven.

I'd have to go back north now, back to Macbeth, away from Crearwy and Madelaine. Epona was right. The future was coming into the present, and I would have to be ready for what would come next. Even if I wanted nothing to do with it.

CHAPTER THIRTY

In the days that followed, I prepared to leave Madelaine. I tried not to mope, especially when I realized that Ute looked even more distressed than me. I was just finishing up packing the last of my new dresses—another haul of gifts from Madelaine—when Ute finally said what she'd been dancing around for days.

"My lady," she began, her voice cracking. "I…have something to ask of you."

She had just closed the bag containing Lulach's belongings.

I turned and looked at her. Huge tears hung on her lower lids.

"What is it, Ute? What's the matter?"

"My lady, if she will have me, I would like to stay on with Lady Madelaine. The staff here is all very kind, and they speak well of your aunt and the Thane of Fife."

I stared at her.

"It's not anything against you, Gruoch. God knows I will miss Lulach more than I can stand. I just… I don't want to return to Inverness."

I crossed the room and took her hand. "Some ill deed was done to you in my house, wasn't it? The child? Is that why?"

"I don't want to discuss it. I beg you to forgive me, but please, let me stay."

"Ute," I said, feeling my heart beat hard. Unbidden, I heard the beating wings of the raven. I closed my eyes, seeking to control the rage. "You must tell me who harmed you. They must pay for what they've done."

Ute turned away. "My lady, I am sorry, but I will not name the man. Perhaps there was some misunderstanding between us. I… I'm not sure. My mind is so confused about it. Please forgive me, but I would like to stay here, if you will allow it."

I reined in my anger. It would not serve me here, especially if Ute had chosen not to speak of it. "Lulach will miss you terribly."

"I know. And I him."

I sighed. "Madelaine will treat you well. I'll talk to her."

"Thank you, Gruoch," Ute said, wiping her cheeks.

I wrapped my arms around her and hugged her from behind. I left her then to seek out Madelaine who was in her own chambers playing with Lulach. The moment I walked into the room, Madelaine's cheerful expression faded.

"What's wrong, Corbie?"

"Ute would like to stay with you. Will that be all right?"

Madelaine scrunched up her face. "Did you quarrel?"

"No. There has been some trouble with a man at court. She won't name him, but she doesn't want to return."

"I see," Madelaine said, and there was an edge to Madelaine's voice. Given the way Allister kept his household, I was sure Madelaine understood very well.

"She is a very loyal and skilled maid. Gillacoemgain employed her for me. She'll serve you well, if you'll have her."

"Of course. I always liked the girl."

I smiled at Madelaine. "I'll let her know."

"And what will you do now?"

"I'll return north. To Cawdor."

"To Cawdor?"

I nodded. "Macbeth and I cannot find our way together. He's a complicated man. I excused his roughness at first, thinking he was just courtly in his manner, but no more."

"Roughness? Has he harmed you?"

What Madelaine was really asking as if he had struck me, hurt me. He had not, but every time I left my marriage bed, I felt ill-used. Was a woman supposed to feel like that after making love to her husband? It had not been that way with Gillacoemgain. Suddenly, I felt ashamed. How could I explain such a thing to Madelaine?

"No. But he's ill-tempered in a way that is unbearable. Sunshine in the morning and thunderstorms by nightfall. When he remembers I exist."

Madelaine pursed her lips together as she mused over the problem. "A streak of madness?" she finally asked.

I looked toward the fireplace. The small flames inside burned cheerfully, the wood crackling. I had given Macbeth a chance. I had opened my heart to him all based on some visions. But Epona was right. Andraste liked to play. Maybe I should not have been so generous toward Macbeth. Macbeth's distempers did smack of madness. "Perhaps."

She frowned. "And they called Gillacoemgain the mad one, but I think you loved him."

"I did. He was not mad. He was a good man."

"And made such a beautiful child," she said, lifting Lulach. "Children."

"Children."

"Go to Cawdor then. Perhaps Macbeth needs a reminder of who you are. We are the blood of MacAlpin's line and not to be trifled with. Macbeth must learn to control himself. Given his whispered aspirations, he's going to need your help."

"Yes."

Madelaine kissed Lulach. "And you, my boy, will one day be King of Scotland. You will rule well and treat your wife kindly. Do you understand?"

Lulach nodded then giggled.

I smiled at them, my heart filled with joy at the sight.

But also sorrow.

It was time to go.

CHAPTER THIRTY-ONE

Lulach and I rode north the next morning under heavy guard. With Madelaine's many gifts, it was necessary to take a wagon. Madelaine had the foresight to pack some household supplies as well. Cawdor would not be expecting me. It might take time to get everything back in order. As we rode, I saw that the harvest season had arrived once more, and the farmers were working their fields, busy with ensuring the safety of their families in the winter months that would soon come.

My heart set on a new course, I rode back to Cawdor. As I passed through the gate and into the walls of the citadel, I felt at ease once more. Cawdor had come to feel like home. I was safe here.

"My lady?" Standish called, crossing the quiet courtyard to greet me. He helped me and Lulach down.

"Standish," I said, hugging him gently.

"We weren't expecting you, my lady. We'll get a room ready for you to rest for the night."

I shook my head. "Will you please provision the Thane of Fife's men so they can return when they are ready? Afterward, I will reopen the castle. I am returning to take up residence once more."

"We had no word from Lord Macbeth about it, Lady Gruoch. There are but a dozen servants here, Macbeth's sentinel, and a handful of men—Macbeth's men."

"Send Macbeth's men back to Inverness. I want the sentinel gone by nightfall."

Standish smirked but quickly tried to hide the expression. "As you wish, my lady. Rhona and Tira are within. I'm sure they will be happy to see you since your maid isn't here."

"Very well. And I need to send a rider to Inverness," I said, pulling a scroll from my bag. I had written Macbeth a very formal letter informing him that the Lord of Moray was returning to Cawdor. I outlined the supplies I needed to be sent from Inverness for the winter.

Standish took the scroll from my hand then nodded. "I'll arrange everything, my lady."

"And I would like some Moray men on the castle. Loyal men. Macbeth's guards can go serve Macbeth. Will you see to it as well?"

This time, Standish smiled, unable to control himself. "Indeed I shall. Go get yourself a glass of wine and warm yourself by your hearth, Lady Gruoch. I'll make things right. Welcome home, my lady."

I smiled. "Thank you, Standish."

I glanced down at Thora who was sniffing the wind excitedly. "Go and see if there is any sign of Eochaid."

Thora wagged her tail then ran off.

I looked down at Lulach. The boy was sleeping in my arms. "Welcome home, Lord of Moray," I said then headed inside.

"Lady Gruoch, we are so pleased to have you back," Rhona said as she and Tira cleaned Gillacoemgain's and my old chamber, refreshing the bedstraw and linens, getting the fire going, and unpacking my things.

"Will Lord Macbeth be joining soon?" Tira asked.

"Well, I've not invited him to do so. I'm guessing no."

Both of the women stopped and looked at me.

I laughed at the expressions on their faces.

"My lady, I'm sorry to hear things are not…" Rhona began then trailed off, seemingly unsure what to say.

"Not all marriages are happy ones. That is common, my lady, amongst those born high and low alike," Tira said. "You and Lord Gillacoemgain…*that* was love."

"Yes," Rhona said affirmatively as she helped Tira make the bed.

"Yes," I echoed, looking into the fireplace. Yes, that was love. Something Macbeth did not understand. Now we would see what he would do. He wanted to be king of Scotland? If so, he needed me. He would either find a way to control himself and make amends with me, or he could try to have me murdered. Try, of course, being the critical point. The raven would never allow such a thing. In the end, I was the Lady of Moray, daughter of Boite, and of the line of MacAlpin. I was the mother of Lulach of Moray, ally to Lord Thorfinn and King Magnus, niece of King Malcolm, and Prince Duncan's cousin. My people were loyal to me. Macbeth? He was an outsider, son of a lord few loved. I didn't need Macbeth to rule the north. He needed me.

The next morning, a courier arrived carrying a letter written in Macbeth's hand. It was simple, stating what provisions were being sent to Cawdor and when they would come. There was not a single word of reconciliation, not even an acknowledgment of the estrangement. Instead, there was a list of cows, pigs, chickens, ale, wheat, and wine.

Standing in the middle of the yard, I could not help but laugh. My loud laughter echoed across the yard. I shook my head then watched as Macbeth's men rode out of the castle and back toward Inverness. In their place, faces I recognized, Moray's men, returned one by one to Cawdor.

I tapped the scroll on my hand then turned and headed toward the stables, passing the empty mews, to the back where I had a good view of the fields. A soft wind blew in, carrying with it the scent of the highlands.

In the end, all my pain had come to nothing. There was nothing between Macbeth and me. But I had secured Lulach's birthright. That was all I had ever wanted to do.

As for me, I would rethink my world, my life, and find my own way once more.

In the name of the Goddess.

As Gruoch, the raven.

CHAPTER THIRTY-TWO

As much as I had wanted Macbeth to ride to Cawdor and express his love and ask my forgiveness, that never happened. In fact, I heard nothing from Inverness except for informative dispatches regarding matters of state. It amused me that for the first time in my marriage, I was kept abreast of the affairs of the country. I would have been better off as one of his constituents all along. In truth, I was relieved to be done with the constant energy it took to keep Macbeth happy. The entire time I was with him, I'd felt like I was walking on glass, always hoping not to provoke him. Life in Cawdor was quiet and blissful.

It was late in the winter when I found myself in the small garden outside the church. This section of the castle had been kept closed. I eyed the room in which Crearwy, Gillacoemgain's sister, had been murdered. I sighed.

It was very silent in the little garden, the snow drifting down slowly in fat flakes. I was all alone.

No Macbeth. No Gillacoemgain. No Ute. No Madelaine. No Eochaid. No Sid. No Epona. No Andraste. No one save Lulach, Thora, and me. I'd sent a messenger to Lochaber, but there still had been no word from Banquo either. I felt very safe in my solitude, and very alone.

That evening, as I sat soaking up the moonlight and ruminating to the point of melancholy, a rider arrived.

"Lady Gruoch? My lady?" Standish called as he neared the garden.

Rising reluctantly, I went to see what was the matter.

Standish carried a torch. The orange light glowed on the blanket of new snow. Alongside Standish was a messenger, a man I didn't recognize wearing the colors and insignia I knew well and had grown to loathe—the colors of King Malcolm.

"A message, my lady," the man said, dropping to his knee. "Urgent," he added.

I opened the scroll and read.

Malcolm was dead.

The note had come from Duncan.

Macbeth and I were to come to Scone before Christmas to pledge our fidelity to our new king.

I turned and looked back at the garden. How beautiful it looked in the moonlight, how serene, how quiet.

"My lady?" Standish asked.

"The king is dead," I said.

"We'll ring the bells."

I nodded.

"My lady," the messenger said. "I'm supposed to return with a reply from you and Lord Macbeth."

I handed the message back to him. "Then you must ride on to Inverness where Lord Macbeth keeps residence."

"Oh," the messenger said. "I was told to come here."

"By whom?"

"The king. King Duncan."

I smirked, thinking over the reasons for Duncan's play. Clearly, he knew Macbeth and I were estranged. Why would he send the message to me? Was it possible he did not trust Macbeth? It amused me that he thought he might have an ally in me. Of all the people in this land, no one hated Duncan more than me.

"Just a small confusion. Word travels slowly. Why don't you take some refreshment before you ride on to Inverness," I told the messenger.

"Thank you, my lady," he said then turned and went to the hall.

I headed across the yard when a second rider arrived. This time, from Fife.

"Lady Gruoch?" the rider called. He dismounted quickly then handed me a message.

"Thank you," I said, taking the scroll. It was from Madelaine. It seemed that Malcolm had died peacefully in his bed, weakened by a coughing sickness. Duncan had sent word to all the thanes, demanding they come to Scone to kiss his ring and pledge their allegiance to their new king. How quickly everyone forgot that Madelaine was

Malcolm's half-sister. Didn't they even consider that she might want to take a moment to mourn her brother?

Tapping the scroll in my hand, I turned and headed inside. When I returned to my chamber, Tira was inside tending to Lulach.

"What is it, my lady? I heard the bells."

"King Malcolm is dead."

She stared at me. "And…"

"And Duncan has taken the throne."

"May the gods watch over us all."

"Indeed."

Two days later, Macbeth rode with a small party through the gates of Cawdor. I watched him from my chamber window. My heart twisted in ten different directions. I hated him, yet desperately wanted to love him. How could a person feel such contrasting things all at once? I was also keenly aware that he was only here for one reason. Macbeth and I must present a unified front before Duncan. If we did not, it would fracture Macbeth's and Thorfinn's hold on the north.

And just what would happen if I did not join him? What would happen if I chose to support Duncan—not that I ever would—but what if?

I cast a glance at Lulach who was sleeping.

Every move I made was for him. What was best for Lulach?

"My lady?" Tira called. She rapped on the door then

entered. "Lord Macbeth has arrived. He's in the hall. He asked that we let you know."

I nodded. "Very well. Thank you."

"Shall I stay with Lulach?"

"Yes, please."

Sighing, I turned and headed toward the hall.

For Lulach.

For Lulach.

But the raven within me was whispering.

Tell him no. Go to Scone without him. Swallow your sorrows and win Duncan's support. Rule the north alone. Kill Macbeth. Bury him. He doesn't deserve your love. Finish him, and be with your druid. Finish him, and avenge Gillacoemgain. Better yet, raise your army and end them both as Boudicca would have done. Daughter of a king. Granddaughter of a king. Blood of MacAlpin and ruler of Moray. Take your crown. As Boudicca would have done. As Boudicca would have done. Level them both. Make them pay.

The voice became so loud in my head that it made my hands shake. I stopped mid-step and gazed out the window, catching my breath.

"Boudicca died, the Romans crushed the Celts, and Boudicca's daughters suffered because of her defeat. Would you have me be so stupid?" I whispered, not sure if I was talking to myself, the dark seed that lived within me, or something other.

Either way, the tirade ended.

I needed to be smart, smarter than Macbeth or Duncan.

For Lulach's sake, for Lulach's heirs' sake, I needed to outsmart them all.

Taking a deep breath, I smoothed down my long skirts, swept back my hair, and painted a smile on my face.

In the hall where I had seen Gillacoemgain stand before the hearth so many times now stood Macbeth. I hated him for standing in that spot.

"How now, Macbeth?" I called.

He paused, seeming to collect himself, then turned and looked at me. "Gruoch."

"Are we for Scone?"

Macbeth inhaled slowly, deeply. "Yes."

"When?"

"In the morning?" he asked tepidly.

"Fine," I said then turned and headed out.

"Gruoch?" he called, but I did not look back.

Now, we would see.

There was a flurry of activity that night as I readied myself for the trip south. Rhona and Tira had a good-natured squabble over who would go to court. In the end, Rhona won out, saying she was old and more likely to die soon without ever seeing any kind of pageantry save some sheep herded through the yard, which made us all laugh. Tira reluctantly acquiesced.

Macbeth did not come to my chamber that night to broker peace nor to pay even a moment's attention to Lulach. I was glad my son was too young to have grown to love Macbeth. He would not, I hoped, ever miss him. Feeling vexed about the entire matter, I did not hold a feast to welcome Macbeth. He could eat whatever scraps my kitchen maids felt like giving him, sleep wherever they decided to light a fire—or not. In fact, I gave no instructions for his comfort at all, and in Gillacoemgain's castle, none were inclined to provide any. For all I cared, he could have slept in the pig shed.

Without a single word spoken to Macbeth and no more than a passing glance when I did finally see him the next day, we took to the road the following morning. The snow was too deep for wagons, so we rode on horseback. Little Lulach, who had no idea he was about to be thrust into the public eye, rode with me. In addition to Macbeth's men, I also rode with four guards of my own, all of whom wore the tartan of Moray. I might ride to Scone beside Macbeth, but I was not truly with him.

We arrived in Scone the following morning. King Malcolm was dead, but it didn't appear anyone minded. In fact, evergreen garlands were hung on the buildings and decorated the castle. The place was busy, full of people and animals. It looked like a horse fair times ten. Everywhere I looked, vendors sold their wares, calling to the visiting lords and ladies and their servants. As we rode through town, many stopped to watch Macbeth and me.

"Scone of the Noisy Shields," Rhona said as we rode down the street toward the castle which sat not far from Scone Abby where Duncan would be crowned. Trumpets blasted as we approached the citadel.

Lulach whimpered then began to cry, the loud noise grating his nerves.

"Don't cry, love. One day, if you become king, you can order them not to blast their trumpets," I said.

Macbeth, who was riding just ahead of me, looked back at me over his shoulder.

I ignored him. If Macbeth thought I'd ever let him into my bed again, he truly was out of his mind. The man had left me to die in the dark, in a pool of my own blood, writhing in pain as his own child died. In such a circumstance, he'd thought only of himself. He hadn't spared a moment to offer me, lying in agony at the loss of our child, a word of comfort. He only blamed me, blamed Banquo. He'd abandoned me when I needed him the most. It was Banquo who had stayed with me, Banquo who had ensured I was cared for. What had Macbeth done? Nothing. I would never forgive him. Whatever I'd hoped Macbeth and I would be, he had broken it completely. I glared at him.

Once we arrived at the castle, we were escorted to the western wing where we were bid to relax and make ready to meet the king the following day. Finally, I had a reason to be glad of courtly life. Macbeth and I had been given separate sections of the castle.

My section of the castle had a large meeting hall and two bedchambers, one for me and one for Rhona. My bedroom was richly adorned with a large poster bed, rich tapestries, and fine furniture. The extravagance seemed excessive. I settled in by the fire, warming up after the long ride.

"Look at all the lords and ladies," Rhona said, glancing out the window. "What pageantry!"

I yawned tiredly. Footmen and maids raced in and out of the chamber bringing wine, food, and news. There would be a grand dinner that evening, but the king would not come from Edinburgh until the morning.

"He isn't here yet?" I asked a maid who had brought a basket of bread and a round of cheese from the kitchens.

"No, my lady."

"I wonder why not," Rhona mused aloud.

The maid smirked. "There was a rumor that he would not come until Lord and Lady Macbeth arrived."

I huffed a laugh. "I suppose he needed to ensure he actually had the north before he proclaimed himself king over it."

The maid giggled then turned and left.

Rhona chuckled. "Have you ever seen him, my lady? What manner of man is King Duncan?"

I bit my lip, wanting to tell her *exactly* the kind of man he was, but I said, "I saw him once. He didn't make a good impression on me."

Rhona harrumphed.

There was yet another knock on the door, but before Rhona could open it, Madelaine let herself in.

"Gruoch," she called merrily, crossing the room to embrace me.

How lovely she looked in her winter furs and an elegant green velvet gown. Her long red hair drifted down her back.

She turned quickly and picked up Lulach, planting kisses on his cheeks. "Oh, my naughty boy, you're growing like a weed. How big you are since autumn."

Lulach laughed.

"Madelaine, this is my maid, Rhona. Rhona, this is my aunt, Madelaine, the Lady of Fife."

Rhona was about to drop a curtsey when Madelaine clapped her on the back and said, "Merry met."

Rhona laughed. "I see where my lady gets her open nature."

Madelaine smiled. "Can you believe all this pomp?" she said, motioning out the window. "My god, there will be a shortage of soap in Scotland."

We both laughed.

"Fife has gone with Macbeth. The lords are meeting in the hall below. Shall we go meet the ladies?"

"By the gods, no."

Madelaine laughed. "Gruoch. Don't you want to see who has a daughter for Lulach?"

"Madelaine! He's just a wee boy."

"I know that, and so does everyone else. Everyone will want to claim the hand of a boy with royal blood."

I blew air through my lips. Sid's faerie princess would be better than some courtly lady.

"Now, let's see what dresses you brought for the coronation tomorrow. Who packed, you or your maid?"

"Both of us."

"Oh dear," Madelaine said then looked back at Rhona. "Did you fix it?"

Rhona laughed. "Yes, my lady."

"Fix what?"

"Gruoch, you can hardly tell the difference between a house dress and a formal gown."

"I can so."

Rhona laughed in such a manner that indicated that clearly I did not. In truth, I hardly cared for a gown one way or another. In fact, men's breeches always appeared far more practical to me.

"Well, I brought some of the new dresses you sent," I said, albeit weakly, in my defense.

Madelaine winked at Rhona and then began picking through my things. I smiled at her, glad to have a mother's comfort at this time. Alone, I would have to deal with Macbeth. But with Madelaine here, I had every excuse to avoid him. And more, while Madelaine knew nothing of the matter, every time I thought about seeing Duncan, my stomach felt ill, and rage made my hands shake. That pompous boy, that user and defiler would become king of Scotland. It was an affront to the country I loved. But I remembered Macbeth's plans. As angry as I was at Macbeth, I still supported his plan to win the crown. Had he asked my opinion on the matter, I might have advised him to stay north. If we stood our ground now, before Duncan was crowned, it would make things easier. But Macbeth had not asked me anything other than how many casks of wine and pigs I needed at Cawdor.

"How is Ute fairing?" I asked Madelaine as she looked through the dresses.

"Very well. She told me to send her greetings."

"She didn't want to come?"

"No. I asked her, but she declined. What about this one?" Madelaine asked, snapping the wrinkles out of a lovely purple silk and velvet gown. The cut of it was much like the holy gown I wore at Ynes Verleath. "It will match your torcs and amulet."

"Yes. That will be perfect," I said, my mind distracted by the idea that Ute had not chosen to come, not even to see Lulach.

"There is a suit there for Lulach as well, and a doublet and pantaloons that match that gown," Rhona said.

"Yes, I had them made of the same fabric," Madelaine said with a giggle.

"Mum, mum," Lulach said, climbing up into my lap. "Mum, dat," he said, pointing to the fire.

I looked at the flames. "What do you see?" I whispered.

"Dat, dat. Banc dere. Banc," he said.

I stared into the fire, for a flickering moment, I saw the image of Banquo riding toward the gates of the citadel in Scone.

Picking up Lulach, I went to the window. Roman-style glass covered the edifice. The view through the thick glass was wavy and distorted, but we had a slim view of the courtyard. Lulach and I watched and waited. Five minutes later, I saw the colors of Lochaber then the Thane himself.

"Banc!" Lulach screamed.

I chuckled. "He cannot hear you, son. He is too far away."

"Who is it?" Madelaine asked.

"Banc. Banc!"

Madelaine chuckled.

"Banquo, Thane of Lochaber," I said, setting my hand on the cold glass.

Madelaine rose and came to the window. We both watched as the Lochaber men dismounted.

"With the chestnut colored hair?" Madelaine whispered.

"Yes."

Madelaine watched until Banquo was out of sight. She sighed heavily then turned to me, pushing my hair behind my ear, then leaned in to kiss my cheek. "My little raven," she whispered. "Lulach saw him in the flames?"

I nodded.

"Boite's grandson indeed. Did Gillacoemgain…"

I shook my head. "No. But he knew, understood." But more, Gillacoemgain was not Lulach's true father. His real father would arrive tomorrow and be crowned King of Scotland.

CHAPTER THIRTY-THREE

The next morning, I woke to the sound of trumpets blasting and drums beating the courtyard. I opened my eyes and stared at the rich drapes. Duncan had arrived. I inhaled deeply then let out a long, slow breath. I would feel nothing. I would remember nothing. Not the rain. Not the mud. Not the feel of him inside me. Not the pain of knowing I carried his children. I would feel nothing. I would show nothing. I was here in the role of Lady Macbeth, mother of Lulach. That was all.

But you are more, so much more. And one day, he shall pay. One day, he shall pay.

Rhona arrived not long after to help me get ready. Footmen raced up and down the halls rousing all the lords and ladies. I bathed and rubbed my body down with perfumes and oils. Rhona fixed up my hair in high looping curls. She set a silver brooch in my locks. Once she was done, we both wrangled Lulach and forced him into his fancy clothes, much to his annoyance. But more, we made sure the boy wore the plaid of Moray.

"I brought this, my lady," Rhona said, pinning the fabric across Lulach's chest with a silver penannular brooch. I recognized the piece at once.

"Gillacoemgain's?" I asked.

She nodded. "I put a cork on the end so Lulach doesn't take his eye out," she said with a laugh.

I smiled. "I thought it was gone."

Rhona shook her head. "I found it by accident myself. It was... Lord Gillacoemgain left it in the chapel."

"Oh," I whispered, touched that Gillacoemgain had the foresight to leave the precious item for his son.

There was a knock on the door.

As I righted Lulach's clothes, Rhona went to answer. A moment later, Macbeth entered.

He smiled lightly but barely met my eye. "If you and Lulach are ready, we should go to the cathedral."

I eyed him over. He was dressed fashionably in red velvet and black silk under a heavy bear cloak.

"Very well," I said then put a cap on Lulach.

Macbeth took my cloak from Rhona's hands and helped me put it on. "You look very beautiful," he whispered.

I raised an eyebrow at him. "Thank you."

"And you, little Lord Lulach. Would you like to go meet the new king?" he asked, picking Lulach up.

"No," Lulach said, looking dour.

Both Macbeth and I laughed. "Well, at least there is something all of us can agree on," Macbeth said with a gentle smile. I eyed him warily, reminded myself not to be fooled again.

We were escorted from the citadel to the cathedral. Pair by pair, we would be processed through the church to the new king who sat on the Stone of Scone. We were expected to profess our loyalty. The footman organized the lords and ladies, sending each pair through. The crowd was thick. I saw many lesser lords and ladies were already seated within. Madelaine and Fife were in the procession line ahead of us.

"Where is Thorfinn?" I whispered.

Macbeth smirked. "North."

"Bold."

"It must begin somewhere."

The footman announced Madelaine and Fife. I strained to look, catching only a glimpse of my aunt's red hair.

"Your aunt," Macbeth said.

I nodded.

"If you will… I would very much like to be introduced to her."

I looked up at him. Macbeth met and held my eyes. I was surprised to find sadness and, I thought, remorse.

"Gruoch," he whispered. "I want to make amends—"

"Lord and Lady Macbeth. Come forward, please," the footman said.

Macbeth set Lulach down, and I straightened his clothes, smoothing down his hair. I took my son's hand, surprised to see that Macbeth held his other hand.

"Come, Lulach. We shall go together like the family we are," Macbeth said then prepared to be called.

I swallowed hard, forcing myself not to be unmoored by his words. I straightened my back, pulling myself up long and tall. Remembering just a bit of glamour, I worked my fingers and pulled an enchantment around myself. I would appear more radiant, more beautiful, and very powerful. At this moment, Duncan needed to see a hint of the raven. He needed to feel its strength and be wary.

"Mum," Lulach said, his eyes wide, a smile on his face.

"Sh," I said, lifting a finger to my lips, grinning when I realized what the boy had noticed.

"Macbeth, son of Donalda and Findelach, Lord of the North and his wife, Gruoch, daughter of Boite, Lady of Moray, and Lulach, son of Gruoch and Gillacoemgain of Moray," the herald announced.

The cathedral stilled.

Everyone knew that if there was any legitimate challenge to Duncan's rule, it would come from me and Macbeth. While Duncan had been Malcolm's favorite, Duncan's mother was the elder of Malcolm's two daughters, I was the daughter of Boite. I was the Lady of Moray. Macbeth held the north. We were the only ones in the room with the power to unseat everything—save Thorfinn who was not here to profess his allegiance. Again, I thought about how we should have stayed north. We should have amassed our armies and ridden south in force, not with fancy clothes and pretty words. But here we were.

There were whispers in the crowd. I heard my name and

my father's. I heard Gillacoemgain's name, Lulach's, and Macbeth's.

"Mum. Mum, Banc," Lulach whispered pointing. I tapped his hand gently, reminding him to be quiet, and thanking the Goddess that Lulach had not simply screamed out Banquo's name as was his usual fashion.

I cast a glance toward the Highlanders and spotted Banquo amongst them. His eyes met mine for just a fleeting moment, but I looked away, knowing my face would betray me if I did not. I could not be soft at this moment. I could not feel anything. I must radiate power. And I must forget the past, forget that the man before me was the father of the child whose hand I held. I needed to forget the smell of the wet earth and the rain. Forget the glow of torchlight. Forget the feel of his hand on my back. Forget the sound of his coin purse falling at my feet, the coins inside jangling.

I set my eyes on the man before me.

Duncan's arrogance and utter joy at having the world at his feet was the first thing that shone through. What I did remember of him, I remembered perfectly. The thin face, fat lips, fair hair, and gangly body were the same. He looked like a child playing at king, like his rich robes adorned with jewels weighed more than he did. He smiled smugly at us.

The raven within me screeched loudly, and I heard the heavy beat of raven wings. My eyes flashed silver, and in that moment, I saw the expression on Duncan's face change. An expression of confusion and fear washed over his face. What had the raven shown him?

I sucked in my breath and held it in, keeping the raven

at bay. A terrible rage washed over me, and all I could think about was killing him where he sat, freeing the stone of destiny from the fungus that sat upon it.

Duncan wet his lips nervously then rose. "Worthy cousins," he called.

I exhaled slowly.

"My king," Macbeth replied with a bow. "May I present my wife and stepson?" Macbeth said, turning to us.

"All men say the Lady of Moray is the most handsome woman in the land. It is not a boast," Duncan said, turning to me.

One day, I will kill you. "Thank you, my king," I said then curtsied.

Duncan stared at me, examining my face longer than expected. "Lady, have we met before?"

Fool! "No, my king."

Duncan nodded. "Perhaps I am seeing your father in your face. I remember Boite. I thought he was a giant," Duncan said then laughed loudly.

I stared at him.

Duncan coughed then looked down at Lulach.

My heart slammed in my chest. What if he realized? What if he recognized his own blood? I curled my free hand into a fist so it would not tremble.

"And this is your *stepson,*" he said, glancing from Lulach to Macbeth.

The comment was meant to wound, and from the fleeting expression on Macbeth's face, it had. Worse, Duncan had seen Macbeth's pained expression and had relished in it. He smirked, looking self-satisfied. His expression enraged me.

"This is Lulach, Son of Gillacoemgain, heir of Moray," I said firmly. To my surprise, my voice echoed throughout the cathedral, the words sounding more like a proclamation than an introduction.

The poignancy was not lost on the assembled crowd. If Duncan nor Macbeth produced an heir—not considering Lulach's true paternity—the tiny boy who would one day be king, would one day come to this very room and sit on the stone of destiny.

"Lord Lulach," Duncan said more formally, inclining his head to my boy. Out of the corner of his eye, Duncan gave me a wary glance.

Good. He had realized I would not let his petty games pass. Perhaps he and Macbeth had grown up together at Malcolm's knee, spent a lifetime tormenting one another and vying for the king's affection and attention, but I would have no part of their cheap slights. I was the daughter of Boite. Lulach was Boite's grandson. Duncan was a cheap version of power, a raping ruler. He was a fool, and I would never again suffer a fool. I narrowed my eyes at him, feeling the raven look out once more.

Duncan looked away. He turned to Macbeth. "Come, cousin. Let's be done with this so we can get to our meal," Duncan said then motioned for Macbeth and me to kneel.

Do not kneel. A daughter of the Goddess does not kneel. Rip out his heart, and eat it before the assembled crowd. Let them see the real you.

Macbeth kneeled.

Inhaling deeply, I followed his lead. I wrapped my arm around Lulach's waist and held him at my side. Lulach did not kneel because he did not know better. And I did not ask him to. His small refusal would not go unnoticed by the gods.

"I, Macbeth, son of Findelach and Donalda, swear the loyalty of my lands in the north to Duncan, king of Scotland."

"I, Gruoch, daughter of Boite and Emer, swear loyalty to King Duncan as the Lady of Moray for both myself and my son, Lulach of Gillacoemgain."

"Lord and Lady Macbeth, I accept your fealty and acknowledge Lulach as the rightful successor to Moray. I bid you go in peace."

With that, we rose and were escorted to a seat at the front of the cathedral close to Madelaine, Fife, and some other lords and ladies I did not know. The bishop came forward then and began speaking in Latin. He said his prayers and blessed Duncan, ending the performance when he set a crown on Duncan's head.

"Long reign King Duncan," the man intoned.

"Long reign the king!" the assembly answered.

Until his reign comes to its end.

CHAPTER THIRTY-FOUR

Duncan stepped off the dais and took the arm of a beautiful woman I had not noticed before. The girl, who would not have been older than eighteen, had long golden hair and wore an ornately embroidered cream-colored grown. A small diadem of gold and pearls sat on her head.

"Queen Suthen," Madelaine whispered in my ear. "Sister of Earl Siward of Northumbria."

Following behind them was an attractive older pair who nodded politely to us.

"That is your cousin and my niece, Bethoc, daughter of Malcolm, and her husband, Crinan, Abbot of Dunkeld. Duncan's parents," Madelaine whispered.

The attendant waved for us to come next.

Macbeth picked up Lulach, and we processed back through the cathedral.

This time, I caught Banquo's eye.

He smiled at me and nodded.

We were escorted back to the castle and into the feasting hall. There, we were seated close to Duncan at the end of the table. I glanced at those around us, my extended family, none of whom had anything to do with me.

"Lady Macbeth," Queen Suthen called. "Please, sit beside me."

Madelaine took Lulach from my arms and sat down beside Bethoc, Duncan's mother. Fife, Crinan, Macbeth, and a man I did not know talked with Duncan.

"My queen," I said, inclining my head, then took a seat beside her.

"Please, call me Suthen. And you're Gruoch, is that right?"

I nodded.

Queen Suthen smiled as she eyed me over, her gaze assessing. "That's my brother, Siward," she whispered as she pointed her chin toward the man. "Duncan speaks regularly of his cousin Macbeth, but he doesn't seem to know much about you or your aunt."

"I'm not surprised. Besides whose bed we lay in, Madelaine and I were of little interest to Malcolm."

Suthen, who was sipping her wine, half spit out the drink as she suppressed a laugh.

Duncan looked up at her, a reproachful glance on his face.

My gaze darkened. I stared at him, daring him to look at his wife in such a manner again.

Acting as though something behind his wife had caught

his attention, Duncan fixed a soft expression on his face once more then turned back to his father who was talking quickly, gesturing wildly as he spoke. I couldn't help but notice the good Abbot's fingers were covered with gold and silver rings.

"Sorry," Queen Suthen said, daintily patting her lips with an embroidered cloth. "I'm unused to such frankness."

I smirked. "I was not raised at court. I am unused to hiding my opinion."

"All the better for it, then. And that is your son?" she asked, looking toward Lulach.

I nodded. "Lulach."

"And his father was Gillacoemgain of Moray?"

"Yes."

Queen Suthen tapped her finger on the side of her glass as she stared at Lulach. I could see she was calculating: Lulach's age, the length of my marriage, and so on. There was no one in the land who did not know Lulach's fate if neither Duncan nor Macbeth produced an heir. And by now, both Macbeth and Duncan should have an heir on the way—yet neither did.

"He is a fine boy. I hope to soon be blessed with a child of my own. Perhaps when Lulach is older he—and you, of course—should come to court. But only if it won't curtail your frankness," she said then smiled. "One day, Duncan and I will have sons of our own. It would be nice to see our children grow side by side, let them grow to love their cousins as our husbands do."

I raised an eyebrow at her. Was she really so clueless

about the true nature of affairs in Scotland, or was she playing? She picked up her wine and sipped once more.

"Indeed," I answered simply. Dammit, what was I doing here?

"Or, perhaps, if we have a daughter... What better alliance could be found? But now I speak like a politician, and I see you're already weary of the conversation. Let's have a change of subject. I understand you were north with Thorfinn of Orkney? Is he the monster they all say?"

Duncan gave his wife a sidelong glance, but he did not interrupt.

"Worse," I said with a smirk.

"And is he married?"

"He is betrothed to a girl from the north."

Queen Suthen nodded. "Of course. My mother and father would have the whole world married off, paired like the beasts of Noah's ark," she said then glanced at Duncan. I could see the look of disgust that danced on her lips. She lifted her wine and drank again.

In that single moment, I pitied her. I had run from Duncan, but this girl had taken my place. I could not imagine what kind of man he must be, how he must treat his wife, but then my eyes fell on Macbeth. No, I knew how Suthen was treated. I was treated the same way.

The meal took far longer than was tolerable. Madelaine chatted happily with both Suthen and Bethoc. I eyed Duncan's mother who, despite being Malcolm's daughter, didn't seem to have any of the blood of MacAlpin in her. How many times could someone have the same conversation about the weather? Bethoc had found at least a dozen ways to consider the subject thus far.

As I listened, I learned that the Crinan, the Abbot of Dunkeld, was actually in charge of the realm's silver—her mines, her coins, her wealth. And money was, it seemed, the only thing that interested him. Despite his wife's sincere passion for the weather, Crinan always returned the conversation to coin.

My head ached. I had ridden south in good faith. I had come to see Lulach acknowledged, and that work was done. There was no other reason for me to stay here. I would not sit for days on end and talk of marriage alliances —or the damned weather.

I cast an eye at Duncan. He was nothing. As I sat and listened, I realized that Duncan merely repeated his father's words and ideas. Crinan was the power behind the throne. I suppressed a sneer.

"How about a hunt, Macbeth? Shall we see if there are any winter stags about?" Earl Siward offered.

"It is far too cold for hunting. If the wind comes in from the west, you will all catch frostbite," Bethoc informed them.

Macbeth smiled at Duncan. "What say you, cousin?"

Duncan shrugged. "There is meat enough here."

"There, you see how smart my son is? No, no. You should not go out. I have heard that if a man lets his beard freeze, it can cause his jaw to crack," Bethoc said.

I cast a glance to Madelaine who was holding her face so still, frozen in such a practiced smile, that I almost laughed.

"Mother, really," Duncan said, rolling his eyes.

Bethoc turned her attention to Macbeth. "You must take care, nephew. And after your long ride south. Well, it's a wonder you all aren't sick."

"Thank you for your care, Aunt," Macbeth told her.

Bethoc smiled, looking pleased with herself.

May the gods save us from fools.

Lulach, seeming to sense my great need for an escape, began to wriggle in Madelaine's lap.

"My little lord has grown tired, I'm afraid," I said, rising to take him from Madelaine. "With Your Majesty's permission, I will take him to rest."

"Don't you have a maid to look after him?" Bethoc asked.

"I do, but I prefer to stay with him. It is a strange place for him."

Bethoc clicked her tongue, but Duncan gave his mother a reproachful look.

"It is good of you to take such close care of your child, Lady Gruoch," Duncan said. "There were times in my youth when I didn't remember what my mother looked like," he added, giving Bethoc a sharp glance.

"Well," Bethoc said, shaking her head.

Before she could discover a way to turn the conversation to the weather, I curtseyed to Duncan. "Your Majesty."

The king, who had risen when I moved to leave, inclined his head. "Cousin."

"My lady," Macbeth said, nodding to me.

"My lord," I added with an inclination of the head. I then turned to Lulach. "Come along, love."

"She is a fine woman, Macbeth," I heard Duncan say as Lulach and I headed out.

"As is Her Majesty," Macbeth said.

I heard Queen Suthen laugh lightly.

As I exited the room, it was all I could do to keep a straight face. It would not do to show my immense relief at escaping. *My lord, my lady, my lord, my lady, my lord, my lady*. Ugh. It was dizzying.

I headed away from the great hall and toward the section of the castle in which I had been housed. As I walked down the stone corridor, I heard someone approach. My nerves on edge, I pulled a dagger from my belt but turned to find Banquo there.

He lifted his hands then grinned at me. "I come in peace."

"Banc!" Lulach screamed then struggled to get down. Rushing quickly on unsteady feet, he went to Banquo.

Banquo picked him up. "Little Lord Lulach, what an impression you made on the fair court." Smiling, he fell into step with me. "I didn't like to see you leave the company alone. We have enemies here at court. Macbeth should have sent someone with you. Since he did not, here I am. As it is, you are watched," he said, whispering the final piece.

So busy with my own thoughts, I had not been wary. Now, as I stilled my mind and shifted my vision with the keen sight of a raven, I noted a man lingering by the window.

"Whose man is he?"

"Northumbria," Banquo said, and we continued on. "Lulach did make quite the impression, reminding everyone in the room that the future of this country is not yet decided, and that, as things stand, the north has more power than the king himself. You need a guard on you and Lulach at all times."

"I brought men from Moray. I'll send for them."

"Not that you were slow at pulling that dagger. A child in one arm, a blade in another. How little you have changed, my Boudicca."

I smiled at him. "I've missed you," I whispered, looking deeply into his chestnut colored eyes. It had been months since we had parted on the shore in the north.

"And I you."

We returned to my chamber, which we found empty.

"Where is Ute?" Banquo asked.

"Ute is a maid for Madelaine now. She's back in Fife. I brought a woman from Moray, Rhona. The servants are, no doubt, feasting as well."

Lulach had fallen asleep in Banquo's arms. He laid Lulach down on my bed, pulling off my child's boots and unpinning his tartan. "In case he rolls in his sleep," he said, handing the brooch to me. He looked at the piece as he did so. "It has the same flower as your dagger."

"Gillacoemgain's. Both."

"Did you quarrel with Ute?" Banquo asked, looking perplexed.

"No. She just… She needed a change."

Banquo frowned. "A change? That doesn't sit well with me."

"Nor with me, but that is how she wanted it."

Banquo looked down at Lulach. "I was told you returned to Cawdor and have been there these months—or south with Madelaine."

"Do you have spies on me? After Thurso, I could not bring myself to stay with Macbeth."

"Not spies, but I do what I can to make sure you're safe. I confess I could not return to Inverness either. Macbeth wrote to me with apologies. He asked me to come."

"You got more than I did. I had not seen nor spoken to Macbeth until we started for Scone."

Banquo frowned. "Is that true? By the gods, he is a fool. He was always a bit unbalanced. I always thought… Well, some people are touched. Who was I to judge? But now, however, I see it affecting those I love. I hate him for it."

"Banquo," I whispered.

Banquo looked at me. Moving slowly, he reached out and touched my cheek. "How beautiful you are. My heart stopped when you walked into that cathedral. I couldn't take my eyes from you."

"Glamour," I whispered.

"It was not the glamour. I can easily see past that. It was you. I missed *you*," he said then stepped in close. His hand gently caressed my cheek, his thumb brushing across my lips. "Macbeth has the only thing I ever wanted, and he is so careless. I despise him." He put his hands on my waist and pulled me closer to him. "Cerridwen."

"I've missed you too."

"My love," he whispered.

I closed my eyes. My body swayed. In this place, surrounded by men I hated and a life I loathed, I found the man I loved once more. In that moment, I had him—but not really. He was mine and not mine. I stepped back.

"Cerridwen," Banquo groaned then pulled me back, setting his forehead on my shoulder.

"It cannot be risked," I whispered.

Banquo inhaled deeply. "No. You are right."

"And…Merna," I added, my hands shaking.

"And Merna," Banquo assented. He pulled back then turned and sat down at the small table. I watched as he poured two glasses of wine. He motioned for me to take the seat opposite him. "Come, my Cerridwen," he said then dipped into his jacket and pulled out some playing cards.

"Are those cards?" I asked with a laugh.

"Indeed they are. We cannot have what we want, so what is left?"

"Games?"

Banquo chuckled. "Exactly. Come. I have a new game to teach you."

Inhaling deeply, I sat down. I picked up my goblet of wine and took a hearty drink.

"Drink again," Banquo said. "It will make it easier for me to beat you."

"How do you play?"

"Everything starts with the queen."

CHAPTER THIRTY-FIVE

Banquo stayed awhile, teaching me his game. After a time, he asked, "How long will you stay in Scone?"

I shook my head. "I hadn't thought about it."

"Me and my men return north tomorrow."

"You're leaving already?"

Banquo nodded.

I turned and looked back at Lulach who was still sleeping. "I've done what I came here to do. Lulach and I will ride with you. You're right that it's not safe here. I'll call the Moray men. We'll go back to Cawdor. Now I just need to find a way to break it to Rhona."

"And Macbeth."

"Damn Macbeth."

Banquo harrumphed but said nothing more. A short while later, Rhona returned and Banquo excused himself so he could go say his farewells and get ready. After I broke

Rhona's heart with the news, I sent her with a message for the men to tell them to get ready to leave.

Not long after, Madelaine stopped by.

"Won't you come along, Gruoch? Queen Suthen is gathering all the ladies for drinks and games. Won't you join them for a little while?"

"No. The men of Lochaber are returning tomorrow. I've already sent word to the Moray men. We'll ride with them. I'm leaving." I was done pretending. I was done playing Lady Macbeth. I was just done with it all. I had done my part, pledged my word on Lulach's behalf, and now I wanted to go home.

"Gruoch. But you can't. Macbeth—"

"To hell with Macbeth."

"Corbie, is it…really as bad as that?"

"Yes."

"If you are having an affair with Banquo of Lochaber, it will complicate matters."

"An affair? Hard to have an affair with a man you're already married to. But that aside, I'm not having an affair with anyone. I don't have anyone. I just want to go home. I cannot stand to look at Duncan's face anymore. Everything around me is a lie. I cannot stay here."

Madelaine stared at me. "What is the matter between you and Duncan? Corbie, I will never forget the fear in your eyes when you learned Duncan was riding to claim you. I have never seen you afraid in all my life with the exception of that night. I don't understand. You never even met Duncan—"

"Once. I met him once. That was enough."

"When? Where?"

"It doesn't matter. He didn't know it was me."

Madelaine stared at me, and for a moment, I felt magic shift around us. I often forgot that Madelaine had been trained in the ancient arts.

"I cannot see, but I smell rain, and I can feel your pain and anger. Corbie, what happened?"

I lifted a hand. "Don't speak of it."

Madelaine shook her head. Saying nothing else, she crossed the room and embraced me once more. "I'll be here in the morning to see you off. Goodnight, love," she whispered, kissing me on the cheek, then she left me alone.

I sent a messenger to Macbeth, letting him know of my intention to leave. And then I sat alone. Part of me wondered if Macbeth would come. Part of me understood that he would not. He had never really loved me. And despite my wish for things to be different, I no longer loved him.

I set my fingertips on my lips and remembered Banquo's words: *Macbeth has the only thing I ever wanted.*

I closed my eyes. Banquo, too, was the only thing *I* had ever wanted. Andraste had me mooning over a man I had not met, a man who was nothing like what he seemed to be. Those visions had been nothing more than shadows. Is that what I had given Banquo up for? Shadows?

Lulach sighed in his sleep and rolled over.

I rose and went to look at him. Lost to dreams, his face was soft, peaceful. As I stared at him, I swore I saw the shape of Gillacoemgain in his features. I sighed. No, I had given it all up for Lulach. With that, at least, I could make peace. I covered the boy then turned to go back to my seat by the window. I was surprised to find someone already sitting there.

The Morrigu.

"My lady," I whispered, taken aback.

Her eyes drifted to Lulach. "Andraste," she muttered then shook her head. Her dark eyes met mine. "Three times Duncan will strike the north. Once he will seek to strike by sea, but he will fail. Once he will strike with bought men, but he will fail. The third time, he will come to my bloody fields like the soldier he should be. There, he will meet my champion," she said then disappeared.

CHAPTER THIRTY-SIX

Rhona and I were busy packing the next morning when Macbeth finally arrived.

"Gruoch," he said as his eyes glanced over our packs. "I received your messenger."

"I'll go to the kitchens for the provisions, my lady," Rhona said then left, scowling at Macbeth as she went.

Macbeth didn't notice.

"I'm returning to Cawdor."

"With Banquo?"

"Banquo is returning to Lochaber. His bannermen have offered to ride with Lulach and me to ensure our safety. I have my men, and if you have a few men of your own to spare, I'll take them."

"But...why?"

"Why?" I shook my head. "False faces hide what false hearts know. I am not keen on staying here and playing games. I came to do what I had to. Now I will go home."

"And what was that?"

"To have Lulach acknowledged as the heir of Moray. I have no use for courtly pleasantries. No use for false faces."

"You will cast suspicion on both of us."

"Why? You're staying. That should be enough. Let them say Lady Macbeth is rude. Let them say she does not like court. If you must say something to excuse me, say only that I am my father's daughter. Say that, Macbeth, and none will question you. My father had no love of court. Boite would not dance to their tune, and neither will I. You, however, seem quite adept at this game. Stay as long as you like."

Macbeth ran his fingers roughly through his hair. "Why must you be so damned difficult to talk to, Gruoch? I would like you to return to Inverness. Things will be complicated now. We should be together."

"If you wanted me to return to Inverness, if you wanted to talk to me, where were you last night as I sat awake waiting for you?"

"I...was..." Macbeth began then looked away, a guilty expression on his face.

I stared at him. *Just where in the hell was he?* I had not intended to trap him with the question, but his expression revealed I had stumbled on something I should not have seen.

I set down the parcel I was holding. "Where were you, Macbeth?"

"With the others, that is all," he stammered. "I just... I have not found the right words to say to you. I don't know how to apologize in a way you will understand. You won't hear anything from me, and everything makes you angry."

"I see. I am to blame. We are done here, I think," I said then turned and picked up the parcel once more. My heart was pounding in my chest, and jealous suspicions washed over me. Where *had* he been?

"You see. You prove my point."

My hands shaking, I turned and looked at him. "I came to you in good faith. I could be sitting where Suthen sits now. You understand that, don't you? But I rode north. Your mind, your moods, swing like a pendulum, Macbeth. I cannot keep up with the sway. You left me in the dark, left me in pain, bleeding, our child lost and my life in jeopardy. I will never forget that you left me alone."

"I have done penance, Gruoch. I have prayed. My priest advises me—"

"Don't tell me what your priest advises. I will not hear it," I said then glared at him. The raven within me flashed with anger. I felt her silvery glow inside me.

Macbeth stared. "The old gods..." he began then said nothing more, seeming unsure what to say.

"Don't talk about what you don't understand. I'm leaving. Send me some men to join Lochaber's party or don't. Stay or don't. I don't care. You were nothing like what was promised to me. And if you don't change soon, you will be nothing to me."

"Gruoch."

"Goodbye, Macbeth," I said then turned to finish my

packing. A few moments later, I heard the door close once more.

I gazed at Lulach who slept. I closed my eyes. For him. I would carry on for him.

I should have run away with Banquo.

A few hours later, dressed in our heavy winter clothes, our packs already delivered to the stables, Rhona, Lulach, and I headed outside. When we stepped into the square, I was surprised to see Macbeth's men there —all of them. And Macbeth himself. He was chatting lightly with Duncan, the both of them laughing merrily.

Madelaine, who had been talking to Banquo, crossed the courtyard to join me. She smiled lightly.

"I wanted to say goodbye," she said, pausing to fasten the ties on Lulach's coat more tightly. "And to have a word with the Thane of Lochaber before I missed my chance," she said then touched my chin. "I like him very much. He is a very good man."

"Yes, he is," I said, casting a look at Banquo who smiled at me and raised his hand in greeting. The morning sunlight shimmered on his brown hair, calling up shades of gold and red. Banquo motioned with his chin to Macbeth.

I cast a glance at Macbeth. He was dressed for riding.

"I am sorry, Gruoch," Madelaine whispered, pulling me into a hug. "I am sorry to see in the flesh what I stole from you. And Banquo… I just spoke a word with him, but it was enough to show me he was the right man for you. I failed you. I'm sorry. If Boite had still been alive, maybe... Oh, my little raven."

"You did your best. It was Malcolm's fault. In the end, I am not sorry for my time with Gillacoemgain. I am only sorry for all the rest of it."

She nodded then dashed a tear from her cheek. "There will be talk, you know," she said, casting an eye toward Macbeth. "With Thorfinn absent and you and Macbeth leaving..."

"I didn't know he was going to join me. But it is as it should be. It is the prelude," I whispered. "Stay safe. Return home, close to Epona so you may stay hidden if things become complicated."

She nodded. "My little raven, and my little love," she said, leaning in to kiss Lulach, who giggled.

Banquo joined us then.

"Banc!" Lulach screamed.

Banquo chuckled. "How would you like to ride with me?" he asked, reaching out for Lulach.

Lulach grinned and nodded.

"They're coming," Madelaine whispered then turned a cheery smile toward Macbeth and Duncan.

"My king, my nephew," Madelaine called happily.

"Alas, the northerners return north," Duncan said. "How shall we entertain ourselves now, Lady Madelaine?"

Madelaine smiled. "Perhaps Queen Suthen will arrange a dance."

Duncan nodded then looked at me. "I am sorry, Lady Gruoch, that Suthen is not here to wish you off. She dislikes the cold weather. In truth, I don't think I've ever seen her out of doors. She even rode here in a closed carriage."

Macbeth and Madelaine chuckled lightly.

Was that supposed to be funny?

"It is farewell for you as well, sir?" Duncan asked, turning to Banquo. "Moray's loyal bannerman," he said, eyeing Lulach in Banquo's arms. "I must apologize. I've forgotten your name."

"Banquo, Thane of Lochaber, Your Majesty," Banquo said, but Duncan had already turned his attention back to me.

"I understand you have the opposite problem of Suthen, Lady Gruoch. Always out of doors. I remember hearing you once provided alms to your people, going from homestead to homestead in Moray."

"Medicines, actually."

"Medicines?"

"There was a fever in Moray. I distributed medicines."

"Oh, well, it is good to win their hearts and minds. Very astute, Lady Gruoch."

I could not repress the half-laugh that escaped me. "If I had not gone, my king and cousin, many would have died of fever. It was more their bodies and souls I was concerned with."

"Indeed? Very well done, Lady Gruoch. I wish you a safe ride north. We are all sorry to see you go so soon," he said, baiting us.

"Indeed we are, Your Majesty," Madelaine interjected, taking Duncan playfully by the arm.

"It's far too cold, Lady Madelaine. My mother is convinced we might freeze solid out here. Shall we leave these northerners and go see if Fife has left us any mulled wine?"

Madelaine laughed a high, false laugh. "Let's hope we're lucky. Farewell, my loves," she said, reaching out to squeeze Lulach's hand once more.

"Macbeth, Lady Macbeth, Lochalsh," Duncan said.

Banquo gave a short bow as he suppressed a laugh then turned. Lulach with him, he mounted his horse.

I curtseyed, Macbeth bowing, then we turned to the horses. I hated seeing Madelaine on Duncan's arm, but the sense of relief I felt at escaping was nearly overwhelming. As we walked toward the horses, Kelpie nickered loudly to me. I guess I wasn't the only one excited to leave.

"Gruoch," Macbeth said. "I want to make amends with you and Banquo. I have asked him to stay awhile at Cawdor. I…will join you there for a time if you will have me."

I flicked my eyes at him.

He had such an earnest impression on his face.

Be wary. Be wary! False faces, false hearts.

I sighed. More than anything, I wanted to be at peace with Macbeth. Would it be so hard to refuse him? It had cost me before to open my heart to him. But, perhaps, if I let him in a little, there would be no harm.

"Very well."

Macbeth nodded. "Good. Good. Then we are settled. I shall get to horse and join you. After all, I can hardly have my wife and son ride out of Scone at the Thane of Lochaber's side," he said then turned and left.

Shaking my head, I climbed on Kelpie. Was that the only reason he was leaving now? To avoid gossip if I had gone alone with Banquo? I frowned. Once more, I swung on the pendulum. I reined Kelpie in close to Banquo.

"Well, Lochalsh, shall we head to the lands where the faeries walk from Eilean Donan to Dunvegan?"

Banquo chuckled. "I suppose if one has never seen a loch, they all look the same. And you, my wanderer, have you ever been in those lands?"

I shook my head. "I've been far, but not there."

"Perhaps you have not been there, but your dagger has," he said, pointing to my boot. The pommel of Gillacoemgain's dagger was sticking out.

"Scáthach," I said.

"Scáthach?"

"Her name."

Banquo laughed. "She is well-named then. That flower on her hilt and on the brooch… You will find it on every standing stone in Skye. Lulach carries the rich blood of two ancient lines. Don't you?" he said, tickling the boy and making him giggle. "Don't you, little lord?

Macbeth reigned in beside us. "Well, Lulach. Ready to ride home?"

"Banc," Lulach said, pointing up to Banquo, making clear he did not want to be moved.

"Indeed," Macbeth replied, his face tightening. He turned then and rode out ahead of us. Alone.

CHAPTER THIRTY-SEVEN

"Good to have you back, my lady," Standish told me, taking Kelpie by the reins as we rode into Cawdor.

"Thank you, Standish. Can you see Lord Banquo's men are provisioned for the return to Lochaber? Their lord will stay awhile," I said.

Standish nodded then eyed over Macbeth's group. Macbeth, his guard, a footman, and two soldiers stayed behind. The rest of Macbeth's party had already ridden on to Inverness. "Lord Macbeth will take residence with us…briefly."

Standish nodded. "I'll see for chambers for both gentlemen."

"Thank you," I said, not wanting to meet Standish's eye. I suddenly felt ashamed at having brought Macbeth there.

Rhona had already taken Lulach inside. The child had been asking for biscuits for the last hour. Tired, my bones aching and feeling weary from the road, I headed into the castle.

"My lady," Tira called happily when I entered. "Welcome back. I swear you were on the road longer than you were there."

I chuckled. "True."

"And how was it?"

"Exceedingly dull. You'd be best to ask Rhona for the details. In the meantime, I would kill for a bath to heat myself back up."

"Of course, my lady. I'll go get it ready for you," she said then headed upstairs.

I turned and went to the unused part of the castle. The small garden was blanketed with a light dusting of snow. I went to the bench, dusted the snow off, and then sat down. I closed my eyes and tried to feel Gillacoemgain's spirit. It did not take long to sense his presence as I always did in this place.

"I'm home, love," I whispered.

My head ached. While it would be better if Macbeth and I could be reconciled, it felt easier to let things be as they were. It was easier to remember Gillacoemgain, to love Banquo from afar, without Macbeth there asking things from me I didn't know how to give. No matter what way I had tried to love him, nothing ever seemed right.

A moment later, I heard movement in the garden, and a soft nose pushed my hand.

I opened my eyes to find Thora there, her tail wagging.

I chuckled. "I see I am forgiven for leaving you behind," I said, petting her head.

"I confess to setting her on your trail," Banquo said then entered the garden. "What a beautiful space."

"It's so lovely in the springtime. I planted all my medicinal herbs here."

Banquo glanced around. "You don't use this part of the castle?"

"No."

His eyes rose to Crearwy's chamber. "I see," he said, his gaze narrowing.

"Don't."

"Don't?"

"Don't disturb her. Or the past. Or anything else there."

Banquo inclined his head. "As you wish."

I rose slowly, my back aching from the cold. "We should go find something warm to drink."

"Macbeth is already inside."

I chuckled. "I'm sure he is."

"He says he wishes to make amends."

"Well, let's see if he can find the temperament to do so."

"Indeed."

Banquo and I headed back to the castle, him going to the hall to join Macbeth while I went upstairs. Tira had my bath ready.

"Will you need my help, my lady?"

"No, Tira. Thank you."

"Very well. I'll be back in a bit to help Rhona unpack

your bags. I need to go find our little lord and give him a good squeeze."

I laughed, waved to her, and then went to my box of medicines. I unpacked some herbs, sprinkling the hot wash water with dried lavender, chamomile flowers, and other fragrant flowers and leaves. I took off my riding clothes and dropped them onto the floor then slipped into the washing tub sitting before the fire. The hot liquid enveloped me, the fragrant herbs filling my senses. I closed my eyes, letting the water wash me clean of my encounter with Duncan, wash me clean of his words, his presence.

Opening my eyes slowly, I gazed at the wash water. The fire from the fireplace was mirrored on the surface. I gazed deeply into the flames reflected there. The sound of raven's wings came to me, and I felt my gaze shift as the raven and I became one. The water rippled. I heard the sounds of rough voices, waves, and wind. A moment later, I saw the image of ships burning and sinking upon a tossing sea. Duncan's banner slowly drowned under the waves. The raven looked around and found Thorfinn at the prow of a longship, the wind blowing back his long, blond hair.

"For Macbeth! For the north!" the Northman called, lifting his ax in the air, his men cheering.

Then the image faded.

I closed my eyes. The battle at sea as the Morrigu predicted. Soon. It was coming soon.

CHAPTER THIRTY-EIGHT

A few days later, I found Macbeth standing in the hall reading a dispatch, his brow furrowed.

I approached him slowly. Things had been stiff and awkward between the three of us. When Macbeth and Banquo were alone, there was an ease between them. But between Macbeth and me, there was still a barrier I didn't know how to pass. I should forgive him and move on, but the raven wasn't sure that was a good idea—at least not yet. I laced my fingers together then approached him.

"What is it?" I asked.

"Thorfinn. His cousin Rognevald has returned from exile. Rognevald is in Norway under Cnut's protection. He is amassing a navy—and he has help."

"Cnut?"

"Cnut *and* Duncan," Macbeth replied, crushing the note in his hand. "Duncan…how many questions he asked me about Thorfinn. Cousin this, cousin that. You are right,

Gruoch. False faced liar. They will seek to oust Thorfinn and set Rognevald in his place."

I shook my head. "If they truly believe you are loyal, they will set Rognevald in Thorfinn's place and then they will send you to destroy Rognevald. Once you have done so and the north is solidified, Duncan will come for you and take it all."

Macbeth stared at me as if the weight of my words was sinking in. "We should not have ridden south. We should have stayed north as Thorfinn did, set our allegiances square from the beginning."

"If you had asked me, that is what I would have advised."

"Really? Would you have? But you are so keen to protect Lulach's claim," he said, his voice hard.

"No matter what you do, it will come to war in the end. Duncan will not be content to see you so powerful. We hold too much sway. Lulach will be Mormaer of Moray one way or another. Since we rode south, I forced the words from the king's mouth."

Macbeth paused then looked behind me. "Banquo? Good god, man, you're ashen. What is it?"

I looked back to find Banquo there, a grave expression on his face. "I must return to Lochaber at once."

"What's happened?" I asked.

"Fleance and Merna have both taken a fever, and they've had no luck healing them."

Macbeth nodded. "Have Gruoch's men saddle your horse. Take whatever you need. Go at once, old friend."

"I'll see to it," I told Macbeth then turned and left the hall, motioning for Banquo to come with me.

From behind me, I felt Macbeth scowling. While Macbeth and Banquo had warmed to one another, Macbeth had not warmed to the sight of Banquo and me together. His jealousy was insufferable. But at that moment, I didn't care about his pettiness. Banquo was in trouble.

Banquo and I headed toward the stables. "I can come with you. We can ride quickly. I'll go back upstairs and grab my medicines. I'll be ready before the horses are saddled."

Banquo shook his head. "They write that the illness is contagious. Several members of my household are ill, and two have died already. I would not risk you there. I'll send a casting to Balor. He winters in Skye. He can walk the old paths and come quickly. The old paths. Cerridwen, your garden," he said then grabbed my arm. "I have no time. The rider just arrived, but it may already be too late. My son. Cerridwen, your garden. I know you said not to intrude, but the worlds are thin there."

I nodded. "Come with me."

Banquo and I headed quickly into the garden.

"This way," I said then led him up the steps to the unused part of the castle. Grabbing a lantern, I led Banquo down the dark halls. The air stilled, and my skin rose to gooseflesh. Taking Banquo's hand, I led him forward.

"I'm sorry to leave you like this," Banquo whispered.

"Think nothing of it. Your son, your wife. You must hurry to them."

"Fleance," Banquo whispered, his voice choking.

I squeezed his hand. An image of my own daughter fluttered through my mind. The thought of hers or Lulach's lives in danger would be more than I could take. I understood Banquo's need for expedience.

The hallway was dark, dank, and filled with cobwebs. We walked to the door of Crearwy's chamber.

"Cerridwen, what is this place?" Banquo whispered.

I shook my head. "I promised I would not speak of it."

Banquo nodded.

"If I can do anything, cast to me. I will come."

"All right."

"Grip the door handle and wish for home," I said, motioning to the door.

"Thank you."

"May the Great Mother and the Father God watch over you and yours," I whispered then stepped back.

I closed my eyes, and pulled magic around me, feeling the great beyond.

Send him home.

Banquo inhaled slowly letting out a slow, steady breath. The air around me seemed to tremble.

The door opened then closed.

I opened my eyes once more. The hallway was very still, very silent.

Turning the latch, I opened the door. My lantern shone into the room, revealing the orange-colored stain on the floor. I cast a glance across the dusty chamber, the cobweb-covered spinning wheel, the decaying gown lying on the bed. There, at the window on the other side of the hall, stood Crearwy's—Gillacoemgain's sister's—shade. The slim girl, her dark hair fixed prettily on a pile on her head, turned and looked at me.

"Sister," I whispered, bowing to her.

A slight smiled crossed her lips. She inclined her head to me then disappeared.

CHAPTER THIRTY-NINE

With Banquo gone, I was left with Macbeth and the awkward balance between us. Late one evening, we sat in the hall reading dispatches. Macbeth, I could see, was growing increasingly agitated as he read. He tossed the scroll he'd been reading onto the table then took a long drink of his ale.

"Is there any news from Banquo?" Macbeth asked, eyeing the message I held. It was a letter from Madelaine.

I shook my head. Neither by paper nor by casting, I hadn't learned anything about what had befallen Merna and Fleance. Part of me thought to cast myself to Lochaber, but I wouldn't intrude where I was not invited. Yet still, I worried for Fleance who was still so young and for Merna. And for Banquo too. He'd said the illness was contagious. What if he'd grown ill as well?

"No."

Macbeth eyed the paper in my hands once more.

"From Madelaine," I told him, lifting the parchment.

He nodded then slid the message he'd been reading across the table to me. I picked it up and scanned the contents.

"When we were south for the coronation, I was told a great deal of silver had been invested in shipbuilding," Macbeth told me.

"Shipbuilding," I repeated, reading over what I dared not believe. Duncan was building an armada off the west coast. All signs pointed in the same direction. When the spring thaw came, Duncan would launch his new armada and join Rognevald in war against Thorfinn.

The vision I had seen in the water was beginning to take shape in the real world. And if the premonition had been true, the first battle would be ours.

"What will you do?"

"We will share what we know with Thorfinn, and we will wait."

"We cannot let Thorfinn be destroyed by that boyish king."

Macbeth laughed. "No, we will not. I have spent my own silver. It is hard at work in the south. We will learn soon enough what Duncan plans."

I raised an eyebrow. "And what have you purchased?"

"Eyes and ears."

Surprised, I smirked. Perhaps Macbeth wasn't as naive about the "good cousin" game as he seemed.

"Gruoch," Macbeth said, his tone careful. "Yule is coming and the celebration of the birth of Christ. I would like to return to Inverness for the holiday. And I would very much like you and Lulach to join me there. We can celebrate together as a family. I…am not comfortable here in Cawdor. I want to be with you, but I would like to go home."

I looked at him, remembering what Banquo had once told me about Macbeth's desire to be at Inverness. And in truth, I could see my servants merely tolerated Macbeth. This was Gillacoemgain's castle. They would never make Macbeth welcome here.

"All right," I said warily, not sure if I was making the right choice.

Macbeth smiled then grabbed a sheet of parchment. "I'll send word to ready the castle," he began then stopped and set down his quill. Reaching across the table, he took my hand. "Thank you, Gruoch."

"You're welcome, Macbeth."

"Now, you must tell me what favor I can give you as a gift you to celebrate the season."

"You've already bought me something."

"I have?"

"Eyes and ears. What better gift could a lord buy for his lady?"

At that, Macbeth laughed. The honest sound softened my heart.

We returned to Inverness within the week. While Rhona and Tira were not happy about it, they only complained a little. Thora, Kelpie, and

Lulach, however, seemed content to return. On the day we arrived, I took Kelpie to the stable to let Elspeth know her favorite vexing stallion was back. But when I searched the barn, I couldn't find her. I did, however, come across her father.

"Samuel," I said brightly, leading Kelpie along behind me.

"Lady Macbeth," he said then nodded. "Pleased to have you back, my lady. And that giant brute of yours."

I chuckled. "Thank you, sir. I was actually looking for your daughter. I know Elspeth was partial to Kelpie. I thought she'd be pleased he has returned.

"Oh," Samuel said, suddenly looking uncomfortable. "I'm sorry, my lady. Elspeth is not here with me anymore. She went back to the glen with our family."

"Is everything all right?"

"Oh, indeed. I am a grandfather now, my lady. Elspeth gave birth to a healthy baby boy not a month ago."

"Congratulations." I was happy for the man and for Elspeth, but a child born out of wedlock still created gossip. "Does Elspeth or her child need anything? Can I send anything to her?"

"No, my lady. That is very kind of you. My daughter and her little one as well," Samuel said then reached out for Kelpie's lead. "Come along, Kelpie. I'm not as pretty as my bonnie lass, but I guess I'll have to do."

"Wish your daughter well for me."

"Thank you, my lady," Samuel said then turned and led Kelpie away. I bit my tongue, not pressing the matter further. No wedding nor husband was mentioned. No doubt the child was that of whomever she'd been with that day in the stable. But it was not my business. Turning, I headed back to the castle, thinking nothing of it save for the lingering sound of raven's wings beating at the edge of my awareness. Odd.

Lulach and I moved back into the chamber near the small garden with the balcony that looked over the river. Over the next few days, a terrible storm blew in. The winter winds whipped against the shutters, and a heavy snowfall blanketed the castle. Macbeth spent more time with us than he had before, and his attentions were not lost on me.

Macbeth was trying.

I should try too.

One evening, after Lulach had gone to sleep, I pulled on my heavy cloak and went to seek out Macbeth. The winter storm had locked us all in the castle. With the Yule celebration just days away, I was hoping Macbeth would be willing to host the servants and hold a grand feast. Perhaps we could even carve a yule log and celebrate the traditions of both religions, those of the old gods and the White Christ. In the least, we could show those who served their lord and lady how much we appreciated them. The idea of a merry event with music, wine, dancing, and cheer sounded like a joy. I hoped Macbeth would agree. And more than that, I wanted an excuse to spend some time alone with him. With Macbeth's many small kindnesses, I was beginning to feel something once more. Not love. But hope, however small, was blossoming in me once more.

Pulling my cloak around me, I went first to the main hall to look for him, but his papers had been cleaned up. I went to Macbeth's chamber. As usual, I found his guard posted outside his door. In the midst of such a terrible storm, did Macbeth fear a troupe of winter faeries might come for him? I grinned at the thought, amused by his slight paranoia.

"Good evening. Is your lord within?"

The man eyed me warily. "He's abed, my lady."

"Already? Is he well?"

"Yes, my lady."

I frowned from the man to the door. On the other side of the chamber door, I heard voices. I caught the sound of Macbeth's voice, but didn't recognize that of the other person whose voice was very low.

"Who is with my lord?"

The man frowned. "Goodnight, Lady Macbeth."

The raven did not like this answer.

Frowning, I moved to go around the man, but he shifted to block me. "My lord asked not to be disturbed, my lady."

"Macbeth," I called toward the door.

The voices within quieted.

"Macbeth?"

There was no answer.

I glared at the man, feeling the flash of the raven in my eyes. "Liar. I will not forget," I told him.

"Lady Gruoch," the man said, shifting uncomfortably. "I'm sorry, my lady. Macbeth ordered me…" he began, but I didn't hear the rest.

Turning, my anger boiling, I headed back to my chamber. I was about to go within when I spotted movement in the small garden below my chamber. There was a hooded figure sitting near the tree. Why was someone in my garden? Already seething, my heart beat quickly. Who would dare to come so close to me and my son? There was treachery afoot at Inverness. The raven was set on edge.

I pulled Scáthach from my boot, extinguished my lamp, and slipped down the stairs. The dagger before me, I stepped into the garden. The snow was so deep it was above my knees. I eyed the ground all around me. There were no other footprints in the snow.

I stared at the robed figure. The person held their head in their hands and wept.

A god?

A goddess?

The air around the figure simmered and waved. For a moment, I saw a hall I did not recognize. Images of stones and the orange glow of fire were superimposed over the snow. I saw the garden and the hall all at once. The stranger was both here and there.

The figure moaned miserably.

Gasping, I recognized a familiar catch in his voice.

"Banquo?" I whispered.

He looked up, his face scrunching up as if he was unsure where he was. The image of the hall around him wavered. I realized then what was happening. His despair had called to me, and I had found him in one of the thin places. Given the raven was already awake within me, it was not a surprise I had heard his distress. Banquo was not at Inverness. He was in Lochaber. But, at the moment, neither of us were quite in one place or the other. We were in the thin place, the place that was neither and both all at once.

"Banquo?"

He wiped a tear from his cheek. "Merna is dead," he whispered.

I gasped. I had been jealous of the woman, but had never wished her gone. In my most desperate hour, Merna had been there for me whereas others who pretended to love me had not. It was Merna who had been at my side when my unborn child died, not Macbeth.

"I'm so sorry. Fleance?"

"Recovering, thanks to the gods. Balor arrived just in time. He was able to heal Fleance in time, but Merna… She was too far gone."

"Oh, Banquo," I whispered, stepping toward him. My heart ached. "Banquo," I said, reaching out to him.

"Don't come too close," Banquo said, motioning to me in warning, "or you will step through." Banquo looked off into the distance. "What will I do now? My son…"

"Bring him to me. Bring him to me, and I shall care for your child. I will raise him alongside Lulach. Bring Fleance when he is well enough to travel—and Morag."

Banquo stared at me. "Are you… Are you certain?"

Tears welled in my eyes. "I will never give you a son in this life. Let me care for your boy as if he were my own. For Merna and for you."

Banquo wept hard.

My heart broke at the sight.

But then there was a sound in the distance, and the dual image wavered. I heard someone call Banquo's name.

Banquo turned and looked at me. "Cerridwen?"

"My heart goes with you," I whispered.

A moment later, the image disappeared.

I squeezed the handle on my dagger then stared up at the moon. My mind whirled. I was furious at Macbeth, sad for Fleance and Banquo, grieved Merna's loss, but also—much to my shame—felt an enormous sense of relief over her death. Merna was a good woman, and her goodness had served as a barrier between Banquo and me. And now… I was ashamed of my thoughts.

"I'm sorry, Merna," I whispered. "You were so good to me. I am sorry I loved him first," I whispered then turned and headed back upstairs.

Merna was gone.

But there was still Macbeth.

When I reached the landing, I heard boots coming my direction. I turned to find Macbeth walking toward me. "Gruoch?"

Scáthach still in my hand, I held the dagger in front of me.

Macbeth slowed. "Gruoch?"

"How now, Macbeth?"

"Gruoch, what is the matter? You're as pale as snow. Have you… Were you crying? What's wrong?"

"Who was in your chamber?" the raven hissed.

"My chamber?"

"Who was in your chamber?"

"I…was with my priest. I was in prayer. It is the time of Christ's birth. I took my prayers in private so I would not disturb you. I know you do not follow the White Christ. My guard always sees to it my prayers are not disturbed."

Lies. He lies!

With the double vision of myself and the raven, I studied his face. Was he lying? Gruoch doubted, but the raven did not. It was all I could do to keep the raven within from stabbing him right then and there.

"Gruoch, is that why you are upset?" He moved toward me.

I stepped back. "I was not crying over you," I snapped.

Macbeth recoiled like he'd been slapped. "You don't have to be so harsh. Then…what is it?"

"Merna is dead."

"There was a messenger? Someone came in this storm?"

"There was a messenger, but there is no one here."

At that, Macbeth paused. Understanding, his expression darkened. "I see," he said.

I stared at him.

"Is Lulach abed? I brought this for him," Macbeth said, holding out a small wooden duck.

I stared at the toy. "He's sleeping."

"No matter. I have a whole barn of them carved to give him in the morning. Why don't you get some rest? This news from Lochaber is upsetting."

Without another word, I turned and headed toward my chamber.

"Gruoch?"

I went inside my chamber, closing and locking it behind me. I leaned against the door and stared into the bright space. The fire was burning brightly. I could hear Tira and Rhona inside their maids' chambers, both of them snoring. The door to my bedchamber was open. I spotted Lulach sprawled out the bed, Thora taking up what little space Lulach had left.

My heart was pounding in my chest. I was filled with rage. But why?

He was with his priest.

That made sense.

Right?

Right?

But if it did, why was I so angry?

He lies! He lies!

I closed my eyes and let the raven wholly in.

I felt a sharp jarring woosh as the raven and I became one. The beating sound of raven's wings overwhelmed me, and a moment later, I flung myself from my body and flew out the window. I glided, an ethereal creature, on black feathers around the castle to Macbeth's chamber. A thing no denser than the wind, I blasted into Macbeth's bedchamber then shifted once more into my own form.

There, lying in Macbeth's bed, was one of the kitchen wenches. A plump girl with long brown hair lay sleeping in the nude. The distinct smell of carnal relations filled the air.

You see! He lies! He lies!

The chamber door opened.

Macbeth stepped inside.

He grinned at the girl then began untying the lace on his shirt. He tossed the little wooden duck into the fireplace.

But then, he felt it.

He shivered as if struck by the cold.

His eyes wide, he turned and looked at me.

Not just me, but the raven.

I shrieked loudly.

The sound rattled everything in the room. The looking glass on the wall shivered and fell to the ground, crashing into a thousand pieces. The wail woke the woman who looked around the room, disoriented. She looked through and past me. She did not see.

Macbeth made the sign of the cross over himself.

I sneered at him then turned and flew back out the window, shifting into my winged form once more. I flew back into my own chamber then slammed back into my body.

I gasped then my eyes popped open.

I fell to the floor, my head hitting the stones hard.

Scáthach fell from my hand and bounced across the floor.

Then the tremor struck.

My back stiffened first, and then my arms and legs started shaking.

"What in the world was—Lady Gruoch!" I heard Rhona call. "Tira, get up, Lady Gruoch is having a fit."

"Oh my goddess, my lady!" Tira exclaimed.

"Her head is bleeding. Dammit, Lord Banquo has gone back to Lochaber. Run downstairs, and find the healer that rides with Macbeth's army."

I heard the door open and close.

Rhona's strong hands fought to hold me still. I shook and shook, unable to control the tremors. The taste of blood filled my mouth.

"Hold on, my lady. Just hold on. Try to breathe, and let it pass. Just try to breathe, and let it pass. Hold on."

"Mum?" I heard Lulach call.

"Your mum is sick, little lord. Please stay abed until we get her well again."

"Mum? Mum?"

I stared at a spot on the ceiling.

A moment later, the image of Gillacoemgain appeared over me, looking down at me with worry on his face.

A realization struck me. I could let go. I could just let go and go to him now if I wanted to. If I let go, if I stepped out of my body, I could stay there with him in the otherworld. My body shook hard, the taste of blood filling my mouth. I could let go and be done with all this pain.

"Mum? Mum?" Lulach called then began crying.

Gillacoemgain looked at Lulach then back at me, a sad smile on his face.

No. It was not time yet.

I opened my lips to whisper.

"Don't try to talk," Rhona told me. "Don't try to talk, my lady."

"An…An…Andraste," I whispered.

A moment later, I caught the scent of flowers, and the world around me and Rhona grew dark.

"Mum. Mum!"

"What the… May the Great Mother watch over us," Rhona said, her eyes wide as Andraste stepped out of the darkness.

Frowning and shaking her head with annoyance, Andraste held my jaw still with one hand while she poured an ice-cold liquid from a small silver vial down my throat. The deed done, she turned and stepped back into the darkness, disappearing once more.

I twitched hard one more time then the shaking subsided.

"Oh, my lady, the gods themselves watch over you," Rhona said in an astonished whisper.

Tira returned a moment later with Macbeth's healer and two soldiers, men of Moray, alongside her.

"We must move her to the bed," the healer said.

"I'll get Lulach," Tira said.

Half-unconscious, I felt hands move me. Rhona explained to the healer what had happened—leaving out Andraste's sudden appearance. Macbeth's man looked me over, looking deeply into my eyes, which I could barely keep open.

"The worst has passed. Does she have these fits often?"

"I don't know," Rhona said.

"Rhona, don't you remember?" Tira asked. "When Lord Gillacoemgain was alive, she had that fit during the council meeting just before—" Tira began but left off, her eyes narrowing as she looked toward the door.

"What's happening here?" Macbeth asked.

"Your wife, my lord. She had a fit, a shaking ailment," the man replied.

"Is she… Is she all right?"

"The worst is over, I believe. I did not see the fit myself, but she seems calm now. She does have a nasty cut on her head."

"We'll attend to it," Tira said. "We have Lady Gruoch's medicines here."

"Your lady may not wish you to use her—" Macbeth began.

"We'll attend to it, my lord," Rhona said firmly.

"Mum! Mum?"

"Mum is sleeping, little lord. She'll be well soon," Tira said.

"I, well, very well then," Macbeth said.

I closed my eyes.

A moment later, I heard Macbeth's footsteps retreat.

"Call me if she becomes ill again," the army healer said then left.

"You men, stay by the door. No one comes in to see the Lady of Moray unless she permits it," I heard Rhona tell the guards.

"What happened?" Tira whispered. "Did something upset her?"

"I don't know. She was out somewhere. There is snow on the hem of her gown. God knows what game Lord

Macbeth played with her now. Take Lulach and get him to sleep in our bed," Rhona told Tira.

"Come along, little lord," Tira said.

I heard Rhona sigh as she opened my medicine case. A few moments later, I felt her apply an astringent to the cut on my forehead. She then applied a salve to the wound. She exhaled heavily then sat beside me and took my hand. "I don't know what happened to you, my lady, but I know one thing for sure. Inverness is no place for you. Only Cailleach saved you from Findelach's house tonight. Tomorrow, we should return to Cawdor where our mormaer's spirit can watch over his wife and son. This place is poison."

I could not speak, but I squeezed her hand.

She was right.

There was no Lord and Lady Macbeth. There never had been, really. My mind replayed scenes, incidents, moments. Suddenly, everything began to fall into place. All the pieces started to fit. I remembered Thorfinn's words about Macbeth's whoring ways. I remembered things that had not been quite right, but I didn't know why.

And then the raven let me see.

Images flashed before my eyes.

Suspicions I had buried because they were too odious, too unthinkable, came to life before me.

Now I knew why Ute had left.

The vision made me gag. I watched in horror as Macbeth did to her as Duncan had once done to me.

Now I knew who the father of Elspeth's child was.

I saw her and her tiny, dark-haired baby boy whom she had named Findelach.

Now I knew about all the others.

There were so many other faces, so many other women. They lined up to fall into in his bed—some willing, some not. At Thurso. At Inverness. At Cawdor. At Scone. I saw his hands on ladies while my back was turned. His hands in the lap of a woman beside him at dinner, his fingers playing between her legs, while I sat on his other side, oblivious to it all.

All the while, Macbeth smiled and smiled, relishing his secret revenges—on me, on Banquo, on Gillacoemgain—enjoying the pain and confusion he caused.

A tear slid down my face.

Now I knew.

And the raven would never forgive.

CHAPTER FORTY

It took me three days to recover. When I was finally well enough to ride, and the storm had weakened to a light snowfall, I returned to Cawdor. I would play the fool no more.

"My lady," Standish said, greeting me at the gate. He searched my face, concern plastered on his features.

I handed him a note. "Standish, will you please send a messenger for me?"

"Of course. To whom?"

"The Thane of Lochaber."

Standish bowed. "As you wish, my lady."

I kissed Lulach on the top of his head. I had brought my son home. And this time, no amount of lies, guilt, nor desire to have things be good—they were not and never would be—would make me go back. Soon, Banquo would come, and my life would be my own again.

Banquo and Fleance arrived a month later. I had apprised Standish, Tira, and Rhona of Merna's death. When they rode in, both Banquo and Fleance looked woefully sad. A small party accompanied them, including Morag.

"My lady," Morag said as I held her horse so she could dismount. "My tired old bones are happy to see you and Cawdor."

"I have a nice warm fire ready for you, Morag. This is Tira and Rhona. They will help you settle in."

"Thank you, Lady Gruoch," she said as she slowly climbed down. "I used to ride the hills half-wild when I was a girl. Now, I think I broke my arse," Morag said, rubbing her backside.

Rhona laughed. "I think Morag will fit in just fine here. Come along. I'll steal some of Lady Gruoch's good wine for you," Rhona said, extending her arm to the maid.

"Banc!" Lulach yelled, making Banquo smile. I was glad to see the expression on Banquo's pale and drawn face.

Reaching out, I helped Fleance down from his father's horse.

"Welcome, my dear. My, how big you have grown. How old are you now, Fleance?"

"I three. Corbie, my mum go to the otherworld," he said, his eyes welling with tears.

"Yes, love. I know. I'm so sorry," I said, hugging the boy.

"You will stay with me now. I will watch over you. I promise," I whispered in his ear.

The little boy kissed my cheek and wrapped his arms around my neck. Given he had always been a sprite-like creature, I expected him to struggle to get down. Instead, he sighed heavily and set his cheek on my shoulder.

"My lord," Standish told Banquo who dismounted. "I've arranged chambers for you and your footman. I'll house your men amongst those of Moray. If you will, Thane," he said, motioning toward the castle.

Banquo smiled softly at me then followed Standish inside.

"Such a sad sight," Tira said. "Lord Banquo is usually so merry."

"These days will be hard for them, but we shall do our best to help."

Tira nodded, and we headed inside.

I'd rearranged the sleeping chambers so Lulach and Fleance were housed together in the room beside my own, Morag with the boys, and Tira and Rhona in the chamber on the other side. To avoid the gossip that would no doubt follow, I asked Standish to prepare a room for Banquo in another wing of the castle. He would not be able to stay forever, but at least for awhile, he would be amongst friends.

I heard nothing from Macbeth.

Nothing before I left.

Nothing after.

We had seen the true sides of one another.

I saw him for the lying whore he was.

And he had seen the raven.

Wounded by the truth, I cut off the broken part of myself so I would not feel the pain. I was the Lady of Moray. Unless he set me aside, which he could not do, Macbeth would never have a legitimate heir—bastards, apparently, would be in plenty.

Macbeth was nothing to me.

Now, I would do as had always been intended.

With or without Macbeth, I would rule.

In the weeks that followed, Banquo and Fleance settled into Cawdor. I even began to see some signs of the mischievous boy who used to bedevil his mother. Banquo, however, had yet to return to his mirthful self.

To my surprise, I found him sitting in the garden in the closed wing of the castle all alone one night. The snow had begun to melt, and the first signs of spring were on the horizon. The place was a wet and muddy mess. Banquo sat staring, tears in his eyes.

I sat down on the bench beside him. "Banquo, what is it?"

He shook his head.

Taking his hand in mine, I gazed at him.

"Is it just…the loss?"

"It's the guilt, the terrible guilt."

"Guilt?

"How many times did I wish I had not married Merna? I wished I had waited for you. I resented her, resented my marriage to her. As she was dying, do you know what she said? She told me 'Go to her now. Go to her. She needs you. And you need her. You love her, and she loves you. Go to her.' She knew all along, Cerridwen. She knew, but she did not resent it. I…wonder about my actions, my choices. I married her while I was in love with someone else."

"As did I when I married Gillacoemgain. There, right there," I said, pointing to the small chapel on the other side of the garden. "But I loved him no less. In truth, I loved him very much. And I still do. You loved Merna?"

"Yes," he whispered.

"Love is a dangerous, confusing creature. We are all her slaves. Gillacoemgain is gone. Merna is gone. But we are still here."

"Macbeth?"

"Macbeth is dust to me. The raven has seen him for what he is. That part of my life is over."

"Then what now?"

"Now, we shall watch the winds. I am the Lady of Moray. I will rule the north as I was intended to do. To that end, I have discovered there is movement in the south. Duncan's fleet will soon set sail to join Rognevald. We will back Thorfinn, and he will have his victory."

"Let's hope."

"No. It is certain. I have foreseen it."

Banquo looked at me, nodded, then took my hand.

"That is good news for the country. But what about us? My staying here breeds gossip. If all believe the Lady of Moray has thrown over her husband for the Thane of Lochaber, it will weaken the north. I…must go soon."

"I'd rather you stayed."

"I would rather stay, but…"

We both chuckled.

I smiled at Banquo then gently reached out and stroked his cheek. He was right, but would it always have to be this way? War was coming. What if Macbeth died?

"Don't think such things. You will live to regret them," Banquo whispered.

"Druid, stay out of my mind," I said, smiling gently at him. I shook my head. "Macbeth has betrayed me. It is done between him and me."

Banquo exhaled deeply. "I hoped he would do better by you. You are so very special. He is blind if he could not see what prize he'd won."

"He is his father's son," I said, my eyes drifting toward Crearwy's chamber. Terrible images wanted to force themselves on me. I blocked them away. Sighing, I asked, "What will you do?"

"I will ride north to Thorfinn."

"Fleance will be safe here and well cared for. I promise you."

"It is a lot to ask."

"It is nothing to ask. He is your son."

Banquo smiled tenderly at me.

"When will you go?" I whispered.

"Soon."

"Soon?"

He nodded. Our eyes searched one another's faces, raising and answering questions neither of us dared speak aloud.

I reached out then and squeezed his hand. My heart beating hard, I rose and left the garden.

Late that night, long after the boys and maids had gone to sleep, I rose. I checked on Lulach and Fleance who were cuddled together like puppies on their big bed, Thora lying alongside them. When I opened the door, Thora lifted her head and looked at me, her eyes glimmering in the candlelight. I smiled at her then lifted a finger to my lips, motioning for her to be quiet.

Thora wagged her tail then laid her head back down.

Morag slept on her bed not far from the boys. She snored so loudly, I thought Thorfinn could have been there in her place. I suppressed a chuckle.

I blew out my little candle and set it aside.

The castle was quiet, everyone asleep.

I crept down the hallway to Banquo's chamber.

The door opened even before I had a chance to knock.

Taking me by the hand, Banquo led me inside.

He turned and closed the door, locking the latch.

He exhaled deeply then took my face into his hands. He leaned in and set a soft, sweet kiss on my lips. His mouth tasted sweet and salty, the taste of honey mead on his lips. The familiar smell of his masculine scent and that of the woods overcame my senses. I fell into the kiss. I kissed him desperately, passionately, setting free years of unspent passion, kisses that had been smothered, love that had been chained.

I set it all free.

I wrapped my arms around his neck and hooked my legs around his waist.

Holding me by my bottom, Banquo carried me to the bed. We started pulling off our clothes as our mouths roved over one another, desperate to make up for lost time, desperate to have that one thing we had both wanted so badly but had denied ourselves due to promises we had made in good faith. Merna, alas, was gone. But she had blessed us and forgiven Banquo all in one breath. And my faith had been utterly destroyed. I could not even fathom the depths of Macbeth's betrayal. One cousin had been no better than the other. In the end, Macbeth was Findelach's son. But he wasn't my husband anymore. His lies had broken the accord between us.

I kissed Banquo eagerly, lovingly.

Laying him down, I slid on top of him and gazed deeply into his eyes. Banquo reached out and stroked my cheek, my hair, touching my breasts tenderly, lovingly. He laced his fingers with mine, the palms where we had made our handfasting touching. My body trembled when those sacred marks met, renewing the promise between us. I leaned forward and kissed him again. Moving gently, I joined my body with that of my true husband. And the pleasure of it was like nothing I had felt in a very long time.

I locked my eyes on Banquo's.

This was love.

This was what love felt like.

Tears rolled down my cheeks.

Macbeth had made me forget. Macbeth had used and hurt me. Macbeth had used and hurt others to hurt me. Nothing with Macbeth had ever been love.

This was my real husband.

This was my soul's mate.

This was love.

This was true love.

And it was everything.

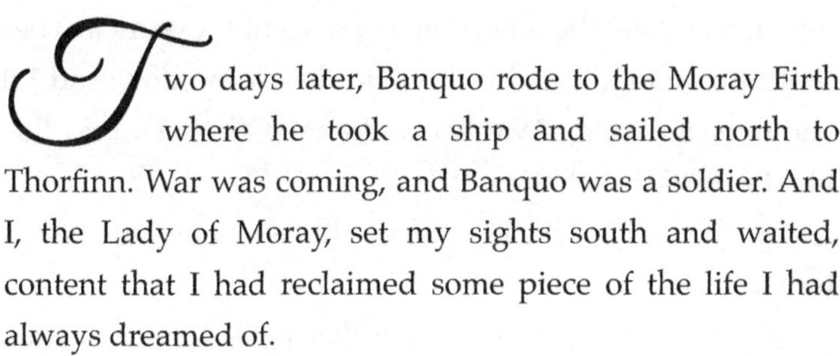

Two days later, Banquo rode to the Moray Firth where he took a ship and sailed north to Thorfinn. War was coming, and Banquo was a soldier. And I, the Lady of Moray, set my sights south and waited, content that I had reclaimed some piece of the life I had always dreamed of.

CHAPTER FORTY-ONE

Long ago, Epona taught me that three was a sacred number. The goddess comes in threes: maiden, mother, and crone. There were nine of us at the coven. And there were nine covens in the land, though I did not know where the others were. I'd spent six years in Ynes Verleath, though it had barely felt like six months. And I'd had three husbands. With the addition of Fleance in my life, I had a third child to love.

In the days ahead, more threes came to be of importance.

Six years. The length of time that passed since Banquo rode from Cawdor. Also, the number of years that had passed since I saw Macbeth in the flesh. And the numbers of years it had been since I'd seen my own daughter.

And another three.

Three wars.

The war at sea that I had foreseen came to pass the

spring Banquo had ridden off to war. Duncan's ships—not the king himself—were soundly defeated by Thorfinn's armada. Rognevald went down with his ship, and the king's force returned south. Once the country was stirred, it did not rest.

Two years later, as the Morrigu had predicted, Duncan built up a new army made of mercenaries from Ireland. Misunderstanding Thorfinn's close relationship with Echmarcach, Lord of the Isles, Duncan solicited the lord's help to land his army on the west coast. This time, Thorfinn and young King Magnus, who had come to live with Thorfinn, met the mercenaries at sea. Banquo, under Macbeth's directive, went with an army and destroyed the troops who managed to make landfall. A second defeat still did not deter Duncan.

It took Duncan two more years to devise a plan to crush the north. In the sixth year of his reign, on one very dull and inauspicious evening, the last and most important three was born.

"Mum," Lulach called as he and Fleance sat with their tutor, both boys trying hard not to learn Latin as I had once done, much to their tutor's consternation. "I think Fleance and I would both learn better if we had a mug of honeyed herbs."

"Oh, aye. Lulach is right. Please, Corbie?" Fleance echoed.

I grinned. At some point over the years, I had made a small pot of the same honeyed herb drink Gillacoemgain favored to soothe my own loneliness. Banquo had been gone for years. For fear of Lulach's and Fleance's safety in time of war, I had not gone south to see Crearwy or Madelaine. The entire country had held its breath waiting to see what would happen next. I waited, grew herbs, raised my boys, and brewed honeyed herbs which Lulach had loved from the first moment. Fleance? Well, any excuse to take a break from learning Latin was appreciated.

I went to the fire where I had a small pot warming beside the cauldron. When I glanced into the large cauldron, I saw a ripple on the surface. Slowing, I paused and looked within. The water pitched and boiled then I saw blood. Unbidden, I heard the raven's wings, and the dark spirit awoke within me.

Look. Look!

I saw the king's ships travel up the east coast. A battle ensued near Aberdeen. In the north, I saw another battle take place in the rough waters between Caithness and Orkney. To the south, I saw Duncan's golden armor shining as he crossed boldly, under the mantle of peace, into the northern districts, a massive English army headed by Earl Siward of Northumbria not far behind him.

Gasping, I pulled myself back before I fell into the fire.

"Mum," Lulach called, rushing to me.

I stared wide-eyed at the flames.

Fleance took me by one arm, Lulach by the other.

"What is it?" Fleance asked.

"My lady?" Tira called, rushing across the room.

"Tell Standish to ready riders at once. I... Bring me my parchment and ink. I must send messages, and quickly."

"Yes, my lady," Tira said then rushed off.

"Mum, what did you see?" Lulach whispered.

I stared at him, looking from Lulach to Fleance. "My boys… War is upon us again."

I wrote first to Thorfinn and Banquo who were together at Thurso, telling them what I had foreseen. Then, begrudgingly, I wrote to Macbeth. Over the years we had entered into a formal relationship. Macbeth treated me like any other constituent in the north, and I was settled with it—for now. He never came to Cawdor. He never asked anything of me. I sought no rumor of him. It was done.

But now, Duncan was coming for us as I had always warned he would. If we were going to survive, we would need to find a way to navigate, not just our enemies, but one another.

As I was taking Macbeth's note to the messenger waiting in the yard, Tavis rode through the gates of Cawdor.

"Tavis?"

"Gruoch, thank goodness. I must speak to you at once."

"Is it Madelaine? Or Uald?"

Tavis shook his head. "All are fine. *All* of them. But I have a message."

"Here. For Inverness," I said, handing my note to the rider who quickly headed out.

"Come inside," I told Tavis, motioning for a groom to come take his horse.

Fleance and Lulach had given up on the Latin and were talking about my news with intense seriousness when I returned to the hall with Tavis.

Tavis slowed when he saw them. "Is that Lulach? The dark-haired boy?"

I nodded.

"He looks like you, and I see his father in his face as well."

I had grown used to the comment and used to pretending it didn't still hurt. "Thank you."

"The other boy?"

"Fleance of Lochaber."

"Ah," Tavis said, his brow arching. He said nothing more, but he didn't have to. I knew Tavis was Madelaine's closest confidant. No doubt he'd been told something.

"Lulach, ask the kitchen maids for ale and food for our guest," I said then bid Tavis to sit.

Lulach nodded then he and Fleance ran off to the kitchen. Together, always together. Thora, who was heavily pregnant—surprising me with a litter of puppies so late in her years—was dozing by the fire. She, like me, had prolonged her life due to her time at Ynes Verleath. But still, she was no young dog anymore. She lifted her head and looked to see where the boys were going. Determining it was too much work to follow them, she looked back at me. Spotting Tavis, however, she rose and slowly came to him.

"Thora," he said, petting her head. "How round you are," he said with a chuckle.

Satisfied she'd made her own greeting, Thora went back to her comfortable spot by the fire.

"I saw a rider leave as I approached. He was moving quickly," Tavis said.

I nodded. "I've just sent riders to Thurso and Inverness."

"I, too, come with news. Duncan is putting it out that he will tour the north this spring, as you no doubt already know. But money is flowing everywhere, and there is a rumor of an army amassing in Northumbria. The southern lords, those loyal to Duncan, have been called to Edinburgh for a meeting…including Fife."

"They cannot think Fife and Madelaine are truly loyal to Duncan."

"Indeed not. Queen Suthen expressly invited Madelaine to Edinburgh for the spring season. But Uald arrived at the castle the very next day—if you can imagine such a thing—telling Madelaine to return to the coven at once, that she was in danger."

I swallowed hard. They would take Madelaine as a hostage, a valuable bargaining piece to use against Fife or me.

"Has she gone? Is she safe?"

He nodded. "She left at once. I saw her and Uald safely there then I rode here as Madelaine asked me to."

"Here you are, sir," Lulach said, returning with a

tankard. Fleance carried a plate with bread, meat, and cheese.

Tavis reached out and ruffled Lulach's hair.

"Boys, this is Tavis. He is a close friend of our family."

"I remember you when you were no larger than a loaf of bread," he told Lulach. "And you, young man, I hear your father is a fine Thane and a good commander," he told Fleance.

"Thank you, sir," Fleance said, setting down the plate.

Lulach smiled at Tavis but his brow furrowed, and he gave Tavis a questioning look. "Is my Aunt Madelaine well?"

Tavis looked at me then back at Lulach. "She is safe."

Lulach nodded, a thoughtful expression on his face. I studied my son. For years, I had seen that glimmer of the otherworld in him. I ached for Banquo to be with me, to advise me on what to do. Lulach was a lord, but the mark on his brow said he was much more. How was I to raise such a child? And now that Duncan and Suthen had two sons of their own, Malcolm and Donalbane, Lulach's claim to the throne was not as strong as it once had been.

Tavis took a long drink of his ale then said, "I will stay here with you if that's all right. And if not, you must take it up with Madelaine, who insisted."

"She does know I have an army at my disposal, doesn't she?"

Tavis chuckled. "Indeed she does. I half suspect she told me to stay here for my own protection."

"You are always welcome."

Tavis wrapped his arm around me and gave me a squeeze. "Little Corbie," he said with a smile.

This, of course, made Lulach and Fleance laugh.

"Laugh again, and I'll call your tutor back. Or, you can go upstairs to your chamber where you can see all the commotion from your window. It's going to get very busy around here soon."

Lulach and Fleance looked at one another then turned and raced away. This time, Thora could not resist, and she trotted along behind them.

"The king will ride north," Tavis said stoically.

The third time, he will come to my bloody fields like the soldier he should be. There he will meet my champion.

"Yes," I said, picking up my mug of honeyed herbs.

Tavis clicked his mug against mine. "When the king is dead, long live the queen," he said then winked at me.

I took a sip of my drink then smirked.

It was time to get ready. The final three had come, and when it was done, my world would turn to right again.

Or so I hoped.

CHAPTER FORTY-TWO

As the next month passed, word began to slowly flow northward. Rumors abounded about the force amassing in Northumberland. And Duncan began to announce loudly and everywhere he went that he would tour the north in the spring, that he longed to visit his cousins. Macbeth wrote, sharing that Duncan had written requesting an audience with Lord and Lady Macbeth. And in Macbeth's letter, he asked for my help preparing Moray for war.

The raven smirked when she read his words. *Fool.* So, now he had a use for me? Part of me wanted to resist just for the pleasure of doing so. But I would not. I would protect Moray because it was my home, Lulach's birthright, and out of love for Gillacoemgain's memory. How had that man become so fixed in my heart and soul? A single year. Not even that. That was all we'd had together, but it had changed me forever.

While the disturbing news came in from the south, at long last, word—in the form of flesh and blood—came from the north.

"My lady! My lady," Tira called, rushing into the great hall one busy morning.

"What's wrong?"

He hand on her chest, pausing to catch her breath, she smiled. "A rider coming toward the castle. Lord Banquo!"

"Please fetch Fleance. He and Lulach are with Tavis in the training hall."

Tira nodded happily and raced out of the room. I inhaled deeply then smoothed down my gown and pushed my hair behind my ears, suddenly feeling self-conscious about the few streaks of silver in my hair at my temples. I slipped the day's messages back into my pocket and headed to the yard.

A few moments after I arrived, I spotted the banner of Lochaber and a party wearing Lochaber's colors ride into Cawdor, Banquo at the front.

My heart beat hard. I restrained myself from running across the lawn to meet him, aware that there were eyes on me everywhere. In Cawdor, we vetted each new arrival and kept our friends close and our enemies out. But coin always speaks, and I did not know for certain if it had bought someone's tongue. I would not have any more rumors surrounding me than already did.

Smiling, Banquo dismounted then came to me.

I took his hands in mine. "Well met," I said, my eyes pricking with tears of joy.

"My lady," he said, lifting and kissing my hands, one after the other. "*My* lady. You are a sight for my weary eyes."

"Come. Take some rest. You and your men."

Banquo leaned into my ear. "We've ridden in from the Firth. Thorfinn has ridden on to Inverness. I must join them there, but I wanted to see you all first."

I nodded.

I linked Banquo's arm in mine then motioned for the others to join us. I led the small party to the great hall where my servants were in a bustle of activity, preparing food and drink for the party.

A flurry of footsteps raced down the stairs outside the hall. I heard a clatter as something was knocked over. A moment later, Fleance—Lulach just behind him—stood in the doorway.

I saw a million emotions wash over Fleance's face. He was nine now, and often it seemed as if he was not sure if he should play the part of a man or still be a boy. He straightened his posture and crossed the room to meet his father as a gentleman might, but the moment he drew close, he threw himself toward Banquo, wrapping his arms around him.

"Father," he whispered.

Lulach crossed the hall and took my hand. I kissed him on his head. It was a happy moment, my family—save one—all together. Soon, I would see Crearwy again.

Banquo led him to a bench.

"What a fine young man you have become, Fleance.

Look how you have grown. You must tell me how you have been. Cerr—Corbie writes that you and Lulach have been studying hard."

Fleance cast a grateful smiled at me, glad to hear I had stretched the truth a bit to please his father. In truth, both Fleance and Lulach were bright boys and one day, Fleance would make a good Thane. But for now, at least, he was far more interested in swordplay and riding. Of the two, Lulach was more keen to learn, if he was not too busy daydreaming.

"Mum, Lord Banquo should take some rest and refreshment. Shall we go check on Thora and her pups? I haven't been by to see her yet today."

I eyed Banquo and Fleance. They needed a moment alone. I smiled at Lulach, proud that he had also seen the need.

"You're right. She'll be wondering if we've abandoned her," I said then grabbed a bit of bread from the basket on the table. "We'll be back in just a bit," I said, setting my free hand on Banquo's shoulder. He took my hand, kissed it lightly, then let me go.

Lulach and I walked to the stables. The spring sun was shining. It cast its rays on Lulach's dark hair, pulling up tints of blue and gold.

"I'm happy for Fleance," he said, but there was a catch in his voice that I understood well. It was the sound of a child who had lost a parent, a child who had never known the love of someone who they wished, beyond everything, they could have known.

I wrapped my arm around his shoulder, burying the secret thoughts about Lulach's true paternity. My mind, instead, turned to Gillacoemgain.

"Your father would be proud of you, my love."

Lulach smiled. "I hope so. When I… When I see him, he does seem proud."

I stopped and looked at him. "What do you mean?"

"Nothing. It was nothing."

I touched the mark on his forehead. "My little love, don't tell me it was nothing. I have told you the story of how you got this mark and what the shape means. Did you see the tattoo on Lord Banquo's brow?"

Lulach nodded.

"Please, tell me what you meant."

"In the garden… Sometimes I see a man there. He watches me, and he seems pleased. And other times, there is a lady there. She often seems very sad, but she smiles at me when I look at her."

"Our blood is special. People from our family are often sensitive to the otherworld. One day, when the madness is done, I will see to it you learn more. But you must not speak of what you see to anyone else save me and Lord Banquo. It is not strange to see spirits. Only special people can."

"Can you?"

"Yes. I see them too."

"Is that my father? The very tall man with the brown hair? He wears the blue and green of Moray. Sometimes he has a falcon on his arm."

"Yes." My stomach clenched hard.

Lulach smiled then took my hand once more. He led me into the stables. From the back of the barn, I heard the sounds of little growls and barks. Grinning, Lulach led me to the stall. Why Thora had decided to have her pups in the barn was beyond me, but the stablemaster ensured she was not disturbed, and we all brought her food and drink. Thora's wild batch of puppies, five in all, rolled around, fighting and playing with one another.

"The stablemaster has been letting them out. They're big enough now to survive on their own, but sometimes they get under the horses' feet, so he pens them up when it's busy to keep them safe."

I opened the gate so Lulach and I could slip inside.

Thora lifted her head and wagged her tail.

"Well, bonnie lass. What a brood you have here," I said, tossing her the bread.

Still true to her mark, she snapped the bread from the air and chewed happily, her tail wagging.

"Mum," Lulach said, looking down.

I followed his gaze to one of the puppies. There, sleeping in the corner, was a puppy I did not recognize. The sweet little bundle had white fur and one roan-colored ear.

"Who is this?" I asked.

I bent down and reached out to pet the little thing. He woke up groggily then went directly to Lulach, his tail wagging.

I glanced back at Thora. "Now what trouble have you gotten us into?"

Thora let out a muffled bark then wagged her tail again.

"Maybe the stablemaster found a runt. Mum, how cute he is! Have you ever seen a dog like this before?"

"Seen? No. But I've heard tell of dogs like these," I said then petted the pup who wagged his tail when he looked at me. I glanced around the stall, and then I spotted it. Where the puppy had been lying sat a single red rose.

I picked it up, inhaling the fragrance. I smiled. "The puppy is a gift for you, Lulach."

"For me? From who?"

I handed the rose to him. The boy's brow furrowed. He inhaled the rose then gave it back to me. "But it's not the season for roses."

"No. Not here, at least."

"Not here, then—"

"The pup is cú sídhe, like Thora."

Lulach laughed as the dog licked his chin. "Thora the faerie dog. Now, that I believe."

I shook my head at Thora. "Did Eochaid buy your silence with treats?"

Thora looked at me out of the side of her eye then wagged her tail.

I rolled my eyes.

"You will need to name him. And one of Thora's puppies will need to go to Fleance or I will never hear the end of it."

"Angus," Lulach said at once.

"Angus?"

Lulach nodded. "It is my favorite name."

"All right. Angus it is. Well, Thora, you suppose Fleance can take one of your bairn off your hands? We'll need to get the pup trained to live in the castle."

Thora thumped her tail, yawned, then closed her eyes and went back to sleep. Couldn't blame her. Her pups were a rambunctious lot.

Lulach and I stayed a bit and played with the puppies. They were cute but wild, and all of them were black like Thora with the exception of Angus.

"Well, Angus, are you ready to see inside the castle?" I asked the little fey puppy who cocked his head at me.

I grinned at him. There was no doubt in my mind that Eochaid had brought the puppy. I only wished Eochaid had stayed. I missed Sid's sweet boy. How old would he be now? Twelve or so? I wasn't sure. With those who walk between the worlds, their age never runs the same, as it does for Thora and me. I gave all the puppies a good pat then turned to Lulach, motioning that we should go back.

Admittedly, I was anxious to return to Banquo.

When we returned to the castle, we found Banquo and his men had finished their meal. Fleance sat beside his father, hanging on Banquo's every word. Upon seeing us with the puppy, Fleance slipped off his bench, but then he thought better of it.

"Father, may I see what Lulach has?"

Banquo looked up, glancing at Lulach and the fey bundle he held, then at me. He smiled softly.

A lump rose in my throat. Here was my love. Our children, not born of a union between us but every bit ours, with us. It was everything I ever wanted.

"Lulach, what have you found?" Banquo called.

"Thora had a litter of puppies," Lulach said.

"And has taken in a foundling," I added.

Banquo reached out for the puppy who greeted him with a lick on the hand. "How unusually colored," he said, eyeing over the dog.

"I've heard stories about dogs like that," one of Banquo's men said, pointing to the pup. "You've found a fey thing, little Lord of Moray. The good neighbors have blessed you with a fine hunting dog."

I glanced at Fleance, whose eyes glimmered with jealousy.

"Let's hope he grows to be as good a tracker as his mother. You know, I believe Thora's other puppies are ready to wean from their mother as well. If we're going to have both puppies in the castle, we'd best start training them now."

Fleance looked up at me. "Both puppies?"

"Have you chosen yours yet?" I asked him.

A wave of gratitude washed over his face. Fleance turned to Banquo, "Father, may I—"

"Of course, of course," he said, and no sooner had Banquo answered than the two boys rushed out of the hall, Angus the fey dog along with them.

Banquo poured glasses of wine for him and me. He handed me a goblet then we went and stood before the fire where we could talk in private.

Banquo smiled. "Fleance has grown into a fine boy. All that wildness is still just behind his eyes, but it seems he has polished off the edges with you there to guide him. Cerridwen, you don't know how grateful I am. Between the battles and the cold and the sea, I had much on my mind. But when I laid my head down each night, I did not worry for my son. You have been a good mother to him."

I smiled softly. I understood how Banquo felt better than he could ever know. It was the same thought that comforted me when I missed and worried about Crearwy. But remembering she was under Epona's care always brought me comfort. "I have done my best."

Banquo exhaled deeply. "There are no words to describe what it means to me."

I reached out and squeezed his hand. "When have we ever needed words?"

While Banquo's' men took their rest, Banquo and I returned to the meeting hall where I had taken up residence as my workspace. It was the same hall in which Gillacoemgain and his men had once met and where I had foreseen their end. Now, I used the space as my own to train with sword and dagger and to plot my way forward.

"With Thorfinn's arrival, Macbeth will call the northern lords to Inverness. Will you come?" Banquo asked.

I shook my head. "I will not step into that castle ever again."

Banquo frowned. "Those who were once loyal to Gillacoemgain may not listen to Macbeth if you are not in attendance. They look to you, not him, to see which way to lean."

"I'll send messages to Buchan, Mar, and the others. In truth, if it were not for you and Thorfinn, I'm half inclined to let Duncan pass and have at Macbeth."

"Cerridwen."

I shrugged. "What difference does it make if I make peace with one rotten cousin or the other?"

"You can't be serious."

"I'm not. But the thought has occurred to me. I do not trust Duncan to lord over my bannermen or me. I have already chosen my burden. I must live with the consequences of my choice to ride north rather than south."

Banquo frowned. "But you… Are you very unhappy?"

I shook my head. "No. Macbeth has left me in peace. The separation was clean and complete. I have been content to raise our sons and think only of my true husband."

Banquo eyed the door then pulled me close.

"I missed you," he whispered.

"I missed you too."

Leaning in, he kissed me hard, his longing and passion matching my own. I loved the feel of him against me, the strength of his arms and chest, the taste of rich red wine on his lips, and the smell of him, his body, his hair. I'd missed him desperately. Our hands roved over one another, and soon, before we did something rash in this very public space, we pulled back. I rested my head on his chest.

"I love you," I whispered.

"I love you too."

"How soon must you leave?"

"Today. I...cannot stay the night here with so many lords roaming about. There will be too much gossip. We will prepare for war, and I will be asked to lead an advance on one of the fronts you have foreseen."

"Then Macbeth believed me?"

"He has put out your prophecy as word from his spies. He believes you. I do not know what he has seen to change his mind, but he has no doubt in your words."

"He has seen the raven."

Banquo snorted. "Good," he said then turned and lifted his goblet of wine. "Cerridwen, in your vision, how far south was Duncan's army?"

"Not far from Cawdor."

Banquo frowned. "I'm concerned for Lulach and Fleance."

"As am I, but Cawdor will be well fortified."

"I think I should send for Balor."

"Send for Balor?"

"My love, Lulach is touched by the Otherworld. And if the fey have seen fit to lavish gifts on him... It would do him good to spend some time amongst holy men. Not only would he learn to navigate the spirit realm, but Balor will also teach him caution. Not all the fey have mankind's best interest at heart. And with Balor, he would be safe. Balor can teach him the ancient roads, him and Fleance. And amongst Balor's men, Fleance and Lulach are not the sons of lords targeted for kidnapping or worse. Lulach will be Mormaer of Moray. And if—when—Duncan is defeated, you and Macbeth will take the throne, Lulach will be the heir to this realm."

"I…" I began, but he was right. Lulach was a valuable prize. It would be wise to send him into hiding much as Madelaine had already done. "Yes, you're right."

"I'll send for Balor at once. Even now Duncan may be plotting to send a man to kidnap your boy."

"The queen wrote to Madelaine, inviting—insisting, really—that she go to Edinburgh. They would use her to their advantage. She escaped to Epona."

"I would never seek to take him from you. It would just be until everything was settled."

"He's still so young," I said softly.

"Yes, but he'll be safe."

I stared into the fire.

He's right.

My eyes flicked to the side where, for just a moment, I spotted the shadowy apparition of Gillacoemgain.

All my husbands are ganging up on me.

Exhaling deeply, I looked into the flames. Visions took shape before my eyes, and in the fields and villages south of Cawdor, I saw war, and fire, and blood.

I closed my eyes. "Send for Balor."

Banquo wrapped his arm around me and kissed my cheek. "We don't have time to send a messenger. I must cast to him. May I make use of this chamber…alone?"

"Of course," I said. I set a sweet, soft kiss on his lips then turned and exited the room.

I headed out into the yard where Lulach and Fleance raced in circles, Thora's entire brood, and little Angus, running after them.

"I'll pick the fastest one," Fleance called to me.

Thora sat watching on the other side of the yard, gazing on in a manner that mirrored my own expression. The sight of it was so ridiculous that it made me laugh aloud. Thora trotted over and sat down beside me.

"Thora, choose your most loyal and loving pup. We shall ask Eochaid to take that wee one to Crearwy."

Thora wagged her tail, and we both watched on, a ridiculous pair, fawning over the children who would soon leave us.

But as I watched them, my thoughts went to the sons of Duncan and Suthen. They'd had two boys, Malcolm and Donalbane. What would be done with those boys when Duncan was defeated? Where would they go? If the king was toppled, his children would grow up plotting their own revenge. I stared at Lulach. Even now we moved to protect him. What was Duncan doing to protect his own boys? I considered Suthen. Would Macbeth have already made plans to kidnap her sons? I chewed my lip as I considered the problem. If those boys fell under the care of the Earl of Northumbria, they'd be turned into adders. What could be done to prevent it? My heart went out to Suthen. Suthen had suffered, I had no doubt about it, and surely she loved her boys as I loved mine. It did not do for one mother to strike at another. I would make no move to harm those boys, and if a time came when I could prevent it, I would do what I could. After all, they were still my blood.

I shook my head, unable to see the way. For now, I had my own sons to worry about. Soon, Balor would come, and Fleance and Lulach would be gone.

CHAPTER FORTY-THREE

As dusk neared, Banquo and his men prepared to depart. Lulach, Fleance, and I gathered around to say goodbye.

"I will return as soon as I can. My son is here. Let tongues wag about you and me as they will, but I will return to see my boy," Banquo told me.

"Balor?"

"He will ride for Cawdor. He and his band are not far."

"You trust him. Completely?"

"With my life. With Fleance's. And with Lulach's."

I sighed heavily.

Banquo squeezed my hand then mounted his steed. Waving to the boys, he and his men then turned and rode to Inverness.

Wordlessly, Fleance came to me. I wrapped my arms around him and pulled him close. "He'll be back soon," I whispered in his ear.

Fleance nodded and pulled himself up straight, trying to look far more grown than he was. Despite his manly posture, he quickly dashed a tear from his cheek.

"Fleance, you haven't told me what you decided to name Thora's son," I said, petting the puppy Fleance held tightly.

"I don't know what to name him."

"I never liked to name anything either. It seemed to me their names should come by them naturally."

"Like the name Angus," Lulach said. "I just knew his name was Angus."

I chuckled. "Angus. It is a good name." I lifted the puppy from Fleance's hands and stared into his little face. He looked every bit like Thora had when I found her that windy morning on the hilltop. My fey black dog, her feet nearly as big as her head. This puppy, however, had a mischievous face. "Well, little wild thing, what is your name?" I asked.

"I…I did have an idea," Fleance said.

"Really?"

"Thor, like the thunder god, and also after his mother. I think it would be good to name him after his mother."

I swallowed hard, hearing the hurt in his voice. Of course he ached. His real mother was gone, and his father had just ridden away again. "I think Thora would like that. And look at him. What a brute he will be! Thor is a perfect name. Perhaps the thunder god will bless him."

"I like it," Lulach said.

"Thor it is," Fleance said, taking the puppy from my hands once more.

"Better get them something to eat," I said, motioning for the boys to go inside.

Nodding, they set the pups down then turned and ran back into the castle, their tired puppies loping along behind them.

"My lady," Morag called, coming up to me with a small bundle wrapped in cloth. "Here you are. I did my best, but there was not much to be had save dried fruits."

"Thank you, Morag," I said, taking the warm bundle from her hand. I kissed her on the cheek.

She patted my arm then headed back inside.

I returned once more to the stables. Thora lay sleeping in her stall with her little brood all around her. She was down to four puppies now. I passed her stall and went to the back. There, Gillacoemgain's mews still sat unused. I had asked Standish to leave them as they were. One day, I hoped, Lulach would learn to love birds as Gillacoemgain once had.

Opening the pen, I lay down some clean straw on a ledge. I opened the wrapped bundle in my hand. Morag had made the tart just as I had asked her to with as many berries and nuts as we had in supply. I could smell the honey and berries. I wrapped the confection back up and set the tart inside the pen. I then stepped outside and looked out toward the pasture.

"Sweets for the sweet," I called lightly. "Eitri, will you

share my words, my gift, with Eochaid?" I called to call the little fey man who had surrounded Eochaid as Nadia did with Sid. "Eitri, please give Eochaid my thanks. And may I ask a favor of my good neighbors? Will you ask Eochaid to do something for me, to take one of Thora's pups to my daughter?"

In the distance, crickets started to chirp.

I smiled.

"Blessed be," I called.

I turned and headed back inside. On my way back to the castle, I stopped at the gate where Standish was organizing the night guard.

"My lady," he said.

"Tomorrow, we will close Cawdor. Call in the first of my bannermen, the most loyal, to guard the castle. No riders or messengers in or out without my say so. Save Lord Tavis, expel anyone from the castle who does not have a place here and prepare the north and south wings to garrison soldiers. How have we done with the stores?"

"We are stocked, my lady. We did it little by little, as you planned, but we are nearly at capacity."

I nodded. "A war in the spring will cost us in the winter. Begin the rationing now."

"Yes, my lady."

I stared out the gate at the open road. "Close the gate tonight."

"Yes, my lady. Lady Gruoch, what have you—"

"Thorfinn is at Inverness. The king prepares his ride north."

"I understand," he said then turned and headed to the gate. A few moments later, I heard the sound of steel and wood as the gate closed and Cawdor made ready.

CHAPTER FORTY-FOUR

The next morning, I found Lulach and Fleance in their chamber watching the flurry of activity below with curiosity.

"Mum," Lulach said when I entered. "The castle is closed, and there are soldiers in the yard."

Fleance stared out the window. "Will my father be able to come back in?"

"Of course. We have closed Cawdor to outsiders."

Both boys turned and looked at me.

"Why?" Fleance asked.

"The king will ride north," Lulach said, his eyes taking on a faraway look.

"Yes."

Lulach blinked hard. "We should go to Tavis for sword practice."

Both boys nodded then turned and headed out of the room, their puppies scampering quickly behind them. But

Lulach paused at the door. "Mum, did you need something?"

I smiled softly at him. "No. Not yet."

He nodded then turned and rushed off.

I gazed out the window, and in the distance, I saw a rider approach the castle. I was startled to see the familiar gold and red colors of King Duncan. I hurried back downstairs and outside.

A footman raced to me. "Lady Gruoch, a messenger from the king."

I crossed the lawn where I met Standish. "Take the scroll. Send the rider away. Get someone ready, and send a rider to track the messenger."

Standish nodded then went to the gate. He paused, speaking to a Moray soldier standing there. The man rushed to the stables. Not long after, he returned on horseback, waiting just inside the gate. Standish went outside, returning a few moments later with the scroll. I heard the sound of hoof beats as the king's messenger departed. The gate opened, and my own rider slipped out. Standish returned, the parchment in his hand.

"The messenger rode north," he told me.

"Thank you. Let me know when our rider returns," I said then went back inside.

Returning to my council chamber, I unrolled the letter, which was written in Duncan's own hand.

It began nicely enough with fine courtly pleasantries. Then Duncan made two moves I did not expect. He wrote that he was sorry to learn that Macbeth and I were estranged and that if it was ever in his power to see his cousin more happily wed to anyone of her own choosing, no matter the lord's station, he would do everything he could to ensure my happiness.

There was his first offer. If I let Duncan pass, if I let him destroy Macbeth, he would bless my union to Banquo without interference. Clearly, the rumor of my attachment to Lochaber had reached the king.

I frowned then read on wherein Duncan sent his regards to Madelaine, hoping she did not find the winter climate in Moray too cold. He said he looked forward to seeing us both, and the little Lord of Moray, in good cheer when he made his visit to the north.

He thought Madelaine was here. Or, at the least, he was trying to determine if she was. No doubt someone had seen Tavis at Cawdor and recognized him as Madelaine's personal guard. Perhaps Fife had put it about she'd gone north as a way to decline the invitation from the queen. That made sense. Either way, I was glad Duncan thought she was at Cawdor. If he did, he would have no reason to look for her anywhere else.

I tapped the scroll in my palm then went to the fire.

So, Duncan wanted to make a deal. What deal did he offer Macbeth? A new bride? An acknowledgment of his bastards? Little Findelach, Elspeth's son, would be nearly six by now.

Should I consider the offer?

What would it cost me, really?

I closed my eyes and thought about Creawry.

Because of Duncan, I had to give up my daughter.

If not for Duncan, Crearwy and Lulach might actually be Gillacoemgain's children, not Duncan's.

If not for Macbeth, Gillacoemgain might still be alive.

Damn them.

Damn them both.

There was the sound of movement behind me. My heart stilled, and a strange sensation crept across my skin.

I turned to find the red-robed Morrigu there, her arm outstretched as she handed my sword to me.

I gripped Uald's Gift by the handle then threw the scroll into the fire.

The Morrigu smiled then disappeared.

I wouldn't bargain with either of them.

One at a time, I would deal with them both.

One at a time, they would both pay.

At this, the raven smiled.

CHAPTER FORTY-FIVE

Several days later, Banquo returned with news. Thorfinn would return to Thurso, Macbeth going along with him. Thorfinn and Magnus would guard Caithness. Macbeth would take half of Thorfinn's navy and his own ships and sail to Aberdeen. Banquo would ride south, leading the northern lords to meet Duncan's English-backed army.

"When I was at Inverness, there was a rider, a message from Duncan," Banquo told me.

I already knew. My man had followed Duncan's messenger to Inverness and had seen him return south thereafter.

"Duncan… He offered to annul your marriage to Macbeth, cancel Lulach's claim, and give Macbeth a new wife, solidifying Moray under Macbeth with the condition that Macbeth turned on Thorfinn."

"I'm sure that led to an awkward conversation."

"Indeed. And I was glad Thorfinn was there to keep Macbeth's response…balanced."

"And what did Macbeth say?"

"That he would not betray Thorfinn."

I snorted but said nothing more. What was there to say, to feel? Macbeth had never loved me. There was no use in pretending he had.

"Macbeth is much changed since I saw him last."

"Changed? How?"

"Not for the better, I'm afraid. There was always an unsteady spark in him, which I am sorry you have seen. That spark… It glimmers more brightly now. Inverness has become an odd mix of priests and—"

"And?"

"And debauchery. Macbeth is uneven. Thorfinn and I spoke of it. Macbeth's words often don't reflect reality, and he sees malice everywhere."

"What do you mean?"

Banquo frowned. "It is one thing to be wary, but another to be paranoid. My Cerridwen, strange shadows surround Macbeth."

"Cursed…or madness?"

"Or both? Whatever his priests are doing for him, they are not keeping those shadows away. Thorfinn spoke to him at length, and he seemed better after. Better, but not right."

My thoughts went to Findelach, Macbeth's father. There was an echo of the past here. Was this what had happened to Findelach? Had he slowly gone mad until he had done the unforgivable? I had seen that streak in

Macbeth, but now… Did I have a responsibility to do anything about it?

"They will sail within the week. I will stay here in Cawdor and rally the northern army. If, of course, you will have me."

"How well Macbeth plays. He cannot ride here himself, so he uses the relationship between us—the one that he so hates—to get what he wants. Hypocrite. And will he be sending supplies for his army from Inverness?"

"Yes."

I nodded.

Banquo scanned around the room. "Have the boys been sparring in here?" he asked when he saw the targets and weapons.

"No, I have been training."

Banquo smiled. "Uald would be proud. But you must not worry. You will be safe here in Cawdor."

"I will not stay in the castle. I will ride out."

Banquo stared at me. "What?"

"I will join you when the time comes."

"But… You cannot."

I laughed. "I can, and I will."

"Cerridwen, you don't know what it's like. The blood. The men. It's not safe. You are a gifted swordswoman, I know, and a Valkyrie at heart, but I can't let you do that."

"My dear, I love you well, but you cannot stop me."

"What if something happens to you? Think about Lulach and Fleance. The boys need you."

"I promise you, I will be safe."

"But Cerridwen—"

"I will ride out," I said, more venom in my voice than I had intended. But it was not me who had spoken the words but the raven. And once more, that dark force hooded my features. "I will ride out, Thane. As has been foretold."

Banquo looked at me then lowered his eyes, seeing that it was not Gruoch who spoke but the other. "Yes, my lady."

I inhaled sharply, feeling the presence of the other—me and not me—fading once more. "Banquo, I'm sorry," I whispered.

He shook his head. "Say nothing of it. I've known all along what you are. I should not have tried to stop you. We will make plans to keep you safe. I expect Balor to arrive tonight. We shall see our sons safely bestowed then we will make our plans for battle."

"Banquo—"

"I honor the words of the Dark Lady, but prophecies do not always hold true. Sometimes our visions are lies. We see things that make us act in one way, but, perhaps, we should not. The gods have been said to plant false visions, stir our emotions, and make us *know* things that are false to see their own will is done. I honor the gods, but I know how they meddle. We may not win this battle, Cerridwen. The numbers... The Earl of Northumbria's army is enormous. Cnut has sent his armada north. There is a chance we could all die."

No.

"Then we will do what matters most and see our sons safely hidden away," I said. But then my thoughts turned to

Andraste. She often riddled, and in the past, I questioned her motives. Was Banquo right? Would the gods be so cruel to give us visions, make us believe lies just to see their own will done?

"That will settle them, but what about ourselves?"

"Ourselves? Well, tonight I will make passionate love to my husband and dare the world to damn me for it."

Banquo smirked. "That, at least, is a plan I can agree with."

In the early evening, I received word that a small band of riders was at the gate.

"They have an odd manner about them, my lady," Standish said.

I went to the gate, climbed the rampart, and looked out to see the familiar face of Balor and that of the druid, Calean. With them were two other young men I did not know, but both were tattooed in a similar manner to Banquo. While the others did not carry the mark of the stag, I saw ravens and other swirling designs on the brow of one of the men. No wonder Standish had thought them odd. These men were amongst the last druids in all of Scotland. And they had come for my son.

I swallowed hard.

It wasn't forever. It was just for a time.

"Let them in," I called.

The gate opened and Balor's party rode inside.

At the same time, Banquo emerged from the castle.

I descended the stairs and went to welcome the party.

Banquo held Balor's reins as the Arch Druid of Scotland dismounted. When Balor finally alighted, Banquo kissed both of his hands in a show of respect, the druid placing his hand on Banquo's head. Balor whispered something in undertones that I did not hear.

"Thank you, Father," Banquo whispered then turned to Calean. "Calean," he said, embracing the druid. I remembered the man from my days at the coven. I had liked him, mainly because he'd argued with Druanne.

Suddenly, I felt eyes on me. I glanced up to see Lulach watching from the window, his eyes on the druids. After a few moments, he turned from them and looked at me.

I inclined my head to him.

He smiled and returned the gesture.

I went to Balor. "Merry met," I told him.

"And to you, Lady Gruoch."

"Calean," I said, nodding to him. "It is good to see you again."

He smiled knowingly. "Lady Gruoch."

"May I introduce my party," Balor said, turning to the unknown men. "This is Beric," he said, introducing a man who wore leaves tattooed on his brow and on his cheeks, symbols of the green god of the woods.

"Lady," he said, inclining his head.

"And Diarmad," Balor introduced, referring to the man who wore the symbols of the raven.

The man put one hand on his brow and another on his heart then bowed to me.

"My lady," he said. And from his tone and manner, I realized it was the other he saw, not Gruoch.

I nodded to him.

"My friends, come take your rest," I said, motioning for them to follow me.

I looked back to see Standish rubbing his chin as he considered the group. He turned and met my eye, nodded, then went back about his business.

I led the druids inside to the great hall.

"Gentlemen, will you excuse me for just a moment? My house will see to you," I said, waving to the servants to bring refreshments.

Balor nodded.

I turned then went upstairs to the chamber from which Lulach had been watching. He was still alone in his room—save Angus and Thora. He was sitting by the open casement looking out.

"Lulach," I called merrily. "Where is Fleance?"

"With Tavis."

I crossed the room and took a seat opposite my son.

"Who are those men?" Lulach asked.

"You tell me."

"They… Well, I can see, but I don't know what name to use."

"They are druids."

"Druids," Lulach repeated as if saying the word made it more real.

"Why are they here?"

"You will go with these men for a time."

"Where?"

I shook my head. "I do not know. Perhaps Lord Banquo can say better than me."

"For how long?"

"Not long, my dear," I said, taking his hand. "The king marches north. He means to remove Macbeth from power, and me along with him. Lulach, you must understand, as the son of Gillacoemgain, you are a very important person. If Duncan is defeated in battle, Macbeth and I will rule Scotland. Given we have no other son, that means you—"

"That I will become king after Macbeth. But doesn't King Duncan have sons?"

"He does."

"What will happen to those boys?"

"I don't know. As was the case for Macbeth, perhaps they will be fostered with Macbeth himself. But, given your importance, it is imperative that when the king rides north, you go somewhere safe. If Macbeth is defeated, Balor will know what to do."

"If Macbeth is defeated, what will they do to you? What would happen to you?"

I smiled as to soothe his worries. "I will be fine. Ladies are treated differently. Duncan would probably give me a new husband, but I won't be hurt."

"Would he give you Banquo as a husband?"

"I don't know."

"That would be good. But what about me? Would they try to hurt me?"

The truth was, I wasn't sure. To protect Donalbane's and Malcolm's claim, they might. But still, something told me Duncan would be more inclined to bargain with me if it came to it. And I could certainly spin a web of lies to ensure a future for Lulach and me. But I didn't want to trouble Lulach with such things. "No, but just to be safe, it is better if you are with Balor. Moray is yours, my son. No one can ever take her from you. But crowns change heads, so you must guard yours well."

"What about Fleance?"

"You will go with the druids together."

At that, Lulach eased. "But not forever, right?"

"No, not forever. Think of it as an adventure. Go see what these men know. Like you and me, they too can see that other side. They will teach you."

Lulach nodded. "All right," he said then smiled. While his words were spoken with certainty, his smile eliciting the dimple in his cheek, there was also a tremble in his chin. It was telling enough. But it was the manner of his expression that caught me off guard. It so reminded me of Gillacoemgain that I stared. Once more, doubts nagged at me. Both Andraste and Epona had told me Duncan was the father of my children. I'd had a vision of Lulach in the hours after Duncan had…assaulted me. But still. I shook my head. No, it was merely wishful thinking.

I turned and gazed out the window. There, I saw Thora pass through the yard, three little ones nipping at her tail.

"One of the puppies is gone," Lulach said sadly. "I looked everywhere for it."

I nodded. I had already discovered the same, but I'd also found the bundle of cloth that had held the fruit tart empty. "Yes. But I think she's all right."

"You think so?"

I nodded. "I know so. Come," I said, reaching out for his hand. "You must meet our guests. Say nothing about them to anyone. Save Lord Banquo and myself, no one will know where you have gone. Not Tavis. Not Morag. No one."

Lulach nodded then slipped his hand into mine.

"I'm not afraid," he said.

I realized that his words were partially for his own comfort and partly for mine. "Of course not. You are the son of Gillacoemgain of Moray and the blood of the ancient line of MacAlpin. There is no more blessed and fierce blood in this land."

At that, Lulach smiled, his heart filling with pride.

And for some reason, this time when I spoke the lie, it felt like the truth.

CHAPTER FORTY-SIX

The night passed quickly, and we did not press Balor and his men to stay longer. As I had done with Lulach, Banquo told Fleance the plan. Unlike Lulach, Fleance was more hesitant to leave, but tried not to show it. Lulach's courage gave him strength. The band of druids waited until nightfall before they prepared for their departure.

"There are spies in the hills all around Cawdor," Balor told Banquo and me.

"How will you slip through unseen?" I asked. "If anyone spies you riding from Cawdor with the boys, they will be at risk. As it is, I worry that someone marked your arrival."

Calean smiled patiently at me. "They will only remember a party passing through, no more."

"And on the road, we are unseen. You have my word, my lady," Balor said. "Epona is not the only one who can pull shadows from the otherworld. Nor step between them, as her most apt pupil is said to do," he added with a wink.

I smiled softly. "My son… Lulach has the sight already."

Balor nodded. "The otherworld shimmers all around him. As if the fey pup is not a sign on its own. But we must teach your son that not all of the golden troupe wish us well. I will do my best to coach him."

"For that, you have my gratitude. I am indebted to you."

"One day, you will return the favor," Balor said with a smirk.

"Indeed?"

Balor looked at Diarmad.

"After the raven has had her day," the man said, once more touching his brow.

"I serve the gods. As they will," I said. And while what I said was true, it was one thing to trust a druid's word, to trust my own faith in the gods, and quite another to give over my son in the middle of the night. But soon, it was time for them to depart.

Banquo, Lulach, and Fleance returned from the stables, both boys on their horses, their puppies stowed in their sacks just like I used to ride with Thora when she was small.

My stomach quaked when I saw Lulach on his horse. He was still just a boy. It was too soon. My resolved slacked, but I put on a brave face. Both boys had turned their gaze to me to see how they should feel. I smiled boldly, like there was nothing at all to fear.

"We're ready," Lulach said.

I went to him first and kissed his hand. "I will see you soon," I whispered. "I love you."

"I love you too," he said with a cheerful smile.

I then went to Fleance. "And you, my sweet. I'll see you safely home in no time."

Fleance looked less certain. He quickly glanced toward his father, for whom he was putting on a brave face, then back to me. I took his hand.

"Corbie," he whispered.

"All will be well. I promise," I whispered. "Have I ever broken a promise to you before?"

He shook his head.

I squeezed his hand. "I love you."

"I love you too."

At that, I stepped back and joined Banquo, linking my arm in his.

Both Banquo and I bowed to the group who in turn nodded to us.

I motioned to Standish, who ordered the men to open the gate. Standish hadn't asked me anything, but his eyes surveyed everything, watching the druids, Fleance, and Lulach.

The druids turned and rode out into the darkness, Fleance and Lulach along with them. My mind tripped over a million things: had I packed enough food for them, did they have enough warm clothes, were their boots new enough, were the puppies old enough, did Banquo select horses who were sure of foot, and on, and on, and on.

And then the gates closed once more.

I left Banquo and climbed the rampart. I scanned the horizon, expecting to see them on the road, but there was no one there. Thinking they'd followed the wall to the river, I looked in both directions, but I didn't see them there either. No matter where I looked, they were just gone.

Standish climbed the steps and came and stood beside me. His arms folded across his chest, he surveyed the landscape, making the same assessment I had.

I looked back at Banquo who waited for me. My confusion must have been evident on my face. Banquo gently touched his brow. I turned back and looked across the landscape once more, a feeling of relief washing over me.

Standish nodded slowly. "You have done the right thing, my lady. It pains you. I see that. But leave it to you and Lord Banquo to find a way to hide Fleance and Lulach in the one place Duncan would never think to look."

"The one place?"

"Under the shield of the old gods," Standish said then smiled. "Where none will find them."

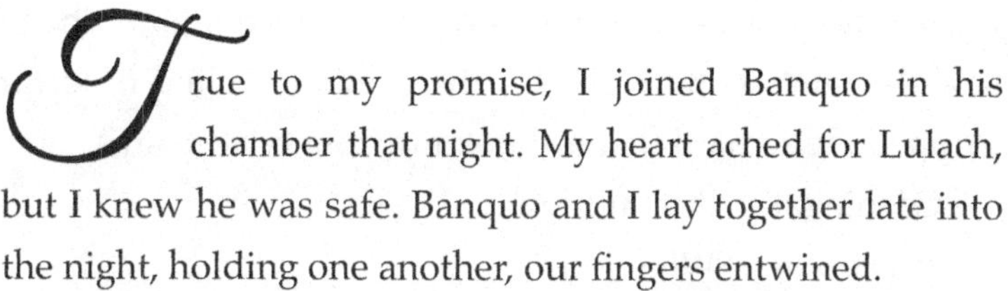

True to my promise, I joined Banquo in his chamber that night. My heart ached for Lulach, but I knew he was safe. Banquo and I lay together late into the night, holding one another, our fingers entwined.

"When we win, what will you do?" Banquo asked.

"What do you mean?"

"Macbeth will go to Scone and then to Edinburgh. He

will need to win back the hearts of the lords he knew in his youth. Will you go too?

"I will go to Scone."

"And after?"

"And after, I will return to Cawdor. I am the Lady of Moray."

"And queen, hereafter."

"If we win."

"We will win." Banquo kissed the top of my head. "I love you, Cerridwen. And so does my son. You cannot know how much that means to me."

"I love him too and his father."

Banquo laughed. "Then kiss me again, lady. Tomorrow the army will begin to fill the fields outside Cawdor. Let me have one last night in a warm bed with the woman I love."

So I kissed him again, and again, and again. And that night, as I lay in Banquo's arms, I had a very strange dream. I saw Macbeth in an elaborate dining hall talking with Banquo. Macbeth smiled and smiled, the face of a friend and madman all at once. Macbeth's eyes shimmered with wild glee. When Macbeth poured Banquo a glass of wine, his hands shook, and he wet his lips in anticipation. When I saw Banquo's hand reach for the drink, a feeling of terror gripped me so hard that it shook me from my dream.

Gasping, I sat bolt upright.

"Cerridwen? What is it?"

I shook my head. "Just…a dream."

Banquo pulled me back down beside him. "You're shaking."

"Banquo," I whispered. "You must not trust Macbeth."

Banquo pulled me close and kissed my bare shoulder. "I don't. Sleep, my Cerridwen, and dream of something nice."

"I'll dream of Sid. She would be jealous to see us here without her."

Banquo chuckled. "There is no one quite like Sid."

"That is an understatement. When it is all settled, we should ride south and see her." But my stomach twisted then, realizing that if Banquo ever saw Crearwy, he would quickly learn the truth. But then, it was Banquo. What harm would it do to reveal the truth to him? "I love you," I whispered, the last of the anxiety the dream had provoked fading. It was just a dream, after all.

"I love you too."

Three days later, a dispatch came from Lord of Mar that the king was on the road north with an army right behind him. The time had come.

CHAPTER FORTY-SEVEN

All across the north, the red banner of war was raised. On the one hand, Duncan sent riders letting everyone know he rode in peace with his brother in law, the Earl of Northumbria, to tour the north. On the other hand, reports of a massive army amassing to the south and ships spied off the coasts came flooding in.

As Banquo had anticipated, not all the northern lords were quick to trust Macbeth. And despite Macbeth's pretty words and rallying at Inverness, I found my hall full of lords and clan leaders who saw the same thing in Macbeth that both Banquo and I had seen, the shimmer of madness and the rotten seed of his father.

"My lords," I said, addressing the assembly. "Lord Banquo of Lochaber will lead the army south. He is a loyal Thane and loyal to the north. This war will have a ripple effect. Duncan seeks to unseat the north and fix his English-loving allies here. We cannot allow this. Cnut and Duncan are playing games. If Duncan defeats us from the south and his armada, combined with that of Cnut's, manages to win in the north, we will be crushed in the middle. Duncan would seat his own puppets in here, men loyal to him and his English factions. And Caithness and Orkney will fall to Cnut. But Duncan is a fool. How long before King Cnut decides little King Duncan is all that stands in his way? We must stop the English incursion now."

"My lady, where is King Magnus?" someone called.

"North with Lord Thorfinn. An armada approaches the northernmost provinces. We will defeat those forces and assist King Magnus, who is now of age and a good and loyal ally, in retaking his throne."

"Lord Macbeth went with his ships? He is not leading his men south?" another man called, a sour tone in his voice.

"No. Macbeth is a ship commander. His skills are best used at sea. A second wave of ships, an English armada, has been spotted near Aberdeen. He will sail to meet them."

That news stirred up some talk, and some grumbling, in the room.

Banquo rose. "My lords, I am well known to some of you and not at all to others. But I assure you, we are ready to ride south. Each day our army expands. We have the men we need. We are a mighty force, and we shall roll over Duncan's army like a wave."

"That's all well and good, but we cannot forget, Thane, that you rode with Macbeth when the former Lord of Moray was displaced," a young man called from the back. I eyed his tartan. He was the eldest son of the Lord of Mar and would take his father's place when the old lord passed away.

"My lords, the Thane of Lochaber can be trusted." I knew there was a rumor about Banquo and me, and in this moment, I hoped it actually served me. But aside from that, the swirling druid's designs on Banquo's arms and on his brow spoke of his true allegiance. "The Thane is loyal to this land, and to the gods."

"And to the future Mormaer of Moray," Banquo added. "My friends, I did not know your mormaer well, and I was not there when he was…defeated. But Lady Gruoch speaks well of Gillacoemgain. I met him once, and he was an honorable man. I am sorry I did not know him better. I am here to ensure Lord Lulach can claim his father's birthright —and beyond," Banquo said. While Banquo didn't say he had chosen the wrong side, he honored Gillacoemgain with his words. And more, he planted a seed in their minds that many had not yet considered. If Duncan was defeated, Gillacoemgain's son might one day be king.

The men eyed Banquo and me then spoke amongst themselves.

"Lady Gruoch," an elder clan leader called from the back. His grown son stood at his side. The man was rail thin with wispy white hair. He had one mooneye. "Many of us remember the day you stood in this hall and wailed like a banshee. Everyone knows you saw Gillacoemgain's doom. Will you tell us, lady, what you see now? What should we do?"

At this, the room grew still and quiet.

Banquo, who had not heard the tale, looked at me.

I touched the amulet on my neck. "We will ride south. And we will win."

And be avenged! And be avenged!

At that, the men nodded in assent.

"My lords, if you have not yet called your men to Cawdor, please send riders at once. We will need everyone's help in protecting the north, protecting your homes and families. Lady Gruoch's men are ready to assist you, as am I. Together, we shall defeat King Duncan," Banquo called.

This earned him cheers. The matter settled, the men dispersed from the hall.

Banquo paused and looked at me. "What was he talking about?"

I shook my head, not wanting to remember. "A vision. I saw Gillacoemgain perish. I saw the fire that took him."

Banquo exhaled sadly. "I am sorry. I was not there when it happened, but I heard."

I stared at Banquo. "Who gave that order?"

"Order?"

"To kill Gillacoemgain. To set that fire?"

Banquo looked away.

"Banquo?"

"It was Macbeth."

My hands began to shake violently, and the sound of raven's wings beat in my ears. I swallowed hard and mastered myself. I nodded.

Banquo eyed the door. "I must go. Thank you for your help. I don't blame them for not trusting me. At times, I don't trust my own judgment in regard to Macbeth. I think we are both deceived."

I stared at Banquo. "What should we do?"

He shook his head. "The wheels are in motion now. It is too late to do anything."

He was right. I inclined my head to him.

"I need to go. I'll find you soon," he said.

"Very well."

Banquo turned and left the hall.

After he had gone, I went back upstairs to my chamber. I opened the trunk where I'd stored all the fancy dresses Madelaine had sent to me, feeling a bit abashed when I realized I hadn't worn most of them. Setting them aside, I dug into the bottom of the chest where I found Gillacoemgain's old armor. I placed the pieces on the bed, determining what would fit. He'd been so much taller than me, so much larger. I picked up his leather jerkin and inhaled deeply. I caught the scent of the material, but just under that lingered Gillacoemgain's smell, a faint perfume of cedar and lavender that had almost faded.

I closed my eyes.

I would protect what was Lulach's.

And at last, I would have my vengeance.

CHAPTER FORTY-EIGHT

Two days later, Banquo began rallying the army to ride south. We would leave just before dawn. A late spring snow blew in, covering the ground with white powder. The weather was strange that day, thunder rocking the clouds. It was as if the sky itself was at war.

The Lord of Mar, playing the friend, rode south to welcome the king. Mar's army, led by his elder son, waited alongside my own men and that of the north. If Mar's deception was revealed too soon, his life would be in grave danger. I worried about the man who had once been so kind to me, the man who had remembered my father and my mother, who'd told the tale of Emer and her harp. I prayed to the goddess to keep him safe.

Alone in my chamber, I stood before the fire. I closed my eyes and reached out with my senses, feeling for Lulach. But no matter how hard I tried, I could not find my son. Wherever Balor had taken Lulach, he had taken him somewhere very deep. I suspected that I would have better luck reaching him if I returned to Ynes Verleath.

The sounds of men and horses rose from outside. It was almost time to go. I closed myself off from the noise and inhaled slowly and deeply. I found the silence and the darkness within.

And then, I called: *Come.*

I am already here. We are one.

The sound of wings filled my senses. Once again, the raven and I melded into one. I lifted my arms, feeling her and me all at once. I was a Valkyrie. I was an avenger.

Pulling Scáthach from my belt, I grabbed my long black braid.

For the Morrigu. For Scotia. For victory.

With a quick flick of the blade, I cut my hair at the nape of my neck. I threw my long locks into the fire.

Thora, who had been lingering around me all day, her tiny brood having now found new owners amongst the soldiers, whimpered.

"I suppose you want to come."

Thora thumped her tail.

"It is war. It will be dangerous. You are not yet recovered from weaning, and in truth, you're not as young as you once were. Stay at Cawdor. Keep the castle safe."

Thora looked at me as if I had just said the stupidest thing she'd ever heard. Only my dog would dare judge the raven.

"Very well. Then you will need to stay beside me and help me fight."

She yipped a small bark.

I turned then and dressed, pulling on a pair of man's breeches, a stiff leather jerkin, and Gillacoemgain's chainmail shirt. I fingered my short hair and then pulled on Gillacoemgain's helmet. I looked out with my raven eyes. Little by little, I could feel that Gruoch was retreating. I was Cerridwen, the raven. Everything around me was brighter than it had been before. I was able to hear far more clearly than I had before. I belted Uald's Gift then slid Scáthach into her scabbard.

I looked at Thora. "Let's go." I went to the door. I had already opened the latch, but then I paused. I went back into the room and dug deep into my trunk. There, at the very bottom, I found a small wooden box. Gruoch's hands wanted to tremble as I removed the lid, but the raven would not allow it. Inside, I found a worn coin pouch stained with blood. The coins within jingled, the small fee my cousin had paid me for the complete alteration of my life. I closed my eyes, remembering Lulach and Crearwy as tiny babies, and the pain I felt having left my daughter behind. I slid the pouch into my pocket and then went to join the awaiting army outside.

Working my way through the scores of men in heavy armor milling about, I went to the stable. Thora followed a discreet distance behind me. I quickly saddled Kelpie, hoping Standish would not spy me, then rode out of Cawdor to join the army of men that had collected around the castle.

The men were falling quickly into ranks. I worked my way through the soldiers, positioning myself near one of the lesser lords of Moray. As the sun began to rise, Banquo came forward and began to rally the army.

"My friends, the Lord of Mar has gone forward to greet the king. The Earl of Northumbria and his army follow a league behind King Duncan. When we attack, the king will retreat to join the earl's army. Duncan does not believe we have had time to prepare. He will not expect our army. And yet, even when he does see us, he will believe he has the better of us.

"He does not."

"When we engage the king's army, the men of Lothian and Fife, loyal to Lady Madelaine, will turn on Duncan and join us. Know they are your allies.

"I will ride with a small group of men to rescue the Lord of Mar, who will be amongst the king's people. The rest of you men stay under the direction of your lords," Banquo said then paused. Torchlight illuminated him. How handsome he looked in his armor, the flames reflecting on him. My vision doubled, and I saw Banquo and Prasutagus together. My once and future husband.

"The king has sent a large portion of his army by ship with the intention of making port at Aberdeen. They seek to surprise us, crushing us from both a frontal assault and a surprise wedge from the east. Lord Macbeth has gone with heavy ships against the king's armada. Echmarcach of the

Isles has joined forces with Thorfinn the Mighty to ensure the safety of Orkney. My friends, the king's plan is as weak as its creator. We have seen through all of his schemes and have moved to counter them. There can only be one result, a result long coming, to this war: King Duncan will be no more, and King Macbeth will sit on the Stone of Scone!"

The men roared. The sound rose up into the night and to the ears of the Morrigu. This song belonged to her.

"Come, men. Let's ride," Banquo yelled, and then the lords turned around and began barking orders.

The army began to advance.

We swarmed across the land that was familiar to me. But looking out from underneath Gillacoemgain's helmet, the nature of the land around me changed. I saw visions. At first, I was confused. Then the Morrigu whispered a truth to me: some lands bleed more than others. Riding beside me were phantom beings, armies from the past. First, I saw the men of Ynes Verleath marching across the land. I watched the phantoms battle, the men of Ynes Verleath against the armies of Dal Riata, Pict against Northman, Celt against Roman. I heard swords crashing together and the grunts of men—and women. I smelled blood.

Then one face stood out. I saw my kin, Kenneth MacAlpin, whose looks reminded me of my father. It was Kenneth who'd finally brought the north under control. It was he who united Pictland with the old Kingdom of Dal Riata and created Scotland. Scotia remembered this union. The Morrigu remembered this bloodshed. The Crone remembered these deaths.

My vision was interrupted by my commander's call to halt. The phantom images dissipated like puffs of smoke. I suddenly became conscious of the passage of time. Lost to the raven's visions, I realized we'd been riding south far longer than I'd realized.

The men began to stir excitedly. Everywhere I looked, men adjusted their weapons. This was what I had been missing all those times when Macbeth and Banquo had gone into battle. This was the truth of war. It was glorious.

I watched as Banquo rode the length of the army to ensure that all was in order. As he neared, I unsheathed Uald's Gift and lifted it into the air. It glimmered in the firelight. He slowed, lifted his hand to salute me, and then moved on. I sheathed my sword and smiled down at Thora.

"You keep out from under the horses' feet when they start charging. Some of these horses have been trained to kick. I don't know how long I'll be on horse, but try to stay nearby. If you lose me, look for Banquo. If something happens to me, get Banquo."

Thora wagged her tail.

It was not long after that when Banquo moved us forward. The lords began to ride more aggressively, and the men around me began to unsheathe their weapons. I lifted my shield and took out Uald's Gift. We rode over a small crest. Duncan's army sat on the other side.

They were on lower land than us, their army only a fraction of the size of our own. Their scouts would certainly have informed Duncan we were coming. As I looked across the field, I saw that the army stood at ready.

Banquo lifted his hand in the air. The lords turned around on their horses and lifted their swords. The men began to scream, cackle, and yell. I joined my voice with theirs. Banquo pointed his sword forward and screamed, "Now!"

I had one moment of clarity when I watched Banquo and a group of men break off—they would go for the Lord of Mar—then I was pushed forward on the wave.

Duncan's army rushed forward to engage our own. My eyes focused as I reined Kelpie to move quickly across the field. I sought out Duncan only to realize he was not amongst these men. Where was he?

When we rode into the army of men advancing upon us, it was like we had hit a massive wall of steel. We came to a stop, and, looking over the attire of the men we battled, I realized we were fighting Irish mercenaries. The men of Fife turned around and joined us, but my attention was lost when a man twice my size came at me in an attempt to pull me off my horse.

His battle-ax slammed forcefully into my shield, making Kelpie shy sideways. Furious, I struck out with Uald's Gift. As the blade swung, it had a silvery sound that made the air shiver. I sliced the man's head from his neck. His face held a moment of awe and fear, and then his body fell to the ground. Seconds later, another man was upon me.

As soon as one man was defeated, another stepped into his place. I rode forward hunting Duncan. Duncan, Lulach's father, the man who had pushed me to the ground and had changed my life in a moment of sheer pleasure, where was he? His action had forced me to birth a daughter whose face I rarely saw. Duncan, the waster, the taker, the user. As I fixed my mind on this purpose, something strange happened. The men who had lined up to meet their death turned and ran away. All of them.

"Give chase, give chase," the lords called.

And be mindful, I thought to myself, that you chase a small army of bought men into a substantial army of Englishmen who had come to fight Scots, as Englishmen were apt to do. As we rode, I spotted Banquo and a small group of men, including the elder Lord of Mar, rejoin the army. I breathed a sigh of relief.

We gave chase. Below me, Kelpie began to lather as I sped across the field, Thora racing to keep pace. After a hard ride, the Earl Siward's army, with the earl and the king at the front, came into view. The lords barked at us to move back into ranks.

"Make ready," the clan chieftain, MacDougall, called.

The men across the field lifted up their voices then charged.

I moved forward with one goal, to kill the man in the golden armor. MacDougall led his men into a flanking maneuver, but that stratagem led me away from Duncan. I left them and raced across the field to join Banquo. He and a small band of soldiers rode directly toward the king.

Once the advance began, however, Duncan, the pompous coward, whirled his horse around and retreated to the back of the army.

"Damn him," I cursed.

When we met the Earl of Northumbria's men, it quickly became evident that we weren't fighting Irish mercenaries anymore. These were well-trained English soldiers. Though I was part of the cavalry, the men I fought against were on foot. Those men had one goal: remove the cavalry from horseback.

One well-armed man after another advanced on me. My position of height made it easy for me to take these men's lives. The raven within me shrieked with pleasure as each man fell. But the men around me, seeing their comrades die, became more desperate to get me off my horse. In a desperate maneuver to unseat me, they began to beat at Kelpie. He was a strong horse, but he was also well beyond his prime. I could feel the anxiety rising within him as he whinnied and kicked. Thora snapped and bit, trying to defend Kelpie as best she could. My concentration on my goal waned as I fought more for my horse than for my vengeance. One man came forward swinging a massive claymore. He had seen the other men try to dislodge me and fail. From the gleam in his eyes, I understood his intention. He was going to cut Kelpie down.

Kelpie felt it too. He began to back up as the man came toward him. I jumped from the saddle.

"Go! I won't sacrifice your life. Go!" I said, slapping Kelpie on the backside.

Kelpie whinnied then took off. My dismount surprised my opponent. It threw him off guard. I took my chance. Moving fast, I spun my sword then ran him through. His claymore dropped from his fingers. When I pulled my sword out of his gut, his still-warm blood sprayed all over my pants. I sneered at him then turned and raced in search of Duncan.

The king was far afield, and the battle of men taking place around me was heavy. Dodging one assailant after the other, I pushed my way through. A young man wearing the colors of Moray was being beaten down by a Northumbrian soldier. I shoved Uald's Gift through the Northumbrian man's back, saving the Moray man's life.

But then the boy's eyes grew wide. "Look out," he called, staring behind me.

I spun and dodged left, but felt the sting of a blade as it sliced my arm. I stared into the face of yet another English soldier. I snatched Scáthach from my belt and stabbed the man in the neck.

The soldier fell.

Offering my good arm, I helped the Moray man up.

"Thank you, sir," he told me.

"Of course," I said, but the man held on to me.

"Purple eyes," he whispered.

I winked then turned and headed off once more.

Weaving around the fighting pairs, I soon had Duncan in sight. Foot soldiers skirmished between him and me, but at last, he was close. Five strong guards stood in a circle around him, one of which I recognized. MacDuff, the man with the badger symbol, guarded his king. My mind flashed back to that stormy night and the mud and the rain. Macduff had held the arrow on me, forcing me to choose between death and rape.

I glared at him and advanced.

Duncan fought, but not much and not well. His guards were strong and well-armed, but they were not invincible. As I neared Duncan, I saw one of his guards go down. Only four were left.

Seeing me approach, one of Duncan's guards turned to engage me.

"Well, wee lad, what are you trying to do, make a name for yourself? I think not. Are you ready to meet your maker?" he asked me.

"My maker wears a red cloak and rides a raven. You might see her here at my side, and she will gladly take your blood," I said as I began to circle around him.

He laughed. "I'll send *you* to that bloody goddess." He lifted his ax and moved to cleave me in half.

I danced behind him. Lifting Uald's Gift, I drove it forward. But much to my surprise, I met with metal. The man had blocked my attack.

"Fancy feet. Does that come from all your lordly dancing? Who are you in that fine armor? My son is going to like that sword of yours."

The raven laughed. "He won't like it much when he finds it sticking out of your gut."

This comment angered the man, and he swung at me. I bent low to the ground and struck my dagger upward. I cut the guard's belly wide open, rolling away before a rain of blood and guts could cover me. The guard groaned and became silent.

Duncan's bodyguards, including MacDuff, now numbered

only three. He would retreat soon. I made way for him again, but someone grabbed my arm. I turned to find Banquo, who was also blood-soaked, staring at me through his visor.

"Thank the gods. Which way, Lady Raven?"

"In the direction of vengeance."

"Let's go."

Banquo and I began to work our way toward the king.

"Your Highness, we must retreat," one of the guards told Duncan, who cursed in reply.

"Let me take the king," I whispered.

I realized then that a thin mist had settled on the snowy battlefield. Strange weather. But I also realized then that if I could get Duncan into the fog, he would be mine.

One of the guards turned. Sizing us both up, he advanced on Banquo. Soon, their swords were clashing.

I rushed toward MacDuff and Duncan.

Both men turned toward me. Duncan held his sword. MacDuff had drawn his bow.

Come the mist. Come the mist.

The fog swirled all around us, enveloping us in a dense mist. I felt the magic in the air.

"Stay close," I whispered to Thora. "Don't get lost in the fog."

"Kill him," Duncan told MacDuff, motioning toward me. As the king retreated, he nearly tripped on one of the corpses lying on the ground.

MacDuff turned to me. "Traitor," he cursed. "Would you kill your king?"

Thora growled and bared her teeth.

MacDuff sneered, leveled an arrow at Thora, then shot.

I gasped.

Thora darted to the side just in time.

Scowling, the man reached for another arrow.

"You," I said, my hands shaking with rage. I pulled off my glove, raised a single finger, and pulled magic from the air.

I scanned the ground, looking at my fallen men. "Wake," I whispered.

Recognizing the gesture, MacDuff lowered his arrow. "Who are you?"

Making an arcane symbol in the air, one Andraste had taught me, I motioned to the bodies of the soldiers, men of Moray, lying on the ground around us.

"Wake," I told them.

Slowly, the dead men, their bodies broken and bloody, rose to their feet once more, their weapons still in their hands.

"Kill him," I said, leveling my finger at MacDuff.

The soldiers rushed MacDuff, Thora joining them, leaving me free to turn on the person I had come for.

Duncan.

He stared at MacDuff. The mist had been so thick that he would not have been able to see clearly what had happened, but he saw his last guard under attack. Duncan turned his attention to me. Seeing me approaching quickly, he moved backward.

"Come, lad. I am your king," Duncan said as he continued to retreat.

"But you are the very man I have come to kill. Would you turn me away now?"

Duncan had long since lost his helmet. His hair was wet with sweat, his face dirty. He looked back at MacDuff. "MacDuff? MacDuff! Where did those soldiers come from? Boy, turn back. I am your king."

I lifted Uald's Gift. "I am no boy. And you are no king. You are a defiler and a cutthroat. And when you are gone, Scotland will know a new ruler."

Duncan laughed then lifted his sword. "You're wrong. Macbeth will never wear the crown." He engaged me, but his moves were clumsy.

I laughed. "Who said anything about Macbeth? Your life, King Duncan, is done. I have come to cut your thread. Don't you see? You've angered the gods, and I have come as their messenger."

"What?"

"I have come as the raven, and the message is death," I said then lunged at him.

Duncan blocked. "I know your voice. I know you. Who are you? You are no man."

"I am the raven," I said attacking again.

Duncan retreated. "No…no, I know you. Who are you?"

"I am the crone," I said as I attacked again. Duncan and I circled round and round each other, attacking and retreating.

There was a sharp scream behind us as MacDuff fell.

"MacDuff," Duncan whispered, pausing a moment, his sword drooping.

I lunged at him again. With the length of my blade, I cut a line down the side of his cheek. Blood poured down his face. He clumsily threw up his sword to protect himself.

"Back away," he stammered.

Gripping Uald's Gift, I advanced on him. Slashing, I cut his leg.

Duncan yelped. "Back away."

"Coward," I retorted, attacking again. This time, I disarmed him. He pulled a dagger from his belt and held it in front of him. The blade caught my attention; an odd blue glow seemed to surround the dagger. Duncan gripped the weapon and backed away.

I advanced on him. "User. Violator," I said as I lunged forward again.

He tried to block with the dagger, but his move was awkward. I stabbed him in the arm.

"Who... Who are you? Your voice..." Duncan said.

"Don't you remember? No. I'm sure you don't. One girl in a hundred. And just how many innocent girls have you forced to ride your cock?" I said, and with an upward slice, I caught him between the legs.

Duncan let out a howling scream.

"Sorry. Does that hurt? I wonder if you ever stop to think of the hurt that nasty little member of yours caused that poor girl you met in the woods. Her or any of the girls like her."

Duncan grabbed his wounded member and dropped to his knees. "G-girl? In the woods?"

"Tell me what you remember," the raven hissed.

Duncan screamed in pain. Blood oozed from between his fingers.

"Tell me!"

"What I…remember?"

"Tell me," the raven shrieked.

"I remember… I remember the rain."

I kicked him over. His dagger tumbled from his hands. The weapon glimmered as it bounced away. I stared at it. There, lying in a bank of pristine snow, lay a silver dagger with a raven on the handle. Hands shaking, I picked up the dagger and turned over the blade. Just below the hilt, I found Uald's smith mark. I gasped.

"Where did you get this?" I seethed.

"What?"

"Where did you get this?" I said, grabbing him roughly by the collar of his shirt.

"Malcolm. Malcolm gave it to me. A family heirloom."

"This is the dagger of Boite."

"What? I don't know," Duncan said then whimpered again, holding his bloody crotch.

I stared at the dagger then back at Duncan once more. "So, you remember the rain. The rain and what else?"

"What? MacDuff? MacDuff, where are you?"

"MacDuff is dead. The rain and what else?"

"The rain?"

"The rain and what else?" I screamed, shaking him

hard.

"A farm girl," he whimpered.

"But why did you think she was a farm girl? Because she was dirty? Now you are dirty. You dirty yourself with your own blood, and, for at least for a few minutes longer, you are a king. What did you do to that farm girl?"

"I... She was not a farm girl?"

"What did you do to that girl?"

Duncan wiped the blood from his mouth. The sound of the army was far behind us. "I took her."

Setting on his chest, I gripped my father's dagger tightly and leaned over Duncan.

"Rape, I think you mean. Can you say *rape*, Duncan?" I set the tip of the dagger on his throat.

His eyes bulged.

"Say it, you filthy bastard!"

"Rape," he whispered.

"What did you do to me?" I asked.

He did not respond.

"Say it."

His lips quivered.

I pressed the dagger in. Blood made a ring around his neck. "Say it."

"I raped you."

"You did what?"

"I raped you."

"Raped who?"

"You. I raped you."

"But who am I?"

He did not reply.

I pulled off my helmet and let it drop to the ground with a thud.

"Gruoch!"

"Your kin. Your own blood. Not a farm girl. Not a peasant girl. Not that it matters. I was a girl who did not want you. That should have been enough. Do you know what I have been waiting for all these years?"

He stared at me. "Gruoch?"

"I have been waiting and training for this moment, the moment when I extract my vengeance, and you live no more. Tell me why I have done this."

"God, God, God," Duncan whispered.

"God has nothing to do with this. Even the White Christ does not condone your sins. Why, Duncan? Tell me why this blade is on your throat. "

"Why?"

"Yes, why?"

"Because," he said and then he stopped.

"Because?"

"Because I raped you. "

I bent low, looking him in the eyes. From inside my vest, I pulled out the coin pouch and held it for him to see. "For your trouble," I said then threw it at his face.

His eyes opened wide. I lifted the dagger into the air and let it drop into his chest again and again. He screamed and screamed. With each stab, I pounded away years of pain and hate. I stabbed and stabbed at his body and loved the feel of it jerking beneath me. The dagger tore through chainmail and leather, burrowing into the flesh. Again and again, I stabbed him, Duncan's blood spraying on me. Then I yanked away his tattered armor. I carved into his chest. From within, I plucked out his bloody heart.

I rose and held the heart above my head. Blood ran down my arms and covered me. "See me, Morrigu. See me, Scotia. See me, Andraste," I yelled into the night. "See my vengeance. See me avenge my father's death. Malcolm's dreams die here. See me, Morrigu! I am avenged! I am avenged! I am avenged!" I squeezed the heart until all its blood had emptied onto me, and then I threw it onto Duncan's corpse, his eyes frozen open, his mouth gaping.

I sneered at him. "The king is dead. Long live the queen."

Continue the Celtic Blood series with Highland Queen, available on Amazon.

ABOUT THE AUTHOR

New York Times bestselling author Melanie Karsak is the author of many series including *The Road to Valhalla, The Harvesting, Steampunk Red Riding Hood, Celtic Blood, Steampunk Fairy Tales,* and more. A steampunk connoisseur, zombie whisperer, and Shakespeare junkie, the author currently lives in Florida with her husband and two children. You can find all her works on Amazon.

facebook.com/authormelaniekarsak
twitter.com/melaniekarsak
instagram.com/karsakmelanie
pinterest.com/melaniekarsak
bookbub.com/authors/melanie-karsak
amazon.com/author/melaniekarsak

Made in United States
North Haven, CT
27 December 2023

46701399R00243